THE SCROLL OF BENEVOLENCE

JOHN TRENHAILE lives in Ashdown Forest with his wife and two children.

He is the author of seven novels. His first, *The Man Called Kyril*, was adapted for television and shown in 1988 as *Codename Kyril*. *The Scroll of Benevolence* is his sixth novel. His latest is *Krysalis*.

by the same author

The Man Called Kyril
A View from the Square
Nocturne for the General
The Mahjong Spies
The Gates of Exquisite View
Krysalis

JOHN TRENHAILE

THE SCROLL OF OF BENEVOLENCE

FONTANA/Collins

First published in Great Britain by
William Collins Sons & Co. Ltd 1988

A continental edition first issued in Fontana Paperbacks 1989
This edition first issued in Fontana Paperbacks 1989

Copyright © 1988 Dongfeng Enterprises Ltd

Printed and bound in Great Britain by
William Collins Sons & Co. Ltd, Glasgow

For Rebecca, my own daughter, with love.

We parted at the gorge and cried 'Good Cheer!'
The sun was setting as I closed my door;
Methought, the spring will come again next year,
But he may come no more.

WANG WEI

FOREWORD

I am grateful to Colonel Kim Suk-Tai, Commander of the Salvation Army's Korean Territorial Headquarters, Lt Col Peter and Mrs Wood, Mrs Dolores Fogle and those other officers of the Sudaimun Corps who, together with members of their families and their staff, worked so hard to overcome the sense of culture shock that a first visit to South Korea can so easily (and did!) provoke. (And not forgetting Dok Yong, who is special.)

The translations of the poems which appear respectively as the epigraph to this book and on page 197 are taken from 'Chinese Poetry in English Verse', Herbert A. Giles, Bernard Quaritch (London) and Kelly Walsh Ltd (Shanghai), 1898. The translation of the poem that ends the book is based on that found in 'The Jade Mountain', trans. Wittner Bynner from the texts of Kiang Kang-hu, Alfred A. Knopf, 1920–1929.

The information concerning CHAPS and SWIFT related on page 342 is taken from *The Times*, Friday, 18 September 1987, report of the proceedings of the International Bar Association.

The principal unit of currency in mainland China is the *Yuan*, and in Hong Kong it is the Hong Kong Dollar.

Qiu Qianwei is pronounced Chew Chi-en Way and Kaihui is pronounced K'eye-Hway.

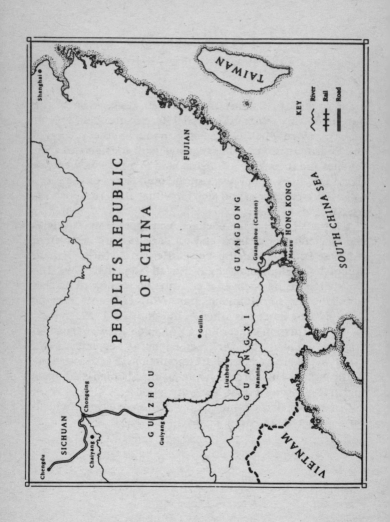

GLOSSARY

Aiya!	Chinese exclamation denoting surprise.
Baba	Chinese word for father; also nickname of the former head of the Chinese Secret Service.
Binguan	Small hotel of the 'Travellers' Rest' variety (Chinese).
Churka	Russian derogatory expression.
Dacha	Russian country house.
Fen	Smallest unit of mainland Chinese currency.
Feng-shui	Literally 'wind-water', (Chinese) system for determining the best location for a new building.
Koujiao	Face mask used to keep out the cold, polluted air or both (Chinese).
Mahjong Brigade	Another name for the Central Control of Intelligence, mainland China.
Maotai	Variety of Chinese liquor.
Pinyin	The official form of Romanization of Chinese script used in the People's Republic of China.
Putonghua	Literally, 'common speech' the Mandarin spoken every day in the People's Republic of China.
Sam-fu	Form of female dress (Chinese).
Sekretutka	Secretary (Russian).
Shao-xing	Chinese wine, not unlike sherry.
Shi de	'YES' (Chinese).

Tai-pan	Chinese slang for head of one of the great Hong Kong commercial houses.
Xin Hua	Short translation of the New China News Agency.

In the beginning . . .

The massacre of fifty-eight men at Gansu-B-Ten airfield did not explode across the front pages of the world's press, nor did it make prime time evening news. It went almost entirely unremarked.

Gansu-B-Ten was located somewhere in China's vast north-west desert. To speak of it as having a more precise location, or of existing in the present tense, is meaningless: because the place had always been used for top-secret projects it never appeared on any of the public maps and its precise co-ordinates are now a matter of speculation. After the killings, this airfield ceased to exist.

Some of the men who were murdered had worked at Gansu-B-Ten before, so they knew what to expect when they arrived there: bitterly cold nights alternating with crinkly-dry days of furnace heat; no recreational facilities; tinned food-stuffs; louse-ridden beds; filthy showers, their tiles overlaid with a patina of grey-green mould and supplied only erratically with tepid water.

The one good thing about B-Ten was its desolation, and that was an advantage only in the eyes of the man who controlled it.

His name was Lo Bing. He came and he went, always dressed immaculately in a well-pressed brigadier-general's uniform, throughout the time it took to install the weapon on the plane; some days he was omnipresent, but mostly he flitted around like a tiresome insect, the clatter of his helicopter distracting the men from their finicky work on the Boeing-747-400 parked in B-Ten's large hangar. His instructions were adamant:

everything had to be done in less than a week. It followed, naturally, that mistakes were made. For the most part they were rectified. Some, however, got overlooked; and this was to have consequences for the elegantly-tailored brigadier-general that could not have been foreseen.

At last all was ready. The Boeing flew off into the dusk one evening and the fifty-eight technicians prepared to be reassigned elsewhere.

Two days later the plane returned to Gansu-B-Ten.

That something had gone badly wrong was obvious; the upper cargo cabin bore signs of a fire and the hull had mysteriously become radioactive. Now Brigadier-General Lo Bing was back on a permanent basis and the technical staff anticipated his anger; but when he confronted them his face remained strangely still. He issued fresh orders. The peculiar equipment they had installed was to be ripped out again – quickly.

Afterwards, the Brigadier-General seemed satisfied; so much so that he announced a party to celebrate the project's success. The fifty-eight technicians were surprised and pleased, for they had not expected recognition. The Brigadier-General flew off in the Boeing-747. Once it was safely out of sight, the airfield's skeleton unit of regulars obligingly produced bottles of *maotai* and *shao-xing*.

It was hardly a sophisticated affair. The bottles were laid out on trestle tables in the large hangar and there were not enough glasses to go around, but nobody minded. The airforce crew did their best to make sure that things went with a swing. After a couple of hours they withdrew, silently locking the hangar-doors behind them. Moments later a helicopter clamorously hauled its way into the sky, but by then the men had become so used to the sound, what with the Brigadier-General's comings and goings, that they did not even hear it. Many of them, loaded with liquor, would have been past caring if they had heard it.

They were at the end of an assignment, and the jollification was heightening their already well established sense of camaraderie. For the one thing these men did have in common was their loneliness. As the personal confidences for which there had been no time before were at last exchanged, it became clear that none of them had any close relatives.

Some of them were just beginning to get interested in this apparent coincidence when a single Fantan—A fighter-bomber came over the horizon at one thousand feet above the ground, travelling in the region of Mach 0.6. As B-Ten came up on his screen, the pilot released two Hughes AGM-65 Maverick air-to-surface missiles, climbed almost vertically, sheered away from the airfield and was gone before his engine-signature could be heard inside the hangar. The Mavericks, however, had greater powers of penetration.

Two days later, Brigadier-General Lo Bing came back to B-Ten for the last time, bringing with him a wing of transports and Colonel Lai Jia Yao of the District Military Commander's headquarters' staff. As they surveyed the rubble-filled crater, once the site of the big hangar, both men agreed that this accident had been regrettable. Colonel Lai was mollified by his superior's ready acceptance of responsibility – one of Lo Bing's pilots had done the crazy thing – and by his offer to take care of all the paperwork. The Brigadier-General also suggested that they would do well to keep the incident quiet; and Colonel Lai Jia Yao, mindful of the adverse effect such things can have on a man's career, agreed with only the briefest of qualms.

One matter, however, did bother Colonel Lai Jia Yao. He confessed himself ignorant of what had been going on at B-Ten and inquired if the airfield was indeed unmanned at the time of the incident, as the sketchy records showed; the Brigadier-General was happy to assure him that such had been the case.

Indeed, the only point of divergence between these two conscientious officers concerned the fate of the site itself. Colonel Lai Jia Yao optimistically suggested that things might just as well be left as they were. The Brigadier-General disagreed, testily pointing out that he had not transported half a dozen bulldozers to the former airfield for fun. At which the Colonel, whose Wartime Hero Medal, first grade, had been awarded for discretion rather than valour, withdrew his opposition, because he was frightened of Lo Bing. His fear had nothing to do with the outward show of Lo Bing's uniform. Lai

15

Jia Yao reluctantly acknowledged to himself that even if this man appeared stark naked, he would still inspire fear. So he ordered the bulldozers to be off-loaded. Three hours later, the job was completed; and sand was slowly beginning to drift across what had once been the runway, filling in caterpillar tracks, obliterating footprints . . .

By the same time next day, there was nothing to show that there had ever been an airfield in this part of the desert at all.

Let alone a mass grave.

ONE

◇

Diana Young was buttoning the last toggle on Dok Yong's quilted jacket when she heard the phone ring in the principal's office along the hall. In *Hangul*, the language of Korea, Dok Yong's name meant 'goodness', although today he was being anything but good. Diana tut-tutted as the little boy swayed under the none-too-gentle pressure of her hands, not helping, not hindering, just standing still in mute displeasure with no trace of a smile. Then Park Son-do came up behind her and said, 'It's for you. From Hong Kong.'

The principal's office was a tight little cube of warm fug, the heat generated by a combination of under-floor heating and a smelly paraffin stove beside the metal desk. Diana was grateful to find no one else there.

'Hello?'

'Diana.'

'Hi, Da.'

'Diana . . .'

Her father's voice sounded faint, as if he were speaking in the next room while she eavesdropped. During the long pause that followed, Diana made connections, tidied up loose ends. Her heart was pumping blood through her veins at a rate they were not designed to bear.

'Diana, you've got to prepare yourself for a shock, I'm afraid. The doctors . . .'

'Rest. You said all mother needed was rest. Tonic.'

'It's not quite that. They . . . they'd like you to come home.'

Diana heard the paraffin heater clank slightly as metal expanded. She wanted to hang onto that sound. It came from

17

the real world of order and stability, unconnected to the Maelstrom her father was about to set in motion.

'Jinny . . . mother's dying.'

It was strange how father and daughter still managed to communicate through the silence. Each could feel the other's pain.

'I see.' Diana was surprised to hear how firm her voice sounded. 'Does she know?'

'Yes.'

'I'll come as soon as I can.'

'Thank you. Ring me at home as soon as you've got a confirmed flight.'

'Yes.' Another silence. 'Is that all? I mean . . . no, that came out wrong. Da?'

'I'm here.'

'Are you all right?'

'I'm all right.'

'How's Mat taking it?'

'Your brother's okay.'

'Give him my love. And Ma, too.' She drew a deep, shuddery breath. 'I love you.'

'I love you too, Diana.'

As she replaced the receiver she was cold, although the room itself seemed stifling. A tremor had begun somewhere inside her; she knew that soon it would manifest itself in her hands, her face . . .

'Bad news?' Sonny stood in the doorway.

'Not good. My mother's . . . ill.' She stood up, suddenly decisive again. 'I have to go home right away.'

'I'm sorry.'

Yes, she thought, looking at him, I can see that you are. His dark eyes were deep and sad. Diana thought of him as the epitome of *mot*, a fine-sounding *Hangul* word for a fine-looking race: handsome, well-built, physically attractive. He was twenty-one, her own age; kind, hard-working, a good Methodist . . . Diana felt the familiar cross-currents of allure and repulsion stir within her and abruptly withdrew her gaze.

'I'll have to see the principal,' she said mechanically. 'Sonny?'

'Yes.'

'Can you help me?'

He did more than that; he gently swept her up and shepherded her through her last hours on Korean soil, gently loosening the bonds of love that bound Diana to the Suwon Children's Orphanage where she had worked for the past three months.

Afterwards there were to be serious gaps in her recollection of that day. She could see herself packing her few possessions in an old suitcase and a tough rucksack that she'd bought when she and Sonny had visited Itaewon; there was an odd, bitter-sweet farewell in the principal's office, with everyone standing up and a tray of quartered Taegu apples that no one ate on the table between them; a last glimpse of the children in the playground gazing at the car, not understanding why the foreign lady who never seemed to get cross was leaving so suddenly; tears, the kind that make your eyes smart with pain, and not just the eyes . . .

Suwon was about forty kilometres to the south of Seoul; the journey to Kimpo International Airport did not take long. Sonny drove.

'When will you be back?'

She wasn't coming back. As Diana reluctantly turned away from the passing panoply of birch and pine, dusted on this March morning with light snow, something told her the truth. This was the end.

'I don't know.' *Coward.* 'I don't know how long mother's got left. I can't decide anything while she's still alive.' Was that her talking? So practical, pragmatic. 'There's a lot of catching up to do. Repairs . . .'

Sonny wanted to ask about that but Diana was once again staring out of the window at the hills, stark and somehow menacing in the dull light. 'Repairs,' she muttered again.

Sonny had never met anyone quite like Diana, and he was definitely in love with her.

Admittedly, he didn't know any other western women. Her

first appearance at the orphanage had shocked him. What was this beautiful, young English girl doing here? That deep, dark brown hair with rust-red tints, combed into tresses to frame her oval face, still faintly freckled like a child's; thick, ripe lips ever parted in a cheerful smile; the casual clothes, the endless resources of sympathy, patience . . . here was a treasure, come from afar. But why had she come?

She was in flight, he discovered. From home, an unsatisfactory course in Oriental Studies, herself. Chiefly herself. Something to do with a past she never talked about, but which glowed at the back of her eyes when she was tired or depressed.

'Diana.'

'Yes?'

'I'm going to miss you.' For some reason he chose to speak in heavily accented English. 'I mean . . . miss you a lot.'

Oh dear, she thought. I've done it again. The wrong signals transmitted in the wrong way. When will I ever learn?

'You'll forget me quite quickly, I think you'll find,' she said and her voice was rough.

'Tangshinun yeppum-nida.'

'Thanks. You're pretty, too. And you're smart enough to know that Koreans ought to love Koreans, English love English. Sonny, I really don't . . .'

But he cut her short by pounding the wheel, all the lines on his young face tautly drawn into a look of frustration. 'Why can't you love me?'

'I really can't love anyone just now.'

'*Why* can't you? I know there's someone. In England.'

'Sonny —'

'Is he better than me? More handsome?'

'That taxi!' He swerved violently, his mind still far from the road, and Diana felt panic rise behind her breastbone. 'Sonny, my mother is *dying!*' She regretted it instantly, of course. Such a bludgeon. 'I'll miss you too,' she blurted out. 'And the children.'

'You must come back!' But the heat had gone out of him. As they pulled up at the airport's security checkpoint and soldiers from Capital Garrison Command began to search the car, Sonny allowed his head to fall forward onto his chest. 'Sorry,' Diana heard him mutter.

'My fault.' But then — Why does everything have to be your fault? she asked herself dully. Always your fault . . .

She bought a ticket, for the first time grateful that her father had insisted on her having a Ducannon Young Trust Card, then found a telephone booth. There was the familiar feeling of tightness that always overcame her when using the phone. Often she would count up to ten rings then count back down again to zero before abandoning the call with a sense of relief that never failed to shame her. Today, however, there could be no question of not getting through. While she waited for her father to come on the line she watched Sonny kick the marble floor outside, plainly at odds with himself. She wanted to open the door, reach out for him . . . but then she heard her father's voice and thankfully turned away.

The Chinese have a rocket-testing centre at Shuang Cheng-ze, by the Jo-Shui river; they call this place 'East Wind'. On the day when Diana first learned that her mother was dying, East Wind Centre had been placed under the sole jurisdiction of Brigadier-General Lo Bing. His ostensible purpose was to oversee the test-firing of a new weapon, codenamed Sledge Hammer, against a Chinese target-satellite. Lo Bing's ostensible purposes rarely coincided with his true intentions.

Major Shen raised a hand towards the nearest screen. 'There,' she said quietly.

Colonel-Professor Ma saw what had attracted her attention. He quickly refocused his scanner to telephoto. The monochrome image blurred and steadied to reveal a satellite floating in the ionosphere, its rectangular wings reminding him of an imperial head-dress. He switched on his chest-microphone.

'Ah, comrades . . . what you're looking at is the Soviet ASAT interceptor, that is, a satellite interceptor. Also known as a hunter-killer satellite.' He could not hear a reaction but could imagine the stirring of interest in the gallery behind him. 'Now that we have established visual contact, we can commence the link-up with the Boeing.' He gave Major Shen's shoulder a gentle squeeze of encouragement. She glanced to her left, where three more technicians sat before identical consoles, and nodded.

'Countdown from ten . . .'

Yang continued his softly-spoken exposition. 'A few seconds from now, the Milky Way computer will, in effect, take over Sledge Hammer, removing it from our hands. Exact co-ordination is essential to success.'

The woman's voice prevailed over his: 'Three . . . two . . .' A row of green figures ran across the foot of the screens and their images seemed to freeze for a second. Ma resumed. 'We now have this situation. Our own space satellite is approaching the Soviet ASAT on a course that deviates only slightly from the one designated on launch, five days ago. As it passes within range of the Russian hunter-killer satellite, the latter's telemetry system will take soundings and register the presence of an armed intruder. It will then destroy our satellite before it can come any closer, thereby releasing a burst of energy that will easily be monitored from the earth's surface by the United States or anyone else who's interested and has the right equipment.'

'One minute thirty seconds, Colonel,' interrupted Major Shen.

'The destruction of our satellite will be exactly coincidental with the Sledge Hammer firing from on board the Boeing-747. At the desks two rows in front of me' – Ma gestured down the control-centre – 'they are in the final stages of linking up with the Boeing. In approximately one minute, we'll see if this thing works.'

He switched off his chest-microphone and took a seat along-side Shen. 'Contact the plane,' he murmured.

As Ma clicked the switch the control room was filled with noise amplified over a distance: background voices, blips, the constant sough of jet-engines. When the flight captain spoke his voice came out much too loud; Ma adjusted the volume control.

'We are having trouble . . .' Someone evidently distracted

the captain for there was a rubbery squeak and everything became muted, as if he had placed a palm over his microphone. '. . . Trouble maintaining this altitude. At four hundred and twenty . . .'

'The 747-400 can cruise at forty-five thousand feet without difficulty.'

'Not with Sledge Hammer aboard, Colonel.' The captain came across as mild, patient. Major Shen felt certain he wore weak, metal-rimmed glasses.

'Never mind; not long to go now. You're monitored here as locked into Milky Way.'

'Acknowledged.'

'The countdown is at' — Ma glanced up —' Minus twenty-two seconds. Secure anti-radiation panels.'

'Closed, locked . . . electronic bolts on.'

'Anti-flash hoods.'

'All personnel checked.'

'Minus seventeen . . . sixteen . . .'

'Switch to automatic pilot on my mark . . . Mark.'

'Acknowledged. Auto-pilot function confirmed.'

In the control room a siren sounded three short blasts. Ma spoke to the pilot. 'You are committed.'

'Twelve . . . eleven . . .' Major Shen cleared her throat. 'All internal electronic systems register function, cleared and active. Co-ordinates will merge six seconds from now.'

'Override arming circuits.'

'Overridden.'

'Prime ignition and restore to automatic.'

'Primed . . . restored.'

'Six . . . five . . .'

'Final monitor MHD generator circuit systems one and two.'

'Go and . . . go.'

'Two . . . one . . . zero . . . plus one . . .'

'Weapon fired!' The Boeing's captain sounded triumphant, perhaps a little surprised. 'I . . .' He shouted something indistinct. 'Smoke. We have a smoke problem. I —'

The audio-channel connecting mission control with the Boeing vaporized into a howl that bordered on the threshold of human tolerance before someone cut it. The red phone at Ma's elbow buzzed; in his haste to answer he knocked the instrument off its bracket and had to fumble around on the floor to retrieve it.

'What has happened?' Ma recognized Lo Bing's quiet voice and he tensed.

'The weapon performed according to specification.' He glanced up. 'We're receiving confirmation right now: the target was destroyed.'

'The plane?'

'I'm not sure.'

'Well, be sure.' And the connection was broken.

Diana had just told her father the flight number and time of arrival when the line went dead; she went on talking for several seconds before she realized what had happened. 'Hello, are you there? *Hello?*'

When she got through to the operator she discovered that there was a fault on the international line. Many complaints had been received. The position was being investigated, but nothing could be done at present.

'A problem with the satellite,' Sonny said knowledgeably when she explained what had happened; and Diana wondered why it was that men always had to have an answer ready. Something to do with insecurity, she supposed. Her father and brother were just the same, although what they had to feel insecure about Diana couldn't imagine.

Sonny picked up her rucksack, which she had left in his care while she made the phonecall. 'And your jacket . . .'

Diana slung the faded denim blouson over her shoulders. 'Turn around.' She did so, with a smile that betrayed reluctance. They had played this game before. Sonny pointed out each word emblazoned in bright yellow across the back of the jacket. 'I . . . love . . . my . . . orphans.'

'Very good.'

'The big red heart . . . it means love? Okay. I big-red-heart you.'

'Sonny, I —'

'Come back.' His voice was very fierce. 'I have to go now,' he said, and because this was a lie his tone became even crosser. 'Goodbye!'

He stalked away towards the escalator that would take him down to the car park, out of her life. She longed to call after him, to apologize for not being satisfactory, but he jumped the first two moving steps and was gone from sight before she could find the right words.

The flight was unpleasant. Diana didn't want to read or eat or drink; she wanted to think about what lay ahead and how she was going to cope with it all. With the smell of disinfectant. People coming up to her afterwards to say how they'd known Jinny since the year dot and wasn't she a lovely . . .

Diana smacked her palms down hard on her legs and said aloud: 'Dramatic!' The two Indonesian businessmen sitting next to her scarcely noticed. They alternated between bemoaning the fall of the Hong Kong dollar, and speculating where Tan Sri Somebody-or-other might have gone with all that money he'd stolen from the Hong Kong and Shanghai. They came down into Kai Tak along with exchange rates and confidence in the British colony's future. Diana, listening with half an ear, felt herself sink with them.

She went through customs and immigration very quickly; people in authority habitually took one look at Diana's face and decided to trust her. As she caught sight of the Rolls with its familiar 'DY 1' number plate she felt a tremor of annoyance: with herself as much as with her father. It embarrassed her to mix jeans and a T-shirt with state of the art opulence. Then the offside front door opened and the driver got out. 'Hello,' he said.

It was a mournful greeting, delivered by a short, undistinguished-looking Chinese in his mid-forties. Diana knew him, but not as a driver of her father's prestigious cars.

'Qiu Qianwei!'

He removed his heavy spectacles and polished them with a corner of a clean white handkerchief, screwing up his eyes to blink at her as he did so. 'I have not seen you for a long time.'

'No.' She put her head on one side and treated him to a proper survey. 'You've changed. You're different.'

'Oh? Carry your bag for you?'

It shocked her to think of this man humping luggage. A bewitching wild animal, trained to do circus tricks . . .

'Tell me everything,' she said as she tossed her bags into the boot of the Rolls. 'Absolutely everything.'

Diana got in beside Qiu, first throwing a newspaper from the passenger seat into the back. A headline caught her eye – 'Arson in Shanghai: Hotels Burn' – and she tut-tutted. So China was in turmoil. Again.

'It must be rotten for you, reading that.'

'Yes.' Qiu's downturned lips indicated profound sadness. 'My son's in Shanghai.'

'What! Tingchen? I thought –'

'His mother took him there, to school.'

'Oh. He must be . . . what, ten now?'

'Yes. His mother thought he would benefit from being some-where more cosmopolitan. We're divorced now, by the way.' He eased the car into the flow of traffic.

'Should I say I'm sorry or glad?'

Qiu smiled. He had a weird smile, one so quick that observers could never be quite sure if it had existed at all. His lips would extend to their furthest limit in an exaggerated attempt to portray good humour, while at the same time his eyebrows rose to make a pair of pointed circumflex accents. There was no emotion in the smile.

'It's nothing, really.'

'But you planned to marry again, I seem to remember. Wasn't there a Taiwanese girl – Lin something?'

'Lin-chun.' His shoulders momentarily sagged under the weight of memory and he was silent for a while. When he spoke again his voice sounded bleak with suppressed emotion. 'It didn't work out. She couldn't bear the thought of never going back to Taiwan again.'

'But she seemed so keen when I met her. Of course, I only met her the one time . . .'

'It was life on the run she couldn't face.' Qiu shrugged. 'You know my story. For years I was a member of the Mainland Chinese Intelligence Service. I was a colonel, a big fish. When I came out to work for your father, that was the end. They would never let me out of their sight. And Lin-chun couldn't face that, you see. So . . .'

He tailed off. They were entering the cross-harbour tunnel, the new one, only recently completed. Qiu gratefully used the echoing roar of closely confined traffic to bar conversation and so mask his depression.

'I'm sorry,' Diana said, as the car ran out into the sunlight. 'And so Tingchen's in Shanghai.' She was anxious to change the subject, for the sadness he radiated was like a virus: catching. 'But the trouble's up at the university, isn't it? I'm sure there's nothing to worry about.'

'No?'

'The present leadership's in control, isn't it?'

'What leadership? Did you read about the border clash with Vietnam? Twenty-one thousand casualties in a *border clash! Aiya!*'

'So what are you doing now?' she asked in a small voice.

'I am your father's personal assistant.' His voice rose. 'That's the job-title. That's what you make someone who's got a head full of useful secrets but who cannot be trusted any more.'

'I'm sure he trusts you.' Seeing that Qiu chose not to waste his scorn on that remark Diana had to prompt him: 'But what do you actually do?'

'I write reports. Analyses of different Asian markets. I lunch contacts. Pick brains.'

'You make it sound terrible.'

'Just dull. That's why I picked you up at the airport. An assignment out of the office, for a change.'

Diana became distracted by her own reflection in the window. She wished she'd made a greater effort before leaving Korea. She wanted so desperately to please her mother, and stained denim wasn't the way to go about that. If only she'd stopped long enough to wash her hair . . .

The scenery had taken on the familiarity of homecoming now: they were running alongside Repulse Bay. Because it was midweek not many people were relaxing in the sticky warmth of Hong Kong's spring, but Diana could see a pair of windsurfers far out in the channel, skating like outsize shark-fins across the flat surface of a sea the colour of an over-chlorinated pool.

Then Qiu dropped a gear in readiness for the climb to the bluff and she mentally braced herself. As if reading her thoughts, he said: 'I'm sorry, very sorry, about your mother.'

'Thank you.' Diana was pained to discover how resolutely she had been putting off any mention of Jinny to Qiu. 'How is she, do you think?' She felt tears prick her eyelids and ground a warning fingernail across her palm.

'So-so.'

'Simon says she's dying,' Diana said flatly; and Qiu stuck out his tongue in the classic Chinese expression of dismay. 'Don't say that, please!'

'Why not, if it's true?'

They were home.

The large, white, three-storey house, built out of the side of a hill, commanded a panoramic view of Repulse Bay; and as Qiu parked the car beside the main entrance Diana had to fight down an impulse to walk around to the terrace for a sight of the sea. She was conscious of an acute desire to put off what was coming next.

The servant opened the door, bobbed and smiled a welcome. Home smelled of home, as always. Furniture polish, an historic blend of cooking smells, lilac air-freshener, whiff of incense from an altar somewhere in the servants' quarters. Such things were identifiable, tangible almost; but Diana could detect something very different. In her nostrils rose the scent of human relationships, individual and distinctive of the surroundings that had nurtured them. Thus the odours reminded her of past events, when people had done or had done to them things that mattered; when words were spoken with love or in anger; laughter; grief . . .

Home and the family. Everything she had fought so hard to escape from over the years. As Diana looked around her, absorbing familiar things, she understood the futility of escape for the first time.

It was the photograph that affected her most.

A large, gilt-framed mirror fashioned into three panels hung beside the stairs on the wall at the back of the hall. She walked towards it, noting how the large expanse of brown-speckled glass made her face glow with unnatural pallor, and stowed her bags by a spindly blackwood table inlaid with mother of pearl that stood underneath the mirror. She glanced down, knowing she would see a half-ring on the wood where she had placed a cup of hot milk when she was seven years old, hearing her father's rage, almost prepared to feel again the flat of his hand across her bottom . . . it was then that she caught sight of the photograph.

Jinny stared back at her from a plain black wooden frame. Taken perhaps three years previously, the colour print revealed a slightly hesitant Chinese woman of indeterminate but not yet 'a certain' age, her features well proportioned, rounded, still unmarred by wrinkles; fine-boned and beautiful, in the prime of life it seemed . . . either the photographer or his subject had covered up the small mole on the hairline, but Diana knew it was there, just as she knew that at the time when this picture was taken her mother's hair was starting to lose some of its former body, her neck was ageing, and the backs of her hands were showing signs of slackness.

The woman in the photograph boasted a good figure: the sumptuous Cardin jade-green dress fitted her to perfection. Her breasts were firm against the material. In those days she had had two breasts, like her daughter.

Diana put down the frame and gazed into the mirror. She adjusted her hair, rubbed a spot of grime from her chin with a handkerchief and made to go upstairs. She had to bypass Qiu, which she did without raising her eyes from the carpet. But at the foot of the stairs she stopped, came back and, to his surprise, laid a hand on his shoulder.

'I'm so sorry,' she said quietly. 'About Lin-chun, I mean.'

Before he could react Diana removed her hand and ran upstairs. She made herself be steady, took a few deep breaths, and walked into her mother's bedroom, the image of the photograph still fresh in her memory.

Reality was different.

'Shot it down!' Sun Shanwang's voice was scarcely more than a whisper of outrage.

'That's what I said. This way . . .'

They were hurrying along a corridor deep underground in Beijing's Military Academy, north of the Summer Palace. Sun shook his head in a vain effort to clear his vision. The chief of mainland China's Central Control of Intelligence was seventy-one years old and he had just worked his way through a sixteen-hour shift, seeking to keep his finger on China's pulse when he wasn't even sure if the heart still beat. Then, as he was preparing to go home for a few hours of rest, the phone had rung and Wang Guoying, chief of staff to the People's Liberation Army, was on the line with more vile news.

'This door . . .' said Wang Guoying.

They found themselves inside a large, scallop-shaped lecture hall. A single spotlight shone down on the lecturer's podium and its solitary, uniformed occupant; everywhere else was in darkness. Wang clattered down the central stairway, closely followed by Sun. Two people who had been sitting in the front row stood up at their approach.

'Controller, this is Xiong Qilai, political commissar, National Defence Commission for Science, Technology and Industry . . . the Minister of the Aeronautics Industry, in charge of our satellite people, you already know . . .' Wang Guoying pointed at the rostrum. 'That officer is Brigadier-General Lo Bing, formerly commander of the Shenyang Military District and now in overall charge of the Logistics Department of the Defence University. He is an expert on space matters.' Wang Guoying paused, licked his lips. 'He will explain how it is that someone has shot down a Ford Aircraft Company telecommunications TCS-7 satellite, which probably contained an intelligence-gathering device implanted there by the United States of America.'

30

The atmosphere became oddly still, as if no one was breathing. Sun felt giddy.

Lo Bing placed his hands on the lectern. 'In 1988,' he began, 'I was ordered to devise a beam-weapon development programme capable of supporting both offensive and defensive strategies.'

His light voice carried easily through the amplification system to every corner of the lecture-theatre.

'I was told that the time element was important and that I should have a prototype in being within three years. This was not as daunting as it sounded. We had reaped the benefit of defections from the Soviet Union's beam weapon research establishment at Semipalatinsk and you will be aware that a number of overseas Chinese employed by the American defence establishment report their progress to us on a regular basis.'

Sun saw how thoroughly he had divorced himself from the content of his brief; the officer's face betrayed no signs of emotion.

'I was given one further guideline. Satellites. It might be necessary to deploy the new weapon in space, against satellites; we were to bear this in mind.'

Sun bleakly noted how 'I' had suddenly become 'we'.

'We decided to concentrate on developing a charged particle beam weapon, using information conveyed to us by the defectors and other informants I have already mentioned. We've made good progress. In effect, we have matched the technology currently available to the two superpowers, Russia and America, but neither country even remotely suspects our capabilities in this area.'

Sun, already well aware of these things, was becoming irritated. 'Are we getting to the point at last?' he snapped.

'The point, Controller, is simple: we have enough expertise to understand what happened earlier today.'

'Continue.'

'At about that time, our rocket-launching facilities started to find favour with the many nations wanting to send satellites into space.'

'Long March rockets?'

'Were made available commercially on an international scale, yes. Certain customers took the opportunity to reach agreement with us that devices prepared by them should be inserted in their satellites, with no questions asked by us. Sometimes . . . sometimes we suspected that such devices had been implanted, even though no such agreement had been reached. But since the customers' satellites were always sealed before being delivered to us, we couldn't be sure.'

'And?'

'And we're reasonably certain that one such device was implanted, without our official knowledge, in a telecommunications satellite sponsored and manufactured by the United States on behalf of a consortium of South-East Asian countries. The Americans would have been particularly keen to make this implant, because the satellite was designed to overfly the Soviet Union at regular intervals.'

'From which I imagine it would also have to spend part of its orbit over China?'

'Yes.'

'So there was America, cosily putting devices into a third party's satellite with a view to spying on the Soviet Union and also on us?'

'Yes.'

'Without our consent?'

'Yes. The Politburo were informed of the dangers. Apparently they decided that the commercial benefits of continuing to lease launch-space outweighed any disadvantages.'

Sun stared up at him. 'Indeed they did. A policy-decision which, in the light of your tale, may need revision. Now: what happened?'

'Today, that satellite was shot down.'

'Who shot it down?'

'We believe that a Soviet hunter-killer satellite, known as an ASAT, may have done it.'

'Why do you blame the Soviet Union?'

'Because our tracking station at Lop Nor monitored a huge outpouring of energy from such an ASAT at the precise time when the satellite was destroyed. Furthermore, it makes sense, in that the Russians may well have learned that the satellite contained an American surveillance device and decided to do something about it.'

Sun realized that the implications of this were terrifying. He still had a lot of questions to ask, but first he urgently needed time to think. He glanced at the politicians. 'Anything to be done, at present?'

'No.' It was the commissar who spoke. 'But this comes at an inconvenient time. We've other things to worry about, let alone a fight brewing between the superpowers.'

'An understatement. I'll monitor the situation and report. Goodnight.'

Wang followed Sun back along the corridor to the lifts. While they waited he had time in which to study his colleague. He did not find the sight reassuring. The controller's body, once so tall and lean, had begun to droop. Sun, long a heavy smoker, had recently begun to wheeze rather than breathe. His yellow teeth resembled fangs, set crookedly in receding gums that were blackened around the roots. His eyes were rheumy and scarcely visible behind his rectangular glasses: the pupils had shrunk to pinpricks, nearly every trace of colour had drained away from the irises. Here was a relic of the Cultural Revolution, a man who in the prime of his life had backed the wrong side and been made to scrub out toilets as payment; tonight, Wang reflected, he looked the part.

Sun bypassed the brass astrolabe that dominated the Tactical School's marble-floored atrium without wasting a glance on it, hobbled down the shallow steps, Wang close at his heels, and climbed into the back seat of a Red Flag limousine. 'Home,' he told the driver. As they drove off he eased his tired limbs back into the soft cushions and said, 'Tell me about Lo Bing. Although I can guess.'

'He was with Mao in Yenan.'

'So was everyone. Come forward a bit.'

'Close friend and backer of Ye Jianying. Got kicked out along with the old boy when we cleaned up the General Political Department in '85.'

'Whose idea was it to give him Sledge Hammer?'

'A sop. Trade-offs. You were asked at the time.'

'I'm asked so many things, I can't remember them all! What sort of man is he?'

'A little dour. Unmarried. Spends all his free time painting austere landscapes in a very old-fashioned style, or so I'm told.'

'Austere, and insolent with it, I suspect.' Sun grunted: a drawn-out despairing sound. 'Damn! We've got it all there, in place, and now this . . . Power, it's like holding a piece of sizzling duck in a wafer-thin pancake. If we're quick enough, deft enough, we can swallow it . . .'

He broke off to nibble a cuticle. His lips made slobbery sounds, reminding Wang of a ravenous man bolting food, perhaps that very morsel of duck.

'And if we're not . . .' The chief of staff enjoyed developing Sun's imagery. 'It'll burn the skin off our hands. What do the doctors say about the Chairman?'

'That we shouldn't expect to have a paramount leader this time next week. At least – not the same paramount leader.' Sun sighed. 'It'll fall to you as chief of staff to hold the centre steady.'

'Men like Lo Bing don't help.'

'No. What really happened, d'you think?'

'The Russians did it, just as he said. Anything else is inconceivable: the Americans would hardly install a bugging device in a satellite and then shoot it down.'

'*Aiya*. What a time for this to happen!'

'I was interested in Lo Bing's progress report, though. Think about Project Steel Nail, the repossession of Hong Kong. What he was saying, in effect, was that Steel Nail can be made to work.'

'But at a cost! If the capitalists get the faintest clue what's happening they'll run away like dogs before we can set Steel Nail up. And with the Chairman dying, they could do just that – run!'

'You really think so?'

'With some of the most powerful factions in the People's Liberation Army standing ready to reverse fifteen years of

34

reforms? No more responsibility land, no more private enterprise, no more joint ventures, no more "socialism with Chinese characteristics" . . . only civil disorder, rioting, rivals at each other's throats . . . yes, Guoying, I think so. I believe they're poised to go right now – some time within the next few days, before the Chairman dies. They'll up and go before we can turn around from crushing our own students.'

'What's that about students?'

'You haven't heard? Last night, we temporarily lost contact with Xiamen naval base.'

'What? I knew it was bad, but –'

'Half the fleet were out on exercises. It was the students! They'd set fire to a telephone exchange and it somehow burned out our circuits as well. We were stuck with a local radio frequency for nearly an hour. Imagine it! One of our prime operational bases, opposite Taiwan, connected to headquarters by two men wearing headphones and backpacks!'

'What were the students complaining about?'

'Lack of books, lack of food, lack of competent teachers. Apparently we lost a generation of teachers during the Ten Terrible Years.' Sun's sarcasm was leaden. 'You know what I hate most about Chinese youth? It's their *solemnity!*'

Wang chuckled.

'Multiply that by a dozen cities, add a few dissatisfied peasants whose neighbours are making two yuan more than they are, throw in Lo Bing and all the other Lo Bings in China . . .'

The telephone buzzed. Sun reached forward to answer it with an impatient click of the teeth. 'Yes?'

There followed a long silence. At last Sun said, 'Thank you. I'm coming in.'

He replaced the receiver, slid open the partition and gave fresh instructions to the driver. 'Sorry,' he said, sitting back. 'But it's not bedtime after all. The White House has issued a statement accusing Moscow of destroying a commercial telecommunications satellite. The Kremlin have denied the charge.'

'Shit!'

'The President of the United States is threatening to recall his ambassador from Moscow, for consultations; the Russians will be bound to retaliate in kind if he does. My people in the Pentagon urgently need instructions, and to be honest . . .' He wiped his spectacles with fingers that shook. 'I really don't know what instructions to give.'

He replaced his glasses. 'When the Chairman dies, there will be chaos. Somehow we have to find a way of saving China. We've got a week, ten days at the most, in which to do it.'

A small, malign-looking bird with dowdy electric blue feathers flapped onto the balcony rail, looking around for something to eat. Diana recognized it as a Formosan blue magpie and wondered what it was doing so far from home. She continued to stare long after the inquisitive bird had exhausted any interest for her. That was so much easier than having to smile at mother.

The sun shone, the temperature had risen into the mid-sixties. From where Diana was sitting she could look down on Repulse Bay, the intense light glittering off its placid waters like so many thousand needles scattered higgledy-piggledy by a naughty child. Her mother's bed had been wheeled out onto the balcony behind her, and Jinny was lying propped up in it like an understuffed pillow, almost indistinguishable from the bleach-white sheets.

'What's the time, darling?' She had been dozing, lulled into a semblance of rest by the warm rays of the sun. Now she was awake.

'Just gone ten.' Diana noted how bright and pleasant her voice sounded. That was good.

The scarecrow in the bed shifted position slightly. At once a gasp of pain was wrung from behind Jinny's clenched lips and her head twisted in an attempt to stem the sound.

Diana made herself approach the semi-comatose figure she called 'Mother', forcing her nose to ignore the smell of disinfectant and the other, less agreeable aroma that always seemed to hover just beneath the antiseptic tang. She held the spout of the plastic flask within reach of Jinny's carmined lips, steadying it while the sick woman sipped. Let her not be sick again, Diana prayed . . .

Her plea went unanswered. Diana did what was necessary, covered the bowl with a cloth and adjusted the pillows so as to ease her mother's head back into a more relaxed position. It would have been easier, she felt, to perform these distressing duties for a total stranger.

'I'm sorry, darling.'

All that was visible of Jinny was her head. The bedclothes came up almost to her chin, revealing only a hint of the plain white nightgown beneath. Diana did not dwell on that area, if she could help it. She knew they had opened up the breast and taken one look before doing some urgent butchery and hastily sewing her mother back together again. Too late, that was the verdict. If only she'd had a scan earlier . . .

Jinny's body had shrunk. There was nothing left of the face shown in the photograph downstairs. The skin sagged into pouches and pockets, making her look frighteningly old, hag-like. She was a strange colour, resembling an ivory billiard-ball that had aged beyond usefulness.

'Is there anything you want?'

'Nothing. Thank you.' The voice was very weak. 'You look so nice this morning, darling.'

Diana was wearing a Tana lawn smock dress in Liberty print, with white sandals. On the floor beside her chair lay a straw hat trimmed with tiny roses, for when the heat grew intense. She did not feel at ease in these clothes, but neither could she bring herself to stay in jeans and a T-shirt.

'I should wear something like this more often.' She looked at her mother, really looked, so that Jinny could see she wasn't repelled, and smiled. 'I'm sorry I didn't always dress up more.'

'Don't . . .' The emphasis, scarcely audible, was nevertheless there. 'You were always a wonderful daughter.'

Diana turned to look out across the bay, a natural movement with which to cover grief and confusion. 'Do you have many visitors?'

'In the evenings. When it's cool. Not too many Chinese.

37

They're afraid of me dying while they're here. They think my spirit might possess them.'

The day nurse came out onto the balcony and spoke to Jinny in Cantonese. Her voice sounded raucous, aggressive. Diana knew it was only the natural sound of the dialect but still she felt uneasy. When Jinny replied in the same tongue, Diana went to stand with her hands folded on the rail, keeping her back to the pair. At last she heard the nurse's crepe-soles retreating across the bedroom's parquet floor.

'Chinese . . . Something I always wanted to ask you, darling . . . the language . . . why do you hate it so?'

Diana shuddered. 'I don't hate it.'

'You do.' There was a long pause while Jinny gathered her resources. She wanted to talk: a proper conversation, not fragmented phrases. 'I've seen it often. I've never asked. Now . . . I'm asking.'

Diana looked inside herself and decided that there was an honest answer to this question.

'It was . . . years ago.' The words came out slowly. 'I was playing with someone. In the garden. We did something wrong. I can't remember . . . you came out. You were so angry! There was a slanging match. You screamed at us both. In Mandarin, and in Cantonese, all mixed up. But not in English. I was so astonished. I just stared at you. You went on and on. You seemed so . . .'

'Say it. Please say it.'

'Alien. I'm sorry.'

Suddenly Diana didn't mind the smell, and the bones that seemed to scrape the inside surface of the skin. She ran across to lay her head on the coverlet and relish the feel of her mother's hand on her neck. She was half-crying. She knew if she gave way completely she would never stop.

'You're half Chinese,' Jinny murmured at last.

'I know! That's what makes it such a terrible memory for me. Ever since then, to me, Chinese has been the language of judgement. Whenever I hear it spoken, any dialect, I shiver. I'm made to tremble by the language of judgement – and it's *my* language!'

It was odd, but by now she was laughing. Jinny's body, too, shook with amusement.

'It sounds so silly,' Diana said ruefully.

'A little. To go through your life, thinking that.'

'I never told you.'

'Why?'

'Frightened you'd be cross.'

Jinny heard her daughter's spoken words and saw her smile, but inside she was making connections that could not be articulated. She knew what Diana did not yet know: that you could choose your friends but not your family; that sometimes the people whose blood ran in your veins just weren't your kind of people at all . . .

'You never were cross, were you?'

'Not often.'

'Will you be cross if I tell you something now?'

Jinny tried to read Diana's expression. 'About the bad time?'

'Yes. When I was ill.'

'Go on.'

'I wasn't really ill.'

'I didn't think you were.'

'I didn't have glandular fever.'

'No.'

'You knew?'

'Yes.'

'Why didn't you say anything?'

'Why didn't you?'

'I couldn't. I'd been in hospital. There was an . . . an abortion. This man, you see. An American, and he was married. In London.'

When Diana stopped speaking the balcony seemed unnaturally silent. The Formosan blue magpie had long since gone. Even the wash of waves against shingle on the beach below was muted.

The touch of Jinny's hand on her wrist made her twitch. She swallowed, lifted her head. Jinny was smiling.

'It's terrible. Isn't it?' Diana's voice demanded assent.

'It must have been terrible for you.'

'It was. I felt unclean. Soiled, you know?'

'My darling, I am sorry. For you and for . . . everything.'

Diana squeezed Jinny's hand, not noticing the spasm of pain the gesture sent across her mother's face. She had been staring down at the bed. Now she raised her eyes and was seized with consternation. Jinny's teeth ground, her head tossed from side to side, her back arched.

Diana stood up, uncertain what to do. 'Nurse!' she cried. *'Nurse!'*

The woman ran onto the balcony, took in the situation at a glance and withdrew. To Diana, obsessed with the need to bring her mother some comfort, it seemed an age before she reappeared carrying the kidney-bowl with its tube of oblivion.

As Diana watched the medication being administered she realized that she was unwilling to go on facing this thing alone. Her father and brother were here, in Hong Kong. She needed them.

Diana entered the bedroom and made a beeline for the telephone.

TWO

⬦

The pilot flew north by north-east from Anchorage; before they had gone more than a dozen miles Gene Sangster had completely lost his bearings. In the snowfields of Alaska it was a grey, sunless day: ahead of him the foggy sky bonded with the white carpet below to form a seamless void. They might have been flying upside down for all he could tell. But the pilot seemed to know where to go, because fifty minutes after take-off he banked to the left and brought them in low over what looked like a makeshift football field.

Sangster stared down with interest. Fluorescent red plastic tags had been strung along a large rope rectangle to mark out an area of snow. A line of men was working across it from side to side, poking the interminable whiteness with long sticks. At one corner stood a single-storey 'instant' building, some fifty metres square.

They came down in a flurry of white powder thrown up by the rotor blades. As the helicopter settled and its engine cut out, a figure ran from the building, holding his parka hood over his head with both hands.

'Mr Sangster?'

'Yes.'

'Major James Guard, 82nd Airborne Division.'

'Rapid Deployment Force?'

'Right. We set this thing up. How much time do you have?'

'Zilch.'

'Best get going, then. Come along in.'

The two men stepped out of their snow-gear and took a quick, professional look at each other. Guard wore uniform.

His head was bald except for a few wisps of hair at the sides: coupled with his white, clean-shaven face the effect reminded Sangster of an egg. The major's expression was that of a closed-and locked security type. Sangster felt at home with him.

'ID?'

Sangster produced his card. The officer looked at the photograph and easily matched it to the original: a tall, slim, thick-shouldered Caucasian; thirty-six; shock of bushy hair, greying at the temples; square face; brown eyes; high, deeply lined forehead; big pores; a pleasant smile revealing two rows of extremely white, large and even teeth; 'peculiarities', none . . . everything tallied. Except the suit, which was a well-cut pearl grey lightweight, with matching tie and a handkerchief in the breast pocket, set off by a discreetly gold-clasped leather belt and beautifully polished leather shoes. Gene Sangster looked a little too much like someone who worked in the media, Major Guard decided, as he ushered his guest through the door to the main room. Personally he would have called that a 'peculiarity'; but then the CIA had its image to maintain.

Sangster's first impression was that the whiteness outside had duplicated itself here: perhaps a dozen lab assistants in white coats, rubber boots and hair-caps were at work in front of white tables or white freestanding instruments taller than a man. In the far corner, a group of people were huddled over a bench. As Guard and Sangster approached they stood upright and turned around.

'Mr Sangster, this is Dr Van Thach of Lawrence Livermore University . . . Mr Cooper, from COMSAT . . . and the gentleman sitting is Professor Wilson, from your own agency. Mr Sangster here is from –'

'Professor Wilson's team.' Sangster smiled around the group, noting how all of them with the exception of Wilson betrayed varying degrees of anxiety at his presence, and wanting them to relax. He knew from past experience that the letters 'CIA' did not have a soothing effect.

'Glad you could make it, Sangster.'

It was Wilson who spoke, in a deep-South drawl. The

professor sat bolt upright with hands clasped on the bench. He could have been any age from fifty to a hundred, although Sangster guessed late sixties. He looked thin but strong. His small head was bright dark brown, as if it had recently been stained with varnish; short hair that was still jet black coated his skull; and his scraggy neck stuck straight upright with a quarter of an inch of empty space between the professor's skin and his old-fashioned, stiff shirt-collar. On his breast he wore a battered gunmetal watch, hanging from its strap like a medal.

'But tell me this: why are you here?'

Sangster spread his hands wide. 'Your guess is as good as mine,' he seemed to be saying; and the professor evidently liked him for it, because suddenly his severe face broke into a grin. 'You want a crash course in satellite technology?'

'If you think I need it.'

'Yup! This thing here' – Wilson took a pencil from an inside pocket and jabbed at a small piece of twisted metal lying on the bench – 'is, was, part of a satellite. Telemetry system, if I'm any judge. Until yesterday, this baby was circling round and around, up there.' Wilson unfolded the index finger of his right hand and raised it slowly above his head, until the arm could extend no further. 'Then somebody shot it down. Blasted it out of the sky. This is all that's left of it.'

'Ah, Mr Sangster, perhaps we need to add a little in-depth analysis here . . .'

Wilson sat back with an elaborate sigh and stared at the ceiling; but Cooper, a short, restless man who evidently needed to be a participant in any conversation, ignored these signs of disapproval.

'Mr Sangster, you'll perhaps be aware that most of the world's long distance telephone traffic is now handled by geosynchronous satellites.'

'They're the ones that stay fixed over one spot, right?'

'Right. By 1987 there were a heck of a lot of them over the equator, and they all had to be in orbit 22,300 miles from the earth's surface if they were to travel at the same speed as the earth.'

'Got it.'

43

'They had too much traffic to handle. Some up-and-coming nations couldn't book enough space and the Federal commission in charge of these things wouldn't sanction another geosynch. We at COMSAT . . . you do know about COMSAT?'

'The American satellite agency. Part of INTELSAT.'

'Right, great. Anyone wants to launch a telecoms satellite, they have to talk to INTELSAT. In practice, they have to talk to COMSAT. Well, a few Southeast Asian nations got together and did just that. They wanted more telecoms capacity. We agreed they could put a satellite into medium orbit, less than five thousand miles up, to take over the morning rush-hour.'

'I'm sorry?'

'Problem was, between nine and one in the morning, local time, everybody wants to make calls. The geosynch couldn't handle them all. So the idea was to put up a small, relatively cheap satellite that'd come over the horizon and cream off Southeast Asia's morning traffic, with the geosynch handling only the residue. With me?'

'I think so.'

'Okay. Now, here's the wrinkle. We had launch problems around about that time, right? Remember Challenger? A lot of our military reconnaissance satellites were falling silent and we couldn't replace them.'

'Bad news.'

'*Very* bad news. So Washington took a look at the map and came up with a neat idea. The client countries wanted China to launch the satellite. We couldn't do it, the Chinese could, their pricing was realistic. The administration here agreed to take a big slice of the cost, *as long as* we were allowed to put in a few other odds and ends, along with the phone channels. Ford Aircraft built it; the Chinese sent it up in March of '88. For a couple of years it flew around the globe once every ninety-two minutes. As it passed over the Composite Signals Org Station at Chung Hom Kok in Hong Kong, it used to download . . . certain materials.'

'Like what?'

Cooper's face clouded. 'I'm not at liberty to –'

'I see. It overflew the Soviet Union and China.'

Cooper looked sullen. 'The point is, Mr Sangster, that this satellite contributed valuable data for the purposes of national defence. And yesterday the Soviet Union shot it down.'

'Why does it have to be the Soviet Union?'

Sangster turned to Dr Van Thach, the man who had asked the question, with a reassuring smile – reassuring because the diminutive scientist seemed astonished at his own presumption in opening his mouth. Vietnamese, Sangster guessed: appearance and name both fitted, as did his general air of feeling he owed the world a living.

'No one else has the technology.' Cooper's voice was sharp and patronizing.

'Is that right?' Wilson drawled softly. He puffed out his cheeks and rolled his eyeballs. Sangster knew both he and the professor wanted to pursue the topic, but for now he put it on hold. 'What exactly happened yesterday?' he asked.

'Interesting question.' The professor picked up the bit of metal from the bench and squinted at it. 'You familiar with the concept of ablation?'

Sangster shook his head.

'Come over here, take a look at this.'

Wilson led the way across to one of the intimidating, man-high instruments and waved a technician aside. 'Electron microscope,' he said over his shoulder. 'Two hundred thousand times more powerful than the human eye.' Sangster bent to the eyepiece at an invitation from the professor, who went on, 'Dehydrated shaving of metal, something off the outer casing's my guess. We don't have everything we need out here. I'll want hard X-rays of what you're looking at and a mass spectrometry reading wouldn't do any harm. So a lot of what I'm going to say now is provisional, okay?'

Sangster nodded.

'The satellite broke up during frictional drag re-entry. Burned up on coming out of the magnetosphere, in other words. There's traces of that. But there's also traces of something else, something uncharacteristic of re-entry.' Wilson gestured at the microscope. 'A lot of the satellite just vaporized. We were lucky to get a piece of the outer casing where

45

whatever it was hit it made contact. That's how ablation comes in: the casing was treated to form a char layer of porous graphite refractory residue as the heat built up . . . oh, the hell with it, there was a finish that radiated energy away from the satellite.'

'All right. What've we got?'

'Any of you guys shoot pool?' Wilson stared from face to face, as if expecting a serious response. Sangster smiled and half-raised his hand.

'Know how to give a ball side-spin?'

'Not as often as I'd like.'

'Same here! But that's what happened to the satellite. It wasn't a direct hit. Something very hot ripped into the side of the casing, the result of impulsive loading's my guess, and just nudged it enough to send it spinning off in a totally unpredictable path. Back towards earth. Alaska, as it happened.'

'You say something hot. What, exactly? A missile?'

'No! Have you any idea how difficult it would be to shoot down a satellite with a missile? Besides, a missile wouldn't have left any remains, like the ones we have here, for us to analyse.'

'Then what could it be?'

Wilson shrugged. 'Laser beam. Charged particle beam.' Again the by-now familiar grin. 'Death ray, Mr Sangster.' He lowered his voice to a mock-conspiratorial whisper. '*Star* wars, Mr Sangster.'

The visitor rested his back against the microscope and smiled. Wilson read his expression. 'You don't believe me,' he said bluntly.

Sangster shrugged.

'I don't believe me, either.' Wilson laughed. 'Trouble is, it's true.'

'I thought everyone had got tired of that stuff.'

'Hardly. For the past couple of years we reckon we've been able to transmit an effective beam over a range of four thousand miles, using a two-megawatt laser and thirty-three feet mirrors. It's called SIPAPU. And if we can do that, bet your last cent the Soviets can do the same. But we've experienced problems beyond the ordinary.'

'Such as?'

'For one thing, a laser beam, although collimated, spreads, diffuses, over long distances. Whoever did that' – he pointed to where the remains of the satellite lay on the bench – 'managed to crack the problem. Either that, or he used a charged particle beam non-susceptible to bending by the Earth's magnetic field.'

'So we're looking for a genius?'

'More than one. Somebody else would have been in charge of solving the superconductivity problems associated with beam weapons. And if, as we suspect, this was ignited from an aircraft, we're also up against a formidable brain in the field of magnetohydro-dynamics. Either that, or they've invented some kind of incredibly advanced nuclear power-pack.'

'So there you have it, Mr Sangster.' Cooper's intervening voice was sombre. 'The Soviet Union has us by the balls.'

'Just a minute.' Sangster thrust his hands into his pockets and began to walk around. 'That's the second time you've accused the Russians. But relations between the US and the Soviet bloc have never been as good as they are now. *Glasnost*, openness, isn't that what the guy said? Detente.'

'Detente and *glasnost* are faked. The Pentagon gamesroom postulates a wargasm scenario, and if we can't –'

'What is a wargasm?' Wilson interjected.

'Uh, escalating conflict situational development.'

Sangster concealed a smile. 'Well now, Mr Cooper, that is what I would describe as a zebra – a very obscure diagnosis indeed. And I have to tell you, it doesn't gel with my department's assessment of the position, right now.'

'Who else could it be?'

'Some European countries have gone a long way down this road. They have the rescources, given the will. And have you thought of China? They have a comprehensive space programme. They've put a geosynchronous satellite into orbit, I seem to remember, and their Long March III rockets are ranked among the best launch vehicles in the world.'

47

'Ridiculous.'

'Is it?' Wilson's interjection was cold in tone. 'For the past two years, all the best superconductivity work has been done inside China. So there's one of the major problems well on the way to solution.' He paused and looked down at his hands, aware that he might be about to offend. 'How many Chinese nationals are at work on SIPAPU?'

There was a long silence. 'What are you saying?' Cooper inquired at last.

'I'm saying that a lot of people have come out of China over the past twenty years, fleeing one thing or another. Some of them ended up here, working for Uncle Sam.' Wilson's glance flickered towards Van Thach, who was staring at the floor. 'Maybe not all of them work for him full time. Not everyone on the payroll can be Yankee-white, thank God.'

'But we have Russian defectors working for us, too.'

'Not on projects like SIPAPU we don't.'

Sangster found the silence embarrassing. He was conscious of Van Thach, affronted but impotent, standing a few feet away from him. It's nothing personal, he wanted to say; we're none of us anti-oriental . . .

'My great-grandfather was Chinese,' said Wilson. He barked a short laugh.

Sangster glanced at his watch and his face tensed. 'Well, I guess I've learned a lot today. Thanks, Professor . . . gentlemen. Major, do you need me any more? Only I'm supposed to be on a plane . . .'

Guard was ushering Sangster out when Van Thach called across the room after them, his voice high and resonant with tension. 'Mr Sangster!'

Sangster reluctantly turned back, his pleasant smile intact.

'Why did you come here? What do you want from us?'

Sangster made a fist and hit the doorjamb, ever so gently. But his pleasant smile was the only answer he had for them.

THREE

◇

Tom Young entered a small room lined from floor to ceiling with safe deposit boxes. He walked to the far end of it, inserted three keys in different boxes and turned them in sequence. The entire wall of safes opened outwards to reveal a simply-furnished boardroom beyond. It contained twenty men, all of whom now turned to face the chairman and chief executive of the Pacific and Cantonese Banking Corporation.

Tom glanced at the boy – all the bank's security guards enjoyed that appellation, irrespective of age or status – who was standing in the corridor, and signalled that he might be released. The boy closed the door, locked it with his own set of keys and stood with his back to it. He felt under his arm to make sure that the stubby Beretta 9mm was secure in its holster before settling down to wait.

The boardroom lay deep underground in the Corporation's lowest vaults: Tom Young's territory. It showed in the way he moved to the head of the long table and took his seat. He looked every inch a chairman. Tall, lean and tanned, he always seemed the picture of health, although by now he was well into his seventies: he might have dried with age, but he had not withered. His manner was abrupt and humourless; his face was long and narrow, its expression cold, and it tapered to the upturned chin, whence a deep line ran up either side of his sunken cheeks to meet at the temple. It evidently cost him nothing to exert authority over a roomful of men each of whom was accustomed to exercise his own autocratic power.

'All secure?' Tom rapped.

The men nodded; a few murmured assent. Security had

49

become second nature to them over the past two years. At irregular intervals, but never less than once a month, they would gather in this room. Each man came accompanied by a 'minder', whose job it was to ensure that no one followed his employer. These powerful men went through this extraordinary rigmarole patiently, even willingly; because unless the very fact of their meetings could be kept secret, their concerted purpose stood no chance of success.

For that reason, each man had to be ready to produce at least one witness to swear that at the time of the meeting he was somewhere else; none of the people inside this room had risen to the top without generating formidable loyalties (not to mention obligations of a personal kind) along the way.

Between them they represented all the most wealthy and influential trading houses of Hong Kong. In addition, their collective personal wealth accounted for nearly one-third of the colony's individual fortunes. Sometime within the next few weeks, they intended to quit the place for ever. Their common intention was to ensure that their assets went with them.

'Then I call this meeting of the Club of Twenty to order. We will take the minutes as read.'

This was Tom Young's idea of a joke. No one took minutes; the risk was too great. A couple of people laughed: Rameses Wong, one of the four Chinese members; and Harry Longman, Hong Kong's property king. Tom cast a sideways glance at the man on his immediate left: Simon Young, his son, who was one of those who did not laugh. He sat staring straight ahead, lips slightly parted, wearing an expression of unutterable sadness. Tom lowered his eyes.

'Mat . . . turn on the screen, would you?'

At the far end of the table a tall man in his mid-twenties stood up and went to switch on a video display unit by the door. As he made fine adjustments to the contrast the picture jumped and one of the figures changed. 'US dollar down three points against sterling,' Mat muttered as he went back to his seat.

'Deutschmark?' Granville Peterson asked. He was one of the

banker-members; these things mattered most to the out-and-out money men.

'No change.'

Mat stared along the table at Tom, who was his grandfather, and wondered how much hung on those three points for the ruler of Hong Kong's most extended bank.

'All right, gentlemen. I'm sorry about the short notice, but you know why. At noon today, Reuters made the first official announcement that China's leader is close to death. Lung cancer and emphysema. The Chairman's the only person who's been holding the show together. When he dies, Hong Kong's going to crash. Anyone disagree?' His pause was token. 'Very well. Benevolence is coming forward. We go within the next few days. I want —'

'Excuse me, Mr Chairman. A point of order.'

Tom didn't have to look to identify the speaker, didn't even have to match up the voice in his memory. Only one person moved points of order here.

'Cumnor?'

A Chinese gentleman sitting halfway down the table on Tom's right leaned forward, nervously twiddling a pencil. Alexander Cumnor was one of the few who had not removed his jacket. As usual, he wore un-patterned clothes of soft colours: a plain, pale pink shirt, contrasting tie of darker shade, grey suit. Nothing ever had a texture, a stripe or a dot. Cumnor made no demands on the human eye. It was often easy to forget he was there at all.

Only in one respect was he distinctive: time obsessed him. He wore three watches; one on each wrist and a third around the outside of his jacket sleeve.

'Are we not going to wait for Peter?'

'Afraid not. I'm sorry to kick off with the bad news, but we're no longer a club of twenty, we're a club of nineteen. Peter Robson chucked his hand in this morning. The partners are all filing their own bankruptcy petitions. He was good enough to let me know. Principal banker, and so on.'

There was a moment of silence; then throats were cleared, anxious whispers flared up around the table.

'That's a sad thing.' Warren Honnyman, the Club's deputy chairman, sat immediately to the right of Tom Young. His soft, broad-vowelled Boston accent did not seem out of place in the patrician atmosphere of colonial Hong Kong which the other members generated; but his loose-fitting Armani shirt and pale blue slacks, worn like a uniform, were a constant reminder that not everything remained the same. 'Tom, is there anything we can do?'

'No.'

'I hate to push you, but . . .' Warren leaned forward to rest his elbows on the table and picked gently at the sides of his gold-rimmed bifocals. '. . . when one of the oldest firms of lawyers in Hong Kong is forced to file for bankruptcy, I can't help feeling –'

'The losses are very substantial. And we have an agreement, do we not: none of us must do anything that could give rise to suspicion on the outside that we might be acting in concert.'

'Will the clients suffer?'

Robert Clancy, chairman of Continental Financial Services, had spoken, and Tom recognized him as one of the clients in question. 'No.'

'But how –?'

'An unfortunate investment, I gather, coupled with a halving of fee income. Beijing took against them. I don't have to remind anyone what effect that can have.'

Many discreet eyes focused on Simon Young, who remained oblivious of them, but Tom continued smoothly as if his son did not exist. 'Now if I may –'

But Alexander Cumnor had risen and gone to stand in front of the screen, anxiously peering at the figures. Suddenly he brought out a leather-bound notebook in which he began to scribble hasty Chinese characters.

'Excuse me,' he muttered. 'I have to make a phonecall.'

He left the room for a short time. While he was away Tom used the buzz of quiet conversation to talk to his son. 'News?'

'Mm?' Simon made an effort to rouse himself. 'No. Nothing. Just the same.'

'Sorry.' Tom hesitated. 'Look, I know this is a bad time to

52

ask, but . . . what about the computer-tape? The Scroll of Benevolence.'

'It's nearly ready.'

'You realize I must have it soon? Without it, we can't get off the ground.'

'I know.'

Cumnor returned and settled down in his seat once more, but his concentration had gone. His gaze was drawn back to the screen again and again.

'Some more bad tidings before we get on. Simon?'

Simon slowly rubbed a hand over his forehead and sat up a little more, trying to filter out the personal grief. He knew that everyone here was sorry for him; he also knew that Jinny's impending death had no relevance to the business in hand.

'As you know, Ducannon Young has been lucky enough to be able to call on three of Hong Kong's largest banks to finance its operations. Unfortunately, that situation changed yesterday. Beijing's leading front man here has just taken over the Asian Industrial Bank. I am, of course, public enemy number one in China. The result is that there will be no more money; and existing loans must be rescheduled.' Again he passed a hand over his damp face, the gesture of one who has been tried beyond his limits. 'In the present climate, I can't raise the necessary funds.'

The silence that greeted this summary went on for a long time. Ducannon Young, 'Dunny's,' had been founded in the time of Dr William Jardine and James Mattheson. None of the great trading houses had a longer or more honourable history. To the men listening it was as though Simon had just announced the collapse of Victoria Peak.

Cumnor placed both hands on the table and levered himself up. 'Simon, I want to say that I am very sorry. It is a tragedy. For you. And for Hong Kong.'

There were murmurs of assent. Mat looked down at his lap and made a face. He found Cumnor pompous, his words seemed wild. Tragedy had no place in this room. The Club of Twenty knew the rules and played by them. He noticed also that none of the representatives of the four other great *hongs* was in any hurry to come forward offering condolences: Adrian de Lisle, John Blake, Peter Carrigan and Martin Panmuir-Smith sat staring bleakly straight in front of them, like officers at a court-martial.

'There is no hope for any of us.' Cumnor had turned his head away from Simon and was addressing the table at large. 'If Dunny's falls, that means the end.'

'I disagree.' Although Mat was a director of Ducannon Young and ran its Taiwanese operation, he was present purely as his father's assistant and so did not usually speak out at meetings of the Club. But this was too much for him. 'We shall simply uproot and move to Taiwan. The bank can foreclose on a few typewriters if it likes. Everything else will be gone. Forgive me, Alex, but you understand these things perfectly well: you've had a place ready in Singapore for months.'

Tom rapped three times with his pencil. 'No more talk of tragedies, Alex. Maybe you did things differently in Melbourne, years ago.' His pause was pregnant with meaning; no one knew too much about Cumnor's early years, or the means by which he'd made his fortune. 'But this is Hong Kong.'

Cumnor sat down slowly.

'As I see it, the Chairman's imminent death, coupled with Dunny's position, means we've no time left. Warren, what's the up-to-date transport situation?'

'I still have to approach the government for permission to use Kai Tak airport in the way we want, but I've targeted the right man.'

'Then get him. Quickly. But be careful. If the slightest word of what we plan leaked out –'

'The People's Liberation Army would be coming down the New Territories within twenty-four hours.'

'They may be coming anyway. I take it we've all seen the latest news on the satellite thing.'

'Our branch manager in Moscow is asking permission to send the families home,' someone said. 'He estimates our ambassador will go within forty-eight hours and he doesn't want any of his staff left behind.' The speaker was Max Weber, vice-president of the largest German trader still left in Hong Kong. Its parent company was renowned for the thoroughness of its international research, combined with rare analytical acumen; an 'estimate' from that quarter had the hallmark of genuine prophecy.

'My God, look at that.' Weber rose to take a closer look at the screen, where the hourly headlines were being flashed up. '"Reports of further student unrest on the Beijing university campus. Tear gas has been used. Conservative elements loyal . . ." Wait a minute, I can't . . . "loyal to the memory of Mao Zedong are believed to be behind the recent disturbances."'

The ensuing, heavy silence was shattered by the telephone-bell. Mat, who sat nearest to it, picked up the receiver. They all saw him swallow and noted how the colour drained away from his face. 'We'll come,' he muttered at last, before he replaced the receiver. For a moment he said nothing else. Then — 'Da?' His voice was soft.

Simon took one look at his son's face and nodded. The two of them rose and made for the door. The meeting had not ended, but no one thought to ask where they were going, or why.

As they entered the complex of tunnels that led away from the Corporation's vaults, Alexander Cumnor's personal assistant, who was leaning against the wall with a number of other 'minders', smiled at them. The assistant's name was Leong; he and Mat sometimes played tennis together. Now he made a mental note that the Youngs were leaving early and remembered to look at his watch. His employer had often reminded him that the KGB were sticklers for precise times and dates.

The doctor came very quickly, as doctors do when the end is near. He was administering a pain-killing injection when Mat entered the bedroom.

'How is she?'

Doctor Stevens gave the pinprick a final dab with cotton

55

wool before answering. 'She'll sleep now, but she may wake in an hour or two. Is Simon about?'

'Downstairs,' Mat said. 'On the phone.'

'Right. I'll have a word.'

Diana was outside on the balcony, watching the last of the sun descend into a bowl of mauve, pink and yellow clouds shot through with stabs of lingering rain: not a gentle evening. She waited for Stevens to leave before she quietly re-entered her mother's bedroom. Because she had been gazing at the day's end for too long, the interior presented itself to her in the monochromes of a photographic negative.

Mat was sitting bent forward over his mother's hand. At the sound of Diana's approach he sat up.

'Don't move.' She pulled a chair close to the other side of the bed. For a long time the two of them sat there, staring at the sleeping face on the pillow, while outside the light died.

Dr Stevens went downstairs to find Simon on the phone to his finance director.

'. . . well, *do it, then!* Goddammit, George, haven't you played this game long enough to . . .' He caught the doctor's eye and had the grace to appear ashamed. 'Look, I can't talk now. Ring you later.'

He slammed down the receiver. 'The reds are hounding us at the moment. Want a drink?'

'No, thanks. Simon, I'm —'

'Yes, of course.' His mood changed instantly. 'How is she?'

'I've got a fine line to walk. I have to control the pain, but if I give too large a dose . . .'

'Yes.'

'There's nothing more I can do for Jinny. But you're my patient, too, as of now. You're to have dinner, and you can have a whisky, a small one, but you mustn't go near the bedroom until after you've eaten.'

'How can you expect —'

'Because she's sleeping and you couldn't do any good.' Stevens' voice was ragged. 'Don't make this more difficult for us both, please. You and Jinny have been patients, friends, for a long time. It's not easy for me, either.'

56

On his way out, he briefly laid a hand on Simon's shoulder and gave it a squeeze.

Mat and Diana came downstairs shortly afterwards. Dinner was a silent meal. Simon scarcely touched his food. At last he laid down his knife and fork with a sigh so soft that it scarcely carried to where Diana was sitting. 'I sometimes wish . . . the waiting was over.' He twisted in his chair until he was facing both his children. 'Do you think that's a terrible thing to say?'

Mat stared at his plate.

'I think . . .' Diana felt tears rise in her throat. 'Oh, I don't know what I think. Part of me says you're right, because this isn't any good for mother. But another part of me . . .'

She would have liked to say, 'You're right to believe it, and wrong to say it out loud. *Wrong!*' Yet that involved judging her own father in a way that wasn't possible; and besides, she distrusted her reactions.

She knew he was labouring under impossible pressures. She remembered him as he once had been: very tall, with smouldering deepset eyes of formidable power, wavy brown hair, a square jaw and two semicircular clefts cut deep around the mouth adding a touch of humour. But of this dynamic captain of industry, the piratical entrepreneur who had dominated the colony like a human representation of the Hong Kong & Shanghai Bank's headquarters, there now remained little trace.

As they were starting to sip their coffee, the nurse summoned them upstairs.

They entered the bedroom to find Jinny awake. She did not move more than her head, but the pain seemed to be in abeyance and her smile said that she knew who they were.

Simon was the first to bend over with a kiss for his wife; the other two followed. The atmosphere in the room had undergone a subtle change. It was extraordinarily quiet, peaceful in a way none of the family had known for days. Mat opened the french windows to admit humid evening air, now cooled by the sea below.

Jinny did not speak. Instead she made a great effort to stretch out her hand. Simon took it gently, aware of how

57

pressure scalded her nerves. 'It's me, darling. I'm sorry I'm late.'

'Good . . . day?'

'Yes.' He smiled directly into her eyes, willing her to believe the lie. 'Pretty good.'

'Mat?'

'He's here.'

Jinny lifted her right hand from the sheet and moved it almost imperceptibly in the direction of her japanned dressing table. The telepathy between husband and wife had not been undermined by illness; Simon knew what she wanted.

'Jewellery?'

Jinny nodded. Simon fetched an elaborate fifteenth-century Korean chest and placed it on the bed beside her.

'Simon . . .'

'Yes. Here it is . . .'

Jinny looked at her engagement ring for a long time. It was, in Diana's view, the most wonderful piece of jewellery in the world: a rectangular sapphire bathed in a sea of tiny diamonds on a thick platinum band. Since the day Simon had paid the earth for it, Jinny's love for him never ceased to enhance its value, each hour adding to the patina of devotion which the ring both represented and enshrined.

'Simon?' This time the single word was intended as a question. Simon looked at Jinny, seeking confirmation of what he already knew, and nodded. 'Yes. Of course.'

Jinny forced her head back to the left, so she could once again look at her daughter. Diana saw what was coming and said, 'No.'

'Diana . . .'

'Please, Ma. *Please* . . .'

But Jinny had already taken Diana's hand and placed the ring in her palm. 'It's a bribe,' she whispered.

Diana, thinking she must have misheard, brought her ear down to Jinny's lips. But – 'A bribe,' she murmured again. 'You have to . . . pay.'

'Anything.'

'It's in my will. A codicil. All . . . there. Funeral. I don't want

58

to be kept in the cemetery. Not like that. Different. All there. Promise.'

'Of course I promise,' she wailed. The ring fell onto the sheet, unheeded. Silent tears were flooding down Diana's cheeks, but Jinny seemed not to notice. The pain, when it came, was fierce. Seconds later, a stream of yellowy-green vomit trickled across the bedclothes to accumulate in an evil-smelling puddle, masking the precious gems' glitter as a pungent reminder that everything is vanity in the end.

They did what they could to make her comfortable. When she was quiet again Diana retrieved the ring, wiped it clean and laid it on the bedside table, hoping it might lie there and be forgotten.

For several minutes Jinny fought to recover: it was as if she had unfinished business to transact, something that could not wait. 'The box,' she said at last. Her voice hardly amounted to more than a tired whisper. 'Inside . . .'

Simon drew an envelope out of the chest. When Jinny nodded, he opened it to find a sheet of stiff paper folded into three.

'Read.'

He put on his spectacles. 'This is a first codicil to my last will . . .'

'Please.'

'I direct my executors that my body shall not be buried in the Crown Colony of Hong Kong, but I desire instead to be cremated and my ashes preserved. Furthermore I request my . . . my dear . . .'

The paper fell onto the bedclothes. Mat reached over his father to retrieve the codicil and slowly read it aloud.

'I request my dear daughter Diana at a time convenient to her to transport my mortal remains to Chaiyang in the province of Sichuan within the People's Republic of China, there to be preserved at the village shrine by my sister Wang Kaihui and my brother Wang Mingchao with ancestral rites in accord with such of the customs and traditions of the Chinese race as they think proper, the expenses respectively incurred by my said daughter, sister and brother to be a charge on my estate.'

He replaced the paper in its envelope, careful to see that the existing folds were respected, and laid it on his mother's bedside table.

Diana reached across the sheet to take Jinny's hands. 'Please.'

'Yes.' But she could not say more; instead she nodded her head and clasped her mother's hands to her eyes, so that she might feel the tears of her assent and be satisfied.

The merest breeze manifested itself in a lifting of the curtain; the air within the room scarcely moved. Nevertheless they all felt it, and all of them glanced around to see what had caused the change. But the curtains were still. When they looked back, Jinny had left them.

For a long moment they could not believe it. Then Simon rose and kissed the dead face, already softening into peace, before blindly turning away. Mat walked quickly to his bedroom, running the last few steps, and slammed the door. Simon waited for Diana to come past him. As she did so she mutely held out the ring, beseeching him to take it, but he shook his head with a smile.

'Please.' She echoed her mother's last word.

He folded his daughter's hands around the ring and gripped them tightly. 'No.'

She expected him to follow her out, but instead he softly closed the door behind her. And in that moment Diana envied him, because he knew how to mourn.

FOUR

◇

The wind harried Konstantin Proshin's attempts to light his favourite meerschaum pipe, but he was a patient man by nature; and anyhow, this was his rest day, so there was no need to hurry. The old Zippo lighter, held deeply within the folds of his suede overcoat, did the trick at last. He leaned his back against one of the three tall pines that sheltered Boris Pasternak's simple grave, just beyond Peredelkino church, and opened the Penguin edition of *Doctor Zhivago*, puffing contentedly.

Every so often Proshin would look up and spend a few moments staring at the headstone. He could not read the inscription from where he was sitting, but he knew what it said. 'Boris Pasternak, 1890–1960.' Proshin approved of that. It sufficed.

Although it was still early in the year, someone had already scattered daffodils and tulips across the mound. Proshin approved of that also. He shrugged his warm coat more closely around his shoulders and returned to the English text.

Major-General Krubykov's messenger boy, a callow *shpick* named Orlov, found his quarry rapt in concentration and for a second was nonplussed. Could this be the expert they were all seeking high and low? Surely such a great brain couldn't be concealed in that tiny, elf-like body? Then Proshin looked up: his head snapped around in a flash to reveal a profile sharp as a jig-saw piece; his gaze narrowed into a hard stare; every limb moved and at once was still. Orlov stepped back, dimly aware that there was more here than met the eye. 'Konstantin

Proshin,' he called softly; although there was no one else around to hear.

'Who wants him?'

The elf's voice sounded unnaturally light, as if he were having a joke; the kind of voice you use to raise a laugh at the expense of some poor booby. An intellectual laugh, Orlov thought in disgust.

'You're wanted. Never mind who by.'

'But I do mind.' Proshin returned to his book, pointedly rounding his back against the *shpick's* dim stare.

Orlov transferred his weight from foot to foot. 'You're wanted by the boss,' he ventured sourly at last.

'Which boss?' Proshin addressed his question to the printed page, but Orlov fancied that was the sense of it. 'Major-General Krubykov. At . . . *once!'*

If Orlov had expected to snap Proshin to attention by shouting, he was disappointed. Proshin put his finger on the page, ran it downwards, inserted a bookmark and rose to his feet. Orlov observed this display of indifference with mounting wrath. He decided that Proshin had had enough fun for one day. As he made to pass Orlov, the *shpick* stuck out a boot.

What happened next was not in the KGB manual. To his surprise and indignation Orlov felt his right arm jerked half out of its socket at the shoulder; next moment the world was describing a whirligig circle, taking Pasternak's tombstone as its centre. The back of his skull connected with the earth at the same moment as his coccyx. Fortunately the winter rains had softened the ground, or he might not have risen again.

Proshin tucked his book under his arm and with his free hand bent to offer Orlov a hand. The *shpick*, mistaking his motives, hurriedly slithered away. Proshin shook his head and sighed. 'Suit yourself. Where is the Major-General?'

Orlov levered himself upright with a scowl and started for the church. Proshin followed, wearing a grin that seemed to split his face in half whenever he saw his reluctant companion apprehensively look around.

A black Zil stood neatly aligned with the stake-fence that, officially, was supposed to protect the church from vandals.

At a gesture from Orlov, Proshin opened the nearside back door and climbed in.

He found himself sinking into a seat of soft brown hide that smelled pleasantly of tobacco and wealth. This was turning out to be a very satisfactory day.

'Konstantin Proshin?'

The voice belonged to a tall, well-built man whose bespectacled watery eyes, blunt, peasant's hands and decidedly cold expression harmonized into an unsettlingly morbid appearance. Yet he wore an expensive-looking blue suit, his nails were manicured and some barber had obviously spent a long time over waving that silver hair.

'Yes. Major-General Krubykov?'

The older man, who occupied the seat next to Proshin's, did not answer. Instead he picked up the car's internal telephone and murmured the single word, 'Go.'

They drove for a long time; Proshin had an idea they were going around in circles. After a while, however, the car turned off the main road and bumped down a stony track between densely planted spruce, birch and pine trees. Suddenly progress was impeded by a red and white horizontal pole across the track. A uniformed sentry inspected Krubykov's pass, made a note in his book and waved them on.

Proshin was not given much of a chance to take in his surroundings. A gravel drive, three-storey *dacha*, huge Grecian urns containing remnants of dead flowers . . . then he was trotting up a broad flight of steps to a pair of dark, studded doors.

The interior was dark and dusty; Proshin could not suppress the tickle in his throat and began to cough. Then he became aware of Krubykov talking to someone else, a figure half visible through the gloom. 'You like it?'

'I'm surprised to see it.' A woman's voice, mellow but a touch strident, as if she were trying too hard to impress. Then the coughing fit passed, his vision cleared, and he saw what had attracted her attention: a huge oil painting of Stalin, hanging at the far end of the hall. Proshin rubbed his eyes in surprise. Then his brain caught up with the knowledge that

Krubykov and the woman had spoken in English and he directed all his attention towards the General's other guest.

Or rather, guests. A sturdy-looking man stood to one side with his hands behind his back, looking up at the portrait. Proshin knew at once he was an American: those shiny slacks with their knife-edge creases, the blue blazer, shock of hair, flash of gold on a little finger, everything pointed to Transatlantic Man.

The woman stood sideways on to Krubykov, no longer interested in the complacent tyrant portrayed above her, but concerned to study one of his present-day successors. She was in her late forties and looked like a hotel matron, Proshin decided; or maybe a very special *sekretutka*, the kind who worked, horizontally or vertically, only for the topmost bosses of all. She wore a black, tailored suit over a white blouse with a choker at the neck; her shoes were low-heeled and plain, her nylons just visible over somewhat chubby legs; her hair, greying now but once obviously blonde, had been swept back into a severe bun. Yet there was something . . . just as the hair had once shone gold, so the face too must have been lovely then.

'It's funny,' the woman said with a smile to Krubykov. 'I had you down as older, somehow.'

'And your photographs scarcely do you justice. They hadn't prepared me for beauty.'

'Or gallantry, in my case.'

'Or flirtatiousness. This man' – Krubykov glanced over his shoulder – 'is Konstantin Proshin, our contribution to the picnic. Proshin, you are meeting Catherine Palmer, Assistant Director of Plans, Central Intelligence Agency; and Gene Sangster of the Agency's Soviet Desk, Executive . . . Hub, is that what you call it now?'

Sangster inclined his head, an ironical smile tugging at the ends of his lips.

'It's cold in here. Let's make ourselves more comfortable.'

Krubykov stalked into a cavernous living-room, its three sets of french windows draped with heavy velvet curtains. Sangster and Palmer sat on an enormous betasselled gold and crimson sofa. At a sign from Krubykov, Proshin seated himself at right angles to the Americans, keeping his face in shadow. The General himself stood in front of a fireplace twice as tall as he was, and cleared his throat portentously. 'Chairman Kazin sends his apologies. Naturally he would have wished to be present, but –'

'He isn't dead yet, then?' asked the woman.

Krubykov's eyes narrowed unpleasantly. Proshin understood that the General had been pleased to keep his end up in the earlier repartee but now was in a mood for business.

'He is not dead,' Krubykov confirmed.

'Is he here? Upstairs?'

'It doesn't matter where he is.' Krubykov took out a cigarette-case and lit up. He did not waste breath on asking the Americans whether they smoked. He knew about their personal habits, just as they were familiar with his. 'The important thing is that we do the deal, yes?'

Proshin leaned forward. A meeting between the archangels of CIA and KGB to transact a 'deal' . . .! When the woman merely nodded carelessly, Proshin admired her attitude. She was cool, that one.

'The situation,' Krubykov went on, 'is bleak. For the past three years we've prided ourselves on the steps we have taken towards peace. Arms limitations, zero nuclear options in Europe . . . I don't have to spell it out.'

'I think you do.' Palmer sounded dismissive. 'We believe it's a front. *Glasnost*, all the rest of it. A continuation of the war by other means.'

'Then why are you here?'

Palmer was silent.

'I assure you, I promise you – we did not shoot down that satellite.'

'You have the technology.'

'We believe we do, although –'

'No one else has it. Apart from us, that is.'

'China –'

'Crap! Sorry, General, but we rule out China. She just doesn't have the know-how. Eighteen months ago they sent a delegation to Lawrence Livermore, to talk about beam weapons. I've read our side's report: the Chinese are still living in the stone age.'

'If you think we're capable of bluffing you, if you say that *glasnost* and so on is play-acting, why won't you believe the same of Beijing?'

'Let me assume you have a point. What about the rest of the evidence?'

'What are you referring to?'

'We detected that energy-burst from your ASAT.' Palmer tossed her head. 'Come on, General. You have a hunter-killer satellite. It fired. Our own satellite disintegrated a millisecond later. What would you think?'

Stalemate. Proshin had been listening greedily to the exchange. Now, in the silence that followed, he woke up to the fact that Sangster was studying him. Proshin's eyes met his and flickered. Why did the American smile at him like that? Always smiling . . .

'Very well.' Krubykov moved away from the fireplace for long enough to deposit ash in a brass bowl. 'It seems there's nothing to discuss.' He paused. 'Would you like me to call your car?'

'Let's talk about your proposal first.'

'You find it attractive?'

'I find it startling. You invite one of my team to work side by side with Proshin here in an attempt to prove that the Chinese shot down that satellite –' Palmer looked around in irritation to see what was bugging Proshin. She found him strange. Those bulging eyes, those quick, nervy hand gestures, they unsettled her. 'He didn't know?' she asked Krubykov incredulously.

'Not until you were kind enough to tell him.'

Palmer shrugged. 'Seriously, General: if we issued you with an invitation to step inside the Pentagon, don't you think that (a) you might find it suspicious and (b) what the hell, you'd go along for the ride? I mean, a chance to see inside –'

'Now listen.' Krubykov held up his hands. 'You háve made a public accusation. Unless you revoke it, our respective ambassadors must be recalled for consultations. From then on, things will escalate rapidly. If *we* thought *you* had destroyed one of our satellites, we would regard it as a hostile act meriting retaliation.'

'An unpleasant word.'

'With overtones I would not like you to miss.' The General's voice was hard, introspective. 'This is far too important to be left to the politicians, the diplomats. We have to sort out this mess using conventional intelligence means. I think that, given time, I can prove the Chinese shot down that satellite. The trouble is, the USA isn't going to believe any evidence to that effect as long as it's produced by the Soviet Union.'

'Which is where Proshin and Sangster come in?'

'Correct. They're to work as a team, shadowing each other, providing instant self-verification.'

Palmer said nothing for a while. She sat forward, hands crossed in her lap, not taking her eyes off the General's face. 'Why now?'

'Now?'

'There have been many times in the past when we'd have welcomed such an approach. You never made it. Why now? Could it be anything to do with the failure of your grain harvest last year?'

Krubykov shrugged. 'Perhaps. I'm not in on policy-making. You know the facts as well as I do: this matter's becoming more urgent with every hour that passes. Share values are falling, crude commodities and precious metals are sky-rocketing, the US dollar's anyone's guess: it's worse than 1987. Why? Because everybody thinks the past three years have gone for nothing. The cold war's back.'

'And you need grain. Wheat. You need it very badly.'

'If you say so, madam.' The sarcasm in that 'madam', accompanied by a stiff bow, caught Palmer on the raw.

'Yes, I say so. I also say we have no evidence, not the slightest, to suggest that China was responsible for this outrage. So now tell me: what evidence do *you* have?'

Krubykov nodded at Proshin. 'Ask him.'

Palmer swivelled elaborately in her seat, as if to stress

67

to Proshin that she was all ears. 'Mr Proshin. Shoot.'

Proshin gazed up at Krubykov in agony.

'The Chinese Boeing-747.' Krubykov's voice was curt.

Proshin's eyes widened in amazement. 'Our computerized graph-plotters,' he began haltingly, 'were set to work to see if we could detect anything suspicious or out of the ordinary connected with Chinese aerospace.'

'And?'

Proshin hesitated. 'It's probably nothing. But one of our reconnaissance satellites was making a pass over north-eastern China at the moment of the attack. We analysed that one first, because we had a particular interest in the PLA's 23rd Army Corps at Harbin, in Shenyang province.'

'Go on.'

'The cameras picked up something that shouldn't have been there.'

'Which was?'

'A civilian airliner, flying through restricted military airspace. A Chinese Boeing 747-400. Strangely, its hump was elongated.'

'So? That's what they call a stretched-top version, isn't it?'

'We've checked out the records of the Shanghai Aviation Industrial Corporation, which assembles Boeings from parts bought abroad. No stretch-top version was ever ordered by China.'

Palmer was silent for a while. Then she said, 'It doesn't add up to much, does it?'

'I don't know,' Proshin replied. 'The manoeuvres were inexplicable.'

'Hey, hey, wait a minute. This is the first we've heard of manoeuvres.'

'I'm sorry. This aircraft was out of control. Diving, spinning.'

'What happened to it?'

'We don't know. Our reconnaissance satellite had passed on its way by then. But then there's the radiation.'

'Explain that, please.'

'Spectrographic analysis showed that the plane was radioactive at the time when we photographed it.'

'Can Mr Sangster see these pictures?'

Proshin looked up at Krubykov, who nodded.

'They could be faked.' Palmer's tone was less strident, more thoughtful. 'However, I'm starting to get your message, General.'

'I'm glad. Do you authorize Sangster to proceed?' Seeing her about to answer, Krubykov held up his hand. 'Please hear one thing first. We know you regard this as a useful intelligence-gathering exercise: by putting Sangster inside the KGB you hope to learn things about us that you do not know already. You deceive yourselves. He will be given no such opportunity.'

'Of course. You really mustn't judge others by your own standards.'

'We have no standards, madam; we are both spies. Now, do you authorize it?'

Palmer thought for a moment, then turned to Sangster, who had sat quietly absorbing the exchange. 'Looks like you're on station, Gene.' Her smile was artificially bright, Proshin thought. 'Take care.'

Sangster nodded and glanced in the direction of his counterpart. 'Perhaps we should talk,' he said, his perfect Russian taking the other by surprise.

'Perhaps we should,' Proshin replied in English.

'Take our guest to work, Proshin. And now, madam . . . we must part.'

She inclined her head. 'It's been a pleasure, General. Something . . . unexpected.'

'One of those things that cannot happen.'

'Precisely.'

'I will see you to the car.'

He returned to the dusty salon a few moments later with a thoughtful frown on his face, to find his assistant, Colonel Fomenko, laying out papers on the table overlooking the lawn. Fomenko, a career officer, was in his mid-forties and had come up by the 'new route', the one that led through university via application and intelligence combined. 'Daily sheets,' he murmured as his chief approached.

'Anything new on the satellite?'

'Nothing. Did it go well?'

Krubykov eyed his deputy curiously. He had spent the past twenty years walking a knife-edge as personal aide to Oleg Kazin, chairman of the KGB, and if those two decades had taught him anything it was the art of self-preservation. Krubykov would not have dared to ask Kazin if something had gone well.

'It went well.'

'She swallowed it?'

'No. Did you expect her to?'

'Not really. The Americans have always operated on the basis that we are at our most deadly when we appear at our friendliest.'

'A correct basis, too. My instructions are crystal clear: preserve the façade for as long as possible.'

'Which necessitates your proving that someone else pointed the beam at that satellite.'

'Yes. But before we can convince the Americans of anything, we first have to find out for ourselves who really did it. That at least doesn't involve any play-acting.'

'And who do you think really did do it?' Without waiting for a reply Fomenko went on, 'Could it be the Americans themselves, do you think? Trying to sabotage detente?'

'No. You've been reading too many Semenov thrillers.'

'Then who?'

'China.' Krubykov removed his spectacles and went across to the window. A ghost memory was plucking at his consciousness, he couldn't pinpoint it while Fomenko rabbited on.

'You really think so? Excuse me, but you're suggesting that the entire Chinese leadership has united itself behind a war-mongering strategy, when according to our best intelligence they can't even decide what brand of tea to serve at meetings between Foreign Ministers.'

'You're so young, Fomenko. You've learned everything and you've forgotten everything.'

'General?'

'China isn't like anywhere else. No, I take that back: it's a little like England.'

'I'm not –'

'MI5 is and always was split into factions, most of them conspiring against each other as well as the elected government of the day. China, too, resembles a nursery full of squabbling babies. So you see, I'm not accusing the Chinese leadership of anything. I don't think they know what's going on in the army; and it's the Chinese army that destroyed that satellite, I'm convinced of it.'

'Could they *do* that?' Fomenko was aghast. 'Without anyone at the top finding out?'

'You're so young. Army factions, in-fighting . . . you can write China's entire history in those terms and not lose anything important.'

'But –'

'Fomenko, remind me of something.'

'General?'

'I can't remember . . . that man in Hong Kong, the businessman, what was his name? You drew my attention to something of his last week.'

'Alexander Cumnor's report on the companies that want to get out of Hong Kong before the Chinese repossess, you mean? The Benevolence file . . .'

'Yes, that's the one.' Krubykov resumed his half-hearted study of the garden. Spring would soon be here; and then the leaves would once again lend colour to the drab little world that had this faded *dacha* as its hub. And perhaps then would be the time to strike at Hong Kong again, to make up for the débâcle of 1988 . . .

'Why would the Chinese army want to shoot down a satellite?' he quizzed his reflection in the glass; but it was Fomenko who, as ever, produced the answer.

'So as to dominate the battleground in the event of war. If you can destroy your enemy's satellites, you can destroy his command control and communications system.'

Krubykov turned away from the window, glasses dangling from one hand. 'Communications,' he echoed vaguely.

FIVE

◇

About a week after Jinny Young died Sun Shanwang received an important visitor at his headquarters in the hills of Haidian to the west of Beijing.

'Ah! General . . . come in, do.'

Lo Bing's eyes, alight with curiosity, roamed around the spacious room. Its elegant wall panels displayed various scenes from a garden in the height of summer, with several human figures deliberately reduced so as to underline their comparative unimportance in the natural scheme of things. A long blackwood table, its top cleared of everything save an inkstone and brush-set, stood by the tall windows overlooking the placid lake outside. Sun sat at one end of this table, facing the door through which Lo Bing had entered. He saw how his visitor's eyes devoured the room's contents, and smiled.

Lo Bing caught the smile and, after a second's hesitation, returned it. 'No mahjong set?' he inquired.

Sun's laugh conveyed conspiratorial respect, as it was meant to. 'I threw it out when Baba died.'

'I do hope you're not going to throw out *all* the brigadier-generals.'

The *jong* in mahjong could also mean a general of lesser rank; Sun vastly enjoyed the pun. 'Not those with a sense of humour.'

During this exchange Lo Bing had been slowly advancing down the parquet floor until now he was level with Sun's chair. The Controller of Central Intelligence stood up and, taking the General's elbow, led him to the nearest window.

'It's very pleasant up here.'

Lo Bing looked through the glass and at once saw the nature of the test facing him. Seated by the side of the lake, in the shade of a feathery birch copse, was Wang Guoying, chief of staff to the People's Revolutionary Army.

Lo Bing felt that too many seconds of silence had slipped by. 'So peaceful,' he murmured. 'Having the place all to yourself.'

'Yes. Of course, it can seem lonely sometimes.'

As the two men moved away from the window, Lo Bing wondered if he had passed the test. The chief of staff had been there, he was no illusion. But if Lo Bing admitted to seeing him, he at once introduced a new dimension to the meeting, and it was not his meeting, it was Sun's. If, on the other hand, he did not own up to Wang's presence, he ran the risk of spoiling Sun's pitch. Then again, Wang was Lo Bing's boss, an important factor in the calculations and machinations of his career . . . as long as Wang was still in favour, not on his way out. The fact that he was here in Haidian, enjoying Sun's back garden, suggested that he was secure. Unless, of course, Sun himself was on the skids . . .

'Do you like my model village?'

Lo Bing presented his host with a smiling countenance. 'Village?'

Sun pointed to the far side of the room where a model occupied a large expanse of floor. As Lo Bing approached he saw that in fact it was a representation of Hong Kong and the New Territories, the border with mainland China clearly shown by means of a red line.

'Most interesting,' he observed neutrally. Hong Kong was always so difficult: a political litmus-test where you never could tell from one hour to the next what colour the litmus would turn. 'Those markings . . . ?'

'Telephone cables. Submarine cables, there and there . . . one to Brunei, one to Guam. Tokyo, there. General Lo Bing . . .'

'Yes?'

'I don't want to waste your time, but I need some advice.'

'Anything at all.'

73

Sun noted how pleasantly he put himself across: mild-mannered, smiling, head always to one side as if anxious not to miss the slightest word that fell from a dear companion's lips.

'Some years ago,' Sun began, 'the chief of staff was ordered to prepare a plan for the retaking of Hong Kong and its associated territories by military action. He enlisted my help.'

Lo Bing's mouth opened. After a moment he remembered to close it again and swallowed hard. Sun pretended not to notice.

'We were instructed to proceed on the assumption that some time during the run-up to repossession slated for 1997, we would find ourselves confronted with a dramatic loss of confidence by the Hong Kong business community, and that it would be necessary to take steps to avoid the consequences. This project – the contingency plan for the military takeover of Hong Kong – was codenamed Steel Nail.'

'This is the first I've heard of it.'

'Good. The scenario outlined to us called for the rapid expansion of Hong Kong to become China's largest naval base, able to dominate the Soviet Union's routes to the Pacific and Indian Oceans, with adequate capacity for an assault on Taiwan; the swift erection of missile silos able to house ICBMs capable of targeting Russia and the American Pacific seaboard; and provision of accommodation for individuals rounded up by the security forces for interrogation.'

Sun paused for a moment. 'You disapprove?' he said sharply.

'I, Controller? Certainly not! An inspired policy, in my view.'

'You're frank.'

'One confidence deserves another.'

'Then let's continue. We knew from the start that time was important. At any moment it might become obvious either that all the largest western-dominated traders and companies were preparing to pull out of Hong Kong, or that an international crisis was building up between Russia and the United States: in either event, the plan would have to be implemented for the sole purpose of protecting our possession.

'The prime objective, therefore, would be to seize and

preserve as many assets as possible in such a way that they could not be removed from the territory. Surprise would be of first importance. Certain tactics were obvious. So, for example, the invasion would be set for 0600 hours, Hong Kong time: just one hour behind Tokyo, ten o'clock at night in London and five o'clock in the afternoon in New York. In other words, at a time when all the major stock-markets would be closed. All communication between Hong Kong and the outside world would be severed, swiftly and efficiently. First, a power-cut, coupled with severance of key underground and submarine cables, and electronic jamming of radio-signals. But that, by itself, would not have been enough. There remained one problem. This.'

Sun pointed upwards. Just below the ceiling hung a small silver ball.

'An Intelsat-5 satellite.' Sun's voice was tinged with gloomy satisfaction. 'The one that handles the bulk of Hong Kong's telephonic, telex and Fax traffic. I'm sure you understand how money can be made to disappear by means of electronic instructions programmed through an ordinary phone line. Granted a power-cut, given radio-jamming, still, an alert bank with a private generator and a sophisticated telecommunications system could drain its books and vaults. It was an unacceptable risk. That's why we decided to involve the Office of the National Defence Industries.'

Lo Bing's eyes gleamed with sudden understanding. 'And that's where my team came in!'

'Correct. You see, there were always two projects, separate but linked. The one depended on the other. The Chief of Staff and I have devoted our energies to Steel Nail. But you were set to work on a project called Sledge Hammer . . . designed to flatten our Steel Nail. Without your Sledge Hammer, our own plan couldn't succeed.' Sun pointed at the ball suspended above the model of Hong Kong. 'From the start, your goal, although you did not know it, was to shoot down a satellite – *that* satellite.'

'And so when Sledge Hammer is perfected . . . you can take Hong Kong whenever you want.' Lo Bing sounded awestruck.

'Not quite. That Intelsat orbits well outside the range of your weapon.'

'Yes, but . . . it would be possible to mount the firing mechanism in another satellite, I'd have thought. Our Long March rockets have proved themselves capable of launching such technology.'

'Good. Please continue your research along those lines. And that's another reason why I invited you here today: I want to know how much longer we'll have to wait for Sledge Hammer.' Sun's gaze had become intent. 'I understand you held a proving demonstration of some kind, at East Wind Centre.'

'Yes, indeed.' Lo Bing sucked in his lips and shook his head. 'Unfortunately, there's still quite a way to go.'

'I'm sorry to hear that.'

'If more resources could be made available . . .'

'I'll see what can be done. But in the meantime, remember the need for secrecy! As far as the army is concerned, Steel Nail's just a game plan, one of the things we set our best generals, like you, to tax their brains. But if it became known to the western businessmen and bankers in Hong Kong, who are so busily making the Middle Kingdom rich, well . . .'

'They would panic. Then they would flee.'

'And the prophecy would fulfil itself. Precisely.'

Lo Bing seemed to be on the point of speaking, then he changed his mind. Each man gravitated thoughtfully to a vantage point near the windows, whence he could see the chief of staff strolling around the garden. All his movements seemed slow, considered. Conservative.

'Perhaps Sledge Hammer can be advanced more rapidly.' Lo Bing's voice was meditative. 'I will have to think about that.'

'Please do. Two factors are at work here. First, the present tension between the United States and the Soviet Union.' Sun spoke with sudden feeling. 'Whoever shot down that satellite has a lot to answer for! Secondly, when the leader dies, it's possible – I put it no higher – that a hardline faction strongly supported by the military will assume a dominant position. That faction has always hated Hong Kong and all it stands for; they're the ones behind Steel Nail. If they win the power-struggle, the army will have to be ready to retake the British colony at a moment's notice.'

Lo Bing hissed, his mask of polite reserve fell away. 'I cannot believe some of the things you've said to me today.'

'And why? When China drifts without a hand on the tiller, when Red Guards are already on the streets again, when students occupy their own university campuses? Do you turn your back on reality?'

Lo Bing stared at Sun Shanwang for several moments, obviously trying to assess what reliance he might place on the old man's words. Sun's haughty face remained implacable. At last the officer looked away. 'I will have to think very carefully,' he muttered.

'Yes, carefully – but not long, I trust.'

The pace of Lo Bing's progress to the doors suggested extreme reluctance on his part to leave. To Wang Guoying, head pressed against the panels of an internal door, it seemed ages before he heard the General say his final goodbyes, and knew that Sun was once more alone.

'What did he make of me?' Wang asked as he entered.

'What we expected. You were here, with me, yet not so with me that I invited you to share our confidences.'

'Do you still think he's our man?'

'I'm sure of it. I've finally managed to identify him as the author of the "dream culture" articles.'

'The what?'

'For months past, someone who signs himself only as "honest soldier" has been writing articles in the Shanghai Liberation Daily. He's been increasingly critical of what he calls China's unrealistic obsession with "dream culture".' Seeing the look of incomprehension on Wang's face, Sun said, 'Try saying it aloud, using different tones.'

'Meng wen?'

'Say it the other way around.'

'Wen meng, wen meng . . .' Wang's eyes widened as suddenly it clicked. 'The Chairman's principal secretary is called Wen Meng.'

'Yes. Someone closely identified with him throughout his

career. An attack on him is the same as a rejection of all the Chairman stands for.'

'And this "honest soldier" turns out to be —'

'Brigadier-General Lo Bing.'

'So what happens now?'

'If you try to remove Lo Bing, there'll be an uprising, probably in Shenyang Military District which he used to command and where he's still got most of his connections. I think he recognized himself when I described the "hardline military faction" waiting to seize power, though I can't be sure.'

'But leaving him in place is like failing to amputate a gangrenous leg.'

'Let's hope not. I've given him plenty to occupy his mind, this afternoon. First, he doesn't know where *you* stand. As for me: he's tending towards the view that I'm a secret hawk, in sympathy with him; he can't think of any other reason why I should brief him on Steel Nail, or why I should suddenly be showing such interest in the progress of Sledge Hammer. Incidentally, he knew all about Steel Nail. He denied it, but I was watching his face. He knew.'

'I was afraid of that.'

'I couldn't manage to get out of him how far advanced Sledge Hammer really is. I dangled Steel Nail in front of his eyes, but although he was tempted, it didn't work. He's keeping that a secret. Guoying, I'm going to need your help.'

'How?'

'We have to find out all we can about this man Lo Bing. I sometimes think you should never trust bachelors: they've got too much time on their hands. But this one's dangerous, really dangerous. I've already opened a file. You've got to work on it your end as well.'

'Any leads?'

'One, perhaps. Lo Bing's got too much money for someone on his salary. We looked into that. He's on a retainer from a company called All Middle Kingdom Cargo Freight.'

'Which is what?'

'A subsidiary of the state airline.'

'What business has he got, taking money from them?'

'He's not the first to benefit from military rank. Oh, and that reminds me of something. It seems logical to me, but let me try it on you. If Lo Bing's got money, secret money, he'll want advice on how to invest it.'

'Yes.'

'Which he's unlikely to get here. So he'll need an ally in Hong Kong.'

'Why does it have to be Hong Kong?'

'It doesn't *have* to be – but think of the advantages. Apart from being on his doorstep, if he makes a friend in Hong Kong, he'll have yet another source of information about what's going on there. Useful for a man who's planning to seize the place, wouldn't you agree?'

'Perhaps. You've obviously been doing a lot of thinking.'

Sun's expression became grim. 'I had a new thought this afternoon, while I was talking to him, and it terrifies me.'

'What?'

'Suppose his beam-weapon is a lot more advanced than he's letting on. You've read the report of the recent test at East Wind Centre?'

'Yes. A cover-up.'

'I think so, too. Anyone reading that report would conclude that he'd been playing around with fireworks, instead of major new weapon technology.'

'Too bland by far. But what are you reading into it?'

'Let me ask *you* some questions. First, do the Americans have the expertise to shoot down that satellite?'

'Yes.'

'Do you think they did it?'

'No. It was their satellite, containing their equipment.'

'But then why should the Russians do it – risk everything for the sake of one spy-satellite?'

Wang Guoying's face suddenly became tense. 'You surely don't think that Lo Bing . . . but why should he –'

There was a knock at the door. Sun Shanwang motioned the chief of staff to silence. 'Come in!'

One of his secretaries entered. 'I'm sorry to disturb you, Controller, but –'

'Well?'

'Beijing Garrison Command reports a large crowd gathering in the south-west of the city. They're being led by some bad elements, leftover cadres sent down to the country for re-education. The city's full of rumours, morale among the Armed Police Force is bad and the Garrison Commander would like to talk to you urgently.'

Sun turned to Wang with a gesture of despair and was about to speak when the aide interrupted him. 'Also, the leader's doctors have sent a request.' The young man's voice was quiet, businesslike. 'They ask you to come at once.' He coughed and shifted uneasily on his feet. 'Please excuse me, but I was told to repeat: *at once.*'

Sun hurried from the room, closely followed by Wang. The secretary, whose name was Zhang Ming Rong, went back to his own office along the corridor and poured himself a cup of jasmine tea from the communal flask. It was a welcome break for refreshment; he had been on duty for nineteen hours now, and the strain was showing through his carefully cultivated façade of sartorial neatness.

He finished his tea, and was pulling the never-diminishing pile of papers towards him with a sigh, when the phone rang.

'*Wei?*'

'Ming Rong . . . Guangpu here.'

The young secretary bit his lip. Guangpu, who worked for the railways, occupied the apartment next to Ming Rong's. He was also standing representative to the local street committee, and as such a person of consequence in the community. Not someone who could be ignored.

'How are you?'

'Busy.'

Guangpu failed to take the hint. 'I was wondering if you'd managed to make any further progress with that problem I gave you.' His voice lowered a tone. 'I hate to ask you to use your connections, but I can't think who else to approach.'

Zhang Ming Rong suppressed a yawn and tried to concentrate. 'I have, as a matter of fact. But the news isn't wonderful.'

'Can you tell me?'

'Not on the phone. Look, why don't you invite the girl to your place tonight and I'll look in on my way home?'

'I'll do that. Say . . . eight o'clock?'

'No.' Ming Rong glanced around the office. It contained four desks, none of them occupied. Everyone had sloped off, exhausted; with Sun gone to the Chairman's bedside, one more absentee wasn't going to matter. 'Sooner. I'm leaving now.'

On his way out he stopped briefly by the table where he and his staff were engaged in completing a two-thousand-piece jigsaw. The picture was of Mount Fuji: enormous tracts of blue sky, a white snowcap, the huge expanse of featureless mountainside, flowers at the bottom. It would take forever; but they always liked to have a jigsaw on the go. The mental stimulation it provided – matching up apparently unconnected pieces through identification of some common factor – was equalled only by the satisfaction of finding something that actually fitted. The parallels with his daily tasks were obvious, albeit too close for Ming Rong to notice them. No one was supposed to leave for the night without first slotting at least one piece into place. Ming Rong chanced upon a segment of blue sky that fitted with almost mystical ease, and left feeling better for having seen something go right that day.

On the bus into Beijing he reviewed the problem presented to him a week earlier by Guangpu. The thing looked simple enough; a couple of unlogged telephone calls had sufficed to unearth the truth. But Ming Rong felt uneasy about that truth. There was nothing he could put his finger on. If he had seen life in terms of an indefinite jigsaw, like the one on the office-table, he might have said that he was tinkering with a piece that seemed to fit but didn't. So what was he going to tell . . . what was her name, now . . . ?

'Comrade Jian, let me get this story of yours straight . . .'

'Please. Ask anything.'

Ming Rong was sitting in Guangpu's comfortable apartment,

a cup of tea in front of him. When he moved forward to take it, the red plastic chair-cover squeaked in an embarrassingly obscene way. Ming Rong coloured, and tried to keep all his movements slow; but it was difficult to feel at ease in this overheated environment of artificial daisies and antimacassars, especially when you were sitting opposite a pretty girl who kept her big glowing eyes fixed on you like an adoring seal-pup.

'At the moment, you're living in this apartment block, which is how you met Guangpu here. You want to get married, you want a bigger apartment, you want to move from Beijing to Shanghai, to live with your new husband.'

'I do.' She might have been taking some solemn vow.

'In order to do this, you need the consent of your unit. Your husband-to-be also requires the consent of his unit.'

'Yes.'

'Your unit's saying that because you're so young . . . twenty-three?'

She nodded.

'Nothing can be done without the consent of your nearest male relative older than you – your parents being dead?'

'Everything you say is correct, Comrade Zhang. I'm so grateful for the care you've taken over my case.'

Ming Rong had to melt a little. 'Well, I'm not really supposed to use my department's resources in this way, but . . .'

'He's a good man,' Guangpu put in eagerly. 'A very important man. You should listen to him. He has good connections.'

Ming Rong put his cup back on the table and the plastic farted again. 'So your nearest male relative was an uncle,' he went on hastily.

'Uncle Chao, we called him. Not exactly an uncle; I think he was a cousin, or something. On my mother's sister's side.'

'And you tried to find him through his last known workplace – the Shaanxi Aircraft factory?'

'Yes. But they said they'd lost track of him.' The girl was becoming upset now. She looked particularly attractive in that state: a kind of succulent disorder overwhelmed her, making her seem vulnerable, in need of protection, of someone to hold her . . . 'They weren't helpful at all. And unless I can find him . . .'

Ming Rong sighed. He had come to the difficult part.

'I have found him. Or rather . . .' He shook his head in irritation, unsure how best to proceed. 'Not found him,' he finished lamely.

A premonition of what he was going to say shaded the girl's face.

'Miss Jian, I'm very sorry, but your uncle is dead.'

Her hands had been lying in her lap; now they entwined and began to twist and turn, the fingers forming strange patterns. 'I see.' The words were scarcely audible.

'Looking on the bright side, I think if I produce his death certificate to your work-unit, they'll maybe change their position on your case.'

'Yes.' She did not seem to be taking it in. 'Poor Uncle Chao,' she said at last. 'I hardly knew him. I saw him, once. Mother used to talk about him, before she died.' Another pause. 'Please can you tell me . . . how did he die? Only I don't think he was very old.'

'No, he was fifty-six. There was an accident. Oh, I'd better go back a bit. The reason why the Shaanxi Aircraft factory weren't helpful is that the army conscripted your Uncle Chao for a special assignment, and the factory was annoyed at losing him. The army sent him to an airfield in the Gansu desert, somewhere terribly remote . . . Gansu B-Ten, that was it. While he was on this assignment, he was driving this ten-ton truck and there was a crash.'

'No. That's not true.'

Ming Rong felt much sympathy for this girl. He could see she was in a state of shock. But it had been a long, tiring day and now he was anxious to get home. 'Yes,' he said firmly. 'I'm afraid we must all face facts.'

'No.'

'Miss Jian —'

'I'm sorry, but you don't understand what I'm trying to say. My uncle couldn't drive. He had epilepsy.'

'What?'

'My mother told me. It was marked in his household registration certificate: "this man may not drive any vehicle". She'd seen it. So whatever he died of, it wasn't from driving a truck.'

SIX

◇

'Well I'll be damned!'

Proshin turned to find that Sangster had stopped in mid-stride and was examining a door, his mouth open.

'What?'

Sangster extended a finger to touch the silhouette of a cossack, complete with fur hat. 'Just like they said.'

Proshin frowned. 'It's the men's room.'

'Yeah. Just like they said. A cossack . . .'

The two very tall and large men who brought up the rear were becoming impatient. Proshin took his companion by the arm. 'Let's go.'

His office was on the second floor overlooking the car park and, beyond that, a concrete suburban wilderness. As soon as he entered he made for the window to lower the slatted blind.

'You don't want me seeing anything I shouldn't?'

'Of course! No, it's to save my eyes. I've been working in half-light for so long I'm used to it. Reflex action whenever I come in, that's all. You don't mind, do you?'

'No.'

'Thank God for that.'

'God?'

'Yes, why not?'

'You're a Christian?'

'No, I'm a Jew.'

Sangster's body became still. Proshin looked up from his desk, saw what was in his mind and smiled. '*Dezinformatsiya*, is that what you think? We're setting out to disorientate you by feeding you lies?' He reached inside his jacket pocket to extract a booklet. 'Here,' he said, tossing it over; then – 'Oh, do get out,' he said wearily to the guards. They exchanged glances and, after a significant pause, retreated. 'We'll be in the corridor, comrade,' one of them said ominously.

Sangster opened the booklet, recognizing a standard fourteen-page Soviet internal passport. He turned to entry number three, ethnic origin; and there, sure enough, was the single, explosive word: *yevrey*. Jew.

He closed the passport and handed it back to the man sitting behind the desk, who smiled.

'You know what we say: "Without a document, you're an insect; but with a document, you're a human being." It could be a fake, of course. Only it isn't.'

Sangster said nothing.

'You don't believe me?' Proshin laughed and swung his legs onto the cheaply-veneered desk. 'Okay, so what do you believe?' he said, pulling out his pipe. 'What did they tell you about me, eh?'

Sangster surveyed him quietly, allowing his usual friendly smile to become, if anything, more pronounced. 'Quite a lot,' he confessed.

'Shoot!'

'May I sit down?'

'Oh! How polite you are! Yes of course, do excuse me.' Proshin waved at a chair. As Sangster pulled it up to the desk and sat down the Russian said, 'Would you like some coffee?'

'Yes.'

'Okay, okay. There are two ways we can do coffee in this building.' He swung his legs off the desk and rummaged in one of the drawers, at last producing a wrench. 'If you go out the door, turn left . . . maybe you'd better kill those two monkeys . . . at the end of the corridor there's a machine. You'll need kopeks. When it starts to make a whirring noise, you'll hear a clang. Like that – *clang! That's* when you hit it with this. Or . . .' He dropped the wrench on the floor and resumed rummaging in the drawer. '. . . We can have this.'

'This' was a flask. As Proshin unscrewed the cap a strong,

fragrant aroma mushroomed out to fill the room. 'Blue Mountain blend,' he said with satisfaction.

'I guess I'll settle for Blue Mountain.'

'Good. Well, this is my little kingdom. Like it?'

Sangster sipped coffee from the blue and white mug handed to him by Proshin and took a quick look around. In truth, the tiny office was not impressive. Apart from the desk and two chairs, a pipe-rack improvised from a jam-jar, several filing-cabinets and racks of unburst computer print-outs in bindings of assorted colours, the only singular item was a large micro-processor complete with screen. Proshin followed the American's gaze. Suddenly he threw himself forward to rest his left elbow on the desk and point with his left little finger.

'They say the pen is mightier than the sword. So it is. But how much mightier than the pen is my Ferranti IBM clone!'

Sangster burst out laughing. After a moment Proshin joined him. 'My name is Konstantin,' he chortled. 'But you must call me –'

'Kostya.'

'Ah-ha! It is in the file!'

'No, I happen to be familiar with the diminutive form, that's all.'

'I see.' Proshin's smile faded. 'I was only joking in part. With that machine, there, I can go anywhere, discover anything. My magic carpet, I call it. If only you know the key, the code, you can open anything.'

'Even the Chinese Milky Way computer?'

'Not that, not yet. But someday . . .'

Sangster had always responded to enthusiasm. It weighed favourably in the scales he used to test his fellow human beings. Proshin was an enthusiast.

'Now! Let us get properly acquainted. Tell me what is in the Company's file on me, I want to know.'

'Well . . .' Sangster placed his cup on the desk and folded his arms. 'It says you're thirty-four . . .'

'But I look twenty. Yes, thank you.'

'You certainly don't look thirty-four. You were born in Lebedyan, central Russia, where you joined the Communist

Union of Youth, and then went on to study at the Institute of International Relations where you spent five years.'

'Good! Excellent! Go on.'

'You were trained at KGB school number 311, in Novosibirsk, where you divided your time between standard operational studies and the Siberian branch of the Academy of Science. Since then, you've been around. Very few people have moved around like you have.'

'Is that so?'

'Um-hm. First you were assigned to the Sixth Department of the First Main Directorate –'

'China!'

'Yes, China, and then you were transferred across to the Eighth Department of the Second Main Directorate, computers. After that –'

'The China time was terrible. Ghastly. Do you know, they sent me to Khabarovsk, north of Vladivostock?'

'No. After that, you were assigned to the Operational Technical Directorate (Computer Services). And you've stayed there ever since.'

'That is splendid. All correct, too. Habits? Hobbies?'

'You like reading, but not translations. You're good at languages. You've had lots of lady friends.' Sangster smiled from the eyes. 'And when I say lots, I mean –'

'*Lots!*' Proshin giggled. 'Oh, good. I would not like to think they'd missed that. Now, do you want to read your KGB file?'

Sangster tried so hard to believe. Finding himself here, in the First Main Directorate's headquarters on Moscow's outer ring-road, that was incredible enough, and that they couldn't fake. But now to be offered a sight of his own dossier . . . 'Sure, why not?'

'You're smiling. Why do you always smile?'

'Do I?'

'Always. I know why you're smiling this time, though. You think I'm joking. Well, let me tell you, Gene . . . I can call you Gene?'

'I guess so.'

'I punched your file out of the computer and the KGB don't

even know I've done it. I set up the system, you see. I designed it. Nobody in the entire service understands computers like I do. That's why they employ me, even though I'm a Jew.' He solemnly jabbed his chest with his thumb. 'Because I'm the best, and they know it. They don't like it, but that's their problem.' He stood up, pushing his chair away. 'And I think you're out of date. Being a Jew isn't so bad these days. There have been . . .', he tossed his head, 'certain concessions.'

Proshin went across to the rack of print-outs and selected one. 'Here.'

For the next quarter of an hour the only sound in the office was that of Sangster tearing perforations and turning pages. At last he threw the wadge of paper onto the desk and sat back.

'Cambodia was the worst,' he said after a long pause.

'Yes, I should think so.' Proshin knocked the dottle from his pipe, a sympathetic expression on his face. 'Although . . . worse than the divorce?'

Sangster's chuckle lacked humour. 'You've got me there.' He shook his head, a man confessing himself beaten. 'No children. That helped.'

'Did you want —'

'What I want, Kostya, is some input from you.'

'Okay, sorry, sorry.'

Sangster was silent for a minute or more, struggling to get himself back under control. Reading the dossier had not been the pleasure he'd anticipated.

'You don't trust me,' Proshin said forlornly.

'I have to trust you.'

'That woman Palmer doesn't.'

'She's not working in the field.'

'So you do trust me!'

'Look, Kostya . . .' Sangster sighed. 'Trust, not trust, we have a job to do. I'm here to assess what you've got. So let's do some work, yes?'

'Right. This is what we know.' Proshin waited for Sangster's gaze to meet his own. 'This is what we are telling you we know. After that, it's up to you to assess it.'

'Agreed.'

'You are aware that we have a satellite-tracking facility at Plesetek, not far from the White Sea.'

'Yes.'

'All relevant feedback comes from Plesetek. About three months ago, our surveillance of China was stepped up by a factor of one-point-five. As was your own. Because that country's in trouble.'

'Yes.'

'Let me expand the data I gave you and Plamer at the *dacha*. One of our ferrets was overflying Harbin, in the extreme north-east of China. It picked up a jetliner owned by an outfit called All Middle Kingdom Cargo Freight. That's a subsidiary of the Civil Aviation Administration of China, the Chinese state-run airline.'

'Okay.'

'Flight number ZG 877, it later turned out. Now that was a cargo-flight, we think, and on the first pass our satellite observed it flying in a straight line, as one would expect. But on the next pass, the ferret detected something different.'

'Which was?'

'A route-deviation. And on the third pass, some ninety minutes later, we were able to calculate by back-tracking that it had made a dogleg. Now why should a civil aircraft on an ordinary flight do that?'

Sangster had no answer.

'I want to show you the plotting.' Proshin reached inside a different desk drawer to produce a file, from which he took a coloured map of north-east China. 'Here . . . the yellow line, you can ignore the figures, the line shows the route.'

'A hiccup.'

'Yes. The third pass showed something else, too: that plane was hot, radioactive. These photographs . . .'

Sangster examined the plates. The red smudge might have been anything.

'Now there's one more thing you need to know. Our ASAT.'

'The hunter-killer satellite?'

'Yes. Our case is that the ASAT was "framed".'

'You amaze me.'

'I hope so. I plan to. Look.' Proshin rested both elbows on the desk and began to move his hands around. 'This . . . my right hand . . . is the ASAT. And my left is flight number ZG 877, okay?'

'Go on.'

Proshin moved his fists until the 'aircraft' was directly under the 'satellite', then stopped. 'Imagine that they're still moving along their pre-determined paths, but we're freezing the frame there. Above both these' – he jerked his head upwards – 'somewhere near the light-bulb, there's the Southeast Asian telecoms satellite, complete with its payload of American spy whiz-kiddery, which of course we knew about.'

'Of course.'

Proshin moved his left hand up past his right until his arm was fully extended. 'Pow!'

'That's very neat. But . . . sorry.'

'You don't buy it?'

'No. For one thing, we monitor the beam, the radiation, and need look no further than the ASAT. For another, more fundamental thing, I'm not here to buy anything, I'm here to be convinced. And I have to tell you that a couple of dud negatives and some lines on a map aren't going to do it. What I want is facts. Facts alone are what are wanted in life.'

'Mr Gradgrind?'

'You read Dickens?'

'Of course. When I was at Oxford. But I didn't know you were a fan of his.'

'You mean it's not in the file?'

Proshin leaned back in his chair, face serious. 'No. A lapse. Presumably it was not considered important. Anyway, coming back to more serious matters, I've been putting our case. I agree that proving it is another thing.'

'So what do you suggest?'

'That we begin where it's easiest: by finding out as much as we can about flight ZG 877.'

'All right. What's the first move?'

'We have to get inside the All Middle Kingdom traffic-computer.'

'So what's the problem? You plug in your Ferranti, break a few codes and there you go.'

'No. There we do not go. I've tried. That system is so heavily protected against hackers that I begin to feel very confident we are on the right track. No one, but no one, protects a civilian airline's computerized records in that way.'

'We're stymied, then.'

Proshin shook his head. 'That's where you come in, Gene. We are going to break into the computer, you and I. But first of all, we need someone to lend us a key to the inner codes, someone who can admit us to the back-files.'

Sangster thought. 'A Chinese employee.'

'Correct. You can speak Mandarin, I think? Fortunately I, too, speak a number of dialects. The Third Department have done some exploratory work for me. They have discovered an excellent opportunity. So you and I are going on our travels.'

'Travels . . . you mean, to *China?*'

'Not at this stage. Later, yes, to China, but right now it would be pointless.'

'So where *are* we going?'

'London. Come on!'

SEVEN

◇

The room allotted to Alexander Cumnor in the North Korean government guest house was so cold that his breath came out cloudy. While Leong, his henchman, walked up and down the room in a vain effort to restore some body-heat, he sat by the window wearing a buttoned-up overcoat, alternately looking between the view and the photograph album on the table beside him. The faraway prospect of Mount Myohwangsan, rising above the birch and spruce forest to the south, was magnificent; but in Cumnor's eyes it could not compare with the splendour of the album.

It contained some of the earliest photographs ever taken in south-east Asia: for the most part they were of Singapore, although a handful portrayed Hong Kong dignitaries, and there was one priceless print of the Empress Dowager laughing aloud. Cumnor had assembled a unique collection; it was his only serious hobby. He frequently carried one of his many albums on trips abroad, as a means of whiling away dead time.

When a car chugged along the rough hillside road, Cumnor barely glanced up. He knew it would be bringing his mainland Chinese contact, who was, as usual, late. He continued to idle through the album, part of his brain awaiting the sound of footsteps in the stone corridor as a signal to put the photographs away and prepare for business.

Someone wrenched open the door. Four Chinese soldiers crashed into the room, grabbed Leong and rammed him up against the wall as a prelude to searching him. Cumnor had time to see his usual contact standing on the other side of the threshold and to register that he was handcuffed. Then a man in a bright green uniform with brigadier-general's shoulder-boards silently entered to take the chair opposite his.

Leong screamed. Two of the soldiers were literally tearing off his clothes, ripping them to shreds, while a third examined each garment; the last man, an NCO, supervised. Cumnor sat still and kept his face bare of all expression, even when the brigadier-general, whom he had never seen before, pulled the photograph album towards him and began to leaf through its pages.

Leong was struggling now. They had stripped him naked; the air in the room was ice-cold. While Cumnor watched, the soldiers turned him upside down and embarked on an intimate search of a body that was already turning blue.

'I like photographs.' Cumnor, hearing Mandarin Chinese, moved his eyes a fraction in time to see the brigadier-general tear a page from the album. 'But this is a bad one.' He continued to gaze at it a moment longer. Then he tore the page in two.

His uniform was clean, the creases sharp. It looked sufficiently new to suggest that its wearer had an obsession about his appearance. His eyes were very bright. He might have been on drugs, but Cumnor preferred another explanation.

'The Empress Dowager.' The bright eyes clouded over. 'Terrible.' His hands moved with the swiftness of a conjuror's.

Cumnor stared at the photograph, now in four pieces. That print had cost him nearly ten thousand US dollars. The action confirmed his diagnosis: the man sitting opposite was mad.

Leong's final scream degenerated into a gurgle. The soldiers dropped him on his head and retreated to guard the door, their NCO handing Leong's gun to the brigadier-general as he passed.

Cumnor glanced at his bodyguard. Words from an earlier phase of his life, years old but strangely resonant, came into his mind: '. . . As you did it to one of the least of these my brethren, you did it to me.' The brigadier-general's glowing eyes underlined the message. This time Leong, the servant; next time . . .

'You requested a commodity.' The brigadier-general took an envelope from his top pocket and inserted it into the desecrated album, like a bookmark. 'Photocopies of the Mahjong file on Colonel Qiu Qianwei of Central Control of Intelligence, formerly Red Dragon, together with letters from his son. Exactly as you specified. I'm prepared to let you have these documents, because they will enable you to apply pressure in an area where your interests and mine coincide.'

Cumnor said nothing.

'Expensive, even for you. But not as expensive as the enquiries you've been making about me. Why so curious?'

'Because I believe a certain brigadier-general, called Lo Bing, will be the next ruler of China.'

The officer thus singled out for greatness continued to survey Cumnor's face throughout the silence that followed. 'I admire your composure,' he observed at last. 'I neither admire nor welcome your inquisitiveness.'

'I think you welcome it very much.'

Lo Bing's eyes widened in anger and for a second Cumnor regretted his daring. Then the brigadier-general smiled. 'I need to be kept informed about what is going on in Hong Kong. I know your business. You deal in information, using it to make money. On this occasion you will use it to save money: your own. Did you know I like to paint?' He tapped the album. 'I prefer that to photographs. When you take a photograph, you have to content yourself with what's already there. But the painter can change things.'

Cumnor inclined his head with an acquiescent smile.

'Today, I'm going to paint a picture of the future, for your benefit. The future of Hong Kong. And of China. And of the Soviet Union, too. A big painting, in other words. A lot of canvas.'

'Yes.'

'So much to say; and time is short. When the Chairman dies, you may expect to see me in Hong Kong. Hours. That's all we have. Hours.'

Cumnor hesitated, took the plunge. 'My usual fees —'

'Will be waived. In exchange for accurate information, I will allow you to escape. I will give you advance warning of when I am coming. But Cumnor' — He tapped the album again —

'you'll keep that information to yourself. I know that some of you are planning to leave Hong Kong. I don't want that. So if anyone *else* escapes . . .'

Cumnor followed his gaze downward to the floor, where Leong was coming to his senses. Lo Bing jerked his head. Two of the soldiers picked up Leong and hauled him to the door. Lo Bing grasped the gun lying on the table beside him. He examined it; then, with a smile that in other circumstances might have been charming, he pointed it at Cumnor's chest.

As Cumnor stared into the glittering eyes opposite he tried to convince himself that this was bluff, there was no danger: had not Lo Bing expressly said that he wanted a new source of information? But in his heart he realized that it was pure chance whether the brigadier-general pulled the trigger or not; because Lo Bing was part wicked child and part mad. But mostly he was mad.

EIGHT

◇

Jinny's will turned out to contain directions for a Chinese funeral. Mat expressed consternation, Diana confusion, Simon weary acceptance.

So there had been all the paraphernalia of Oriental death to contend with: employing the *feng-shui* man to select a propitious day for the rites; clothing the corpse in the white dress she had worn on her wedding day and then preserved for this very occasion; parading through the streets of Hong Kong behind a motorized bier bedecked with golden flowers, an old black-and-white photo of Jinny as a girl fixed above its windscreen. There had been two uniformed bands, professional mourners, twenty more biers in the cortège and, bringing up the rear, a straggling procession of friends and acquaintances who could be relied upon to get lost at every turning.

As Diana surveyed this sad ending to her mother's earthly existence she likened it to Christopher Robin's Expotition, attended by all of Rabbit's friends-and-relations. 'It's simply a Confused Noise; that's what I say,' mused Diana, quoting from memory; and so it was.

Simon, Diana and Mat walked immediately behind the coffin. The two men refused to wear the traditional hemp hoods and gowns of mourning, although Diana, bitter because things were being done half-heartedly and without conviction, told them they should. Before they'd gone very far she realized she was wearing the wrong shoes, so that a blister formed between her third and fourth toes. By the time they reached the crematorium she had a raging headache.

The party afterwards was a strain; Diana could hardly conceal her relief when at last the crowd began to thin out. But then Simon had disappeared, leaving her to stand on the step by herself, shaking hands, bowing, smiling through it all with the silent dignity of a queen.

Just when she thought there could be no one else and was wearily closing the door, somebody lurched against her.

'Sorry,' Qiu Qianwei said thickly. 'Missed my footing.' He seemed to be a little drunk.

'Goodbye, Qianwei.'

He wanted to say something, but the expression on Diana's face kept the words in his mouth, so he got into his car. Almost as soon as he had turned out of the driveway he pulled over, a little way down the hill from the Youngs' house, and switched off the ignition. For a few moments he sat motionless, staring out of the windshield. Then he flipped open the briefcase lying on the passenger seat to reveal a shortwave radio-set.

Diana shut the front door and leaned her back against it. Tears, suppressed for too long, were breaking through her closed eyelids. She ran upstairs. In her haste to get away she allowed her black silk jacket to slide off her shoulders. As Mat picked it up he felt a mixture of grief and gratitude. Diana had been wonderful, a real source of strength. He wanted to tell her so, but now wasn't a good time so he merely folded the jacket, anxious to avoid creasing it.

Simon laid a hand on his shoulder. 'All right?'

'Yes.'

'We need to talk. Come into the study.'

Mat followed him, laying the jacket on a chair beside the door. He had always liked this beautiful room: very much Simon's own creation. Besides the desk it contained a number of bamboo cabinets that housed his *limian-hua*: assorted glass bottles painted on the inside by very patient craftsmen. Simon and Jinny had spent most of their marriage lovingly creating this fabulous and by now extremely valuable collection; it was like a monument to their time together. There were comfortable leather armchairs and sofas, Chinese wall-scrolls, a huge fan, many low tables bearing assorted knick-knacks in porcelain or brass or jade; but it was not an exclusively oriental room. Like its owner, it shaded into the occident when least expected: the eye might travel along the wall opposite the window, past the fan, past three matching watercolours of scenes from Lhasa, and so to a Constable landscape – behind which lay Simon's wall-safe. But it was a harmonious place. Many things contrasted; nothing jarred.

Here was a remote and peaceful sanctum from which to rule an empire that, in its arrogant prime, had stretched across half the world from Caledonia to Cathay.

'Duncannon Young's going bust.' Simon's tone was the matter-of-fact kind people use to relay the weather report.

'Wait. When did you last sweep this room?'

'Today, lunchtime.'

'We'll do it again. No problem.' Mat's tight smile was barely visible. He went over to a lacquered cupboard standing between the two windows that overlooked the swimming-pool and brought out a leather case. The hide was faded and had roughened to the texture of used blotting-paper, but the bag's contents were ultra-modern: an electronic bug-detector.

The moment Mat turned on the master switch, a red light in the outer casing flashed urgently and a painful screech shattered the silence.

He hastily adjusted the volume control. The noise faded. Simon stood up and came around the desk, a finger raised to his lips. Mat delved into the leather bag and produced a metal spatula at the end of a cable, which he plugged into the side of the machine. Carrying the case in one hand and the spatula in the other, he began to quarter the study.

It took him just under a minute to trace the bug. It was somewhere in Diana's black silk jacket.

Mat put down the machine and quickly carried the garment out of the room. As soon as he returned, Simon broke out, 'What did you –?'

But Mat violently shook his head and again switched on the machine. This time it remained silent; the light did not flash.

'Who do you think could have done it?' Mat asked.

'God knows. Diana must have spoken to a hundred people today, more perhaps. People all around her. Jostling. Pushing.' Simon lowered himself back into his chair. 'In this house,' he said. His voice was unnaturally high. 'In our own home.' He slumped with his head on his chest, and there was silence in the room for a long time after that.

The words 'Ducannon Young is going bust' echoed in Qiu's headset with perfect clarity. He heard the next exchange between father and son with sinking heart, but only when the shriek of the bug-detector reverberated through his eardrums did he slowly remove the earphones and switch off the receiver.

It was dark now. From where he was sitting he could see a few lights on the hill north of Repulse Bay. Some of them winked as the breeze rustled branches to and fro across his vision. It was turning into a muggy evening, ripe for thunder. Thin rain, barely more than water vapour, moistened the windshield. When Qiu got out of the car, oppressive heat weighed down on him like an extra layer of clothes.

There was little traffic; the Young residence stood several turnings off the nearest major road. He quickly scuttled into the shadows of the hedge opposite and made his way back down the drive towards the house.

At last Simon wearily reached out to switch on his desk-lamp, mounted in a big brass shell-casing. 'We'll call the police in the morning. Right now, I have to tell you some things, Mat. You've never had a real overview. This is how it goes. In the years when you and Diana were away at school, the Ducannon Young group was among the first five *hongs*. It had everything: ships, hotels, refineries, insurance companies, banks ... all the things you need to make twentieth-century commerce work.'

'They used to rag me about it at school. They all thought

you were some kind of emperor, gliding around in a different coloured Rolls every day of the week.'

'They weren't far off beam, not in those days.'

'So how did we get into this mess?'

'First, there was the crash of '87, coupled with that business over the desalination plant I built. Then I managed to upset the mainland Chinese. Well, you know about that, of course, you were involved. Beijing's been hounding Dunny's ever since. We spend months preparing to tender for construction contracts, only to find some Red-sponsored twopenny-halfpenny outfit underbidding us by five percent.'

Mat sighed. 'I suppose that sitting in Taiwan I do sometimes put my head in the sand. I'd heard rumours, of course, but –'

'Most of the rumours that have been going around are true. The point is, the Chinese set out to bring us down. And they've succeeded.'

'Are you sure about this?'

'Yes. Why do you ask?'

'Because we're not the only ones who've done badly. Hong Kong's going down the chute, isn't it?'

'It's true that times are bad.' Simon shook his head impatiently. 'But that's not the answer. Last year the only thing that kept us afloat was the European and American operations, and they account for less than a quarter of our entire turnover. It's Dunny's we're talking about here! The biggest and the best! And we've never been profligate, we've run the group properly with sensible gearings and profit ratios and dividends. So how is it that second-rank companies are managing to weather the storm and we're not?'

Mat had no answer to give. 'Is that why you joined the Club of Twenty?'

'I saw it coming, yes. Your grandfather, Tom, of course, was keen to go, quit Hong Kong, right from the start; he persuaded me. At first, I just wanted to up sticks and take the next plane out, but he told me that was stupid. We had to fool Beijing as to what our real intentions were. If all the companies who wanted to leave did so as and when they felt like it, this place would fall apart. There'd be a mad scramble. Panic. Rioting. It nearly happened in 1987 and we learned from that. So when the top twenty traders leave Hong Kong, their departure has to be very carefully orchestrated. They must all go on the same day, at the same hour.'

Mat looked perplexed. 'There's things I've never understood about the Club of Twenty. I mean, for a start, how can we take everything with us? The office building: you can't take that, and who'd want to buy it off you?'

'Right. Now's the time for you to hear some answers. I need to brief you properly, in case anything happens to me. I only wish I'd done it before. Actually, the mechanics are easier than you might think. Very few Club members have fixed assets of any value in Hong Kong. Most of ours are in Singapore, the Philippines, Korea, Paris, Bonn. We have an office building here in Hong Kong, yes; also a ship-yard, a wharf or two, three major hotels, and that's it. We sold the construction side when the going got too rough for us. Our last remaining property development will go next week, though no one knows that yet. The hotels aren't a problem: even when we quit, there'll still be plenty of people wanting rooms. The office building is leased, now; we just stop paying rent. And we take the contents with us, in packing-cases.'

'But what about the money?'

'Telexed out. By submarine cable and satellite.'

'You can't just do that! Can you?'

'Certainly you can. And it'll be automated, too. That's what's at the heart of the Club's plans: a computer-tape, designed to link everyone and take their assets out at the very same second. It's the most secret aspect of all: the Scroll of Benevolence, we call it. Ducannon Young Electronics have been planning it for years. We're selling up and we're leaving: but no one'll know that until we've actually gone.'

'I didn't know any of that. It's staggering.'

'I kept you in the dark because I had to. Everyone had to be sworn to total secrecy, or it was never going to be any good.'

'So when's the off?'

Simon hesitated. 'It can't be more than a fortnight away now.'

'A *fortnight!*'

'I said we had things to discuss.'

Once inside the front gates Qiu stood for a moment, weighing options. A semicircle of gravel fronted the big white house. He skirted it noiselessly, keeping to the lawn, until he reached the flower-beds where his feet would make no sound. The façade was in darkness, so he risked taking a peek through the nearest window, but the curtains were drawn and he could see nothing.

He tucked himself into the darkest corner, where the porch met the main wall, and stood there with his eyes shut and his palms against the stucco, listening. Somewhere a long way away a car's horn tooted. Nearer to where he stood, what sounded like big, dried out leaves scraped and shuffled across some hard surface. Nothing else stirred.

Qiu knew this house well, could summon its floor-plan into his mind's eye as readily as a computer-operator might put a page of numbers on the screen. Simon Young's study was at the back, at ground level, overlooking the pool and, beyond that, the bay.

Still keeping to the flowerbeds, Qiu inched along the wall until he reached the end. He risked a glance around the angle of the house and saw that someone had switched on the electric lanterns used to illuminate the poolside bar. Annoying . . .

He slithered around the corner of the house. Here he was on paving-stones, and they were noisy things. Qiu bent down to slip off his shoes, knowing he would have to carry them. The alcohol he'd drunk during the afternoon had not lessened his agility. Professional, practical instincts dinned into him by the People's Liberation Army still held sway across the years: a shadow made more noise than he.

Slowly, slowly he made his way along the side of the house until at last he reached the shore of the sea of light centred on the pool. His heartbeat was steady, but faster than usual. He had crossed the Rubicon now; if someone found him there, with his back flattened against the wall, no explanation, however ingenious, would serve.

The merest glimmer of light showed through the curtains that draped Simon Young's study, drawing him towards it like a navigational beacon. He eased himself further along the wall, inch by silent inch, knowing that now he was squarely within range of the poolside lights.

Mat puffed out his cheeks, looked as if he were on the point of speaking and remained silent.

'Say it.'

'We're leaving in a fortnight. What about Diana?'

'Her going to China, you mean?'

'Yes. I know it was in mother's codicil and all that, but . . .'

'What matters is that Jinny's last wishes be respected. I can't pretend I like them, because China's an unstable place right now. But Jinny's codicil was quite clear, and Diana's keen to go. I think she must go.'

'As long as she doesn't hang around there. Does she know anything about Benevolence?'

'Nothing. And that's the way it's got to stay.'

'Right. Good. I wouldn't be happy at the thought of her going to China with that hanging over her.'

'Quite. The fewer people who —'

There was a soft knock, followed by Diana putting her head around the door. 'Can I . . . ?'

'Of course, love.' Simon jumped up. 'Are you all right?' he asked, shepherding her to an armchair.

She nodded and made a good stab at a bright smile, but the ravages of tears weren't so easily hidden. 'I just felt a bit . . . lonely, upstairs.'

'We all need a drink,' said Mat. 'You were terrific today, really terrific.'

She looked at him gratefully. 'So were you.'

Simon had gone across to the drinks cabinet, next to the window overlooking the pool. 'What'll it be, Diana?' he called.

'Scotch, please. Water, half-half. And ice.'
'Son, can you give me a hand with the ice?'

It took Qiu five minutes to traverse the section of wall between the corner of the house and the window. At last he had his ear against the glass. For a moment the jumble of words inside the study made no sense. Simon was speaking: '. . . Son, can you give me a hand with the ice?'

Qiu's ear was pressed so hard against the glass that it hurt.

As Mat joined his father by the drinks cabinet, Simon said, 'All that stuff about Benevolence, we've got to keep it to ourselves, of course.'

'Absolutely.'

'If the mainland got even a whiff of it, they'd stop us. They'd use *any* means to stop us.'

'What exactly do you mean by "any"?'

'Invasion. Repossession by force.'

Simon saw his son's look and shook his head. 'I'm not joking. Scotch for you?'

'Er . . . please.'

Before turning away from mixing the drinks, Simon raised his glass to Mat and said, 'Benevolence.'

As they drank, Diana summoned up another brave smile. 'To Benevolence,' she called. 'Although I haven't the –'

Qiu was listening so intently that he did not hear the footsteps until they were perilously close. Only when a raucous female voice shouted in Cantonese: 'You! What do you think you're doing?' and simultaneously the conversation inside the house came to an abrupt halt, did he realize that it was long past time to go.

Mat was first to react. He threw back the curtains in time to see a shadowy figure race alongside the swimming-pool towards the steps leading down to the beach. Then the servant blocked his line of sight, staring after the escaping shadow, and Mat swore. Next second he was rushing out of the study in the direction of the terrace-doors.

He grabbed the servant's arm. 'Who was it?'

'Don't know. Come out, look one look, he see me, he run.'

'He? Man?'

She nodded.

'Where? At the window?'

'Right, right.'

Mat dropped her arm and sped along the terrace, realizing, too late, that he'd forgotten to bring a torch. Halfway down the rickety staircase that zig-zagged across the cliff face he stopped to listen. His mouth was dry, his knees were shaking; did the spy at the window have a gun? A knife? Where was he? Could he see Mat? *Why was it so quiet?*

Below him, nearly at the beach or so he judged, other footsteps suddenly pounded first on wood, then on shingle. Mat stilled his breathing and got a grip on himself. There was no way off the beach, except by sea. Suppose there was a boat waiting . . . No moon. He peered down in vain.

If he went for reinforcements, the intruder might escape. But by following him, Mat put his head in a noose. How desperate was his quarry? What had he got to lose by being captured?

He continued down the stairway, but slowly this time, pausing every few steps to listen. The scrunch of stones was not repeated. He could hear neither outboard engine nor the clunk of oars. Either the man had swum away. Or he was waiting.

By now Mat had reached the bottom step. As his foot made contact with the shingle it kicked something soft. He bent down; but before he could identify his catch a stone was dislodged somewhere by the water's edge and he stood upright.

Mat had known this beach since childhood; even in the dark it held no surprises for him. A narrow, crescent-shaped belt of stones, a jetty, outcrops of weed-covered rocks at either end.

But the spy would not know the layout. To him, everything would be a potential source of noise or blunder, and therefore of detection.

Mat picked his way as far as the water's edge. Right or left?

Even as he dithered, however, he heard the rush of feet; he was halfway through the turn when a head butted into his side, robbing him of breath and balance; as he fell into the surf, strong arms grasped his ankles and shoved him hard into the shallows. Mat spluttered, gagging on salt water as he rolled this way and that in an attempt to retrieve his balance on the stones. By the time he was up and had shaken the water from his ears, all he could hear was the sound of footsteps racing upwards along the wooden stairway.

When he finally made his way back to the terrace it was to find it empty. Simon and Diana met him in the doorway of the study.

'Did you see him? He came back up?'

'We heard steps . . . my God, you're soaked!'

'I'm all right, Dad.' Mat shivered. 'I need a towel. Christ, I feel cold all of a sudden. Have you telephoned the police?'

'Yes. Peter Reade should be here any minute.'

Mat, halfway up the staircase, was struck by a recent memory. 'When Peter comes, get his people to search the beach at the foot of the steps.'

'Why?'

'Because I'm almost certain our visitor left a souvenir behind. I could be wrong, but I think Peter's going to find a pair of shoes.'

NINE

◇

The man who brought Lei Fuguo to the dingy basement at the plebeian end of the Royal Borough of Kensington and Chelsea described himself as attached to the Chinese embassy, but Lei thought that improbable. The man did not have a *Han* look about him; much more likely to have come from Mongolia, and nobody from the minority races was going to gain diplomatic accreditation abroad.

Why, then, did Lei agree to go with him? Perhaps it was simply because he felt the dead weight of authority's hand and knew it was time . . .

As he got out of the car in a broad street of anonymous, five-storey terraced houses he looked around him with a shiver. Despite the porticos and balconies, he knew this for a seedy part of town. Myriad bell-pushes beside each front door, newspapers blowing down the soiled pavement with its dog turds and blobs of chewing-gum, skips taking up much needed parking spaces . . . Baron's Court, perhaps. Something about the high, unbroken line of houses on either side of the shabby street suggested a degree of restraint, which he found unnerving.

They descended some steps to the basement flat of a nearby house. The door opened without warning. Lei thought it odd, but at this stage he was uneasy, rather than frightened. Fear came a moment later, when his guide pushed him through an inner door and slammed it shut. Lei glanced over his shoulder to see a felt-covered panel set flush with the wall. There was no handle on the inside.

'Mr Lei.'

Hastily he turned around. The small, bare room enjoyed only the subdued light cast by an angle-poise lamp, positioned at one end of a table behind which sat two men. It was the man on Lei's right who had spoken. Lei saw a dark, mercurial figure, insubstantial yet somehow ominous: an official with concerns altogether weightier than his slim frame portended. This man sat forward with his hands folded on the tabletop, head slightly to one side, as if testing the accuracy of his identification.

'Yes.'

'Sit down.'

Lei saw that a chair stood halfway between him and the table. As he nervously advanced towards it his attention was caught by the other occupant of the room. This man's suit was crumpled-looking, his tie-knot loose; he sat well back in his chair with hands thrust into pockets and enough stomach protruding for Lei to see that one of his shirt buttons was undone. He looked young, strong and coarse: a typical red barbarian. Lei did not like him.

The first man was speaking again. Lei tried to concentrate, but the fear was building now, swirling about the room like gas. By contrast with his companion, the first man seemed neat, well-groomed . . . *contained* was the word that drifted into Lei's mind.

'I want you to understand at the outset that there is almost certainly nothing we can do for you. I say this because I do not want to raise your hopes unfairly.'

Lei gawked at him. 'I am sorry,' he faltered at last, 'but I do not understand. I was told –'

'You were told that the police were conducting an inquiry of great delicacy concerning a senior employee of the All Middle Kingdom Cargo Freight Company.' The smaller man's voice scarcely rose above a whisper, but Lei heard it with the utmost clarity. 'And that your embassy was co-operating. Yes. You were told these things. And they are true.'

As the two men continued to gaze at him with unhurried, arrogant curiosity it dawned on Lei Fuguo, with a sudden rush of visceral terror, that the senior employee they referred to was him, AMKCF's London branch manager.

They know nothing, he told himself. This is bluff. Tansy has not spoken. Be still, be silent. *Above all else, be silent!*

The second interrogator (Lei already thought of him thus), the coarse-grained one, yawned loudly without bothering to put a hand before his mouth. His colleague took no notice. He seemed to be in charge. Certainly he did all the talking. All the whispering.

'Unfortunately you do not enjoy diplomatic immunity. Yours is a commercial appointment. English law will take its course.'

The second man unexpectedly sat up. He pressed a switch in a small box, the kind that contains remote controls for TV sets; next second a huge photograph was projected onto the wall above the inquisitors' heads.

Lei tried to swallow but he was breathing too fast and he choked. They waited for him to recover, then they allowed him enough time to look over his shoulder and notice the projector in one corner, its cone-shaped beam coldly illuminating an ever widening space as it expanded towards the far end of the room.

He turned reluctantly, already aware that the photograph was of him: Lei Fuguo.

But the details were harder to take in. Who was that strange, shifty-looking old person? That close-lipped artificial smile, those small, pig-like eyes, who did they belong to? Then, as perception heightened, came other, sadder questions: Is my face truly so wrinkled? The fold of lizard-skin beneath the jaw, is that mine? Do I squint? Why do I choose to brush my thinning hair straight back from my forehead when it makes me seem so cruel?

Is that how Tansy sees me?

The smaller of the two men sat back a little, resting his folded hands on the lip of the table. He did not take his eyes off Lei. For a long while he kept silent. When he did speak his voice was even lower than before.

'Lei Fuguo, fifty-eight, unmarried, father dead; mother

110

living in family homestead outside Xining, Qinghai Province; secretary Young Pioneers, Xining twelfth city branch; distinguished airforce career, transferred to civil administration, Qingdao military district, transferred to Beijing second in command of ATC; project manager for CAAC, branch manager for AMKCF, why did you do it, Mr Lei?'

'Yes.' The other man pushed his chair back with a brutal movement; the sound of its legs grating set Lei's teeth on edge. 'Why?'

His voice twanged with suppressed rage. Lei knew that if this man, the coarse one, gave way to the violence bottled up inside him like lava in a capped volcano, he would be terrible beyond imagining.

'Do . . . what?'

For a while his persecutors neither moved nor spoke. Then the second man, the one with the twangy voice and the trace of an accent — was it American? — took out a handkerchief and blew his nose. He held the cloth away from his face, looked into it, held it up to his eyes. Something about his own catarrh seemed to fascinate him. Before long it was fascinating Lei, too. His lips parted, his breath came more quickly. What could the big man see there?

The man slowly raised his eyes from the soiled handkerchief and stared at Lei. It was as if his perspective had changed, but the subject-matter of his observations had not. The peace of the room was disturbed only by the whirring of the projector's fan. With another of his abrupt, angry gestures the big man threw away his handkerchief and stabbed at the control-box.

Now it was Tansy staring back down the beam of light. By a superhuman act of will Lei managed to keep every muscle of his body motionless. His wasted lips formed the serene smile that he had long ago prepared for use in this moment. Knowing it would come.

His left eyelid betrayed him, though. At first he experienced it as a slight tickle. He tried to control it, but the tickle became painful in its intensity. Lei felt their eyes upon him and sensed they were reading the one, manifest sign of his guilt. They knew now. Of course they knew.

It did not occur to him that in the dim light, with the projector beam almost in their eyes, they could not see his face at all.

He made himself look up. Even in monochrome she was pretty. So small, but perfectly shaped, as yet without any of those monstrosities other men found so desirable: bumps and hillocks and challenges of one sort or another. Tansy was tall and straight and her backbone had not yet developed its natural feminine curve. Her thin face with its big, round deepset eyes: how often had he peered into them, seeking their innermost recesses only to discover laughter and innocence. Yes, and shyness too. Modesty.

The blonde hair showed up the colour of moonlight in the black and white projection on the wall. You could not see the pony tail. But if you stood quite close to her, if you placed a hand on the girl's shoulder, laughing reassuringly, telling some story, a joke perhaps, your fingers could run all the way down from the elastic band to the ends, while your chest tightened to the point where it hurt to breathe, and other, less tractable physical changes began . . .

Again the rasp of chair legs. The big man came around the table, making Lei flinch, but he did not approach him. Instead he began to walk up and down, his silhouette breaking through the photographic image on the wall, while at every turn he flicked his wrist and the picture changed.

Tansy swimming. Tansy on her bicycle. Tansy with two schoolfriends, their faces creased in what might have been uncontrollable laughter or petrified screams. Tansy in her mother's kitchen, occupying the very seat nice old Mr Lei Fuguo in the next flat used to take when Tansy's mother, who was divorced and sometimes desperate, could stand no more and went out for the night, leaving her daughter in charge of their kindly neighbour . . .

'Why did you do it?' the whisperer asked again. His interest had deepened; he genuinely wanted to know the answer, the real answer, before the law exacted a formal one.

The other interrogator stopped, turned and looked down at the Chinese as if anticipating a response any second now.

When it did not come, however, he merely resumed his measured pacing, unperturbed by Lei's silence.

Flick. Flick. Flick.

Tansy inside. Tansy outside. Tansy alone. Tansy with others.

'Mr Lei, it will help if you talk. There must be a trial.' The whisperer sounded infinitely patient; Lei knew he did not care how long this took. They would all stay together, here in this cramped, windowless room, while outside, unbeknown to the three of them, night alternated with day.

'At the trial, the child must give evidence. She is just ten years old. The court will contain perhaps a hundred people. There will be the judge, the jury, lawyers. There will be reporters, many reporters. There will be representatives from your embassy. There will be employees of the Foreign and Commonwealth Office, here in London. While the child is giving evidence, all these people will be looking at her.' The whisper died. 'At *that* point, only at her . . .'

Lei said nothing. He was transfixed by the image on the wall above. It showed Tansy clutching Mao-Mao to her breast. Mao-Mao was a cuddly toy panda. A present from China. He had given it to her. He could remember the occasion perfectly. He had said she was a good girl, a very good girl, and she deserved a present, only she must promise not to tell anyone. Tansy said nothing at first. But when he showed her the panda, its head peeping out of the paper bag, she had smiled; and Lei had felt his heart ease within him. Only . . . his serene smile slipped a fraction. Only, she had hardly uttered a word since then. She had looked at him a lot, and often she cuddled the panda to her, keeping it between the two of them like, well, almost like a shield . . . but she had not spoken, not really spoken, at all since that day. Even though he had been left alone with her, often, after that.

'In prison,' the whisper resumed, 'some attempt will be made to protect you from the other inmates. But you must understand that in this country a certain view is taken of offences such as yours. Convicted murderers and robbers see themselves as morally superior to prisoners who fall into the category in which you will find yourself. They think it is their duty to measure out the kind of retribution that English law denies itself.'

The coarse man placed his remote-controller on the table and went to stand beside Lei. The Chinese felt his body shrivel. He knew that this man would beat him. He was going to vent that appalling rage, at last. He made no move to defend himself. None whatsoever.

The big man laid a hand on Lei's forehead and firmly but without rancour pushed it back until he could stare into his eyes. He stayed like that for a full minute, or it might have been an hour; Lei didn't know. The eyes above his were filled with nothing more than simple curiosity.

When the man released his grip, Lei's head fell forward onto his chest. As if from a very long way away he heard the quiet one murmur to his companion, 'There is a phone in the next room. The police . . . if you would be so kind?'

Lei wanted to shout 'No!' His brain commanded that. He opened his mouth. But what came out was a retching gulp of a shriek. It rolled up and down the scale in a mockery of yodelling. When his breath was exhausted, Lei hauled in another lungful and began again. And so it went on, for a minute or more, until at last the coarse man stepped up to the Chinese and struck him, first with his right fist and then with his left. He put a lot of effort into those two blows.

Lei broke off in mid-stream. He did not snivel or moan. In less than a second he traversed the gulf between utter loss of self, and total self-control. The change came about so suddenly that the very silence seemed to echo with a numbing beat.

'There is a way.' The whisper now belonged to a surgeon, a bringer of healing: it still promised pain but now there was a hint of salvation as well. 'There may be a way.'

'Anything. Anything.'

Lei addressed the words to his chest, but the surgeon heard. 'We have been asked to . . . to mediate, you could say. We are not the police. We stand halfway between the police and you. Do you understand?'

Lei raised his eyes to a point between the floor and the

owner of the monotonous whisper that from now on would always echo in his mind.

'We need to have access to AMKCF's database, including its backfiles. The database is well guarded. The information we seek is kept, by you, in scrambled form. We do not have a descrambling unit. You do. It is attached to the terminal in your offices in Grosvenor Gardens. In order to access it, we need your Cryptag.'

The deal was not one that required elaboration, not even to someone in Lei's present state of mind. The neat, quiet man, unfolded his hands for the first time and stood up, pocketing the remote-controller. Then the two interrogators left. The door opened for them as if by magic; they went out, softly closing it behind them, leaving Lei Fuguo to meet, if he could, the fixed, soulless gazes of Tansy and her Mao-Mao.

'We have a problem.' Gene Sangster's voice no longer twanged with rage, but there could be no mistaking his concern.

'What?' Proshin asked.

'Does it matter?' said a third man.

They were in a kitchen two doors away from Lei's 'cell': Sangster and Proshin (who no longer whispered) facing each other across a table with mugs of coffee between them; and a bearded, bespectacled representative of the KGB's London *referentura*. This last man, in Sangster's view, looked too like Leon Trotsky for his own good. It was this 'Trotsky' who had inquired whether it mattered.

'I think it does. We're operating in the heart of London, SIS don't know we're here, the police don't know we're here, the CIA haven't a clue where I am —'

'You worry too much, Sangster.' Trotsky looked at his watch. 'You should get back to Lei.'

'Never mind him for a moment.'

'But you must understand our reasoning.' Proshin tried hard to sound placatory. 'There's no serious prospect of the KGB winning DI5's or DI6's agreement to this. And the CIA evidently does not trust British security, or it would have advised them of your participation.'

'I understand; what I'm saying is that things are difficult enough without blackmailing Lei Fuguo. We have a real problem.'

'I disagree,' said Trotsky, looking at his watch again. 'Anyway, there's no time.'

Proshin eyed his compatriot malevolently and with an inclination of his head beckoned Sangster to lean forward.

'You examined his eyes.' He used Cantonese, knowing that the third man wouldn't understand. 'Is that why –'

'Yes.'

'And?'

Sangster rubbed two fingers across his lips, as if trying to identify a bad smell lingering on the skin. 'That Chinese,' he said, very softly, 'will talk.'

TEN

◇

Mat heaved Diana's tote bag onto the scales. 'What have you got in there? It weighs a ton.'

'The usual. Some clean undies, spare jeans, shirts – two of yours incidentally, I pinched them from the laundry-basket – soap-powder, books.'

'You might have asked about the shirts.'

'Sorry.'

As Diana searched for her ticket a passenger in a hurry cannoned into her, sending everything flying. Mat knelt down and began to gather up the contents of his sister's handbag. He was puzzled by the number of cards she seemed to be carrying. 'London Library?' he said, holding one of them out to her.

'Yup. Gosh, I'd forgotten that one.'

'These are all library tickets?'

'I belong to more libraries in more countries than anyone else I know. Got them all?'

'I think so.' Mat reached out for a small purse-like bag, but Diana snatched it from his hands and stuffed it into her rucksack, blushing furiously. Mat thought about asking her if she was on the pill, then decided not to. It was none of his business.

'No Eau de Patou?' he asked, to skate them over the awkward moment.

Diana chuckled. 'Not in Chaiyang.' The reference was to an enormous bottle of perfume Mat had bought her for Christmas, years before: it was now so old that it smelled peculiar, but she could never bring herself to throw it out. Diana was not a

117

thrower-out by nature; besides, it was a present from Bean Sprout and as such entitled to an indefinite preservation order.

Once the check-in formalities were completed, Mat and Diana faced that uncomfortable hiatus when it was still too early to go through the gate, but there was nothing to do to pass the time landside.

'Want a coffee?'

'No, thanks. I think I can see the bookstall over there. Wonder if they've got the new Clavell . . .' Diana set off briskly, leaving Mat to bring up the rear. As she lifted the paperback from the shelf he caught up with her and said, 'Your coat.'

'What about it?'

'Don't you think it's a bit provocative? The red heart, and so on?'

She looked at him in amazement. 'The Chinese adore children. How can "I love my orphans" upset anyone?'

'They won't understand the language. All they'll see is the red heart; and they might just understand that wrong.'

'Oh, ridiculous. Have you got ten dollars?'

He paid for the book, brushing aside her proffered contribution, and bought himself a *Morning Post*. 'Still think I'm being ridiculous?' he asked, tapping the headline.

Diana, busy trying to find an empty pocket for her book, gave the paper only half a glance. '"Chairman Dead?" . . . they wouldn't say that if they knew. And they'd leave the question mark off the end. It's just a rumour.'

'Pretty prevalent rumour, these days. Look, it isn't too late to call the whole thing off, you know.'

'Sorry, Bean Sprout, but I'm really looking forward to seeing Chaiyang again, and Aunt Kaihui. I need to get away for a while. Think. Regroup. Give my love to Da, tell him not to worry, take care.'

'And you.' Suddenly his face was anxious. 'Please don't stay in China too long.'

He leaned forward to kiss her; with that, she was gone.

As Mat left the concourse, Qiu Qianwei turned to a Chinese standing by the counter and nodded.

The two men sauntered over to the Malaysian Airline System's first class lounge on the other side of the departures level. Although they had neither tickets nor boarding cards, it was obvious that the attendant knew both men and was not inclined to challenge either of them; after she'd let them enter she studiously avoided looking their way again.

The lounge was otherwise unoccupied at that hour of the morning. They settled themselves in the corner farthest from the door, screened from curious eyes by a line of potted palms.

'Fetch me a glass of water.'

Qiu obeyed without hesitation, bringing an orange juice for himself. The other man, whose Mahjong designation was North Wind, took a sip from the glass, rolled water around his mouth, swallowed it, and drained the rest of the contents in a trio of noisy gulps.

'Now,' he said, banging the empty glass onto the table. 'There's a lot of mess to be cleared up, and I don't just mean the shit we saw out there.'

North Wind was about forty years old. His puffy cheeks, receding forehead and protruding jaw, all covered with flaky grey skin, went together to make a decidedly ugly countenance. Something about him – perhaps it was the trail of saliva on the lower lip of his ever-open mouth, or the greasy gleam on his brow – reminded Qiu of animate things that lived in shells.

'Can we be quick?' Qiu pleaded. 'I must get back.'

'Mr Young will miss you.' North Wind's bubbly voice dripped sarcasm. 'Such a valued *servant*.'

Qiu flushed. 'He's a generous employer.'

'And you feel guilty about what you're doing to him. I understand.'

'No! It's not that.'

'Oh, I think it is. Just remember your child, Qiu. Tingchen's growing up now. A fine, ten-year-old boy. His mother takes good care of him. You wouldn't like anything to upset that, now would you?'

Qiu looked down at his glass of juice and was silent. North Wind sat back, allowing his voice to rise a tone.

'It must have looked such a clever set-up to you. There you were, a former Mahjong agent, safe in the arms of Ducannon Young. "Send us Colonel Qiu's son," says Mr Young to the Controller. "Get Tingchen out of China, or we'll give all the wonderful technology we invented for you to America."' He leaned forward. 'Only Sun Shanwang didn't want to play. He called the bluff. "You do what you like," he said to Mr Young. "But we'll keep Tingchen here. Oh yes. *We'll keep him!*"'

When Qiu raised the glass his hand was shaking. It shook so much that some of the juice ran down one side, over his fingers. North Wind, seeing the effect his words had produced, was well satisfied. He offered a pack of cigarettes with a smile that contrasted oddly with what had gone before.

'Is there a letter?' Qiu asked, too eagerly, as he accepted a cigarette.

'No. Why, were you expecting one?' North Wind sniggered in a soft, pappy kind of way. 'Letters from your son have to be earned. Maybe next time.'

'I've obeyed orders.'

North Wind shrugged.

'I don't want Diana Young harmed.'

'She knows about Benevolence. She's chosen to visit the mainland at a most difficult time.' North Wind inhaled, lifted his head and blew a fine jet of smoke at the ceiling. 'In those circumstances, whether she's harmed or not can't be said to be altogether within our control. It's certainly out of *your* control, Qiu.'

'You should give me the chance to work on her undisturbed. She likes me. We're friends.' He paused. 'I'm prepared to come back to China if necessary.'

'Are you indeed?' North Wind was startled to hear that offer. 'I'll report back what you've said. If you're quite sure.'

'I am.'

'Such a pity, then, that so far you haven't managed to discover anything about Benevolence. Listen to me. We think we know what Benevolence is for.' Suddenly he smacked both palms down on the table, making Qiu jump. 'There's nothing more important on the agenda. Do you understand?'

'Yes.'

'Then don't whine about not harming the girl.'

As he spoke these words North Wind stood up. Qiu did likewise, but the other man shoved him back into his seat. 'No. Give me five minutes.'

He left the lounge. Two European businessmen were waiting to check in for the Cathay Pacific flight to Singapore. One of them must have decided on the spur of the moment not to travel that day, for he picked up his briefcase and left the terminal, using the same door as North Wind. It must have been a truly unlucky day for flying: because when his colleague saw Qiu Qianwei emerge from the MAS lounge, he, too, deserted the check-in queue. Fixing his eyes firmly on the hunched shoulders and shuffling feet ahead of him, he set off in discreet pursuit.

ELEVEN

◇

Allowing for the time difference between London and Hong Kong, it was at about the same moment as Diana's plane took off for Canton on the first stage of her journey to Chaiyang that Sangster and Proshin arrived in Grosvenor Gardens.

They sat on the back seat of an anonymous maroon Ford with Lei Fuguo between them. Trotsky was in front next to the driver. The emotional atmosphere had sunk disagreeably far below freezing. All along their intention had been to milk AMKCF's manager and then enjoy an interval for planning their penetration of the computer. Sangster's assessment of Lei's mental state altered everything. It also marked a turning point in his relationship with Proshin. The Russian hadn't hesitated to side with Sangster. Overriding Trotsky's protests, he'd insisted that they make their entry the same night.

Nothing was as it should be. A bright moon swung over London, shining down on its deserted streets through cloudless skies, while a harsh wind siphoned along Grosvenor Place to sting the skin and swiftly render ungloved hands useless.

'It's bad,' Sangster concluded as they slowly drove past the target building. 'Wide street, that square in front, exposed main entrance . . . like doing Fort Knox at high noon. Is that a cop over there?'

Trotsky half turned towards him. 'There are embassies in this district. Some of the police carry guns.'

They circled four times, alternating two broad orbits around Victoria Station with two narrow ones in the immediate vicinity.

'Layout?' asked Sangster. They had found space in a resident's-only-parking street and were sitting quietly with all lights extinguished.

'They've recently taken over some of CAAC's accommodation. Fourth floor suite.' The driver seemed to be the man with the homework. 'Avoid the lift, it's unreliable. Three simple locks on the street door, two deadlocks and a Medeco high-security cylinder mortise job. No alarm. Time-lock on the entrance to the AMKCF suite; Lei can deal with that. Four rooms at executive level, two on either side of a central corridor. Washroom, small kitchen.'

'Back entrance?'

'No.'

'What, not even a fire-escape?'

'Lei's office is at the rear of the building. It has a window. Outside the window there's a balcony shared with the next-door building. If there's a fire, the instructions are to climb across the balcony.'

'Jesus Christ! What's above?'

'The roof.'

Sangster looked at his watch. 'Listen to me, Mr Lei.' No response. He took the arm of the Chinese and gave it a shake. 'We three are going to walk down the street, nice and slow, but not together. The man next to you will be your escort. You go first. I shall be some way behind. You'll let us in through the street door, yes?'

Lei nodded.

'Yes?'

'Yes.'

Sangster looked across him at Proshin. 'You ready?' He spoke in Russian. They had established a ground-rule for their own protection: when on duty, if either man wished to talk he must use the other's native language. The burden of making sense of a message had to rest with the communicator.

'Yes.' Proshin, obedient to the rule, gave his assent in English.

They got out of the car and stood for a moment on the pavement. Sangster stretched extravagantly, just another late night party-goer returning home. It was three o'clock, the street was deserted. 'Car?' he murmured.

'I will get rid of it. It's too risky for our people to be exposed here.'

'If you say so. But that means we don't have any backup and we don't have an express route out if things go wrong.'

'Then we had better hope they don't go wrong.'

'This is amateur.'

'So let's go home and forget it.'

Sangster glanced at Lei. The Chinese swayed slightly, as if he had had too much to drink. His eyes stared straight ahead, intent on some closed-circuit vision.

'No.'

'Then *move!*'

Proshin gave rapid instructions to the driver, who argued. Proshin started to wave his arms around. 'For Christ's sake!' Sangster breathed. The Russian banged his fist on the ledge of the driver's window and spat a dozen words at him. The car pulled away and was soon lost from sight.

Proshin began to walk, one hand looped through the crook of Lei's left elbow. At the end of the street he paused, looked right and left, then hurried around the corner, out of Sangster's vision. The American followed more slowly, noting the light traffic configuration where the side street joined Grosvenor Gardens. Nothing suspicious. But then it was early morning, London was at its lowest ebb, its (the satellite jargon came easily to Sangster now) perigee.

At the corner he paused, hands in pockets, for long enough to establish that the three of them were alone in the street. Opposite he could see the boundary wall of Buckingham Palace, brightly illuminated by orange street-lamps. To his left, the road curved as it approached Hyde Park Corner. The policeman he had noticed earlier was nowhere to be seen. On patrol, presumably . . . which meant he might be back any second.

Proshin had already reached the redbrick building which housed AMKCF's London operation and was dragging Lei up to the glass double-doors. Sangster joined them just as the Chinese was inserting the first key in the lock. A final swift look to right and left along the still deserted street, and they were in, the door closing softly behind them.

Entry, target.

Count seconds.

Seconds . . . As they climbed the stairs a subconscious part of Sangster's mind was already telling them off, keeping time.

At the top of the last flight of stairs Lei produced a key and a plastic wafer the size of a credit card. He inserted this in its slot above the wall-mounted keypad and tapped out some numbers. There was a click, the door opened. Lei stepped inside, automatically feeling for the lightswitch. Luckily, Proshin guessed his intention. *'Don't . . .* do that.'

He eased the door shut and stood close to Sangster, sniffing hard. A grey rectangle was just visible, some feet away. Proshin felt for Sangster's hand and pointed it at the shape. 'Window. Back of the house.'

'Check.'

'Light?'

Sangster hesitated. 'Okay.'

Proshin found the switch Lei had wanted earlier and pressed.

The office suite was tatty. The carpet needed mending; someone had evidently spilled coffee over it. There was no disguising the facts that one big room had been partitioned off into cubbyholes, and that every expense had been spared.

'Your office, Mr Lei?'

The Chinese pointed. 'End, on the right.'

Sangster quickly led the way. He turned on the light to reveal an office in tune with the shabbiness outside. In one corner, next to a water-cooler, stood a desk with a computer terminal and screen.

'Cryptag,' Proshin snapped.

Lei moved forward, offering another piece of plastic, but Proshin waved it aside. 'Log on yourself. And don't try to be smart: I'll be watching you.'

Lei sat down before the screen, inserting his plastic tag into a slot beside the terminal. Proshin turned to Sangster and addressed him in Russian.

'A useful gadget. That card is a resin block containing a radio receiver, transmitter and micro-processor.'

'You're kidding.'

'You can speak English if you want, this is not important. I'm serious. He's just put the card into an interrogator unit and typed his personal password. When the tag's been authorized, it receives a radio wave carrying a number code. The tag does a calculation on that number and transmits the result along with instructions to the interrogator. If the result is correct, the interrogator instructs the database to open for a fixed period of time.'

'And the KGB can't fake these things?'

'No. Each tag's programmed and graded, so that its owner only gets the information he's entitled to. We've got to hope that Lei's senior enough for our purposes. Ah! He's *in!*'

Information was scrolling up the screen. Proshin went to stand at Lei's shoulder. 'I'm going to give you a recent date and a flight number. First, I want the logged flight-time and its cargo manifest. Then I want to know precisely where the plane which flew that flight is going to be every hour of the next thirty days. Got it? Here is the date . . .'

Three hundred and ninety seconds; and with each one that passed Sangster became more uneasy. Nothing he could identify, nothing to pin down. By the pricking of my thumbs, something wicked this way comes . . .

The rest of the quotation hung on the outer edges of consciousness, mocking his attempts to lure it closer. He backed away from the screen, now busily sifting through untold stores of information, and embarked on a dissection of his surroundings.

The office suite was very small. First he checked the window at the rear. There was the balcony he'd heard described earlier. Sangster lifted the window a half-inch, to make sure it wasn't locked.

It wasn't locked . . .

By the pricking of my thumbs,
Something wicked this way comes,
Open locks . . .

126

There was another window at the front of the building, near the entrance to the suite. Sangster padded along the corridor and, standing to one side, looked out. He could see trees in the public garden opposite, a car cruising along the street, two young women walking very fast. Somewhere in the distance a police car's siren blared insistently.

Open locks . . .

He took a peek inside the other three rooms, the WC and the kitchen. Scarcely a kitchen: just a sink and a power-point; a kettle and a cupboard.

Sangster went back to stand in the doorway of Lei's office. Proshin was frantically jotting down notes, every so often exclaiming with satisfaction. By now he had replaced Lei, who sat behind the desk with his head in his hands.

The siren was drawing closer.

'Excellent!' Proshin breathed. He found time to glance back at Sangster, excitement glowing in his eyes like red coals. 'They'd put it all onto a backfile, just as I thought, but Lei has the superiority. Wonderful!'

Open locks . . . whoever knocks!

'Kostya!'

The Russian looked up sharply. 'What? Can't you see I'm —'

'Is that thing, that card, is it interactive?' Sangster's voice reverberated with tension. 'Does it tell the computer who's logged on and what he's asked for?'

Proshin stared into space, uncertainty taking the place of exhilaration. 'It's possible . . . but the technology's so advanced that —'

'*Whoever* gets in, *whoever* unlocks the computer, the machine's going to know! Even if that someone's got a Cryptag. Lei! Is that right?'

'Yes. This computer is linked to the Milky Way terminal in the Chinese embassy.'

'*What!*' Proshin grabbed his shoulders and started to shake him to and fro. 'Why didn't you tell us?'

'You did not ask.' There was a strange look in Lei's eyes; an expression bordering on inexplicable triumph.

Sangster had come into the room now. When Proshin swung around to face him, Lei took advantage of this change of position to squeeze out of his chair and inch his way towards the corridor.

'You hear that! Why should a civil airline have its computer linked to China's main military database? What kind of secrets are they protecting here?'

'To hell with that! If the Cryptag was put in at the wrong time of night, could it ring a bell in some precinct house, not just the embassy?'

'Well . . .'

'*Could it?*'

'Theoretically it —'

'*Could it, could it, could it?*'

Suddenly the police siren was no longer travelling, it had come to rest. It was resting outside in Grosvenor Gardens and the car's revolving light cast blue beams on the ceiling of the corridor. Sangster and Proshin rushed out in time to see Lei begin a sideways trot through the beams, arms held up to his face, gathering speed until at the end he was running. As he smashed through the glass his body turned outward and up, so that he resembled a diver doing a back-flip.

'*No!*'

But Sangster's warning came too late: Proshin had run to the corridor's end and was already looking out. A long way below he could see something dark and shapeless draped across the pavement, with two uniformed figures looking up, first at it, then at him . . .

'*Out!*'

Through the window at the back of the house, onto the narrow balcony, test the window of the house next door, locked, of course it was locked . . .

Sangster glanced up and clutched his companion's arm. 'Follow!'

He stood on the ledge of the open window and hauled himself onto the roof parapet, leaning down to pull Proshin up behind him. They were standing in the sliver of space between the low wall and the roof's steep, slated incline.

'Over there, look . . .'

Kostya followed his gaze: a square of some material that wasn't slate, three buildings further down . . . Sangster led the way, stumbling along the narrow gap until they were standing directly underneath the skylight.

'I'm going to lean backwards until I'm resting against the roof. Climb on my shoulders. Fast! It's our only hope!'

Proshin stepped into Sangster's cupped hands, hauling himself up with a series of grunts until at last his own hands made contact with the edge of the window. It had been left open an inch or so. He managed to release the catch. First his head went through, then his shoulders, then his waist was resting on the ledge.

'What's down there?' Sangster grunted.

'Can't see. Have to chance it . . .'

Proshin manoeuvred himself around through a semi-circle and hung from the ledge. 'Here, hold onto me . . .'

Sangster grasped the Russian's outstretched hand and angled the inner sides of his feet against the slates, rather as a skier climbs a mountain. The effort of maintaining his balance while hauling a heavy, moving load upwards, was too much for Proshin. Just as Sangster's hand grabbed for the ledge he drew a deep breath and dropped. He landed on an uncarpeted floor some ten feet below, without a scratch.

'You okay?' Sangster had somehow preserved his hold on the ledge and was peering down at him.

'Yes. Be quick.'

By the time Sangster had fallen into the attic, Proshin was already at the door. 'It's open!'

'Run!'

They skated down four flights of unlit stairs, not caring how much noise they made. At ground level they caught sight of the revolving blue lamp through a half-light over the front door and ran for the back of the house. Lavatory. Window locked. Proshin smashed through it, using something heavy that Sangster couldn't see. But as they slipped into the mews the American began to worry about that glass-shattering something.

They were in a narrow lane at the back of Grosvenor Gardens. To the left, orange street lights. They hurtled towards the gap. When they were still ten yards short, a white car screeched to a halt across it.

Sangster was running neck and neck with Proshin. He turned his head, saw the gun coming up, *'Don't!'*

He lashed out in a clumsy sideways punch, not quickly enough to prevent Proshin from firing. The shot flew over the car. Its driver, already half on to the pavement, ducked back inside. Sangster bounded onto the bonnet and launched himself into the street. Proshin, less agile, tried to run around the police car's rear fender, only to find a second officer barring his way.

Sangster risked one glance and sped on, screwing up his eyes and ears in protest at the inevitable shot, the wasted death.

As he raced into Grosvenor Gardens he heard shouts to his right. The first group of police to have arrived on the scene had spotted him. He turned left, heading for Victoria Station, panic at his heels. There was nowhere to go . . .

Then a car driving slowly along Grosvenor Gardens sounded its horn once. The driver changed down with a violent rev of the engine and threw it into a U-turn. Sangster looked over his shoulder. Proshin was racing for the intersection; behind him Sangster thought he saw a policeman doubled up, both hands squeezed over his crotch. The car drew into the kerb, not quite stopping even when the back door flew open and hands reached out to haul Sangster inside. He landed across someone's lap. Seconds later, another man descended on top of him with a grunt, knocking all the wind out of his body.

Then they took off as though needling for the front at Brand's Hatch.

'I thought you'd got rid of your people,' Sangster gasped as

Proshin wriggled off him. The Russian launched into a tirade against Trotsky, who laughed.

'You have complaints?' he said. 'Address them to our ambassador, please. No, we knew you would fuck this up, so we hung around. Your thanks can wait.'

The driver circled Hyde Park Corner on two wheels and sent them swinging into Piccadilly. But the sirens were coming up behind them very fast now.

'I hope you like naked women,' Trotsky observed to Sangster with a smile. He seemed to have brightened up; perhaps it was the prospect of being chased all over London by British policemen.

'Naked —'

The driver braked hard. As Proshin bodily chucked him out of the car Sangster briefly became aware of flashing, multi-coloured lights, an archway framed with pink bulbs. Suddenly he was half-falling and half-running down steep steps, two at a time, towards a door. As his foot landed on the last step the door opened to reveal a block of darkness, through which heavy-metal music suddenly pounded. Sangster skidded over the threshold and crashed into a chair. Then Proshin was picking him up and dusting him down.

'Where the hell —'

'This is my club.'

'Your *what?*'

'Club. Soho.'

Somewhere to Sangster's left a bottle broke, followed by the sound of a fist meeting bone.

'You'll like this place,' Proshin added hopefully.

'But the others —'

'By now our colleagues will be on their way to a safe house, with new licence plates. The driver is very good; don't worry. He will not be caught. So we'll have a drink, relax, yes?'

Sangster had recovered his breath. There were many things he wanted to say to Proshin, like: how dare he carry a gun in London; did he always operate in this incredibly haphazard, lunatic fashion; how was he going to explain the death of Lei to his masters? But his body wouldn't let him. The relief came too suddenly, it was too extreme. So what he actually said was: 'And the naked women?'

He could scarcely hear Proshin's braying, joyous laugh over the noise of the fist-fight that was getting into its stride somewhere close by in the darkness.

TWELVE

◇

Diana looked around the hall of the rebuilt house in wonder. 'It's *huge!*'

Kaihui smiled as she shook the water from her umbrella, then beckoned. 'Come.'

She led her niece through into the kitchen. Diana paused on the threshold, convinced she was the victim of a skilfully manufactured illusion.

It wasn't just that the room had been expanded to approximately four times its previous size. There was fluorescent lighting, a tall blue refrigerator, an electric stove and a gas burner next to it. There was a huge table and there were taps over the sink. Under the sink stood a washing-machine. On a dresser, facing her, was a television set. It was on. The picture's colours left something to be desired, but that was scarcely the point.

Diana remembered the kitchen less well than she could recall other parts of this house, although certain impressions stayed very definitely in her mind. In 1988 there had been no running water, no electricity, no TV. She had known that her return to Chaiyang would be fraught with emotion and memories. Nothing had prepared her for the sheer number of traumatic changes that had taken place over the intervening years. Diana felt her knees begin to wobble. She reached out for the table and lowered herself into a chair.

She was exhausted.

Rain had boiled around her from the moment the bus left Chengdu, Sichuan's provincial capital, early that morning. She had stared out of the window through an opaque glass-bead curtain, vainly trying to penetrate the clouds that hung suspended from the heavens in murky great folds. Just before dusk, the bus had driven into the village.

She saw at once that there had been changes in Chaiyang. The mud-brick houses which she remembered from her earlier visit had mostly gone, to be replaced by modern two- and three-storey buildings sheltered from the elements by red tiles. Several old cars were parked in front of the biggest house . . . of course, there was a road now. And there were poles carrying cables for electricity and telephones. When she'd last been here, the only poles were for carrying things across your shoulders.

But if the village had changed, so had her aunt. Diana remembered Kaihui as an old, tired peasant woman with calloused hands and one set of clothes: baggy trousers, torn jacket, both in faded grey. Who, then, was this upright woman who had recently had her hair permed and wore a brightly-coloured *sam-fu*?

Kaihui had been poor but cheerful, worn but lively. Now she was something else and Diana couldn't yet fathom what.

'Zhaodi?' she said, pulling herself more upright. 'Where is she?'

'Gone to market, with Mingchao. They will be back day after tomorrow.'

Mingchao was brother to Kaihui and Jinny; he had married Zhaodi during Diana's previous, enforced stay in the village. She was disappointed not to find them both at home.

'Excuse me, miss. My name is Lingchu.'

Diana, startled, looked around to see a young man emerge out of the shadows by the back door. From the sound of his voice (he had spoken in English) and his general appearance, he could not have been more than about eighteen, but his face was lined and tense. A white bandage covered half his forehead, including the right eye; the visible part of his skull was shaven almost to the skin, leaving it looking as though someone had scattered fine ash over him.

'Goodness! What have you done to your head?'

The youth smiled bleakly. 'I? Nothing. It was the People's

Armed Police.' Seeing her lack of comprehension he went on, 'I used to live in this village. My parents still live here. I am . . . was a student at the Number Three Technical Science College, in Chongqing.'

'Was . . . ?'

'Two weeks ago, a few of the younger teachers and some of the students tried to reintroduce political struggle sessions. The police broke them up. There were many arrests. I was going into the college when the raid was nearly over. The police thought I was one of the bad elements, so they picked me up.'

'And beat you up?'

Lingchu nodded. 'At least they let me go. Many friends are still in prison. But my travel permit has been endorsed: I have to stay in my home village until they tell me I can leave.' He nodded at Kaihui. 'Auntie there asks me to be your translator.'

'Your English is very good.'

'It's not bad.' There was something majestic about this young man's acceptance of her judgement on his monotonous delivery.

Kaihui interrupted, saying a few words in subdued Chinese. 'Yes,' Lingchu said. 'We should all eat now. You must be very tired, miss.'

'Diana. My name's Diana.'

Lingchu did not reply, being too busy helping Kaihui extract a pair of enormous chickens from the electric oven.

Diana was ravenous. After dinner she helped Kaihui clear away the dishes. To her surprise, however, she found the sink full of dirty clothes left to soak. 'Why not use the washing machine?' she asked.

Lingchu came to her rescue. 'No water.'

'But . . .' Diana gestured helplessly at the taps.

'Not joined to anything.'

Diana turned away from the sink to address her aunt. 'You have a washing machine?' Lingchu translated; Kaihui proudly nodded. 'But no running water?' Kaihui heard Lingchu out and nodded again. 'Also a bath upstairs,' she added. 'And a shower.'

'I think I'm losing my bearings.'

Kaihui spoke at length. Lingchu smiled at Diana. 'Your aunty thinks we should all sit down and talk some more now.'

They sat around the big table, with Lingchu opposite Diana. Kaihui brought ginger tea and while they sipped the pungent brew she began to speak. She went on for a long time, with increasingly elaborate gestures, and every so often Lingchu would say 'Mm'. When Kaihui at last ran out of steam, Lingchu cleared his throat.

'Your aunt says she's very happy to see you,' he began. 'But she's sad her sister's dead. She received your letter, so she knows why you're here. She agrees with your late mother's plan. She wants her sister's ashes to be placed at the village shrine.'

It was hard to judge from Lingchu's face what he made of this. If he scorned such peasant superstitions it certainly didn't show.

'Um. Next: Zhaodi and Mingchao have a child. A boy. He's called Yongcai.' Lingchu's lips spread in one of his rare smiles. 'Upstairs asleep, right now, but you can see him in the morning.'

'Yes, we'd heard. Please tell Kaihui my mother was very happy about that.'

Kaihui listened to Lingchu with a faraway look in her eyes but said nothing.

'That is all the good news.'

'Really?'

Diana's glance around the kitchen was ironic, but Lingchu either failed or did not want to understand. 'Chaiyang is different now,' he said. 'We have electricity, telephone, TV. The production team is very successful. The land here is good, fertile. We can grow two rice-crops each year; corn, melons, many kinds of fruit. Peanuts. Sweet potatoes.'

'When I was here last, you only grew rice.'

'Yes. But now there is more than enough rice, so land was released. There was a . . . a . . . *xiao shou*.' Lingchu made a face and knocked a fist against his forehead. 'When you ask people to state what they will pay, all peoples together . . .'

'Auction?'

136

'Yes! The Brigade ordered an auction. So some peoples in Chaiyang have much money, have saved, and those peoples buy the biggest lands.'

When he was on the point of speaking again, Kaihui interrupted him. Lingchu heard her out with good grace, but there was the hint of a wink in his one visible eye as he turned to Diana. 'She asks me to say that she has fourteen hogs.'

'Oh.'

'She also asks me to tell you the troubles here. So that you will understand why you cannot stay.' He paused. 'You could be in danger here.'

'*Danger?* But . . . but I'm family. I mean . . . aren't I?'

'Yes, and it is a rich family. And you come from abroad. Nor do you look Chinese. This village is divided. There are two, three . . . fictions?'

'Factions.'

'Ah! Do you remember Weidong?'

'He used to sell booze, didn't he? Oh . . . he was the bar keeper.'

'That's the man. He is in prison.'

'Why?'

At first, he and his family were wealthy. They bought land. But, he starts to drink too much *maotai*. Then he brings in a snook.'

'A what?'

'Sorry . . . snook-er table?'

Diana bent her elbow and imitated a pool-shot.

'Right, right. Then he start to gamble too much, too much. He lost. He can't snook well.'

'So he had to sell the land?'

'Not at first. At first he tried something else. He bought films. You know . . . videos. And a machine. He shows . . . showed? . . . videos at his house, for money, and many people pay – not just in Chaiyang, but from other villages as well. Then he starts to buy bad videos. Yellow videos.'

Diana had not heard the term before, but she could guess the meaning. 'What we'd call blue-movies.'

'I think so.' He lowered his voice and covered his mouth in

such a way that only Diana could see his lips. 'Sex.' He removed his hand. 'Very bad,' he said aloud. 'But people go still, pay even more money.'

'So why's he in prison?'

Lingchu nodded at Kaihui, who grimaced and broke into a torrent of Mandarin. Lingchu had to hold up both hands to silence her.

'Your aunt says she has a big mouth. And . . . excuse me . . . she does. One day she and Mingchao are in the market at Chongqing. They meet friends. They talk – about Weidong. Public Security Bureau men overhear. They come to Chaiyang.'

Diana looked from face to face, their yellow complexions waxy under the harsh light, and suddenly sensed the concern of a family under siege. Chaiyang was split down the middle, and her relatives had contributed to the rift, perhaps even made it.

'The PSB find many things in Weidong's house. Not just videos. Also, two hundred telephones.'

'*How* many?'

'At that time, we do not have telephone lines in Chaiyang; not like now. Weidong bought the telephones for when the lines came, so that then he can sell them to the villagers.'

'But is that crooked?'

'He bought them from a cadre, who had signed for them, and there was . . . oh, I don't know the words . . . you know, it was corruption. Is that how you say it?'

'You mean, this cadre was taking bribes?'

'Exactly! So they arrested the cadre. Then they arrest Weidong. Now he's in prison and Weidong's family won't speak to this family any more. Some people in the village think one thing, some another. Understand?'

'Yes.' All too well, she thought despondently.

'Weidong had to sell his land.' He hesitated. 'Your aunt bought it.'

Lingchu and Diana looked at each other, saying nothing for a while.

'I hadn't planned on staying long,' she said slowly. 'But I've

138

come to do something here, I . . .' She made her decision. 'I'm sorry if it means more trouble, but I'm not going to leave right away. Too much like quitting.'

'You can't, even if you want to. There isn't another bus for a week.'

Diana felt depressed. There were things about China that she liked, some that she loved; but the country never failed to overwhelm her with a sense of helplessness and confusion, problems without end or solution.

'I want to go to bed now. I'm very tired.'

'I will tell your aunt.'

'Thanks, Lingchu,' Diana said as she shouldered her pack. 'See you again while I'm here, I hope.'

Kaihui had given her the same room the whole Young family had shared on their last, enforced visit, although now it contained just the one bed, complete with mosquito net and a chamber pot on the floor. Diana dumped herself down on the edge of the bed and sighed. Above all she would have liked a bath, but setting up a wash on the grand scale in Chaiyang took longer than she was prepared to spare from good sleeping time. So she undressed, wrapped herself in one of Mat's shirts, splashed water over her face, and lay down. She fell asleep as if sandbagged.

Diana had no idea how long she'd slept when a reverberating crash of thunder knocked her out of bed.

She had been floating on the surface of sleep, wrestling with a ghostly voice that echoed down a bad phone line, warning her of disaster to come. The voice was spectral, indescribably evil. When the thunder exploded over Chaiyang with the immediacy and fury of a grenade, the shock propelled Diana upright, out of sleep, into the full expectation that the owner of the horrible voice would be at her side. She threw herself away from where she took the voice to be, and came to lying half in bed and half on the floor, with the sheet wrapped around her legs like a tight-fitting shroud.

Slowly she managed to disentangle herself. Her head was splitting with a tension headache; her tongue was thickly furred and tasted of bile. She was suffocating. But when at last she could open the window it was only to admit a warm, wet wave of rain-soaked air, thick as invisible fog and redolent of the excrement which covered the fields beyond.

She leaned her head against the frame, wishing she hadn't come. No matter how firmly she reminded herself that she was obeying her mother's dying wish, she couldn't deny the reality of her feelings. She wanted to be back in Korea, with her orphans. Safe.

She drew in several deep breaths, trying to ease the pressures that bore down on her, but found no relief. Suddenly lightning forked directly overhead, to be followed a second later by another hideous peal of thunder: it was as though the sky wanted to rip itself apart. Something made her look down into the street – perhaps it was the sound of Kaihui's hogs, moving restlessly – and as she did so an enormous trident of light flickered out of the black sky. For an instant the lane below turned a lurid white.

Not a dozen feet from her, looking up at the window, stood a tall figure with his feet wide apart and hands on hips.

Diana, startled, jumped back. Her fright soon wore off; she made herself push aside the billowing curtains and lean far out into the drizzle, scanning the street below. Before long the storm obliged her with another of its dazzling tree-root patterns. In the split second for which the lane was lit sickly-pale, Diana saw only straw, an open drain, the wall of the house opposite; but of the dark, phantasmagorical figure that had frightened her to the boundary of educated reason, there remained no trace.

THIRTEEN

◇

Warren Honnyman came into the downstairs bar of the Mandarin Hotel with the familiar light step that Simon, who was watching from one of the dark niches, always found unusual in so large a man. But then perhaps that was what a United States marine's training did for you . . .

Warren sat down next to Simon, helping himself to a man-sized handful of peanuts and smiled up at the Chinese waiter who was already at his elbow. He asked after the waiter's children, discussed the weather, imparted a stock exchange tip and finally got around to ordering a Löwenbrau as if it were some kind of unimportant afterthought. Simon watched the waiter depart and made a face.

'I don't know anyone else in Hong Kong who manages people like you and Rachael.'

'Oh, my lord, it's easy.' Warren grabbed another fistful of peanuts, his lunch for the day, and sat back. 'For Americans, it's easy. Wasn't it Miss Manners' father who told the children that the servants now outnumbered the family and that this was a situation that took time to get used to – say all of three minutes?'

'You make it sound simple.'

'It *is* simple, if you only treat a human being *like* a human being.'

'That's what they taught you in the Marines?'

'Naw! That's what I learned out here, in two weeks, watching the Limeys look down their long noses at everyone.'

'I see. How is Rachael?'

'In fine fettle. Incidentally, ah . . . she asked me to remind you that she's supposed to be coming around to sort through Jinny's things.'

'It's very kind of her. But finding the time, that's the problem —'

'It won't get any easier. You look all chewed up.'

Simon grunted. 'Haven't cried so much since I was a kid.'

'Well, and why not? Jesus, what kind of shit doesn't cry for his wife when she dies?'

Warren's drink arrived. He took a long pull from the tankard and looked around. The bar was crammed with its usual midday assortment of businessmen and tourists, but the very crush of numbers guaranteed its own privacy. He concluded his survey by leaning forward and saying confidentially, 'There's a rumour going around town I thought you might know something about. Did you hear about the border thing?'

Simon lowered his eyes. 'Why should I hear?' he prevaricated.

'Because you and the legendary Assistant Commissioner of Police, Peter Reade, sweeper-up-of-shit by appointment to the extremely rich, are like that!' Warren snapped his fingers.

'What did you hear?'

'Nearly three hundred "ills" made a rush for the fence last night. The guards turned on the juice: quick-fried Chinese takeaway.'

Simon stared into his empty glass. 'I heard they rushed the fence, that's all. Two years, a year ago, I'd have laughed at the rest of it.'

'And now?'

'Now . . . I'm not sure.'

Warren lowered his voice. 'Time to go.'

'Only days away now.' Simon swallowed back his whisky and wiped his mouth. 'Are we still secure?'

'Yes. Funny you should ask: I've just this minute finished making my latest contribution to security. I'm going out with a bang. Snakes and coffins. Statewing's just won a contract for river transport inland from Canton, up the West River as far as Liuzhou. Know it?'

'Vaguely.'

'Liuzhou, believe it or not, is China's coffin city. Mention the place to a mainland Chinese sometime and watch his face fall – bad luck to talk about it, I guess. And then there's the live snakes: one million of them are routed annually through Wuzhou for export to Hong Kong and God knows where else. Some big honcho up north decided they were spending too much on airfreight, so he's putting the trade through Liuzhou. And there's the usual "muck and truck" as well, of course.'

'But why you? For hundreds of years the Chinese have managed their inland river trade for themselves, without complaints.'

'And without profit! There's no discipline. What's built up over the years is a mishmash of pirates and smalltime operators who can't be trusted to get from one end of the Pearl estuary to the other within contract deadline. Beijing took a grip on the thing, asked for tenders for a forty-eight hour lighter service with all the state enterprises forced to use it. We won.'

'Competition?'

'TNT, of course; you'd expect to find the market leader. But they've been steadily laying off their shipping interests over the past decade and couldn't provide the set-up in time. Everyone else was just small fry.'

'You're going to lose money on that.'

'Uh-huh.' Warren shrugged. 'It's always been Benevolence policy; you know that as well as I do. Everybody has to believe that we're staying – has to be made to believe it. Once word got out that we were on the run, confidence would collapse and so would Hong Kong's infrastructure. Therefore, if new business comes along, take it. In particular, if Beijing produces any kind of proposition, snap it up!'

'All the same, to do it so close to Benevolence . . .'

'Look at it from the other side. Statewing's the biggest transporter in the Pacific Rim. If we hadn't bid, what would the little guys in their Mao suits have thought? Maybe they'd have gotten out their abacuses, added up two and two and for a wonder made four.'

'I suppose so.'

'Look, Simon, if you're celebrating a new contract with

mainland China, the last thing the authorities are going to do is conclude that the contractor's about to forsake the Orient forever.'

'Let's hope so.'

'Statewing can swallow it. We'll be leaving behind some rented lighters, twenty tugs and half a dozen old junks that the auditors wrote off around the time of the Opium Wars.' Now Warren drained his tankard and banged it down on the table. 'But I'm going to miss this place.'

'We all are. One thing at least I'm glad about: Jinny won't have to uproot.'

'It would have been terrible for her. How are the kids taking it?'

'Pretty well. Mat doesn't say much, just works himself all hours of the day and night. Diana's in China. Jinny wanted her ashes to . . . go home.' His voice cracked. 'I had to let Diana take them.'

For a moment there was silence. Then Warren said, 'Did I hear right? Diana's in *China?*'

'Yes.' Simon glanced up and saw the worried expression on his friend's face. 'Why, what's the –'

'After all you went through when you were there? And since then, over that Taiwan business?'

Simon nodded.

'Look, I don't want to worry you, but . . . well, China's in a mess, right now.'

'I know. Diana's a sensible girl.'

Warren sucked in a deep breath, shaking his head. 'Risky. For the Lord's sake, Simon, when's she due back?'

'Soon. I told her to come home quickly. Warren, she's a grown-up, for heaven's sake!'

'Does she know about Benevolence?'

'Of course not! Do you think I'd let her go to China with something as dangerous as that inside her head?'

'Suppose Chinese intelligence thought different. Suppose they got hold of her and gave her the third degree.' Warren's tone was brutal, intentionally so. 'Had you thought of that?'

'You're fantasizing.'

'Simon, why won't you see it?' Warren began to check off the points with his fingers. 'One. She's alone. Two. She's in a China that's shown every sign of heading to hell in the fast lane. Three. She's a Young, they've no reason to love her.'

'All right, there's an element of risk! Do you think I'm the kind of father who'd stop his adult children taking risks?'

'No. Rachael and I have three daughters, they've all flown; what they do is, has to be, their business.' He took a few deep breaths, calming himself down. 'Simon, because I love you and because I loved Jinny, I'm not going to say you were wrong. But I'll give you a piece of advice now and I want you to promise you'll listen, okay?'

Simon saw he meant it, that Warren would physically detain him until he'd had his say. 'I'm listening.'

'Don't . . . don't, I beg, I implore you, let any other members of the Club know that Diana's in China.'

'Why?'

'Because now I will tell you something.' Warren rested his hands on his knees, elbows outward, and glowered at Simon over the tops of his glasses. 'The way the Club feels right now, the way the markets are behaving, if any one of them thought there was a chance, however slight, of Benevolence coming into the open . . . you would find yourself left here alone. And I do mean alone.'

Simon gazed at him in silence. 'Diana . . . knows . . . *nothing!*' he said at last.

'I believe you. Others may not. If they thought there was a risk, no matter how small, of Diana undermining Benevolence, my bet is that the Club would abandon you. And I'll tell you something else, Simon.' His voice was charged with foreboding. 'If that's all the punishment they felt like handing out, I'd call you one hell of a lucky man.'

FOURTEEN

◇

Diana would never forget her first sight of Chang Ping.

She had climbed up to the shrine in the hills above the village. The cave lay behind a small clearing, grey with ash deposited by thousands of fires over hundreds of years; a small pile of bamboo leaves was still smouldering in one corner. She approached quietly, her footfalls making no sound on the moist soil, and pushed aside the half a dozen creepers that shielded the cave mouth from prying, hypercritical eyes of politically sound but spiritually empty cadres.

He was in the act of kowtowing.

She stood transfixed and watched. He knelt, keeping his weight well back but not quite resting on his heels. He raised his hands to either side and bent forward until forehead and palms touched the earth: literally 'knocking head', kowtowing. He reversed his hands and clenched them into a fist three times, with a pause between each. Then he turned the palms down again and rose to his original position. He repeated this ritual thrice.

He stood up, placed his palms together in front of his face, held the position for a few seconds as if praying, then bowed. He dropped his hands to his sides, waited a second and turned.

'Who's there?' His voice sounded annoyed but not in the least fearful. Although he spoke in Chinese, Diana could guess the meaning.

'It's me . . . Diana Young.'

'Oh, yes.' Now he spoke English. 'I've heard about you.' He brushed past her, leading the way out of the cave. 'My name's Chang Ping.'

Once Diana had got over the abruptness of his greeting she began to notice things. He looked strong: about five foot eight but stocky with it. His shirtsleeves were rolled up above calloused elbows to reveal the beginnings of powerful, rounded biceps and his movements were those of a lithe boxer. He was about her own age, she reckoned, or a little older, and stunningly handsome. Sexy, oh yes. His body and the way he used it tuned directly into that part of Diana which said things like, 'Let's get our clothes off *now!*', the sly part of the human psyche which boys were forgiven for paying attention to and girls never were.

'Hello,' she said shyly.

He studied her face with a frown. After a while his silent scrutiny made Diana feel uneasy. She stepped back and started to notice details.

His clothes were old. The pink shirt had faded irregularly in the wash, so that some parts of it now were almost white, giving it the look of marbled strawberry-and-vanilla ice cream. His loose trousers had once been properly categorizable as corduroy but the cords had worn flat, leaving bald patches here and there. Only the black cloth-and-rope shoes looked new.

The silence had gone on for far too long. 'It's odd to find a young person kowtowing in China,' she said, her voice uncertain.

'My *nai-nai* . . . my paternal grandmother was devout. She looked after me when my parents were in the labour camp. I'm hot. Let's move.'

He went first, not asserting himself, but someone had to lead and he was naturally equipped for the job – or so Diana rationalized to herself as she fell into second place.

They sat on the side of the hill overlooking the village's paddy-fields. The rain had stopped and although clouds still draped themselves low across the landscape there were gaps through which a watery sun might shine. Far below in the plains, blue-jacketed peasants wearing pointed straw hats were engaged in the occupation of their fathers and their forefathers. Diana leaned forward, hugging her knees. Chang Ping lowered

147

himself down at right angles to her, resting his weight behind him on his hands. After a while he plucked a blade of long grass and meditatively began to chew it. He seemed to have no intention of speaking again.

'You've been sent here for re-education, right?'

He stared at her, as if testing the question for traps, before removing the grass from his mouth. 'I'm a troublemaker.'

Diana believed him: he looked the part. His skin was flawless, save only for a mole on the left side of his jaw, from which sprouted a small curly hair. His brows were thick and perfectly level, ruling off narrow, gulls-wing eyes. A rounded, dimpled chin was the only discordant feature on a face otherwise square and strong with character. And perhaps a little cruel as well.

'What sort of trouble do you make?'

Half a minute of silence went by. 'Political.'

'What sort of political?'

'I can speak English.'

'You certainly can!' Diana laughed and some of the tension evaporated. 'A few of my English friends can't speak it as well as you do. Since when's it been a political crime, though?'

He smiled at her for the first time. It was a rich smile. 'I wish you could laugh again,' he said. 'When you're sitting as you are now you look good.' He paused; Diana knew his inquisitive eyes were upon her face. 'When you laugh, however, you are . . .'

'I'm . . . ?'

Her prompting annoyed him. 'When you laugh, you are something.' His voice came out roughly.

'Thank you.' It was so unexpected that she faltered over the words.

'I have heard that your mother was Chinese and your father is an Englishman. Is that so?'

She nodded.

'You do not look Chinese. Yet there's something oriental about you.'

She gazed back at him, finding it easier now that a smile

148

seemed to hover permanently around his lips. 'You mentioned your own parents. Something about a labour camp. Could you tell me . . . I mean, if you don't mind, that is.'

But he did mind. He looked away then back at her face several times before beginning to speak. 'I was born in Wuhan,' he said reluctantly. 'My father was the producer of a local TV news programme. Mother was a paediatrician.

'Intellectuals, in other words.'

It was the wrong thing to say. The smile vanished, the cold stare returned. 'Odd, you like to apply these labels. I thought it was only we Chinese who did that.' He swept the hair off his forehead in a quick gesture of irritation.

He had strange hair. It seemed to have great body, standing away from his scalp and falling in a single wave from one side of his head to the other, the parting absurdly far down to the left. It was the kind of style that androgynous pop-stars once liked to cultivate: the only androgynous thing about his almost excessively masculine appearance.

There was a long pause. 'The villagers tell me you've come to lay your mother's ashes to rest.'

'Yes.' She didn't want to talk about that just then. 'You said your parents were in a camp . . .'

'I did.'

'Well . . . ?'

'Well what?'

'Why were they in a camp?'

As usual, he took time to consider her question. 'I was at middle school. So were my sisters. The cadres made us write criticisms of our parents. You think that's terrible.'

'Not at all. We know a lot about the cultural revolution now. The pressures on you must have been dreadful.'

'I can't remember the pressures.' His voice held a trace of contempt. 'I remember that when we did a harsh criticism of mother or father, the cadres praised us.'

He got up and stood with his arms folded, staring down the hill. Diana felt unhappy. A moment ago he had touched on important things which would remain with him like a thorn in the flesh all his life . . . yet here she was thinking that he

149

had the most beautiful, athletic body she'd ever seen . . .

Chang Ping glanced around. 'What?'

'Nothing. I . . . go on.'

'You cried out. As if you were angry.'

'I was cross with myself, that's all. Please do go on.'

He kicked the ground a couple of times. 'There was a trial. Our denunciations were . . . were evidence. So our parents were sent to labour camp.'

'I see. I'm sorry.'

'My father has been rehabilitated. He is back at work. Mother's . . .' He kicked the ground again, looked at the fields then at her, squinted up to the sky, eyed her once more. 'She is a few *fen* short, now.' He tapped his forehead. 'Because of words I wrote to win the cadres' praise.'

'Do you really believe that? If you hadn't done it, they'd have found someone else who would – a patient of your mother's who'd say she quoted Confucius, or something.'

He considered her through eyes that were warm with sadness and deep remorse. Diana saw how he had suffered and felt sympathy flood through her. He'd done wrong, but he had also repented; and she liked him especially for that. 'What happened afterwards?' she asked.

'I decided to become a model student,' he said reluctantly. 'To make myself safe.'

'I don't understand.'

'All Chinese know that another cultural revolution is as near to them as this grass is to my tongue.' He looked at the blade with distaste and threw it down. 'I wanted a secure job. So I had to receive a good education first.'

'Did you succeed?'

'Yes.' He seemed disinclined to elaborate.

'But now you're here. What went wrong?'

There followed the longest silence so far. At the end of it, all he said was, 'I'm not too sure. It's worrying. Often I cannot sleep at night.'

Diana had an inspiration. 'Do you walk about the village, when you can't sleep?'

No answer.

'Was it you I saw last night, in the storm?'

Another interminable silence. 'Maybe.'

'But . . . why? It was pouring . . .' She felt almost angry on his behalf, much as a mother might want to chide her irresponsible son. But he only laughed. 'You think it's funny,' she said; and then was cross with herself for sounding over-sensitive.

He became serious again: too quickly for Diana's liking, because his laugh was magical.

'No. Nothing in Chaiyang is funny. Sichuan province is not funny.'

'Why do you say that?'

'You haven't heard about the marauders?'

'No.'

'Some students have banded together and taken to the rural districts. It is very serious for the authorities. At the university campuses, they can control; but out here, there are no police.'

After Diana had been quiet for a long time Chang Ping said, 'I'm sorry. I didn't mean to worry you.'

'Nobody wanted me to come on this trip. When I got here, even my aunt said it was dangerous.'

'You should go home, then.'

'There isn't another bus this week.'

'Then we must hope the countryside stays quiet.' He stretched out a hand. 'Shall we go back now? It's late.'

She allowed him to help her up. Chang Ping led the way, as before. After a while the earth path became studded with flat stones and the going was easier. As they came out onto the plain through the last of the bamboo groves he stopped and pointed.

Diana's eyes travelled over the flat, watery expanse of rice fields to the other side of the valley where the hillside climbed steeply into a pale heat haze. But, she realized, it wasn't all haze. In one place, a column of smoke pushed up urgently into the sky like an evil, embryonic genie.

They quickened their pace along the dike. The early evening silence was broken only by the occasional light splash made by a frog landing in the water or a fish piercing the muddy surface. Diana and Chang Ping had nearly caught up with the last group of peasants, still cleaning off their hoes, when again he came to a sudden halt.

Less than a quarter of a mile distant, a file of people was wending its way across the flat landscape at right angles to their own path: black figures against the green, they seemed to float over the surface of the paddies like ghosts. Diana realized that their dike was lower than the one supporting her and Chang Ping, but still there was something ominous about these swiftly moving silhouettes now nearing the eastern side of the village.

'How odd,' she said in a low voice. 'The leader looks as if . . . as if he was crucified.'

'He's got something over his shoulders.'

They both knew what it was.

'Let's go back to the shrine,' Diana said. 'We can –'

She was interrupted by a loud babble of Chinese. The man with the gun had deviated from his original path where it joined another dike and was advancing towards them, rifle raised in both hands. Chang Ping shouted something back. The gunman did not reply in words; instead he merely lifted the barrel and gestured with it towards the village.

As they passed the armed stranger Diana saw that he was wearing tattered green army fatigues, a peaked cap emblazoned with a bright red star and an armband bearing yellow Chinese characters. He looked exhausted. He kept chewing the lips of his thin, narrow mouth as if seeking sustenance which ordinary food couldn't provide.

'What does it say on his arm?' she murmured as they walked past.

'It says: "Revolutionary Guard".'

'What?'

When they reached the village square it was to find everything in pandemonium. The new arrivals were twelve in number, all clad in the same rough and ready uniform. They had rounded up the villagers and herded them into the square; now they stood in a loose circle, brandishing sticks and howling slogans.

Occasionally a braver spirit among the village men stepped out of the circle, or yelled abuse at one of the Red Guards. Whenever this happened, two or three of the newcomers would immediately attack the villager, beating his shoulders, arms and legs with their staves. One of them had a makeshift flail consisting of a ball attached by a chain to the end of what looked like a billiard cue. Diana saw it and shuddered.

Only the leader remained aloof from the mêlée. He stalked around the square, eternally chewing his lips. At last he went up to the wall of the largest house where there was a metal bath hanging from a hook and knocked against it with the butt of his rifle. He kept up the clamour until the villagers fell silent, all except for one baby which resolutely continued to bawl.

The leader raised his head, looking for the source of the noise, and spoke a few words. His companions laughed.

'What did he say?' Diana whispered.

'That the baby is a good revolutionary baby: it doesn't knuckle down to authority easily. Ssh.'

The gunman shouldered his rifle, unhooked the bath and dropped it on the ground, where he used it as a platform from which to address his reluctant audience. The harangue went on for a long time. When he'd finished he beckoned his nearest colleague, who stepped onto the bath in the leader's place. He produced a slim, red-covered book from his top left pocket, held it up and began to gabble.

By this time Chang Ping had steered himself and Diana to the centre of the village circle, protected by bodies on all sides. 'What's happening?' she breathed.

'The leader says his name is Wen Zaofan: Wen Rebel. But that name belongs to an older generation. He is lying. They've formed a Work Team as a revolutionary tribunal, with the consent of the Party committee in Chengdu and –'

The guard on the bath stepped down, to be replaced by another.

'What now?'

Chang Ping drew in breath with a hiss and shook his head. 'This is old stuff. They're reciting the oath of loyalty to Mao

Zedong. "Chairman Mao . . . " then his name ". . . has finally come to your side. I will always be loyal to you. I will always be loyal to your thought. I will always be loyal to your Revolutionary Line.'

'Whose side are they on? They're leftists?'

'They are anti-Chairman . . . or at least Wen is. I guess there are factions here.'

Wen had been studying the villagers. Suddenly he pounced. He ran forward, grabbed someone's ear and dragged him to the front. Diana, standing on tiptoe saw with a pang of unease that it was Lingchu.

Wen shouted at him. The boy kept shaking his head, refusing to look up even when the gunman jerked him by the chin. At last two of the Red Guards came forward and lifted Lingchu onto the upturned bath. Wen handed him his red book. Still the boy shook his head. Wen stepped up beside him, swung back his arm and struck him over his bandaged eye.

Lingchu tumbled off the bath with a squeal. He lay squirming on the ground, both hands over his head. When one of the other guards kicked him, Diana had seen enough. Before Chang Ping could stop her she had pushed through the crowd to the front and was standing with hands on hips, glaring at Wen.

'*Stop that!*'

The silence was immediate.

Wen Zaofan took a while to register that it was a foreigner standing in front of him. Once the truth dawned, his eyes opened wide into a look of haughty astonishment. He shot out an arm and spouted Chinese, while scanning the villagers' faces as if to seek the perpetrator of some crime. Diana guessed he was expressing outrage that they should harbour a foreign she-devil.

'That's *enough!*'

Wen retreated half a step. Diana was so much taller than him. Everyone saw it. The Red Guard knew he must do something but he was perplexed. Diana could sense that he had never had dealings with a westerner before.

She treated him to a look of contempt before kneeling beside

Lingchu and helping him rise. She was about to lead him back to the group of villagers, but Wen grabbed her arm and swung her around to face him.

This time there was more than surprise in his eyes, there was anger and also a perverted lust: the kind that has its wellspring in enjoyment of others' pain. Diana stepped back, only to find herself flattened against the wall of the house that had supplied the bathtub.

She pulled her denim jacket higher on her shoulders; something jingled in one of the pockets. As Wen continued to advance he made his right hand into a fist and kneaded it into his left palm. He smiled at Diana, trying to keep her attention on his face and away from his hands.

Diana felt inside her pockets. Coins.

Wen had begun to swing his fist in and out of the palm.

Diana waited until he was mere inches away. Then she hit him squarely on the bridge of the nose. She used her fist, with two-*fen* pieces threaded between her knuckles, and she swung her arm around at right-angles to her body so as to get every ounce of strength she possessed behind the blow.

The force of the attack, inspired by blind desperation, all but knocked the Red Guard off his feet. He shrieked in pain and sank to his knees, holding both hands to his face. When at last he tore them away, blood spurted from his right brow where one of the coins had slicked through the flesh.

Diana's heart was thumping like a bird's. The coins fell from between her fingers. She flattened her hands against the damp wall. Wen straightened up slowly. Now there was a methodical sense of purpose about his actions. He reached out for Diana – gently, as if anxious not to startle a dog that might bite – and wiped the blood away on a corner of her jacket, continuing to rub until only a pink blotch remained on his skin. He was breathing heavily. Between those thin, reptilian lips she could see his teeth, stained yellow by nicotine: two of them crossed crookedly and one of the top canines was missing. His skin smelled of tobacco smoke and days-old sweat but his breath was surprisingly sweet, as if he had been chewing mint leaves.

Diana felt sure that behind his studied calm Wen was

almost as scared as she was: knew it because part of the acrid smell filling her nostrils was essence of fear, the skunk aroma that the body treacherously puts out through the pores when least wanted.

He spoke to her softly, words Diana did not understand. Wen shrugged and jerked his thumb towards the villagers, telling Diana to join them. She looked at him, sensing a trick, but his face had become a mask of unconcern.

Diana took a step forward, off the wall. Wen made no move. She skirted around to his left, giving him a wide berth, but he remained still, staring at the point on the brickwork where her head had rested a moment before.

Diana took another step. Wen passed out of her peripheral vision. Suddenly she saw Chang Ping's face tense into an expression of horror; the villagers cried out in a mixture of warning and fear and revulsion; the snap of the webbing on Wen's rifle made her break into a run. But the rifle-butt thudded into the back of her skull with the noise of an explosion; her eyeballs ballooned to twice their normal size; gouts of pain pumped through her head, and as the vomit stirred in her stomach the ground came up to meet her.

When she awoke she had no idea of time. One minute there was darkness inside her brain, the next there was darkness outside as well, but the transition eluded her. She felt very ill. The back of her head throbbed in a dull ache, enlivened with spasmodic red-hot pokers of pain.

After a few moments she realized what had woken her: her bladder was going to burst. When she struggled to sit up the top of her head seemed to fall off. She tried again, but nothing worked, not her legs, not her arms. She lay back and, while tears of frustration and shame trickled down her face, she relieved herself where she lay, beating the sheet with clenched fists, until at last she was empty. Drained.

She dozed, woke again, this time to the knowledge that she was in her bed at Kaihui's. The curtains were open and there was enough moonlight to illuminate the familiar surroundings. Someone had entered the room. Diana felt one of her ankles being shaken. 'Who's there?' she moaned.

'*Ssh!* It's me – Chang Ping.'

'Oh, God . . . I thought you were . . . oh *God!*'

'Not so loud.' He quickly came towards her, laying a finger across her lips.

'What happened?' Diana's voice was thick, it did not sound like hers. 'I remember . . . he hit me.'

'You hit him first.' He paused. When he spoke again he sounded admiring. 'The villagers got very frightened when he hit you. But they shouted down the Red Guards. This is a good village. They don't like bullies. The Guards started to argue among themselves again. They're still at it.'

'How did I get here?'

'They made some of the villagers carry you. Then they asked me all kinds of questions about you. They think you are a capitalist roader, come to subvert the region. Once you're better, they're going to try you.'

Diana's head was starting to clear. 'Try me? But . . . I'm not a criminal, I haven't done anything.'

'In their eyes, you have. You are a foreigner, you have been seen at the shrine and therefore you are religious, you have money for travel.'

'But what will they do to me?'

'I don't know.'

'And how did *you* get here?'

'They "arrested" me, for being in your company. Then they told everyone to go home and await orders. They chose Kaihui's house as their headquarters. They're all downstairs now, arguing like a dozen devils. They put me in one of the upstairs rooms, but I got out.'

'How?'

'The lock was nothing.'

'Isn't there a guard?'

'There was. Not now.'

'What –'

'I got rid of him. Don't ask questions, please.'

Diana stared over the side of the bed in the direction his voice was coming from, but his face remained lost in shadow.

'Diana, we have got to get out of this place. Can you stand?'

'I . . . I'll try.' This time when she sat up her head remained in place; after a pause, she was able to swing her legs off the bed. She was sopping wet and there could be no disguising the smell of urine. Chang Ping said nothing; she was grateful for that.

She realized she was still wearing her day clothes. 'I need to change,' she muttered.

'Hurry.'

'How are we going to get out?'

'Window.'

'I ought to see Kaihui, tell her —'

'There's no time!'

He went to the door and opened it a crack. The passage was in darkness. Diana waited until he had closed the door behind him before she took off her jeans and hurriedly struggled into clean ones. The inside of her head was still beating a tattoo. When she touched the wound she yelped with pain and her hand came away sticky, but the bone felt sound.

She stuffed her few things into her rucksack and pulled on the door-handle. Chang Ping was holding it shut. Feeling her tug, he peered through the gap. 'Ready?'

'Yes.'

They listened. Many voices were raised in argument downstairs. 'Poor Kaihui,' Diana murmured.

'Don't worry. All Chinese peasants have played this game before. By tomorrow you won't find a phone, a TV, anything of value in this village. Everyone will be a poor worker again. *Please* be quick! I'll go first; then you can stand on my shoulders.'

Seconds later he had climbed out of the window. Diana awkwardly slung her legs over the sill, feeling for his shoulders with her feet. As she jumped he caught her around the chest, then took her hand and quietly led her through the dark lanes until they were on the threshold of the paddies. There they stopped and looked back. Chaiyang was in total darkness. Only the sound of penned water-buffalos and restless hogs disturbed the spring night.

'Come *on!*'

In the dark, with only a veiled moon for guide, they had to pick their way from dike to dike, every second dreading to hear the splash born of a wrong step or the sound of pursuit behind them. Not a breath of air stirred the aroma of stagnant water and human excrement, China's age-old natural fertilizer. Diana could not disguise her relief when the ground firmed beneath her feet at the start of the rise towards the valley's end.

It was cooler once they had left the plain and every so often they came upon the welcome scent of jasmine, or some other night-blooming flower. When at last they reached a clearing Chang Ping called a halt. While Diana slipped to her knees he stood on the lip of the depression he had found and looked back the way they'd come. It was like staring into a vast black crater.

'Chang Ping?'

'Yes?'

'Something's been bothering me. Where did Wen get that gun?'

'The army.'

'But . . . why should the army give weapons to students?'

'Because once the students have got out of hand, the army can put them down and seize power. Don't you understand how these things work?'

'So what are we going to do?'

'Chaiyang's close to the provincial border with Guizhou. There's no guarantee things'll be better than in Sichuan, but we'd have a chance.'

'Which direction do we go?'

'South. Look! That's light I can see over there. Dawn. So south is . . . that way.'

Diana stood up and hitched her rucksack over her shoulders. Her horizon divided: below eye-level, in the distance, all remained dark; but above that she could see a thin yellow streak flecked with orange and red where the sun would appear. Chang Ping started up the path. He had gone only a few yards when he realized he was alone and turned to find that Diana was still where he had left her, gazing down into the valley.

'What's the matter?'

'My mother,' she said as she slowly caught up with him. 'I never did leave her ashes at the shrine.'

'Kaihui will attend to it.'

'Yes.'

'I want us to be out of sight before sunrise. Please!'

Diana took one last look at Chaiyang. She raised her hand, waved, then deliberately set her back to the place from which half her bloodline had run across the centuries, through Jinny, into her.

The tepid dawn air thickened into heat haze shortly after sunrise. There was a path of sorts, although sometimes it disappeared into the undergrowth for yards at a time. Exercise did something to ease the pain in Diana's head, but the sight of snakes sunning themselves on rocks along the path scared her. Once a green one slithered in front of her and she jumped back with a cry. After that Chang Ping cut her a stick of bamboo, using his red-handled Feng Yuon pocket-tool, China's answer to the Swiss army knife, and made her beat the path with it as she walked.

It soon became baking hot beneath the low roof of foliage. Sweat poured down Diana's forehead into her eyes; it soaked her shirt and chafed her socks against the skin. Chang Ping plunged on ahead, until she could scarcely see him through tangles of rhododendron, bamboo, wild mango-trees.

At last they came out onto the top of a ridge. The air was still humid but at least there was a breeze. Another valley, not unlike the one that harboured Chaiyang, opened up in front of them to the south, but by now the sun was fully risen and Diana could see clumps of azaleas sequinning the hillside.

'Can you see the stream down there?' he asked.

'Yes. Oh, for a wash and a drink!'

'Then I will go on to that town.'

He pointed. Diana caught sight of a cluster of red roofs. Smoke was rising from several of them, but it was not like the previous afternoon's smoke, harbinger of civil unrest: this ascended sweetly into the new morning light, telling of breakfast, scalding hot tea, rice-gruel . . .

'Why can't we both go?'

'Because it may not be safe.'

'So what are we going to do: wait here for ever?'

'No. We'll lie low for a while. When I'm in the town I'll try to find out where's safe. Then we will go there. But I don't want to risk you being seen.'

They climbed down to the stream. 'You'll be all right here alone?' Chang Ping asked anxiously.

Suddenly Diana panicked. She began to shiver. 'I . . .'

He put an arm around her shoulders and held her close to him. The tang of his sweat was strong. It pulled her round.

'I *will* come back.' His eyes radiated conviction. 'I know that you would come back for me.'

'Yes.' She looked up at that, stared into his deep eyes. 'I would.'

'Trust me.'

Chang Ping waited only long enough to scoop several handfuls of water into his mouth before setting off downhill again. The path was more distinct on this side of the ridge and he made good progress. He looked back several times to wave, but before many minutes had passed he was lost from Diana's view.

It did not take him long to reach the town's outskirts and locate the largest shop in its main street. He went quickly to the back and sought out the manager. 'Where is my old uncle?' he demanded.

If the elderly Chinese behind the counter was surprised to hear the *Ko Lao Hui* triad password, he gave no sign of it. He nodded his head towards a door shielded by a threadbare curtain and went on totting up figures on an abacus.

As Chang Ping pushed through the curtain he saw at once that the officer Sun Shanwang had sent to him was his own age or younger, and a flash of jealousy stabbed his heart.

FIFTEEN

◇

Qiu Qianwei squinted at the restaurant's ceiling while he thought it over. Lo Bing . . .

'He was a general?'

'He *is* a general.'

'Commander of a military district – I forget which one.'

'It's not important. But you have the right man.'

'Mm. Our roads did not meet.'

'So the records say. It's useful to have your personal confirmation.'

An anonymous cadre had come from the mainland. He did all the talking, while North Wind, Qiu's usual contact, kept watch through the latticed screen that separated their private alcove from the main restaurant. The newcomer was younger than Qiu, very tall and thin; he wore a white sleeveless cotton shirt outside his creaseproof slacks and looked no different from hundreds of other workers enjoying their Saturday evening off, in this noisy eleventh-floor restaurant near Kowloon's Ashley Road.

Now he leaned forward to rest a forearm on the table while he sipped tea. He continued to smile over the cup, treating Qiu with just enough deference to make him suspicious.

'The Controller has certain proposals in mind for General Lo Bing,' he remarked. Qiu blinked; he wasn't accustomed to receiving gratuitous explanations from the mainland. 'Aspects of his history are, however, obscure. All brigade cadres and ex-cadres are being consulted. You will please think about this.'

'Yes.'

'The Controller did ask me to raise one other matter. It concerns Diana Young.' The mainlander finished his tea and poured more, remembering to top up Qiu's cup before his own. 'Your offer of help was noted.' The other man drank. 'With gratitude.' Another sip, a warm smile. 'And, with regret, refused.'

'I see.'

'But information — that's another thing. The Controller's becoming increasingly anxious to know what the big companies here plan to do when the Chairman dies. It's clear from what you overheard on the night of Mrs Young's funeral that Diana Young may know something about this Benevolence plan of theirs?'

'Yes. That was my impression.'

'In the light of your "impression", as you call it, Controller Sun has devised a plan for dealing with her. I'll outline it; you, in turn, will kindly comment.'

North Wind's concentration on the scene beyond the lattice had not wavered. Now he stood up. A table directly in his line of vision had been occupied for rather too long. Three men sat there, not talking. Their bill had been paid but still they sat there.

As North Wind emerged from the alcove one of the three men rose, spoke a few words to the others and went out. North Wind continued on his way, as if in search of the toilet, but now he was unsure what to do. He hesitated by the door, next to the fish-tanks, until the departing diner had summoned a lift and been whisked down to the ground floor; but by then the hostesses were staring at him coldly, for he stood in the way of arriving guests and was about as welcome as a pike in a stew-pond.

He quickly returned to the alcove to find Qiu on the point of rising. 'You were followed.'

'No, I checked.'

'I don't care, you were followed. Three of them, sitting in the main room — don't look round, you fool! One of them's gone.' North Wind could scarcely contain his impatience. 'Comrade, had you finished?'

163

'Yes.'

'Then we get out fast.'

The three of them hurried towards the door. As North Wind drew level with the table that had attracted his attention earlier he tripped, fell and reached out to save himself. The cloth went flying. Tea spilled everywhere. By the time the two remaining diners were on their feet, however, Qiu and the cadre from the mainland had disappeared.

The cadre ran down two flights of stairs and rested ten minutes on one landing before summoning an elevator. By that time, he reckoned, the opposition should have cleaned themselves up and headed for the nearest exit. He descended to street level, walked one block south, hailed a cab and asked to be taken to the Hilton. But no sooner had the cab crossed the harbour via the old tunnel than he paid off the driver and ducked into Marsh Road. He boarded a tram, rode a couple of stops and before long was lost in the maze of seedy alleys around the Wanchai district. It was a slick disappearing act, but this man's youthful looks belied his experience. Unfortunately, however, on this occasion the slickness was wasted, because no one was interested in him at all.

Qiu was a different matter.

On leaving the restaurant, Qiu had straightaway taken the lift to the second floor. There he had followed a passage to the back of the building and used the service staircase to gain access to the street. It was a narrow thoroughfare, barely more than a footpath between two high-rises, with much of the space occupied by refuse-bins and crates of empty bottles. Qiu turned right, away from Ashley Road, and began to run in the direction of the bus-terminal. He crossed Kowloon Park Drive without mishap, elbowing his way through the late night crowds with the assurance of someone who knew Kowloon well. But as he reached the terminal his luck ran out.

He paused to allow a double-decker to reverse from its dock. When a car slowly drew up on the forecourt behind him he did not hear it; was aware of nothing, in fact, until a strong hand took his arm and enfolded him into the car with one uniformly smooth movement, so that the next thing he knew he was sitting between two men on the back seat and a gun was pressing into his abdomen.

The man in the front passenger seat turned his head until his profile showed up clearly against the stream of oncoming headlights. Something about the set of his jaw struck Qiu as familiar. 'Traffic's heavy,' he said quietly in Mandarin. 'We're going to have to take this nice and slow. A stupid man might risk jumping out.' He turned his head a fraction more. 'Just how stupid are you, Qiu?'

It was as the speaker had predicted: the car travelled slowly. But at last they were heading north-west out of town, on the road to Tsuen-Wan, with only a few other cars to impede their progress.

Qiu's mind was busy. He'd known from the start that his hosts weren't Royal Hong Kong Police or any other kind of authority; such powers took their suspects openly, with a reading of rights and all the other outmoded ceremonials British justice seemed to require. Then he'd heard the voice coming from the half-seen profile of the man next to the driver and at once a name had slotted into place.

Leong something-or-other. Alexander Cumnor's Leong.

The car turned right and began to wend its way into the foothills, evidently following the road-signs to Shung Min reservoir. Qiu tried not to think what convenient execution-grounds reservoirs had always made and savagely concentrated on Cumnor.

Qiu had spent the first part of his career in the Chinese Central Control of Intelligence's elite Mahjong Brigade before 'defecting' to work for Simon Young. Both jobs in different ways gave him unparalleled access to information about overseas Chinese businessmen: the *huaqiao* so beloved of Beijing's New Dealers, the-ones-who-will-enrich-the-motherland. How was it, then that Cumnor had always managed to remain a mystery?

As the driver changed gear and the engine began to labour against the incline, Qiu strove to recall what little he knew. Age: forty-nine or thereabouts. Three quarters Chinese, one-quarter third generation Australian: on the father's side, which explained the western name. Nothing known about his early years, except for that extraordinary, unproven rumour which refused to die: Cumnor had entered a Jesuit seminary to train as a priest.

Then came the start of the public record. When he was in his mid-twenties he had become a reporter on a Melbourne tabloid, manoeuvred his way into the financial editor's office and in no time was chalking up profits on tips acquired through honest and not so honest sources. Before long he'd made his first big investment, a local radio-station that was going bust.

Fourteen years later he'd sold out to one of Murdoch's consortia, handing over five newspapers, two of them nationals; sixteen radio stations; a half share in a production company; and three business magazines.

Then he disappeared.

Qiu stared ahead. Innumerable moths hung suspended in the night, splattering to oblivion against the glass. Once a larger creature, a bat maybe, thudded against the windscreen, spun around like a child's windmill and dropped off the bonnet. Darkness. Only darkness.

There were trace-records on the file, unverified sightings, almost everywhere. Vietnam, Burma, Cambodia, Laos, Beijing. Never in the west. And never a hard, corroborated, up-to-the-hilt identification. Where had he been during those five lost years? It was a good topic of conversation during the lengthy tea-breaks favoured by intelligence cadres labouring in Bow String Alley. Had he been in Moscow all along, as some suspected? Or was the official line correct: Cumnor had been erecting a screen of cross-held nominee companies with ulti-mate owners who lived in Panama, or Grand Cayman, or nowhere – a suitably discreet, stable platform from which to boost the next phase of his career into orbit?

Suddenly he was back. He came to Hong Kong, bought a comfortable house near Cape D'Aguilar and looked around for something else, something bigger to buy. Within a week he had lighted on New Kowloon Properties, heading for trouble and without a white knight in sight. Until, that is, Alexander Cumnor rode to the rescue.

He hived off the non-property assets into companies under his control, all of which instantly — some said miraculously — became profitable. The property portfolio, by that time the largest single collection ever assembled under one umbrella in the Far East, ended up being vested in a holding company whose owner eventually turned out, to nobody's surprise, to be resident in Beijing.

The car began to climb a stony, rutted track and a few minutes later came out onto a depression cut in the side of the hill. Piles of sand and stones showed up in the headlight beams. The car slowly described a circle until it was pointing back the way it had come. Qiu saw a high corrugated iron shed, a cement-mixer, the beginnings of a conveyor-belt carrying buckets, two or three prefabricated huts. Then the lights died.

'Get out.'

He obeyed. Leong frisked him expertly, not content with feeling the outside of his clothes but inserting his hands between garments and skin.

'Fold your arms and keep them that way. Walk to the farthest hut.'

Shortly after the New Kowloon Properties carve-up, a certain Robert Zhao had disappeared — executed by a Mahjong unit under Qiu's command — and the colony's *cognoscenti* had sat back in the comfortable expectation that Beijing, now in need of a new commercial front-man, would give Alexander Cumnor the job.

'Wait.'

The two men who had sandwiched Qiu in the back of the car remained one on either side of him. Leong went ahead to the hut and rapped on the door. It opened immediately, carving a wedge of yellow light in the clearing.

But Cumnor had surprised everyone. As soon as it became known that Zhao wasn't coming back he had gone public with a marked antipathy to the Reds: neither a popular nor an easy move in the closing years of a decade that had seen Britain cede Hong Kong to China. By now he was indisputably the man to meet if you wanted to talk big deals with a Chinese flavour but strictly no communist involvement.

'Go in.'

As Qiu crossed the threshold he remembered one more thing about Cumnor: you had to keep your word to him, because he was in a position to mobilize Triad muscle. Which seemed surprising, when you tried to marry it up with the softly-spoken, genteel man who now rose to welcome Qiu as if he were an honoured guest.

'I am so sorry about all the nonsense,' he murmured. His English was accented but grammatically perfect. 'We weren't sure of your situation this evening. There seemed to be several factions competing for your attention.'

'Several factions' seemed an odd way of describing the newcomer from the mainland and North Wind. Qiu inclined his head but said nothing.

'Do sit down.'

Cumnor nodded at Leong, who now entered the hut and arranged a chair for Qiu before withdrawing, closing the door behind him. Qiu sat; then he cast a brief look around. A small wooden hut, on one wall a ground-plan; several yellow hard hats; electric fan; table; ashtrays everywhere. A typical site-hut, were it not for the single Mahjong tile lying face up on the trestle table.

Red Dragon.

Cumnor saw how his eyes were drawn to it and smiled. There was a touch of sadness in that smile. 'A long time ago,' he said.

Qiu pursed his lips and shook his head.

'But then,' Cumnor said, pocketing the tile, 'times have changed for us all.'

Behind his calm, resigned mask Qiu was aghast. No one, *no one* knew that he used to hold the rank of Red Dragon in the Mahjong Brigade.

'It is important for us to have a discussion. If we're seen together in Hong Kong, our meeting's bound to get back to the wrong people. So again, I'm sorry for all this' – he waved his hand – 'but it was necessary.'

Qiu fidgeted and cleared his throat. 'Assault and false imprisonment are never considered necessary by an English court.'

168

'You're right.' In his eagerness to agree Cumnor leaned forward, a bespectacled schoolmaster making his point. 'And if I cannot convince you that this meeting was truly necessary . . . then of course it is to court that you must go. Only it will not be necessary, for I'll compensate you out of court.'

Qiu considered him without appearing to. His eyes never deviated from the black rectangle behind Cumnor's head where the window was, but all his attention stayed fastened on his host. The patternless suit, the pink tie, who truly needed three watches? That fussy shake of the head . . . was he effeminate? They said he had kept one throwback to his Jesuit years, just one: he was strictly celibate.

After a while Cumnor deduced that Qiu did not intend to speak again. 'It's late, I won't keep you,' he said. 'I want to talk about Simon. In particular, I want to talk about him and his daughter, Diana. Ah! That moves you, I see.'

Qiu cursed the involuntary shiver of his shoulders and resolved to keep closer watch on himself.

'It moves me, too. Simon is a friend of mine, but he's not himself, I think you'd agree? In a moment of extreme folly – excuse my rudeness – he allowed his daughter to go back into China at a time when, to put it mildly, that country is hardly its usual serene self.'

'Yes.' The word was wrung out of Qiu, for all his caution.

'He needs to get her back. My information is that she may be . . . delayed.'

Qiu's expression remained impassive. 'Delayed?'

'The two men you dined with tonight were from the mainland. They have means of finding out about Diana Young and her whereabouts. You know this, and it distresses you as much as it distresses me. True?'

Qiu said nothing.

'Well, let me go on for the moment. It so happens that I have commercial contacts, on the mainland. These people are important. They're in a position to get something done if they've a mind to. I'm suggesting an alliance.'

'Alliance?'

'Between you and me, your knowledge and my knowledge

169

to be pooled, used for Diana's benefit. And her father's too, of course.'

'Why should I believe that?'

'Because his interests and mine overlap. For the sake of benevolence, if you like.'

It was brilliantly done. The last remark, casually tacked onto the end of another sentence that by itself was unexceptionable, could be taken in one of two ways. A kindness, perhaps that's what Cumnor meant, a favour to a friend. Or . . .

'Benevolence can be costly,' Qiu said slowly. 'How far are you prepared to see your resources stretched?'

'Resources can be made available.' Cumnor's voice was hushed, scarcely even a whisper. The two men looked at each other for a long time, after that. Neither wanted to be the first to break the code.

'You see, Mr Qiu, my contacts on the mainland are rather more extensive than rumour suggests.'

Qiu said nothing.

'I can understand why you don't believe me. Perhaps these will help persuade you.' Cumnor produced a couple of envelopes which he handed to Qiu. 'From your son.'

Qiu stared at him, wanting to believe, unable to make the necessary psychological adjustment. Suddenly he snatched them and ripped open the envelopes. The calligraphy was familiar, too familiar. *My father. How are you? I am well. I expect you are busy . . .*

'Where did you get these?'

'Certain friends of friends owe favours for favours. Can we please leave it vague?'

'What do you want from me?'

'Want?'

'There's a price, isn't there? Letters like this cost . . . what?'

'They are a gift. To cement a new friendship. Ours.' Cumnor paused. 'Of course, if you could see your way to sharing some information with your new friend . . .'

'Such as what?'

'I need to know Simon's thinking.'

170

'You want me to spy on him, in other words?'

Cumnor waved a deprecating hand. 'I just need to be kept abreast of his thoughts, that's all.'

Qiu stared at him. Who are you working for? asked a small voice inside his skull. Simon? Sun? Cumnor . . . does one more employer make that much difference?

'Mr Qiu, a clever girl like Diana must have picked up a great many things about her father's business, over the years.'

He made an effort to concentrate. 'You think so? As far as I could see, she had no interest in money.'

'I do not necessarily equate interest with the bare making of money. But I'm intrigued by your assessment, very. Tell me: which do you think would prove more costly in the long run – exerting all the influence at our command to extract Diana from China, or leaving her there to the mercies of your dinner companions?'

'I'll have to think about that.'

'And central to that question is another: what does Simon plan to do about his predicament? Men under pressure sometimes do strange things. How much time do you need to think it through?'

'Cost-comparisons such as the one you mentioned require much thought. A day?'

'No more.'

'A day.'

'Then we will, with your permission, meet again this time tomorrow?'

'Where?'

'Mr Leong will set up the arrangements and notify you.'

'All right.'

'And . . .' Cumnor's delicate smile almost became a chuckle. 'The court case? For assault?'

'Can be deferred for the moment. Diana's more important.'

Three words. Three quite unnecessary words. Qiu wished the King of Hell had cut out his tongue the instant before it could shape the first of the seven deadly syllables. Cumnor stiffened, just for a second, but it was enough to tell Qiu that his slip had been noticed, its nuances analysed.

'We were friends. Are friends. She's the best of the Young family.'

'I see.' Cumnor stood up. 'We'll all go home now and sleep on this. My party will use the car you came in. There's another vehicle parked near here; it has no history and is at your disposal until tomorrow, when it will be collected from the Ducannon Young garage. The keys are in the ignition. Does this meet with your approval?'

Qiu nodded.

The car, a brand-new middle of the range Ford, was stationed behind another of the site huts. Qiu sat in the front seat smoking while Cumnor and his men made ready to leave. As soon as they had gone he extinguished his cigarette and stepped quickly out of the car. He crawled around it twice, probing the underside with his hands. Then he opened the hood, but it was pitch dark and apart from the feeble flame of his lighter he had to depend on touch. Nothing.

He bit his lip. It was a long walk back to Hong Kong and he couldn't rely on hitching a lift. Some of the villages in the New Territories were still primitive; a lone night-time trekker could not be sure of reaching his destination safely. But the thought of getting into that Ford and turning the ignition key unnerved him.

Qiu was still hesitating when he heard a sound behind him and wheeled around sharply. The noise might have been a human moan or machinery creaking, he couldn't be sure.

There was no wind; the night breathed stillness. But Qiu was not alone in this godforsaken spot.

The sound came again. This time there could be no doubt: a voice. He stared into the darkness. The big corrugated iron shed.

He could smell danger: a mixture of electricity and his own sweat. Every inch of his skin prickled, his brain transmitted only one message – get out, fast.

Suppose this was a set-up? What if Cumnor had arranged for Qiu to be found at the scene of a murder, the only suspect. Why? *Why?*

Cumnor had been clever. Two temptations, two repulsions.

A car that might spirit him away, as long as it wasn't booby-trapped. And a moan equally dangerous to ignore or heed. Two negative poles and two positive.

Earlier, Cumnor had implied that Qiu was being watched, followed: 'Factions competing for your attention.' Factions, plural . . .

Qiu fingered the letters from his son, seeking comfort from that tenuous thread of contact with his past. *What did Cumnor expect him to do?*

Qiu swiftly, silently, made his way to the iron shed. It was more of a barn than a shed, he discovered; one of the two narrower sides had been left open to the elements. As he reached the threshold the sound came a third time.

He advanced in total silence, counting his steps. When he reached twelve, a torch shone into his eyes, arms pinioned his own, he felt the handcuffs click onto his wrists, all was confusion and loud noise; then Assistant Commissioner Peter Reade of the Royal Hong Kong Police stepped through the crossbeams.

'I've been wanting to do this for a long time,' he said. 'You're going to tell me everything, Qiu. About your mainland contacts. What's happening to Diana Young. Whereabouts on the mainland she is, right now. Who's with her. Why. And if you don't . . .'

Someone standing behind Qiu hooked his legs out from under him. Apart from the feeble light thrown by the torches it was dark in the shed, but the unseen assailant had no difficulty in finding Qiu's crotch with the toe of his boot.

SIXTEEN

◇

'How much longer are we going to stay here?' Diana asked, as Chang Ping abandoned his roadside vigil and came to sit beside her. But he merely shook his head and fanned himself with his pointed straw hat. He was tired.

That morning, he had come back to Diana after a couple of hours, laden with booty: enough food to last them a day; some stout shoes; two hats, necessary protection against the sun's rays; bottled water; and, treasure of treasures, a map.

With its help, they found a road along which they walked for three hours without seeing a single vehicle, until at last they stopped to eat. Then Chang Ping stood for a long time, staring back the way they'd come.

'I don't understand,' Diana said wearily, after he had again made himself comfortable beside her. 'Why don't we just go back to that town and wait for the bus?'

'You don't have a travel permit for this region.'

'So what? We just explain about the Red Guards and –'

'There were Red Guards in the town. I had to dodge from house to house.' He smiled tightly. 'I have told you this already.'

'I know. Sorry. But we're just roaming around in the wilderness, aren't we? You say to head south, but there's nothing except miles of mountain passes and an empty road.'

'Yes, but we have this problem: I am Chinese; you aren't. You do not have a particularly oriental look, even though you are one-half Chinese. You're a foreigner, no mistake. And foreigners aren't welcome here. So we must keep to the small roads. Sooner or later, a car, a lorry, must pass by. This road leads to the highway between Ganshui and Zunyi. Once we get to Zunyi it's not far to Guiyang. Then there are trains, buses. You'll be able to get back to Hong Kong.'

Diana was dazzled by this, the longest consecutive statement she had ever heard him make. She longed to believe it!

The afternoon dragged on until at last the light began to fade. Diana knew that the short, grey dusk would soon end and they would be faced with their first night in the open.

She discovered a miserable trickle of water oozing down the face of a rock. As she did her best to wash she found herself yearning for that bottle of Eau de Patou left behind in Hong Kong. The thought put her in mind of Mat and home. Better not think like that . . .

She returned to find Chang Ping unwrapping some more of the food. She was only thirsty and did not want to eat. He squatted next to her. 'Maybe we should rest here overnight . . .'

'Is it safe?'

'As long as we remain calm, we shall be all right.'

'Do you really believe that?'

'Yes, I do. Look at me.'

His eyes glowed; in the dusk they were more than ever beautiful. Chang Ping was no longer exhausted; he looked so resilient, so full of strength, that it seemed natural for Diana to reach out for his hand. But then she frantically woke up to the fact that she was sending the wrong signals and quickly released him. 'Sorry.'

'Why?' His smile deepened.

'I thought it wasn't very clever to touch you, that's all.'

'Chinese people don't spend much time thinking about things like that.' His voice contained a hint of reproof. 'The average Chinese man would not assume anything bad just because a woman touched him in friendship.'

'Sorry.'

'In the West, is it the same?'

'Oh, yes. Men and women can touch each other without . . .'

When she tailed off, his gentle smile seemed to say, 'Yes,

175

you've been a bit tactless, but you're forgiven and indeed it makes me like you more.' After that they sat together for a long time, not talking, while the last of the light faded away. Diana found herself comparing his silence with Park Son-do's garrulousness. Korea, Sonny . . . all that seemed so long ago now.

At last Chang Ping said goodnight and crossed the road in search of a place to sleep. It had become a degree or so cooler; the faint odour of damp stone penetrated Diana's nostrils. She had nothing soft to sleep on. After a while she gave up trying to find a comfortable position and was content to lie on her back, staring wide-eyed at the starry sky.

She was miles from anywhere, in a remote part of China, alone, apart from Chang Ping; but the enormity of her situation did not alarm her. Indeed, she found it adventurous, almost thrilling. There might be danger, yes, but it wasn't quite real.

The peace, though, that was real . . . She imagined herself flying in a jet, thousands of feet above Sichuan, looking down on the vast, uncluttered landscape beneath. Was there a wakeful passenger up there, doing just that, she wondered? Such solitude, for the most part unobtainable in the hurly-burly world, brought its own kind of joy.

Suddenly she knew with certainty that her mother was close by and she raised her head, half-expecting to see Jinny. But there was only darkness. Diana closed her eyes, revelling in unsought happiness. Her mother was here, to left and right, before her and behind her . . . it will be all right, a voice seemed to say. No matter how bad things may look, you will be safe.

'Mother,' she murmured. 'Oh, mother, I'm so glad . . .'

Her last thought before she slept was that she had not felt so free, so peaceful, for years.

She awoke to hear Chang Ping say, 'There won't be any sun today.'

He was right; dawn came, but the sun remained hidden. Instead, a thick pall of cloud hovered mere hundreds of feet above their heads. It was as if the rain intended to ambush them, waiting for the moment when they were most exposed before unleashing itself.

The landscape was dreary, unchanging. Every twist in the road between high granite walls revealed not the hoped-for plain, but another escarpment rising to a nearby range, its peaks lost in cloud. The heavy atmosphere bathed Diana in a mixture of perspiration and its own moisture that sullied her beyond any possibility of scrubbing herself clean. The stream in which she'd washed twenty-four hours ago had no more reality than a faded photo in grandmother's scrapbook.

They stopped for a rest. Chang Ping squatted by the roadside and smoked incessantly. The buoyant optimism of the night before had deserted Diana by this time. She was terrified at the prospect of being left in this desert place, alone. For now she was becoming obsessed with the idea that all along Chang Ping might have planned to lure her away from Chaiyang and then maroon her. She could think of no reason why he should want to do such a thing; but that brought no comfort.

Diana was about to ask him what he was thinking when she heard an engine.

The acoustics were maddening: every time they thought the machine that made the noise must come into view, the sound died away again, blocked by some bend in the road. But at last it rose to a crescendo, at the same time ceasing to echo, and they saw a small lorry.

It squeaked and grunted its way to a stop; the brakes still functioned but evidently they required lengthy notice. A head leaned from the cab to shout at Chang Ping, who was standing in the middle of the road waving his arms. Then the head twisted a fraction and its owner caught sight of Diana.

She might have found it comic if only she hadn't been so tired. The driver was a small old man whose eyes barely reached above the dashboard. Now those eyes had widened so much that even from a distance Diana could see white all around the pupils.

He had to force open the door; it yielded with a sullen clunk. When he swung his legs out they stopped a long way off the ground, so that he had to jump down to the road. He was wearing typical peasant uniform: baggy blue shorts from which two hairless beanpoles descended to straw sandals, and a blue jacket several sizes too generous around the chest. When he trotted up to Diana she saw two smudges at the corners of his eyes, smudges the colour of the snot dripping from his left nostril.

He walked right the way around her, evidently not believing what he saw. He smelled of body-dirt and the vinegary, shitty, stale-tobacco aroma Diana likened to used underwear that had spent too long in a warm place waiting to be washed. When he opened his mouth to speak she saw that he had no teeth at all.

He advanced on her, holding his head critically to one side, withdrew, advanced again. This time he ran a hand down one of Diana's arms before making a circle with forefinger and thumb and then staring at her through it. He half turned towards Chang Ping and said something that sounded like, 'Jern ker par.'

Chang Ping spoke ingratiatingly, but the old boy waved him down while continuing to stare at Diana. 'Jern ker par,' he said, over and over again. It was obvious to Diana that if she had been a horse he would not have bought her, not even to boil her down for glue.

'What does "jern ker par" mean?' she snapped at Chang Ping.

'Um . . . I don't understand his accent.'

'Come off it, what does it mean?'

'It means "How frightening".'

'Frightening?'

'Yes.'

'Me?'

'You.'

There was a long silence. 'Why?'

'He's never seen a western woman before.'

Diana stared at the ugly, semi-senile face hovering a good few inches below hers. 'Will he help us?'

'I haven't asked him.'

'Well *ask!*'

He raised his eyebrows in what might have been amusement.

'Now listen,' she said. 'I've hardly slept. I've got blisters halfway up my thighs. I can't walk another step and I'm exhausted. You fix it so that this man takes us somewhere, anywhere civilized, yes?'

'I will try.'

'Good. Do that. But just remember – if he so much as lays a finger on my body again, I'm going to kill him.'

She could see from the look on Chang Ping's face that he believed her. She almost believed it herself.

Chang Ping began to speak. From where Diana was standing she could not see the lorry-driver's expression, but the way he nodded his head suggested that he was minded to help. The negotiations took time. More than twenty minutes passed before Chang Ping came across to Diana and said, 'How much money do you have?'

'About twelve hundred Yuan.'

'Don't let him see it. I've got him down to a hundred for a ride into Guiyang.'

'Great!'

'Ssh, don't get excited. He thinks we haven't much money. I've told him I'm a language student and you're my teacher from Chengdu University, we went to visit my parents and ran into Red Guards. He doesn't believe me. That's why he wants a hundred. It's going to get worse the farther we go. This man's a peasant. When we start dealing with district Party committees, the price will go up.'

Keeping his body between Diana and the driver, he took some notes from her purse. A few moments later the deal was done and Diana was climbing into the cab.

Chang Ping sat between her and the old man. The lorry trundled off down the gradient, slowly gathering speed. Eventually Diana dozed off. But the suspension was terrible and after a while the incessant jolting woke her up. She found her head resting on Chang Ping's chest with his arm around her shoulders. For a long time she continued to lie like that, ignoring the battering motion of the truck, because it felt cosy

179

and somehow comforting. His clothes smelled of sweat but it was a manly odour far removed from the nastiness emitted through the driver's pores.

'Ten o'clock,' she heard him whisper drowsily. 'Good progress . . .'

The landscape had changed. Mountains were still part of the scenery but now they kept their distance, a low range to the left and a higher one much further away on the other side of the flat road, which now ran due south. The peaks were overlaid with a skein of soft mauve cloud, but above the plain there floated a disc of bright blue sky. After days of pressure-cooker heat Diana found refreshment even in the mild feeling of sunburn where her forearm rested on the sill.

They drove through the town of Zunyi, a dirty, featureless place, without incident; of Red Guards there was no sign. The driver stopped to allow Chang Ping to buy food, and shortly after that they found a shady spot by the side of the road where they could eat their picnic lunch.

Afterwards Diana left the two men dozing and got up to explore. On the right of the road, a sandy expanse led gently down to the side of a river, which here had narrowed and at the same time picked up flow. Some rocks projected into the stream from the bank, as if someone had started to build a ford before thinking better of it; these had created a rough and ready weir.

She sat on the biggest rock with her feet dangling in the water. They were still red in places but the worst blister had wept and begun to heal of its own accord; now that she was riding she no longer needed to wear shoes and the cooler air of the plains was obviously doing the raw places good. The water, neither warm nor cold to the touch, felt wonderful. She was just debating whether she dare slip off her clothes and go for a swim when a voice behind her said, 'We must go now.'

'In a minute.'

'We have no time.'

Diana twisted around so that she could look at him while

180

leaving her feet in the soothing water. 'What does a quarter of an hour here or there matter?'

As usual he was staring at her face as if he wanted to memorize each feature.

'Why do you always make the decisions, Chang Ping?' Her voice was polite but firm.

'Do I?'

'You know you do.'

'Do you mind?'

She hesitated. 'I'm not sure. Sometimes I'm glad you're taking charge: you know the language, the country. But sometimes . . .'

'What?'

'Sometimes I'm not sure if we ought to have left Chaiyang. Maybe we'd have been safer there. In the long run. Even with the Red Guards.'

'You can't be serious.'

'We ran away so quickly. It was a bit impulsive. Wasn't it? Don't you think so?'

He was quiet for a while. Then he said, 'I suppose there's no reason why you should trust me.'

She looked at the ground between them and said nothing.

'You realize I have the same problem?'

She flushed. 'I don't know what you mean.'

'I'd done nothing wrong, but they sent me down to the countryside anyway. There I meet this foreign girl who tells me she's brought her mother's ashes to their last resting place.'

'It's true,' she flared.

'Diana.' His voice was very low. 'Please listen to what I am actually saying. You have to admit that your story is an unusual one.' He hesitated. 'I've even wondered if you were . . . planted on me.'

'Planted!'

He smiled, but did not look away. 'To throw me off balance and make me confess to something. I've heard of them using beautiful girls like that before.'

Diana kept silent. He was right, in a way, to think she didn't

181

trust him; but he did not understand the reason. He did not realize that he had become a little too good to be true.

At last she spoke; but because she was facing the river he could not catch the words. 'What?'

'I said: at least you think I'm beautiful. You said you'd heard of them using beautiful girls to trick people.' Diana laughed. Suddenly she would have given all she possessed, and mortgaged all she'd ever hoped to have, for a sight of his face.

'You shouldn't laugh,' he said. 'Chinese women don't attract me. They do not have hair like . . . your hair is red, in some lights. Your skin is fair. You have . . . you have freckles. Your eyes are alive. When you smile, they flame.'

He stopped, confused. But when Diana started to say something he rushed on, 'You are tall. You walk with confidence. You have so little fear. When I watch you stride, I think . . .' He shook his head. 'I'm sorry.'

'What for?'

'I've never talked to a woman like this before.'

Diana knew she had to put an end to this, however much his words moved her. *Because* they moved her. She jumped off the rock, the water coming halfway up her legs. Her right foot made contact with some object floating in the current: a soft, soggy ball that felt like rotten fruit. She looked down. She screamed. But it was a silent scream. Her hands blocked her mouth, ruling off the sound.

The decomposed body of a tiny baby had come to lodge against her foot. Chang Ping caught her as she toppled forward, robbed by shock of all muscular control, and awkwardly carried her to the shore.

He looked around for some shade but there was none, so he laid her on the sand and knelt between her and the sun's rays. Diana stared up at him, through him, lips drawn back to reveal her teeth clenched together. Suddenly she leapt up, pushing him aside, and began to run bent over almost double, clutching her stomach. She realized she was heading back to the polluted river and veered to one side. Vomit fountained up from her stomach and she fell to the ground again.

Chang Ping sat her up. 'Breathe!' he commanded.

When she started to cry he sensed the worst was over. After a few minutes her tears dried up and she allowed him to wipe her face. 'It was a girl,' she croaked.

Chang Ping nodded.

'"Bathing the infant." That's what they call it.'

'Yes.'

'Because the state says you can only have one child, and because boys are good and girls are bad. So if you're unlucky enough to have a baby girl, you drown it. Like a kitten.'

He knew she wasn't talking to him at all, but to someone he couldn't see, so he made no response.

But now Diana had begun to view the dead baby in a new light. She had wanted the means to break free of Chang Ping's spell-binding words, and some malevolent local god had heard her.

'Chang Ping. Listen to me. I was going to have a baby, once. But I had an abortion instead. I don't know if it would have been a boy or a girl. All I know is that it's dead.'

Diana stood up with difficulty and wandered off towards the lorry. She heard him running and half turned, but before she could complete the movement his arms met around her waist, his chin was resting on her shoulder, and then he was rocking her to and fro. Diana was too muddled to know exactly what she felt. All she knew was that she did not resent him.

At last he freed her, and, without looking at each other, they returned to the truck. The old man had woken up. He yawned, scratched first his crotch then his scalp, and climbed into the driver's seat. Diana stood aside for Chang Ping to arrange himself astride the gear-lever before hauling herself up to sit beside him. This time she kept her distance. No part of her body touched his.

The sky grew overcast, humidity increased, rain began to fall. It stayed like that all afternoon, until at last they drove around a steep bend and ahead of them lay half a dozen giant smokestacks belching forth black pillars that seemed both to support and generate the murkiness disfiguring the sky.

'Guiyang,' Chang Ping murmured. 'The sun is unusual here;

that's how it got its name. "Rare and precious sun." It's a terrible place.'

The road ran between factories enlivened only by the occasional flicker of a welding torch or floodlights illuminating vast empty spaces devoid of any apparent purpose. A filthy river bordered by warehouses, tangled high-tension cables, TV aerials competing like bracken for highest place, here and there a dilapidated temple . . . the outskirts were so mournful that Diana wanted to weep again. By now it was nearly dark outside.

Then the driver turned sharp right and the truck was accelerating down a side-road.

'Where are we going?' Diana sat up. 'This isn't the way into town.'

But Chang Ping said nothing. She grabbed his arm. 'Tell me!'

All of a sudden he was different. She began to struggle with him. He resisted. She tried to scratch his face, but he was too quick for her and she found her wrists seized.

The truck turned left into a narrow street lined by two rows of high buildings and ran slap up against a roadblock.

All was confusion and shouting; but by the light of smoking torches Diana could just make out the green caps, the red books held shoulder-high, many shadowy faces contorted by hatred into fanatical devil-masks . . . then someone wrenched open the driver's door.

SEVENTEEN

◇

Proshin's cab was seven and a half minutes late at the Garden Hotel rendezvous. Sangster got in and the two men were driven around the overlapping red-and-white poles, out of the police cordon area.

'Talkative?'

'Yes.' Proshin nodded at the driver's back. 'He's our man and anyway he doesn't speak English.'

'Is Annabelle in?' Annabelle was their codename for the aircraft that had flown flight number ZG 877 the day the satellite was shot down.

'Not yet. Airport security's been doubled.'

'Shit.' Sangster slumped back in his seat and stared at the cab's ceiling.

He knew when they first began to plan the mission that it was hopeless, but he didn't realize quite how hopeless until he landed at Canton's Baiyun Airport a few hours before and saw the newspaper headlines. 'Chairman: The Last Hours.' The streets had been even more crowded than usual, although the Public Security Bureau and Armed Police were out in strength. People behaved in an orderly way, for the most part, but they were restless.

Sangster had with him only a small overnight case. He checked into his hotel and unpacked enough belongings to give credence to his cover as a director of a herbal tea company based in Milwaukee. Then he went to meet Proshin at the Garden Hotel.

'It will get worse.' The Russian's diagnosis interrupted Sangster's reflections with ugly abruptness. 'Canton's full of rumours. Our driver friend here likes to be called Pete. Pete's brother-in-law is a cabby; this is his cab. Brother-in-law listens to all the gossip in the back seat. Today he's heard everything, from outright martial law coming down the pipe, to the Politburo announcing democratic elections, to the restoration of the imperial dynasties. I exaggerate, but not much.'

'Troop movements?'

'Uncertain.'

'Where are we heading?'

'This is the Jiangcun road. We're north of the city, not far from the airport.'

'Roadblocks?'

'Not when we left.'

'What's our cover?'

'Dinner at the house of a local tea-merchant. It won't stand up if they check.'

'Nothing stands up. I have bad news, my friend. I'm not at liberty to tell you what it is, but I'm going to tell you anyway.'

'You've warmed up. What have I done to deserve such trust all of a sudden?'

'You've been assigned to a suicide mission with me. I want you to die happy.'

'Tell me.'

'The president is going to cancel the grain treaty with the Soviet Union.'

'There will be . . . escalation.'

'Probably.'

The two men stared at each other, but it was dark in the taxi and neither could read the other's eyes.

The driver had entered a maze of narrow streets in what looked like a suburb of Canton. Now he pulled up beside a tall building that showed no lights. Everyone got out. Sangster saw it was a warehouse with barred windows, many of them holed. Next to the padlocked door was a board showing numerous businesses: cloth-cutters, a ball-bearing manufacturer, several import-export concerns giving no indication of what they might deal in. Pete, the driver, unlocked the door and motioned them inside.

They climbed all the way to the top, where they entered a small office containing so many filing cabinets that the only desk blocked the doorway; Sangster and Proshin were forced to clamber over it before they could sit, and even then Sangster had to make do with a corner of the desk. The single bulb cast an insipid light over dusty papers, spiked bills, a rubber-stamp holder and other assorted junk. Not much business got transacted here.

Pete disappeared along the corridor, to reappear a few moments later carrying two sets of white overalls. 'Size okay?' he asked Proshin in the Cantonese dialect.

'We'll check. These are the real thing?'

For answer, Pete unfolded one pair to reveal an All Middle Kingdom Cargo Freight logo on the left breast. Underneath it was a plastic badge-holder containing a photograph and some writing.

As the two men began to put on their overalls, Sangster examined Pete. The Chinese, barely out of his teens, looked a regular scallywag. Long hair, jewel in left earlobe, thin moustache, shades dangling from the gap in his shirt, jeans, leather jacket . . . a typical-looking specimen of Chinese youth on the make.

'Your people were lucky to find him,' he remarked casually to Proshin, in English.

'They didn't. He's a British legman.'

'I thought our mutual friends were being kept out of this. Or was that only in London?'

'No, here as well.' Proshin, aware of Pete lounging in the doorway, smiled at Sangster as if they were enjoying some personal joke. 'He thinks he's working for the British.'

Sangster felt all the skin tense along his skull and fought hard to keep his expression serene. 'And if he finds he isn't?'

'He won't.'

'But —'

'What choice did we have?' Proshin's tone was impatient. 'You know that the only people who ever got a hold in China were DI6. We have to use their men.'

'You didn't just fix that overnight, did you?'

'I don't know what you mean.'

'I mean you must have infiltrated the Brits' Hong Kong operation.'

Proshin did up the last of the buttons. 'What if we did? This conversation's unnecessary.' He rounded on Pete. 'Face masks?'

Pete vanished for a short while and returned carrying a couple of *koujiao*, the broad white masks worn by many Chinese as protection against cold or pollution. Sangster put his on.

'Not bad,' Proshin said. 'We still have to do something about the eyes.'

Pete produced a box of theatrical make-up from one of the filing cabinets and went to work on Proshin. He was no expert, but then he didn't have to be. All they required was a superficial narrowing of their eye-sockets coupled with a slight upward slant to the corners. In this light, when viewed from eighteen inches away, Proshin merely looked bizarre. But tomorrow night conditions in the field would be different.

'Do you trust this guy?' Sangster growled after a while.

'Yes.'

'Tell me.'

'The British recruited him two years ago. He tried to enter Hong Kong illegally, along with his mother and sister. Father's dead. They were caught. This man told the British that he worked in the post office here. The British asked him if anyone knew he'd fled; he said no. So they offered him a deal. His mother and sister could stay; but he had to go back, before anyone realized he was missing. Once back, he had to work. As long as he worked, he'd be paid; what's more, his mother and sister would be found a home and money. But if he slipped up . . .'

Proshin left the sentence unfinished. Pete started on Sangster's eyes.

'Did he slip up?'

'Never. He has contacts – oh, does he have contacts! Some of them take the breath away.'

'That makes me suspicious. Why should someone like this have contacts?'

'Because as a post office worker he has power. He can speed things up or make them even later than they were before. So people come and ask him favours. And in return, they do him favours.'

'Going by the back door.'

'Right.'

'What exactly does he do?'

'He's number three in charge of all registered letters, parcels and packets.'

'Foreign or inland?'

'Both. What do people put into registered mail?'

'Valuables.'

'The kind that can easily be transferred to other people. Money, jewellery, rare stamps. Embarrassing documents.'

'Wonderful.'

'If someone had asked the British who they'd most like to net that night . . . He'll be caught, of course. Greed. Greed finishes everyone like him, in the end.'

Throughout the conversation they had never once referred to the Chinese as Pete. He might not understand English, but he would recognize his chosen name.

'What do you think?' Sangster said, getting up from the desk.

'I wouldn't like either of us to try to pass for Chinese at check-in tomorrow. But we won't be checking in, will we?'

Proshin was looking at the window. Sangster saw at once what had caught his eye: a new light somewhere in the street. He heaved a filing cabinet aside and looked out.

'*Shit!*' Sangster wheeled around. 'There's a police car outside!'

For a moment his brain refused to function; then brutal rage at the thought of his own gullibility flooded over him and he was left with only one desire: to put his mark on the man who had done this. He vaulted the desk, hands going for Pete's throat. But Proshin restrained him.

'Please,' the Russian said quietly. 'Don't make trouble. There's been a slight deviation in the dress rehearsal, that's all.'

Then Sangster saw that he was holding a gun.

EIGHTEEN

◇

The room was poorly lit by a white, wall-mounted globe encased in a mesh cage, but there was enough light to make Simon Young glad that it wasn't any stronger.

'What have they done to you, Qianwei?' he whispered.

Qiu slumped low on the other side of the table, neck resting on the chairback. His eyes gazed up at the ceiling. They were empty. He showed no sign of having heard.

Simon sat down and glanced around the bare cell. Concrete walls stained by damp, puddles of water, streaks of faded whitewash, a row of metal clothes-hooks nailed to a board along one side . . . it was cold and musty in here, but then the basement was almost on the waterline.

Something about this place unnerved him. Simon could not identify the source of his fear. Was it the hooks, so innocuous-looking? Or the off-white streaks on the walls? Things had happened here he would rather not know about.

His eyes strayed to the Chinese opposite. Qiu had not moved. He was alive and not alive. A zombie.

'Can you hear me?' Simon said. He wiped a hand across his brow and tried to concentrate. It was difficult to do that at three o'clock in the morning, just after receiving confirmation that China's leader was within hours of death. Soon the stock exchange would open; then Hong Kong would plunge into a vortex the length and depth of which no one could forecast.

'Qianwei,' he said aloud. 'Can you . . . can you try to listen to what I'm going to say?'

For a moment Simon wondered if Qiu's mind had gone. He looked like a derelict: no jacket or tie, torn shirt, one shoe on,

191

the other missing, dirty face, that angry yellow-and-purple ring around his neck . . . could anyone look like that and still be wholly human?

'Qianwei, Peter Reade asked me here. You're being held in Eucliffe, just by Repulse Bay. I gather it's his intelligence complex now.'

No response.

'You must listen to me. The Chairman's about to die. I need your help.'

For a moment nothing happened. Then, very slowly, Qiu raised his chin, as if some invisible puppet-master were tenderly hauling on the string. Simon fixed his gaze on the eyes opposite, willing them to focus.

'Reade's told me many things tonight. He says he's had you watched ever since you came to Hong Kong to live. He was convinced you'd keep up contacts with the mainland. For a long time he couldn't prove it. Then he found a pair of shoes on the beach, the night of . . . that night. He traced the shoes back to the shop. They'd been paid for by credit card.' Simon paused. 'Your credit card.'

Qiu's head did not move, but there was a subtle change in him. Before, his eyes had merely been on the same level as Simon's. Now they were looking. They were registering another presence in the cell.

'I've seen the file, Qianwei. It explains a lot of things we didn't understand before. For instance, it was you who planted the microphone in Diana's jacket at Jinny's funeral. And there's other things. So I think that Peter's got it right.'

Qiu's lips twisted into a contemptuous smile.

'I think Peter's got it right,' Simon slowly repeated. 'And I don't know what to do.'

It was impossible to read Qiu's expression.

'This is hard for me. I feel stupid. I always realized that when the Mahjongs kept your son back in China, there'd be a risk you might betray me. Because I chose to ignore that risk, now I've been tricked by someone I thought I knew. But I can overlook it. I think I can even see that you don't go to prison.'

Qiu's lips briefly rose in a sneer before reverting to their usual state of downturned disapproval.

'I haven't come here to talk business. I want to talk about Diana.'

Simon allowed the silence to expand for a long time. Qiu's face underwent several changes. First, he lowered his gaze: did it suddenly, as if Simon's words had belatedly assumed meaning. His eyes flitted from side to side, seeking a way out. He breathed in sharply through his nose.

'You know who I mean by Diana? My daughter. Your friend.'

'Friend?'

Simon shivered. The sound Qiu had just made was a bubbly croak. The way he swallowed showed how painful it was for him to speak.

'She called you her friend. Often.'

'I have no friends. None.'

'Qianwei . . . if it *was* you that night, the night of Jinny's funeral . . . you would have overheard certain things. I need to know what they were.'

'Because of my *friend*, I suppose?'

'Right now, Diana's the most important person in the world to me.'

'Why now? For the first time? After all these years of buying things and selling things . . . people?' Qiu broke off to rub his neck, circling his head around in an attempt to ease the pain.

'I've always cared about my family. Just as you've cared about yours. Which is why you're here tonight, isn't it?'

'I don't see —'

'Tingchen.' Simon sat back, spreading his hands along the edge of the table. 'How old is he now?'

The Chinese said nothing.

'Let me see . . . when we were all prisoners in Chaiyang together, he was . . . six, I think. Diana was teaching him English, remember?'

'I remember! Oh yes, I *remember*.' Qiu spat out the words as if they tasted vile. 'You kidnapped my son, held him hostage, so that they were forced to come and get us!'

'Wait a minute. Your own people, the Mahjongs, were quite ready to use Tingchen as a pawn.'

Qiu looked away. 'They decided he would be better off with his mother. They were right.'

'Is that so?' Simon pushed back his chair and sat with hands folded in his lap, studying the Chinese. 'Is that really right?' he said quietly.

'He's my son. I should know.' Qiu's voice had become stronger, less rough.

'I don't believe you. Tingchen was kept back in China, despite all my attempts to bring him out –'

'*Your* attempts.'

'Yes. I tried. You know how hard I tried.'

'And yet you failed. So now you're paying for these things. These failures.'

'And my daughter's got to pay too?'

'Yes! I've lost everything. You have lost your wife and now your daughter is gone from you. So? Diana will doubtless return when she feels able to look you in the face again.'

'What? Why shouldn't she look me in the face?'

'Your daughter's not led a happy life, Simon Young. She confided things to me that weren't considered fit for your ears.'

'You be careful what you say.'

'Why? Do you think I can be made to suffer more than I'm suffering now? Do you know what Reade did to me? He hanged me.'

'*Hanged* you?'

'Oh yes, very good – your big round eyes widen, your face conveys shock.'

'But this is a British colony!'

Qiu blinked at him, unable to follow the line of thought. Simon shook his head. 'I just can't believe it. Peter *tortured* you?'

'Yes. When I refused to talk. He's not a patient man.'

The silent seconds ticked by. Simon stared at Qiu, perhaps seeing reflected in the other man's eyes a colony he had helped manufacture to a specification that now was revealed to him for the first time. Eventually he took a pack of cigarettes and a box of matches from his pocket and pushed them across the table.

'You don't smoke,' the Chinese remarked as he lit up.

'I just thought you might like a cigarette.' Simon's control snapped for an instant. 'Does every bloody thing I do have to be marked down on the scorecard?'

Qiu picked a shred of tobacco from his teeth, giving himself an excuse not to look at Simon. 'You let me down,' he said at last, as if ruling a line under the topic. 'I betrayed everything I once regarded as sacred, on the strength of your guarantee that you would get my son back. None of your other arguments, promises, counted. Ever.'

'Do you think I don't remind myself of that, every day of my life?'

'I'm glad. But it makes no difference. I betrayed my country. You betrayed me.'

Simon waited while the Chinese smoked his cigarette down to the end and stubbed it out on the floor. 'Tell me about Diana. You said she couldn't look me in the face. I want to know what you meant.'

Qiu lit another cigarette. 'She had an abortion. You knew that? No.'

Simon stared at the table between them. 'I didn't know. I . . . I suspected there was something . . .'

'You surprise me. I didn't realize you could be sensitive to your family's emotional needs.'

'I remember . . . I know the time you mean.' Qiu had succeeded in touching Simon on the raw, he couldn't think of the right words. 'I remember how awful she looked,' he faltered at last. 'How wretched she must have been. I felt so helpless, then.'

'You surprise me,' Qiu repeated.

'Because I love my daughter?' The anger showed through now. 'You, as a good Chinese, a good family man, surely you understand that? I only wish she'd felt able to ask me to help her.'

But Qiu merely blew a stream of smoke into his face and

195

said, 'Our dealings are finished. I won't tell you anything.'

When Simon spoke again, his voice made the other man start: neither of them had said anything for an interminable time. 'You've come a long way.'

Qiu rearranged his legs slightly and lit a third cigarette from the butt of the last one.

'Your grandfather and your great-grandfather before him were mandarins. I remember you telling me that, once, long ago.'

Qiu said nothing.

'Yet your father was with Mao Zedong in Yenan, a trusted helper and friend. He had the foresight to send you away to the west, to be educated.'

'You play another instrument, but it's the same siren tune.'

'You're an educated man, a thoughtful man. An economist.'

'I'm a soldier. I know how to fight. I've forgotten the rest.'

'Yes, forgotten. They took everything from you. I think I'd want to forget, too.'

Simon spoke slowly, spinning out time while he cast about in desperation for some way of getting to his adversary. Nothing worked. Nothing could penetrate such defences of human coldness.

Qiu's eyes were closed. The two men sat like that for what might have been minutes or hours, Simon couldn't tell. His mind wandered here and there. At one point he found himself thinking of Jinny. She had gone from him so totally, without leaving anything of herself behind. Yet tonight, for some reason, he felt close to her. It was as if she had come to be with him when he needed her, carrying the habit of a lifetime through into death.

He had no home to go to, when this was over; just a house empty of everything except memories. Two men in a cell, neither of whom had a home. Qiu had lost his wife and child; Jinny was dead and no one knew where Diana might be. Yet life had once been different for these two men . . .

No home . . .

Simon slowly raised his head. Perhaps . . . a long shot. 'Home' was always somewhere, if you went back far enough.

And – 'Yes!' he heard a voice say inside his head, knowing, without astonishment, that it was Jinny.

He began to speak: hesitantly at first, but then with greater confidence.

> *Chuang qian ming yue guang*
> *Yi shi di shang shuang*
> *Zhu tou wang ming yue*
> *Di tou si gu xiang.*

It was Mandarin Chinese, half spoken and half sung so as to bring out the tones. The poem drifted through the dank air of the cell to vibrate chords, different chords, deep within each hearer.

Qiu bowed his head. Simon slowly repeated the poem, this time in English.

> *I wake, and moonbeams play around my bed*
> *Glittering like hoar-frost to my wondering eyes;*
> *Up towards the glorious moon I raise my head*
> *Then lay me down – and thoughts of home arise.*

Simon's gaze never deviated from Qiu's face. 'Li Bai, China's greatest poet. Every Chinese child knows those lines – is born knowing them. You can't translate a poem like that . . . the song of the exile. Forced to live in an alien land, he sees the moon. And remembers. And weeps.'

He leaned forward across the table, so that they were almost touching. 'We've both lost. But Li Bai's poem goes on, along with the white moonlight. That's the same then, now and always, no matter where home may be . . .'

Qiu's eyes remained closed. 'I . . .'

Simon leaned forward still further, terrified of destroying the frail resurgence of life in the man opposite. 'What?'

'I . . . should not have said what I did about your daughter. Not . . . polite.'

'You wanted to hurt me.'

Qiu bit his lip and nodded. His face was moist with sweat;

Simon sensed he had embarked on a struggle with some terrible inner demon.

'You wanted revenge, Qianwei. Because I failed you.'

'No!' At last his eyes opened, his self-control broke. 'It was because you still have a child, children. And I . . . and I . . .' Qiu buried his head in his arms. It took Simon a while to accept that the Chinese was weeping. When realization did dawn, he walked swiftly over to him, taking his chair with him. He sat down and, after a moment's hesitation, placed his arm around Qiu's shoulders.

'When a man loses all his hopes . . .' Qiu's voice sounded dull against the table-top, but Simon could make out what he said. '. . . He discovers things about himself. Bad things. I don't believe I'll ever see my son again. I wanted to hurt you, because I was jealous! And I despise myself for it!'

'Perhaps you will see Tingchen. One day.'

'No. No.' Qiu sat up, putting aside Simon's arm. 'I don't expect that. But for you, it's different. For you and your child, there's a chance.' He paused to inhale a shivery breath. 'Diana's alive. She's all right.'

There was a gap in Simon's consciousness after that. Somehow he must have moved the chair, for they were once again facing each other over the table, and another cigarette dangled from Qiu's mouth. Simon looked at the Chinese and wondered how far that pitiful expression mirrored his own.

'It's true you've been working for Sun?'

Qiu's hesitation lasted only seconds. 'Yes.'

'Information in exchange for Tingchen's welfare?'

'Yes.'

'Diana?'

'Sun's principal interest is in Benevolence. He wasn't pleased with me, because I never found out much about it. That's why he wanted Diana.'

'What on earth has she got to do with it?'

'She knows about Benevolence.'

'But she doesn't! I never told her a thing about it.'

'On the night after the funeral, I overheard you all drink a toast: "To Benevolence," something like that. Diana said she

198

would join in the toast, I heard her! And I told Sun that.'

'But she didn't realize what she was drinking to. Oh, my God! Where is she now?'

'I don't know exactly. All I know is, she's being taken in charge by someone she won't suspect. He's leading her south, via Guiyang. Then they'll take the road to Nanning, and the river.'

'So she's coming home?'

'Maybe. Everything depends on how co-operative she is.'

'I could have stopped her. Warren said I was a fool . . .' Simon t'cha'd angrily and shook his head. 'What's your position now?' he said abruptly.

'I have no position. I'm a prisoner.'

'Suppose I got you freed?'

'I don't understand.'

'You're the nearest thing I have to a contact with my daughter. Has your control, or whatever you call him, missed you yet?'

'I shouldn't think so.'

'What if you simply went back on station, as before? That's what Reade wants, too: a double-agent in touch with the mainland. Who would you really be working for – Peter and me? Sun? Cumnor?'

Qiu looked down. 'Cumnor?'

'Peter Reade told me about the letters they found. Letters from Tingchen. You told him Cumnor had given them to you.'

'If you know about that, then I think you understand. The only loyalty I have left is to Tingchen. My son.'

'Yes. I do understand.'

'Whatever I said, you could never believe it. Not now. You see, I *want* to get out – but only so as to try to find my son. Nothing else. That's my position, as you put it: I'd be working for me. For myself.'

'I could believe you. Because I *have* to! You're all I've got. And remember: I can always put you back here again, by pressing charges. You'll never be more than a footstep away from Eucliffe.'

'So what you're proposing is yet another deal . . . how many times have I dealt with you, Simon?'

'Too many. But this is the first time we've bargained as equals. You want your son. Whatever you said just now, you're still hoping to get him out, I know that. Okay – go to Cumnor, see what you can screw out of him. Just help me get my daughter back. Child for child.'

Qiu gazed at him in silence for a long time. 'I will go back on station, to use your phrase. If that's what you want. Not because of any deal. Because I think it's . . . it's best.'

Simon nodded and stood up. As he reached the door Qiu called his name.

'What?'

'Be careful of Alexander Cumnor.'

'Why?'

Qiu outlined what had happened before Reade and his men had taken him.

'I don't get it,' Simon said. 'Why should Cumnor want to bother about my daughter?'

'I'm not sure. But if he, too, thinks that she may know about Benevolence, she'll become a potential source of danger in his eyes.'

Simon thought about that. He did not like it. 'But even if you're right . . . what could Cumnor do?'

'I don't know. Just . . . take care.'

'I will. Thank you, Qianwei.'

The door opened and Simon was halfway through it when suddenly he turned back. 'Is it true what you told me about Reade? He hanged you?'

Qiu nodded. The physical act so obviously pained him that it provided its own corroboration.

Simon found Mat upstairs, in the act of replacing the telephone-receiver. 'That was the chairman of the stock exchange.'

'And?'

'He's agreed to suspend the floor for twenty-four hours from nine-thirty tomorrow morning.'

'Thank God! But that won't help us in London or New York.'

200

'Dad, you'd better hear the latest: I spoke to Reade ten minutes ago and he told me that the authorities no longer have control of southern China. General Fu Quanyou, he's the commander of Chengdu Military Region, has asked for reinforcements. They monitored his transmission here two hours ago.'

'What answer did he get?'

'There are no reserves available, I quote, "in the present crisis".'

'They actually said "crisis"?'

'Yes.'

'My God, my God . . .'

'Rachael Honnyman tried to speak to me just before we left to come here. It's about Warren's river trip, you know, the inaugural run? She's worried to death. She was asking –'

Simon gripped his son's arm. 'Honnyman! He's due to go up-river, when is it, tomorrow? Today!' He looked at his watch. 'By Christ, it's nearly six o'clock. When's he leaving?'

'He may not leave at all now.'

'Oh yes he will, if I know Warren he will. And that's the answer.' Seeing the look of bewilderment on Mat's face he exclaimed with impatience and said, 'Tell you in the car. All that matters now is grabbing Warren. Get me there – just *get me there!*'

NINETEEN

◇

The truck's nearside fender sent flying one of the Red Guards who manned the roadblock outside Guiyang. For several moments, all was confusion. Chang Ping roughly forced Diana down into the narrow space between the floor and the dashboard.

'Keep still!' he hissed. 'Don't move until I tell you.'

'I can't –'

'Shut *up!*'

The driver stood in the road, surrounded by about a dozen Red Guards who shouted and waved their arms in threatening fashion. At first the old man adopted a meek stance by holding his cap in his hands and keeping his eyes lowered. But slowly his resentment simmered up, until eventually he began to answer back in monosyllables, enraging the rabble still further.

The guard who had been knocked down staggered to his feet and pushed his way through the ring. He rammed his face up to within a few inches of the driver's and began to scream at him. The old man retreated a pace, then threw his cap on the ground and punched his accuser.

To Diana, squashed underneath the seat, the noise-level seemed to treble. Chang Ping muttered something and jumped from the cab.

Diana heard him shouting above the hubbub. Suddenly the sound of a loud crack penetrated the darkness inside the truck's rusty interior. Someone groaned. Diana knew instinctively that it was Chang Ping. She crawled across to the driver's side and peeped through the crack between the half-open door and the bodywork.

He lay on the ground. In the poor light cast by random torchbeams Diana could just make out a dark stain on his shirt. She saw that most of the crowd were young: students, probably, although some of them were armed. It was a rifle-butt that had felled Chang Ping: its owner stood astride him, brandishing his weapon. There was some muted cheering, but Diana sensed that the mob were no longer certain; this must be their first taste of blood.

In the excitement over Chang Ping the driver had been forgotten. Now he ran forward to help the young man stand, but another swing of the rifle-butt knocked him flying. When Diana tried to swallow she found she had no saliva left.

She shut her eyes and tried to think. The crowd was nerving itself up for anything. No one else could stop them. So she had to do it.

Impossible! You've never driven a truck before . . .

If not me, who?

She began to construct a plan. Nobody'd seen her yet; it was her only advantage. The driver had left the engine running. Somehow it would be necessary to start the lorry moving forward, but slowly. First, get in the driving seat. Next, release the handbrake . . .

She backed away on all fours until she could go no further because the crankshaft-casing prevented it. Then she wriggled until her spine was rammed hard up against the seat, and began to writhe upward. As her head emerged level with the steering wheel, she heard glass shatter.

The sound unnerved her. She raised her head far enough to look out of the window. Fortunately no one was looking at the truck, or they could not have failed to see Diana's white face staring through the windscreen. What she saw terrified her.

They had dragged Chang Ping upright and hauled him to the side of the road, where two men held him by the arms. When a spectator smashed a bottle down, one of the men holding Chang Ping arranged the latest shards into a rough circle with his feet.

Somebody carried forward a white dunce's hat inscribed

with Chinese ideographs and stuck it on Chang Ping's head. Then the two men holding him viciously forced his arms up and one of them kicked the backs of his legs.

He went down with a curious cry: a mixture of grief and pain and, perhaps more than anything else, surprise.

Diana had been putting off making a decision about Chang Ping. He had told lies; and, on the outskirts of Guiyang, he had actually fought with her. She did not know who he really was, or what he might do to her. But she could not leave him to the mercy of the crowd; and now was not the time to consider why she could not.

She swiftly forced herself into the driving seat, released the brake and struggled to find the clutch pedal. The truck began to roll forward. Several heads turned. At first no one realized the truth: that a third passenger had been overlooked. Then Diana's thrusting right foot found the clutch. She pushed down with all her might. No give! She trod on her right foot with the left, levering herself out of the seat and weighing down on the pedal.

By now people had begun to surround the lorry, already moving at five miles an hour, and several were poised to jump on the running-board. As one youth pulled himself up by the door handle it came away in his hands. Diana wrenched the stiff gear lever for all she was worth, and took both feet off the clutch.

The truck lurched forward with a tremendous jolt that seemed to punch its way up her backbone. Just in time she remembered to pump down on the accelerator. Three more jolts and the truck was no longer in danger of stalling. Diana, peering through the windscreen, saw people scatter out of her path.

'Chang Ping,' she shouted. 'Jump. *Jump!*'

As the truck rolled past him he looked up, grasped what was going on and somehow managed to get to his feet. The people guarding him seemed fazed by the sight of the truck in motion; they looked away from him just for an instant but it was enough: Chang Ping began to run. Diana remembered in time that somebody had torn off the handle. She leaned over at a dangerous angle and managed to release the door from the inside.

Fists pummelled on the bodywork. Diana took no notice. Chang Ping was level with the door. As he reached up to grasp the sill of the open window someone tried to tackle him around the knees, but he got a foot on the running-board.

'Go!' he cried, as he threw himself inside.

Diana pushed down on the accelerator; the lorry bucked forward; first gear reached the end of its tether and howled in protest. Above the anguished revving Diana heard several bangs and thought, 'The engine's bust!' But when the truck continued to move, she knew they were shooting. Desperation prompted her to try a change of gear. The headlights revealed open road. They were away.

At last she had time to spare for Chang Ping. She turned to see him slumped in the passenger seat, one hand clasped to his shoulder and his lips forced back in a grimace of pain. A puff of breath escaped from between his clenched teeth; then he fainted.

By now she was going at twenty miles an hour. The road twisted and turned past lakes alternating with fields of rice. She stole a look in the cracked rearview mirror: one set of headlights that disappeared and came to life again, according to the bends in the road.

Now she was doing forty.

Chang Ping groaned and lifted his head from his chest. 'Wha . . . wha's happening?'

'They're following us.'

'Been . . . shot.'

Diana took her eyes off the road and the truck juddered dangerously near the verge. 'Badly?'

'Don't think so.' He made an effort to sit up, wincing with pain. 'My shoulder. Hurts . . . *aiya*!' He chewed his lower lip, took a deep breath and went on, 'This road leads . . . to a forest. Huaxi. Twenty kilometres outside Guiyang. Want you to . . . to drive as fast as you can. See the forest. Get inside it. Village.'

'What?' Diana's voice was shrill, panicky. 'Speak up, can't you!' She risked another glance in the mirror. 'They're gaining on us.'

'They know . . . road. Faster.'

'I'm doing –'

'Faster!'

Chang Ping seemed to be recovering. 'I have a plan. We are going to abandon the truck. Then we'll set fire to it. But the people behind us will think we are still inside. Understand?'

Diana nodded.

'When we've passed the village and are in the forest, you must drive very fast for about a mile. Then, when you can't see their lights behind us any longer, stop. There are cans of petrol in the back.'

'How do you know all this?'

'Later. Listen. You must help me push the truck into the forest. So that it smashes against a tree. Then we pour the petrol over the truck . . . then . . . run.'

'Where to?'

'I know a place.'

'How?'

But he shook his head. 'Look for the village.'

Diana grimly assessed her situation; she was driving an old truck with which she was unfamiliar along a road she had never travelled before with a young man who had been wounded in a country that had gone mad. *Never mind, don't think, don't stop . . .*

Suddenly the road levelled out and began to run dead straight across a plain, with a shallow river on one side and paddies on the other. Diana strained her eyesight to the end of the headlights' wedge. 'There's something up ahead. White . . .'

'The village! Good!'

The needle was nudging fifty. Almost immediately the road inclined upward and once more began to weave about. Now they were hemmed in by trees on both sides. Chang Ping craned his neck, trying to penetrate the darkness.

'After the next turn,' he rapped suddenly.

Diana wrenched on the wheel, braked and brought the truck squealing to a halt.

'Don't switch off!' Chang Ping, holding the door with one hand and the frame with the other, lowered himself to the ground. Diana had already tossed out her rucksack and run around to the back of the truck. There, sure enough, under a tarpaulin, were two cans of petrol. As she pulled the first of them to the tailgate she raised her head and thought she heard, far away and masked by the breeze, the sound of another engine.

Chang Ping hobbled over to her. 'You must run the truck off the road so that it falls down the hill. Got it?'

'I can't!'

'You're doing fine, just fine. Think how much you've done already. Wonderful! Now get in the truck.'

No, she couldn't do that. Nothing in life had prepared her for anything of the kind. Then Diana remembered the penalty for failure. She climbed back into the cab. 'Look after my rucksack,' she snapped. 'It's all we've got!'

She shifted into first gear and released the brake. As the lorry began to move under its own weight Diana sketched out a series of moves in her mind. Then she faltered. The truck continued to roll while she told herself she couldn't do it. Faster, faster . . . *You have to do it! You have to do it now!*

She disengaged gear and slid sideways until she was half in and half out of the cab. With her left hand gripping the doorframe she wrenched down hard on the wheel with her right, at the same time slithering to the ground. She landed awkwardly, fell and shrieked as the truck's offside rear wheel passed within an inch of her face. There was a succession of loud noises, followed by a bang and the tinkling of glass as the truck hit a tree trunk.

'Hurry!' she dazedly heard Chang Ping scream from the darkness. 'They're almost here. *Hurry!*'

As Diana got to her feet she registered with amazement that she appeared to be unharmed. 'I can't see,' she wailed. 'The truck's lights went out!'

But she could hear. The engine noise that had distracted her earlier was much closer now.

'Here! My lighter . . .'

A tiny flame sparked into life. 'Mind the petrol!'

'Be *quick!*'

She snatched the lighter from him and stuck it in her pocket before lifting the cans and rushing off in the direction where she guessed the truck must be. More by luck than judgement she found it at once, stumbling up against the tailgate in the darkness. Open the cans . . . The other engine was too close; she guessed it would have to turn just one more bend and then it would be upon them.

All she had was Chang Ping's cigarette-lighter. If she tried to ignite the truck with that, she'd be incinerated with it. A dreadful fear numbed Diana's brain. So close, she'd come so close to succeeding, only to be thwarted at the last minute, failure, capture, torture . . .

Torture. That word broke the spell. She ran back a few yards, yanked out her handkerchief, knotted one end of it around the lighter, lit the other, then flung the flaring, weighted missile as hard as she could.

A loud crump battered against Diana's eardrums; a smothering wall of heat rammed into her and she ducked, holding both hands over her head. She could see a melange of oranges and yellows expanding outward and upward, carrying with them the acrid smells of blistered paintwork and burning rubber. Then came the clank of metal buckling in extreme heat. The truck stood out as a silhouette haloed with bright, angry colours and framed by empty night.

Diana was just coming upright again when the petrol tank exploded. She flung herself flat on the ground, waiting for slivers of metal to tear her apart, but they never came. Suddenly a hand gripped her arm and she screamed.

'It's me,' a voice whispered in her ear. 'We've got company. *Stay down!*'

The ground was soft and wet; Diana tasted soil. She raised her head to see the truck still burning merrily between them and the road. Higher up, flame glittered on metal: a vehicle.

Men were starting to pick their way down the slope. Two of them carried rifles, several others had staves. But as they approached the truck the heat soon became too much for them, forcing a retreat.

Diana held her breath and prayed. Please let them go away; let them just assume that we've been burned to death, and leave us. *Please . . .*

She had been staring at the ground. Now she raised her eyes to the ridge where she'd seen the men a moment ago, to find it empty.

The sound of their engine took a long time to die away. Sometimes the night breeze made it seem as if the Red Guards' vehicle was coming back again, but finally all mechanical noise ceased. Diana scrambled up and gave her attention to Chang Ping.

He lay on his back with his eyes closed. In the light from the burning truck she could see that the top half of his shirt was black with blood. Diana tried not to think about the state of his knees.

'Can you stand?'

He nodded feebly and made the attempt. 'The bullet must have grazed my shoulder. It hurts, but I don't think any bone was broken.'

'Your knees?'

'I can manage.'

'What next?'

'We have to walk. A mile, maybe two. I know a place where we can be safe.'

Diana stared at him in disbelief. 'How will we find the way in the dark? Have you been here before?'

'Yes. I have travelled the road we were meant to follow, not just once but several times.'

'*Meant* to follow?'

'Diana, I know there are things I have to explain. But this isn't the time. We must get under cover before morning light. Then I'll tell you everything, I promise.'

She wanted to scream, 'Tell me now!' but sense prevailed. Her thinking had undergone a change over the past few hours.

Once safely away from Chaiyang she'd initially viewed their plight as annoying, rather than desperate. Now she was beginning to grasp that the perils facing her were of a different order of magnitude. Physical violence had become commonplace; it was only through luck that so far it had not been exerted against her.

She was in danger, real danger. She might never see her home or her family again.

'We'll go on now.' Chang Ping's voice once more sounded confident, resourceful.

He was part of the danger.

As Diana shouldered her rucksack and trudged up to the road she sometimes faced that thought and sometimes sheered away from it. He was not what he seemed. And that, she realized with a shiver, is another reason why you didn't force him to tell you the truth just now. Because you're frightened of what that truth might be . . .

Without even the cigarette-lighter to guide them progress was frustratingly slow, but once they'd managed to find their way back to the road it became easier. When first light appeared it brought some relief, but also a new anxiety: would they reach their destination before dawn? Fortunately, Chang Ping seemed to have excellent sight and there came a moment when he turned off the road with a reassuring show of authority.

They climbed onto a sandy bluff studded with isolated pines and there, in the half-light, some hundred feet below her in the neck of a valley, Diana saw a collection of dun-coloured buildings. 'What's that?'

'It's the Huaxi Hotel. The official tourist *binguan* where visitors stay. But we're not going there. Look – can you see?'

Diana followed the direction of his pointing finger and could just make out the corner of an old-fashioned Chinese pavilion peeping out from some birches and other, heavy-foliaged trees she didn't recognize. It was to the right of them, less than a quarter of a mile distant. A red-brick path wound along the side of the valley between this tiny building and the hotel.

Chang Ping limped off towards the pavilion. Diana stayed where she was.

'Coming?' he called over his shoulder.

'Who's there?'

'I don't know. But I think no one.'

'Aren't you expecting somebody?'

'Not any more.'

He turned and went on, as if indifferent to whether she followed or not. After several seconds of indecision, Diana set off along the path after him.

A dreary dawn had materialized by the time they reached the folly, for so Diana now thought of it. Sulky wind blew raindrops from the branches into her face and hair. She reached a puddle-strewn paved yard in front of the building at the same time as Chang Ping and looked around.

This place had been neglected for many years. Red paint was peeling away from the low, ornamental balustrade in large patches; many of the paving-stones were cracked and all were covered with green moss over which the wind had scattered thick layers of autumn leaves – several seasons' worth, Diana guessed. Someone had smashed a window and left the shards lying in the courtyard. A withered cherry tree hung forlornly beside a dried-up fountain, its skeletal fingers casting a ghostly pall over the front door.

The door was padlocked, but when Chang Ping fished a key out of his pocket Diana felt no surprise. His having the means of access to this gloomy place now seemed a part of some deep-laid pattern: lines on a blue willow plate which would one day form a cohesive whole.

There was nothing inside the square pavilion except a pile of rubbish untidily swept into one corner, some ashes where a fire had been and the smell of damp decay. Diana could see white mould running along one of the window sills. It felt rubbery; when she touched the frame her finger sank in as if the wood had turned to putty.

Chang Ping prodded the ashes. 'Someone's been here.'

'Who?'

But he merely flopped down with a deep sigh. Diana unslung

211

her rucksack, threw it on the floor, and went to stand over him.

'Okay. Explanation time.'

Instead of embarking on a story, however, he raised his head and smiled up at her. 'First, I want to say something.'

'What?'

'Until last night, I just thought of you as a fine person. Too fine for me; out of reach. You were beautiful, kind . . . And you'd suffered, too, as I had: the abortion . . . But after seeing what you did tonight . . .' He shook his head like a man who is suspicious of his own reactions. 'I can't keep it to myself any longer. Sorry, but I'm in love with you.'

TWENTY

◇

Dense, early morning mist still shrouded Shek-O as Simon roared up to the Honnymans' house to meet Warren's car turning out of the drive.

'Stay there,' Simon snapped at Qiu. 'I don't want you involved.'

With Mat at his heels he ran across to the Cadillac and slid onto the back seat next to Warren. 'Diana's still in China. She's in great danger. We've had a tip-off. Chinese Central Intelligence *is* after her, like you said.'

Warren snatched the spectacles from his brow. 'Oh, Jesus Christ!'

'I need your help.'

'Me? But I was just on my way to the harbour. The lighters, you know? We're due in Liuzhou in less than two days' time.'

'You're going right up into the area where she is. Somewhere between Guiyang and here. Look for her, find out what you can, ask around. Dammit, an English girl's going to stick out like a sore thumb in that part of the world.'

'Okay, okay. Calm down.'

'Have you got a radio with you? Good enough to reach Hong Kong?'

'Yup. That's part of the deal with the mainland: continual contact with cargoes. But, Simon — I'm not optimistic. I'm slated to meet everyone from the mayor through the commune cat. If I start wandering off-track, they'll notice. And they'll do something about it.'

'I know, but . . . she's my only daughter, I —'

Simon could not continue. Abruptly he turned to look out

of the window into the wall of white mist. Warren laid a sympathetic hand over his. 'I understand. Anything I can do, I *will* do.'

'I want to come with you.' Mat had rested his arm on the back of the front seat and now was gazing steadily at Warren. 'Okay?'

'But Mat, there's paperwork . . . it took forever to fix visas, you know the hassle with the mainland . . .'

'You're a big man today. They love you. Why? Because when China's falling apart you're going right in there, with a smile and a handshake and a brand new contract. And if you tell them you want me on board –'

'We have to talk.' Simon's voice was harsh with a mixture of fatigue and reproach. 'Outside, please.'

Father and son got out of the car. Warren watched them as they stood on the boundary of the mist.

'Don't do this to me,' Simon said. 'I'm asking you. Not telling.'

'I have to do something. I can't just –'

'Benevolence is imminent. That means Dunny's leaving for Taiwan. Your Taiwanese contacts leave everyone else's standing.'

'But –'

'I *need* you, don't you realize that?'

'There are plenty of other executives –'

'How many sons do I have?'

Mat was silent. Simon stared at the ground for a long time before continuing. 'It's hard to talk like this.'

'Yes.'

'A bit late in the day.'

'Maybe.'

'Mat.' A pause. 'Mat, please . . .'

Mat looked into his father's eyes, saw the pain there and felt his own resolution drain away. 'Asking Warren to help's a pretty long shot.'

'We don't have any other kind. And if you go, you see, you might not come back. To lose everyone . . .'

Mat exhaled in a loud sigh. Hearing it, Simon knew he had

won. The victory was as joyless as victory can be. 'Come on,' he said quietly, putting an arm around his son's shoulders. 'There's a hell of a lot to do.'

When they returned to the Cadillac, Warren was looking at his watch. 'I really do have to go,' he said anxiously.

'I'm not coming,' Mat said. 'Thanks for waiting, anyway.'

'I'm glad. I'll see that the guys at base liaise with you every step of the way.'

They thanked him and got out of the car. By now the mist was clearing; a pale lemon sun had begun to make its unseen presence felt. Qiu was fully awake. 'How did it go?' he asked wearily as Simon settled into the scat beside him.

'There's not much he can do, but he's promised to try. Mat, let's get going – you drive.'

'Where next?'

'The office. Today's going to be . . . I'm dreading it. Qianwei, I want you to go back, meet your contact as if nothing has happened. But from now on you tell us everything you get from him *as* you get it. Understood?'

'Yes.'

'You've really only got one task: to find out where Diana is.'

'You're crazy,' Mat muttered from the driver's seat. 'How many times does he have to let you down before you stop trusting this guy?'

'Your son's right,' Qiu said. 'The history of our relationship has hardly been satisfactory.'

'No. But Diana's life's at stake. So I'm going to trust you, because I've got no choice.'

'You have very little time left, I should think so.'

'Why do you say that?'

'You recall what I told you last night, about China's *real* plans for Hong Kong after 1997?'

'Of course.'

'The thing you must remember is the leadership-crisis scenario.'

'When a leader dies, China goes into turmoil unless someone takes command within twenty-four hours.'

'Yes, and one way of seizing the initiative is to launch an assault against an easy target: intellectuals at home, Hong Kong or Taiwan abroad. I must tell you, Simon: if there's to be an attack, it will come very soon now.' Qiu's voice was sober. 'Today or tomorrow at the latest. And then Diana, well . . .'

They were running into the outskirts of Central when the car phone buzzed. Without taking his hands off the wheel Mat said 'Respond' and the occupants of the car heard the caller say, 'Alex Cumnor for Simon Young.'

Simon leaned over the seat and picked up the phone, cancelling the loudspeaker. 'Hello, Alex, Simon here.'

'This must be a quick call. It concerns a project of concern to both of us.'

'Go on.'

'Certain friends of mine in a foreign country have recently received interesting despatches from Moldavia.'

Simon stiffened. Moldavia was the Benevolence codename for mainland China. 'Yes?'

'It is suggested – very strongly suggested – that we may expect intervention by Moldavia in the Chad project within the next few days.'

For Chad read Hong Kong. 'Serious intervention?'

There was a pause. When Cumnor spoke again his voice sounded hushed. 'Extremely serious.'

'What's your position on this?'

'I'm in the course of summoning a project-quorum: you're my first call. The project has to be implemented immediately. I repeat, *immediately*. Phase one should begin no later than tonight.'

Simon turned white. 'You can't do that!'

'Why not?'

'It's impossible for Dunny's to make arrangements that soon.'

'The arrangements have all been in place for months past.'

'I'm not ready. The Taiwanese end –'

'*We have to go.*'

'Alex, please. My daughter, she's . . .'

'Family concerns must take a back seat now. I don't see how –'

'She's in China.' Simon almost choked out the words.

For several moments Cumnor said nothing. At last Simon heard him murmur, 'Thank you,' just those two words; then the line went dead.

'Blast!' Simon repeated the oath more quietly, as if recognizing its futility. He was about to speak again when Mat made a right turn and a crowd caught his eye. He braked. 'What the hell –'

'Looks like a riot,' Simon said, twisting in his seat. 'That's a branch of the Great West Oceans Bank . . .'

The phone buzzed again; Simon reached forward to lift it off the hook. 'Simon Young.'

'It's Mary, Mr Young.' Mary Street was his private secretary. Her voice sounded strained; Simon wondered wearily what new crisis had emerged.

'I thought you ought to know two things at once: *Xin Hua* have formally announced that the death of the Chairman is imminent. And the Great West Oceans Bank has declared itself in default and shut its doors.'

'My God, why? That bank was as strong as the Bank of China.'

'That's the point, sir. It was *part* of the Bank of China. I really do think you should come in as soon as possible.'

'On my way.'

As Mat accelerated down Princess Margaret Road his father sat back slowly and muttered, 'It's begun.'

TWENTY-ONE

◇

Sun Shanwang might be old, but he still knew how to move quietly. When he touched Zhang Ming Rong on the shoulder, his secretary shot upright like an old-style military catapult.

'Controller, you . . . you startled me.'

Sun looked down at what he had been doing. 'The sky's nearly finished.'

'Yes. The snowcap's the worst thing.' Ming Rong's voice was not quite steady.

'You know it's five o'clock in the morning?'

'I didn't.'

'Everyone else went home long ago. Yet you're still here. Why?'

When Ming Rong said nothing, Sun rested his buttocks against one of the desks and surveyed the young man thoughtfully. The Controller had a lot of problems to cope with, but just at this moment his mind was preoccupied with something comparatively trivial.

'You're starting to appear slack. Yet you're not really slack. It's almost dawn, yet here you are, still working. Why doesn't all this effort get translated into results, like in the old days?'

Ming Rong stood to attention, hands by his side, and looked straight ahead. That way he didn't have to meet the Controller's eyes. 'I'm sorry. I wasn't aware —'

'You were aware.'

'Sorry.'

Sun lit a cigarette, then, as an afterthought, offered one to his secretary.

'Woman trouble?'

218

'No, Controller.'

'Money? Housing? Parents? The three "Big Concerns"?'

'None of them are affecting me.'

'Then what? Come on, Ming Rong, don't make me have to gouge it out of you. You're too good to waste your talents. Look at me.'

Ming Rong looked. His chief was smiling.

'We'll have a talk now. What we say won't get written down. But things are desperate here and I need your full attention. So tell me: what's wrong?'

After a short struggle with his conscience and his fear, Ming Rong decided to come clean. 'You're right to criticize me. I've been a fool. I've been using departmental resources to find out some things.'

Sun Shanwang sniffed a couple of times. 'What things?' he said cautiously.

When Ming Rong told him about Miss Jian and her search for the missing Uncle Chao, Sun was annoyed. 'Do you really think you haven't got anything better to do with your time? Especially now.'

Ming Rong hung his head.

'All right. It's forgotten.'

'Excuse me, but . . . it isn't so easy to forget. There are things coming out that, that . . .' He tossed his head, as if trying to clear the demons from it. 'Controller, I'm holding information which is dangerous.'

Sun stared at him. 'To you?'

'I don't know. Maybe to a lot of people.'

The Controller pulled up a chair. 'Tell me.'

Until that moment Ming Rong hadn't realized how much he'd been longing to share the burden with someone.

'I began by chasing up my contacts in the airforce, to try and find out what Miss Jian's Uncle Chao was working on when he died. My friend came back within two days. There was no record of any man or any project either. What's more, he advised me to lay off.'

'Sit down, Ming Rong. You make me fidget, standing like that.'

'Thank you. Well, I didn't lay off. I spent a lot of time pursuing it.'

'Which is why you've been neglecting your regular duties?'

'Yes. I got obsessed.'

'A strong word.'

'It was all so strange. But in the end I did piece together a story. There *was* an ultra-secret project of some kind, being developed at a factory near Lanzhou, in the northwest. The time came to test it. They chose Gansu-B-Ten.'

'What?' Sun was startled.

'It's an airbase in –'

'I know what it is. Proceed.'

'A lot of highly-skilled technical people were drawn in from all over the place. They had two things in common: a background in the aerospace industry, and no close family ties.'

Sun frowned at him. 'How many people are we talking about?'

'Fifty-eight.'

'Coincidence?'

'Maybe. Except they're all dead.'

Sun's lips repeated the words but no sound came out. '*All* . . . dead.'

'Then I started to approach the problem from different angles. I selected three names at random and invented some excuse to find out about each name. I pretended to be a work-unit secretary, a policeman investigating a theft and a post office employee trying to deliver a misdirected parcel. And I got three quite different stories. One name belonged to a man who'd been killed driving a truck: that was Uncle Chao. Another man had contracted pneumonia and died of it. The third had got into a brawl and been stabbed.'

'What did you do then?'

'I took six more names and went through the exercise again. And I got the same three cover stories, in different combinations; this time there were three brawls, one pneumonia and two truck-accidents.'

'The *same*?'

'Word for word, almost.'

Sun's spectacles had slipped halfway down his nose. Now he pushed them back and sat up, wrestling with the implications of what he'd been told. 'I had no inkling of any of this. Yet if what you say is true, it's precisely the sort of thing that the airforce security section ought to have drawn to my attention.'

'Controller, I agree.'

'Is that all? I mean, it's more than enough, but have you —'

'One more thing. I checked up on all the names. In most cases, I ended up making my enquiries to the same organization, which claimed to have employment records relating to these men.'

'Claimed?'

'Yes. It had rented the airfield for test-flights, at least that's what they told me.'

'What organization is this?'

'A company called All Middle Kingdom —'

'Cargo Freight.'

'Yes! Controller, you *knew!*'

'I didn't know anything.' Sun heaved a deep sigh. 'But now I'm beginning to. Ming Rong . . .'

'Controller?'

'Do you know anything about particle-beam weapons, laser-beams, that kind of thing?'

'Very little. The Americans and the Russians have equal capabilities in that field, don't they?'

'Yes. Now here is something you don't know: China, too, has equal capability. At least . . . I *think* so.'

Ming Rong stared at him.

'Someone has been very busy making sure that China develops her own Star Wars weaponry. Someone connected with All Middle Kingdom Cargo Freight. A certain brigadier-general called Lo Bing.'

Ming Rong wasn't sure if Sun was addressing him or musing aloud.

'Someone who's got a long way, but who hasn't perfected his weapon yet, or he'd have made his move before this . . .'

'Move, Controller?'

'He's developed this remarkable weapon and he's keeping progress secret, even from me. I can think of only one reason for that. Lo Bing wants power.'

The other jigsaw, the one inside Ming Rong's brain, acquired a further piece. His eyes widened. 'Does what you're telling me have anything to do with the satellite the Russians shot down?'

'Russians . . .' Sun Shanwang frowned at him. 'Now why should the Russians want to shoot down a satellite? I keep asking that question, and no one answers me.'

'But if it wasn't the Russians . . . Controller, what exactly are you telling me?'

'I am telling you . . .' Sun looked at the floor, as if seeking the rest of his sentence there. '. . . That you must find the answers which so far have eluded me.' His voice sharpened and he came to himself, no longer musing. 'I was angry when I first heard what you'd been doing. But I'm not angry any more. On the contrary: you may have done the most important piece of work the department's handled all year. From now on, you're to devote yourself to this full-time. Find out what you can about All Middle Kingdom Cargo Freight: who's really behind it, what it does. I want a proper report; type it yourself, no one else is to see it.'

'Certainly.'

'It is urgent, urgent, *urgent!* Do you understand?'

'Yes.'

'At the moment this Lo Bing doesn't know where I stand. Maybe I'm on his side, maybe not. But I can't hold him in baulk for ever. It may already be too late to stop him.'

'I'll get onto it straight away. What do you want me to do after I've written the report?'

Sun remained lost in reflection for a moment. Then he jerked his chin towards the jigsaw and, with a smile that Ming Rong could not analyse, said, 'Start building the mountain.'

TWENTY-TWO

———— ◇ ————

Chang Ping's declaration paralysed Diana. After several moments had gone by, he pointed at the rucksack. 'Do you have anything for my shoulder in there, please?'

'What?'

'My shoulder.'

With an effort she pulled herself together. 'Yes. And for your knees. But you have to stop talking nonsense and tell me everything.'

'I will.'

'Can you take off your shirt . . . that's right. Ugh! I think I can staunch the bleeding with a handkerchief . . . let me look at it.'

The wound was a deep gash some two inches long but not very deep. Diana rummaged around inside her rucksack and brought out a bottle of all-purpose disinfectant. 'This,' she said with a certain satisfaction, 'will hurt. Give a good scream; it helps.'

She smiled into his eyes, distracting him from what her hand was doing, and dabbed firmly. He shuddered; a moan forced its way through his lips, but he did not faint as she had half expected him to. When she'd finished disinfecting the gash in his shoulder she made him hold the handkerchief in place while she fixed it with two elasticated plasters. Then she turned her attention to his knees.

'Trousers.' And when he hesitated – 'Look, do you want me to help you or don't you?'

He eased them down. Diana inhaled sharply. It wasn't just the blood, though that looked bad enough; tiny pieces of glass were still adhering to the flakes of skin.

'Just as well I like to keep my eyebrows plucked,' she said brightly, fishing tweezers from her bag.

'What are you going to do?'

'Get the glass out. If I leave the pieces in, they'll fester. Have you had tetanus jabs?'

'I'm not sure. Maybe as a child . . .'

'We have to get you to a doctor. Soon.'

'No.'

'Chang Ping –'

'I said no. Not yet. It's too dangerous.'

Diana bent over his left knee, saying nothing.

She tried to approach her task like a proper nurse, treating his body as a lump of meat, but while she methodically worked her way left and right, up and down, across his knee, her eyes could not help straying. First to his feet . . . they were hard and bony, with thick toenails the colour and consistency of horn; but the pale yellow skin of the insteps was perfect. Its softness, when combined with the gentle colouring, reminded Diana irresistibly of a favourite labrador puppy. Poacher, that had been its name . . .

His legs were muscular; she noticed how whenever she jogged him, making the calf vibrate, no drooping pocket of flesh rippled along the underside. The thighs thickened very little as they rose towards his crotch, but the pigmentation darkened by several shades, even though it was obvious that his skin hardly ever saw the sun.

He was wearing thin blue underpants, and he kept his legs clenched together in an effort to prevent her seeing the place where they joined. The elastic was tight around the tops of his thighs, leaving indented rings that vanished and reappeared as she adjusted his position. Blue suited him, setting off his paleness.

Now she began on the right knee. Her concentration was slipping; the tweezers stabbed, prodding Chang Ping into a rictus of agony.

'Sorry.' She wiped a hand over her forehead, suddenly feeling desperately tired.

'What were you thinking about then?'

224

Diana looked full into his eyes, her lips creased into a wan smile. 'It doesn't matter.'

'I think you're being too shy. You were thinking about me, then, weren't you?'

'Chang Ping, *please!* Don't be an idiot, we've got enough problems without your playing the fool.' She tried to make herself sound responsible, full of practical common sense. 'If I think about you at all it's because I'm trying to sort out the lies you've told me.'

She unpacked a shirt, held it up to the light and sighed. 'Mat's. Oh well – at least it's clean.' She tried to tear it but the hem defeated her, so she felt around in the rucksack until she located her nail-scissors and soon had the shirt reduced to neat strips.

'One for each leg,' she said, coming back to where he was lying, now propped up on his elbows. She bandaged first his right leg, then his left.

'Comfortable?'

'Not too bad. Thank you, Diana.' When he smiled at her, she smiled back.

'One last thing . . .' Diana had left the knot of the bandage on his left knee loose. Now she undid the knot, crossed the ends, smiled one last time and pulled as hard as she could.

His scream sickened her, but she continued to tighten the ends as if she were throttling an assailant and her life depended on it. Chang Ping's back arched, his torso shot upright; one of his hands flailed at her face but she easily avoided him and when he raised the other hand from the floor he fell backward, bereft of support.

Chang Ping fainted. When he came to he was lying on his side. He tried to move his hands but they were trussed behind his back. His ankles had been knotted together. He couldn't move; and the more he struggled the more he suffered.

Diana sat down, folding her legs beneath her. 'So there you were, thinking I was a nice person. Sorry.'

'You are a good person.' He had recovered some of his composure and now was gazing back at her through calm, meditative eyes. He was not in the least frightened, she could see that. 'You're hard on yourself.'

'I'm going to be hard on you.'

He shook his head and smiled. 'No. You saved my life. Why did you do that, Diana?'

He'd managed to disconcert her, and that made Diana angry. Now that she had him bound and helpless at her feet, she told herself that she did not know why she had bothered to save him.

'No, it's my turn to ask the questions. Let's start with something easy: is there water near here?'

He continued to study her without speaking.

'All right.' She began to shoulder her rucksack. 'It seems we have to part. I hope whoever you were expecting will come and find you soon. Goodbye.'

She had not stood fully upright before he was calling to her. 'Diana, don't go.' He bit his lip. 'Please.'

She could see suffering in his eyes, but knew she must not relent. 'Water. Where is it?'

'There's a spring . . . behind the pavilion. Fifty yards up the hill . . . keep to the left.'

It was as he said: Diana found a thin cascade dribbling from a rock-fissure. She pushed aside a few ferns that were blocking the flow and splashed water over her face and hands before collecting some in a bottle. She did not hurry. By now the clouds had drifted away to reveal patches of blue sky. Steam was rising from the greenery that surrounded the pavilion and as Diana approached the courtyard a misty, golden ray of sun slanted through the trees to transform the little white house into something more magical than its dilapidated self. She felt like Snow White. The comparison amused her, but also cast a shadow. There was still a sorcerer to be dealt with.

She found Chang Ping lying in the same position, his forehead bathed in sweat. Diana knew he had been struggling. 'You'll only tire yourself. They're good knots. I was a Girl Guide. Have some water.' She held the bottle to his lips and he drank greedily.

'Good.' Diana sat down a few feet away from him, out of range of a sudden lunge. 'The truth, please.'

'I'll tell you everything. I should have realized you'd see through it. I told them you would.'

'I sometimes wonder why "they", as you put it, chose you for this in the first place. You're pretty inept at times.'

He smiled weakly. 'Thanks.'

'Think about it.' Diana surprised herself with her own calmness. 'First of all, you seemed to know the area so well; surprising, if you really had been exiled there as a punishment. There was that wonderful map you found in the middle of nowhere. Then there was the old man, the one in the lorry. We hadn't seen a single car all day and along he came, nice and pat.'

'Is that all?'

'No. For a long time I was too stupid to notice, though. Then I began to think. You told me about your parents. Very moving it was, too. But I don't think that's the Chinese way; at least, not when you meet someone, a foreigner, for the first time. And why were you at the shrine, anyhow? It seemed strange . . . until I began to think that maybe it was done to impress me, make me like you. Am I right?'

He nodded. 'Although I did tell you the truth about my parents.'

'That wasn't all, though. When I woke up, after that guy Wen knocked me out, you told me the villagers had shouted down the Red Guards. And I remember thinking: That's odd. Especially as the villagers didn't like my family much, or so Lingchu said.' She glanced at his face. 'Ah! So you didn't know that. Careless. They ought to have told you my aunt was unpopular in Chaiyang. Sloppy briefing.'

He was silent for several moments, while he thought things over. 'If you knew all that, why did you save my life, back there in Guiyang?'

'I've told you, it's my turn to ask the –'

'If you don't answer my question first, really look inside yourself and find the true answer, you won't understand what I'm going to say. Probably won't even hear it.'

227

She stared at him, trying to shake off the unease his words inspired. Although he had been wounded, and now was helpless, his inner strength seemed undiminished.

'I needed you if I was going to escape. You know the language, the country; I don't.'

'Even though you didn't trust me any more, after what happened in the truck?'

'I couldn't just leave you to that bunch of maniacs back there.'

His eyes did not blink. Diana knew he was waiting to hear the true answer. That irritated her further. But instead of attacking him, she became defensive. 'I mean, it was bad enough having to leave the driver . . .'

After a long pause he said evenly, 'Is that all?'

Diana had been toying with the water-bottle. Now she flung it from her as hard as she could. 'I'd started to like you.'

Chang Ping nodded as if satisfied. 'You want to know who I am, why I'm here.' He paused. 'It's bad.'

'Go on.'

'Can you untie me first?'

'No.'

'At least help me sit up. I can't speak to the floor.'

'I like it that way.'

Chang Ping sighed. 'A lot of what I told you was true. My parents . . . my mother never recovered. She was so brilliant, so dedicated. Now she's mad.'

Diana retrieved the water-bottle and took a drink.

'I wanted to get above things. I wanted to make sure I would be safe if the bad times came back. That's why I set out to be a model student. I wanted to join the Party. I was ideologically sound. So when they recruited me at university –'

'That's the second time you've mentioned "they". Who are they?'

He examined her through screwed up eyes, as if wondering whether to trust her. 'Have you ever heard of something called the Mahjong Brigade?'

Diana had the water-bottle halfway to her mouth. Now it jumped in her hands, spilling liquid down her front. 'I've heard of them.'

'Then you know what they do?'

'They're spies. The Central Control of Intelligence.'

'Seventh Department, yes.'

'And what will they do to you when they find you've betrayed them by talking to me?'

'I don't intend that they should find out.'

'What?'

'I don't want the old ways any more. I want to go to Hong Kong.'

She stared at him in surprise. 'You want to defect, is that what you're saying?'

He nodded. 'If there's going to be another revolution, as the Brigade think, my job won't be any real shield. I could still become a target, like anyone else.'

'You know where your own best interests lie, in other words. No wonder you fell in love with me.'

He was shocked; it showed in the way he looked at her.

'You want out, anyway,' she said hurriedly. 'So now I suppose you're going to help me get back to Hong Kong?'

'Yes.'

'And you expect me to *believe* that?'

'Why not?'

'Because that's exactly what you're supposed to have been doing until now – following Mahjong orders. What's so different – apart from the fact that you're tied up and I'm not?'

'You saw what happened at the last roadblock.'

'It looked pretty much the same as what happened in Chaiyang.'

'I wasn't beaten up in Chaiyang. I didn't have my knees cut about. No one tried to shoot me.'

'Oh, poor baby! Presumably they thought you weren't making much of an impression on me, time to hot up the act, was it?'

'You don't understand. There wasn't supposed to be a roadblock in Guiyang. We were meant to have a clear run, as far as Nanning. Those people we met were running wild, they weren't Mahjongs. I went up to them, thinking they were Controller Sun's men, and –'

'Sun Shanwang?'

'Yes. Do you know him?'

'I've met him.'

'*Met* him?' Chang Ping gazed at her in wonderment.

'Go on.'

'I . . . I went up to them and I told the agreed story, that you were my English teacher. That's when they turned on me. They accused me of being an intellectual.'

'Which you are. And the driver?'

Chang Ping's face tightened. 'He was one of ours. I think . . . we shan't be seeing him again.'

Diana held her head in her hands. 'This is all so . . . so wild! What really happened in Chaiyang?'

'It was play-acting. The Red Guards and so on. The idea was to make you trust me, rely on me. As you guessed.'

'It worked,' she said sadly.

'Yes. That's why earlier I asked you to examine yourself for the real reason you saved my life.'

'You think anything's changed?' She meant it to sound sarcastic, but the words came out wrong.

'It's obvious that many things have changed. The plan was for us to stop in Guiyang for the night. When you were asleep, I was supposed to come out here and meet my contacts. But now there's nothing, no one.'

'What was the *point* of all this?' Diana felt exasperated; she stood up and began to walk around, swinging her arms. 'Why on earth should Sun Shanwang waste all this time and energy on *me*?'

'Don't you know? Can't you see?'

Diana glared at him. 'If I could, I'd hardly ask you!'

'It's because of something you know. I was ordered to find out about it.'

'What on earth could I know that would interest Central Control of Intelligence?'

'Benevolence.'

Diana's eyes widened, her mouth fell open. 'Oh,' she said. 'That . . . '

'You do know, don't you?'

230

'No. I don't even know what the word means. Once I heard my father say . . .'

She tailed off, needing to keep silent while her brain moved across the dark, unattractive landscape opened up by his revelation. Someone had talked. It couldn't be her father or Mat and no one else knew that *she* knew . . .

'Who told you about Benevolence?' she asked.

'My director.'

'No, I don't mean that. What was the source in Hong Kong?'

'You know.'

She looked at him and saw that he wasn't arguing with her; he was hoping she would save him the embarrassment of spelling it out. In that moment she knew who it was, who it had to be.

'Qiu Qianwei.'

A shaft of rage ran up Diana's backbone, making her head spin with the intensity of it. 'I see.'

'Please can I get up now? I have cramps and they're very bad.'

Diana hesitated; but somehow she knew he wasn't going to hurt her, so she untied him and helped him sit up with his back to the wall.

'Let's go over it again, Chang Ping. You were planted on me. Told to make yourself attractive, be nice. Win my trust. Then you were meant to screw the secret of Benevolence out of me.'

'Yes.'

'Literally? Pillow talk?'

'I don't understand.'

She could see he didn't; he wasn't faking. 'Never mind. And now you say you're in love with me.'

He nodded shyly.

'Which is what you were supposed to say anyhow?'

'No. No one ever told me to say that.'

'So since when have you been in love with me? When did all this . . . blossom?'

He ignored the irony, or perhaps was simply unaware of it. 'I liked you at once. Then, when we left Chaiyang you were

231

strong. You didn't complain. I'd expected you to be different. I really started to like you very much.'

'You were pretty cool about it, then! You didn't give me much of a clue, you know.'

'That is my way. I'm sorry, but when you spoke about the abortion, then, that's when I –'

'I still think you're lying!' Her voice was uncharacteristically harsh. 'Especially when you say you want to defect. It just all seems so . . . so convenient, somehow.'

'I think I can make you believe me. I'm going to tell you something, a secret your father would spend a fortune to have. But I'm going to give it to you for nothing, and you can tell him. All I want you to remember is that I told you. Then your father will help me, I think.'

'Go on, then. Convince me.'

'The Mahjong Brigade has its own training institute. I was sent there for my final semester – a great honour. There was a mix-up. Because of it I learned something I shouldn't. About Hong Kong.'

'What kind of mix-up?'

'One afternoon we went swimming. Lots of different classes. Afterwards, in the changing-room, I put on the wrong jacket. It looked exactly like mine. We were late, I was frightened of missing class – they were strict, punishments were harsh. I didn't notice that the security clearance tag was different.'

He ran a hand across his forehead, as if straightening his memories. Diana noticed that he was sweating.

'There were hundreds of students there, the lecturers couldn't hope to know us all. They just looked at the tags. Imagine how distinctive your denim jacket makes you.' He pointed at it. 'With "I love my orphans" on the back, that big red heart . . . if a friend saw that, he wouldn't even have to look at your face, he'd know it was you.'

'I suppose it's possible.'

'That's what happened. I was racing along the corridor when an officer appeared in a doorway and shouted at me. He was furious. Why was I late, and so on. He hauled me inside a lecture-room. The lights were already out for a slide show;

if there'd been proper lighting, maybe this wouldn't have happened. Then it started.'

'What started?'

'The lecture. On the future of Hong Kong.' Chang Ping swallowed and drew a deep breath. 'On the *real* plans for Hong Kong, after repossession in 1997.'

Suddenly Diana was all attention. 'They actually told students that?'

'This class consisted of some very unusual students. They were to be infiltrated into Hong Kong, to prepare.'

'And you were mistaken for one of them?'

'Yes. I was scared.'

'Why?'

'I thought that if the authorities realized I knew something as important as that, when I shouldn't, they'd take steps to ensure that the information didn't spread any further.'

'You mean . . . what exactly do you mean? That they would . . . *kill* you?'

'I don't know. I really don't know. Afterwards I found the other student, the one whose jacket I'd taken. He was scared, too. When he found his jacket was missing, he hid, hoping it would turn up. We discussed what was best. We decided to keep quiet. I'm glad we did. The things they told us in that lecture . . .'

'What things?'

'Concentration camps. Nuclear missile silos. Plans for developing it into the biggest naval base we have. Three divisions of troops permanently stationed there. Martial law. Curfew.'

'Now I know you're lying. Beijing's always said there won't be any changes in Hong Kong, not for fifty years at least.'

'Do you believe them?'

Diana had always taken the official statements at face value. But now she wasn't sure; and it irked her that the first seed of genuine doubt should have been planted by Chang Ping.

'The naval base . . .' she said slowly. 'So they'll take over HMS *Dartmouth* . . .'

'HMS *Tamar*.' His lips tightened. 'Please feel free to question me. Try to trap me, if you want.'

'You're lying.'

She waited for a reaction but none came. Chang Ping stared down between his legs, no longer caring if she believed him or not. 'All right,' he said wearily. 'You can turn me in. Find a policeman. Tell him who I am, what I told you.'

'I wouldn't do that.'

'Why not, if you think I'm lying?'

'Because it's a mean thing to do,' she said hotly. The fervour of her reaction underlined what she already knew: he sounded convincing. He was getting through to her. But . . .

Doubt, doubt, doubt. Where was the rock of certainty she craved?

Diana's gaze strayed to his knees. He looked a sorry sight sitting there with bloodstained strips of her brother's shirt around his legs and his trousers concertinaed over his ankles. He didn't appear particularly threatening, or untruthful, or violent; just rather sad. A touch pathetic.

'If *you* want to get to Hong Kong . . . and *I* want to get to Hong Kong . . .'

'Yes?' He looked up at her hopefully.

'Perhaps we could trade. If you'll help me here, in China, I'll do what I can for you when we arrive. How's that?'

'It's fine. You *do* trust me, then!'

Diana did not answer him directly. 'I think we should both sleep now,' she said. 'You're not fit to move yet. It's daylight, and that's dangerous for us. There isn't any food. We should rest until nightfall. Then we can decide what to do next. I've got to think. I'll keep watch, if you like.'

Chang Ping wanted to protest, but he was too exhausted. For a while he watched through half-closed eyes, as if trying to work out what she was thinking; but soon he slid down to the floor, adjusting his trousers first, and turned his back on her. Before long his breathing had become loud and regular. She waited another ten minutes to make sure he wasn't shamming before she got up, absolutely silently, shouldered her rucksack and slipped out of the pavilion.

Diana took pleasure in the way puffy clouds scudded across the face of the sun, translating their antics into playful shadows on the path in front of her. It was like emerging from prison; with every step she took the air seemed fresher, cleaner, the way ahead less fraught with difficulty than she had supposed.

She felt guilty about leaving Chang Ping, because he'd been wounded and if Red Guards found him he'd be defenceless, but Diana knew she couldn't have helped him in a fight, and anyway, his chances of escape must improve without her. She looked like a foreigner, that was the problem; she'd only hold him back. Or so she rationalized it to herself.

She knew she was vulnerable, without a man to keep her company; but there were two sides to that, as well. She could not bring herself to trust Chang Ping again. Which was best — to shelter with someone you didn't trust, or strike out on your own? It was a dilemma. Diana knew that whatever she did would probably be wrong. All that mattered was making a decision, then keeping to it, acting on it.

Suppose he did love her? Really love her . . . ?

His words kept echoing in the back of Diana's head; and for some strange reason they moved her. He'd not had a very happy life. She felt sorry for him, in a way. And he was handsome, more than handsome. He was beautiful . . .

She'd never believed in love at first sight. But some people did.

Could a Chinese love a westerner? Why not? And if that was right, presumably a European girl could fall in love with a Chinese . . .

He needs me. I'm the only chance he has, or is likely to have, of getting out . . . I needed him, at first. But now it's the other way around. And I'm running away . . .

Stop it! This is how they want you to think. Every move was planned, right from the beginning. All part of the trap . . .

Engrossed in her thoughts, Diana turned a bend in the path and witnessed the rape.

Luckily she had some prior warning; without it, she might have suffered the same fate. She'd been half-consciously aware of raised voices. Just before she rounded the turning, which would have brought her into full view, she realized the significance of what she could hear and came to a halt. A large eucalyptus tree blocked her view of the wooded slope below the path. Now she crept close to its bole and peered around it, glad of the cover afforded by the tree's thick screen of leaves.

Three people were struggling some fifty paces down the bank. A few saplings and some scrub stood between Diana and the protagonists, but she had no difficulty in seeing all that happened.

There were two men and one woman. The woman was young, almost certainly still in her teens: her long black hair was braided into two plaits. She wore a pink apron, from which Diana guessed she worked at the hotel. The men seemed slightly older. Their clothes were western: faded blue jeans, T-shirts; and one of them wore a black leather jacket. The other man had long, unkempt hair and a moustache, with a few hairs at the chin in place of a proper beard.

As Diana focused on the scene below, the man in the leather jacket pushed the girl over and threw himself on top of her. She continued to pummel him with her fists; then she must have changed tactics, because suddenly he howled and Diana could see a streak of blood on his cheek. He raised a clenched fist and brought it down hard on her face.

The girl did not struggle so violently after that. Her body continued to move, but feebly, as if she had reached the end of her strength. The man raised himself to a kneeling position and threw off his jacket. Diana had a glimpse of his bare legs; then the other man came between her and the appalling tableau of violence below.

This second brute knelt at the girl's head and began to rip up her dress. Rags and tatters of cloth went flying. Then he lowered his body across the girl's face, enabling Diana to see that the first attacker was already at work, thrusting into the girl with vicious pumps of his thighs, each accompanied by a loud grunt.

He slowed a little and raised his head, eyes closed, as if to savour the moment of orgasm. Then he jumped up quickly and turned away, pulling at his trousers, while the second man hurried around to take his place. He finished very fast and appeared discontented about something, for as he rose he spat at the girl.

What happened next was over and done with so quickly that Diana could scarcely credit what she'd seen.

The girl suddenly came back to life. She rolled over and drew something that glittered from the remains of her apron. Next instant she was up and leaping towards the mustachioed man, one hand held high. He must have heard her coming, for he started to turn, but the force of her assault overwhelmed him. Blood spurted from his neck in a stream and he fell backward. The girl tumbled on top of him. The other man ran off down the hill and was almost immediately lost from Diana's sight.

The victim managed to stand up. She was crying. Suddenly, however, she stopped wailing and allowed her hands to fall listlessly to the sides of her naked body. Then she pounced on the knife, still sticking out of the dead man's neck, and raised it in both hands.

Diana, realizing what she was about to do, shrieked 'Stop!' But the girl dug the knife down in a long sickle-sweep, bending double as it entered her abdomen, and tumbled over.

Diana could hear the girl groaning. All the strength went out of her legs. She sank to the ground, where she knelt, watching helplessly. She knew she ought to try to do something. But she could not. She was too afraid.

After a while the girl's groans entered into a tortured rhythm: each breath a low shriek, then a pause, then a rattle as the air escaped . . . over and over again. And always that dreadful movement of the body, the dog run over in the road but not quite finished off . . . Diana forced herself to stand up. She went down the hill very slowly, and part of her acknowledged she was hoping the girl would die before she reached her.

She had her wish. When Diana was within a few feet of the human wreckage that, she now saw, had once been an exceptionally pretty person, the girl's right hand stretched out in a muscular spasm, she lifted her chin, the hand formed itself into a claw . . . a final rattle that sent a mixture of blood and sputum oozing down the side of her mouth signalled the end. The head fell forward, the hand slowly unclenched.

Suddenly Diana realized that the wood was quiet – deathly quiet, how vivid the phrase seemed! An oppressive silence hemmed her in on every side. The very trees seemed to be listening.

She turned and fled back up the hill. She did not expect to get as far as the pavilion. She knew that any second now a man would stand out in her path, coming from behind a tree, and then she would be dead, like the girl who lay on the slope with a knife in her belly. And that was how it happened. She was sprinting, the landscape had become a blur, and there he was, just as she'd feared, standing in front of her with arms outstretched.

She fought, using her fists and forearms, kicking, biting his hands, but all the while tears poured down her cheeks, for she knew it was helpless, you couldn't fight animals like that, they were invincible.

If I had a knife I'd use it.

But she did not have a knife.

TWENTY-THREE

◇

Colonel Fomenko disliked his Taipei hotel, although he could not exactly say why. Perhaps it was the long, underlit corridors and the silence within them, the sense of emptiness; as if he were the only guest staying in this high, dark pile beside the river.

The boy took him and his bag to a cramped suite and left in too much of a hurry to collect a tip, as if even he had his suspicions about this place. Fomenko looked around the living-room with mixed feelings. It was pleasant to be in a foreign country, on generous expenses; but something told him that it would be wise to go back to Moscow at the earliest opportunity.

He opened the connecting door to the bedroom. In the dim light he could see just enough to make him more uneasy: the oval bed was draped in what looked like satin, and there appeared to be a superfluity of mirrors.

Fomenko switched on the bedroom light.

For a second he did not register what the lump in the bed actually meant. Then his reflection in the glass opposite seemed to ripple up and down. He swallowed, and took out a handkerchief, which he used to wipe his palms. Two minutes later he was on the eleventh floor, being admitted to another suite of rooms, much more generously endowed than his own. Later he was to have no recollection of how he got there. Leong, who opened the door, saw the Russian's white face, noticed how his handkerchief had been mangled by the convulsive movements of his hands, and shrugged. 'You're late.'

Alexander Cumnor did not look up from the desk where he

was initialling alterations to a document. 'Come in, Fomenko.'

'There is . . . there's a body in my bed.'··

'Yes.' Cumnor inscribed his initials, turned a page, moved on.

'You knew!' ·

'Yes.'

'But . . . how?'

'Because I own this hotel, I know what goes on here.' Cumnor raised his eyes for the first time. There was no emotion in them. 'Everything.'

Leong brought a chair and guided Fomenko into it. The Russian sat down. He was trembling. Cumnor reached the foot of the page, appended his full signature, and pushed the document away.

'You were followed from the airport by a member of Taiwan Garrison Command's National Security Bureau. We have disposed of him. We resent having to do that, Fomenko. It sours relations between ourselves and the Taiwanese government. Krubykov ought to have used someone who knows how to evade these difficulties. He will be invoiced for the cost of setting matters straight; tell him that.'

The Colonel stared speechlessly as Cummor picked up a telephone and dialled a number. He listened for a moment, then replaced the receiver without speaking.

'I'm told that you brought the money, and that the amount is correct.'

With a start, Fomenko remembered leaving his case in the suite downstairs. Krubykov had ordered him never to let it out of his sight. 'I –'

'You are going to depart very soon, although not, I'm afraid, in the first class comfort that brought you here. We must transact business quickly tonight. There will be nothing written down.' He glanced at the watch on his outer sleeve. 'So listen carefully.'

Fomenko made an effort to straighten up and pay attention.

'Krubykov wanted a name. The name is Lo Bing, have you got that? Brigadier-General Lo Bing.'

Fomenko nodded.

'Lo Bing can control large sections of the Chinese military. He will probably emerge as the new leader. Do you understand?'

'Yes.'

'He will make his move as soon as the Chairman's death has been officially confirmed. My information is that he is already dead, but that that fact is being kept secret while those with most to lose from his passing struggle to preserve power. In my view, they will not succeed.'

Fomenko gaped at him. 'How do you know all this?'

'That is not Krubykov's concern. It certainly is not yours.'

'But . . . when you approached us, it was merely about the Benevolence project. Getting money out of Hong Kong . . .'

'The scope of my inquiry has broadened considerably. In order to ensure my own position, I have had to be very thorough. I don't think you understand the real nature of my business.'

Fomenko, eager to please, shook his head.

'I buy and sell information, on a grand scale. I am an information broker, just as other men are stockbrokers, or powerbrokers. Like a stockbroker, I must sometimes purchase a product far ahead, in the hope that one day it may be worth something. In this case, Lo Bing, whom I have been targetting for years. And, again like a stockbroker, I must know where – and when – to place the commodity. It's no good just buying knowledge, unless you have a prospective buyer in mind. See?'

'Yes.'

'In this case, the placing was less of a headache than usual. Can you guess why? It's because Lo Bing is interested in opening discussions with the Soviet Union, once he has the power to do so, and he knows that I am uniquely placed to oil the wheels.'

Fomenko's eyes opened wide. 'Discussions . . . what about?'

'That will become clear when the necessary introductions have been made.'

'And you will act as go-between?'

'I'm prepared to act as mediator. For a fee.'

241

'How much?'

'Three million Swiss francs.'

'I'll have to –'

'It is not negotiable.'

Fomenko felt a little of his habitual confidence return. Urbane negotiation was one of his fortes. 'I'm afraid it will have to become negotiable, Mr Cumnor. We don't really need you. If Lo Bing becomes China's leader, we can contact him by telex.' Fomenko's smile was bland, his tone disdainful. He was actually starting to enjoy himself. 'So unless you –'

'You will find that Lo Bing supports my position on this.'

'Oh? A Chinese general . . . brigadier-general did you say? Hardly a prime threat to the Soviet Union!'

Cumnor smiled thinly. 'Think again. China presents herself to the world as a scientific backwater. Nothing could be further from the truth. The South-East Asian communications satellite was shot down by Lo Bing's people.' He paused. 'Would you perhaps describe that as a threat?'

Fomenko leaned forward in his excitement. 'Can you prove this?'

'That is hardly my business. Krubykov knows exactly what he's paid for: accurate advance information concerning what will happen when the Chairman finally dies. I have nothing else to do with it. But there is one more thing he should know: Lo Bing himself asked me to tell you about the satellite. As a gesture' – again that thin smile – 'of good faith.'

Fomenko's shallow reservoir of confidence was once again exhausted. He used the soiled handkerchief to wipe his brow. 'We're hardly likely to credit such a . . . a bizarre story without proof. You must see that.'

'Again, I feel you do not understand the position. There is a corpse in your hotel room. An employee of the Taiwanese government. My staff here see nothing, say nothing.' Cumnor reached for the telephone. 'This line is as secure as anything can be, in Taiwan. Mr Leong will remind you of Krubykov's home telephone number, should you have forgotten.' He handed the receiver to Fomenko, who took it as if hypnotized.

Cumnor drew another set of papers towards him. 'Remember,' he said as he uncapped his fountain pen, 'things will start to happen the moment the Chairman's death has been confirmed. Speed would be an advantage to someone in your position, Fomenko.'

TWENTY-FOUR

◇

At about the same time as Colonel Fomenko was coming to
grief in Taipei, a police patrol car began to cruise along the
western perimeter of Canton airport's outer security fence.

Sangster sat in the back seat alongside Proshin. 'Pete's
brother has pretty good contacts for a cab driver,' he com-
mented drily.

'Even down to our present chauffeur, yes. An excellent *cai
gou yuan*, a fixer. But there are limits. This man can take us as
far as the depot; no further.'

'It's enough.'

'I hope I'm forgiven.'

'It was one hell of a shock. When I looked out of that
window last night and saw the light flashing –'

'You flipped. Yes. I would in your place, I'm sure. But
without this subterfuge, we wouldn't have got within a mile
of Canton airport tonight. Now, are you sure you've mastered
the new arrangements?'

'Yes.'

'Remember the mask . . .'

The two westerners wore their white overalls and round hats
of the kind used by catering staff the world over. On the left
breast of each pair of overalls was a two by half-inch badge
bearing the logo of AMKCF; beneath that hung an identity-
card. Now each man pulled on his *koujiao*. Only a thin strip
was left between the bottom of the surgical-style cap and the
top of the mask.

There was a final adjustment to be made. Proshin took a
pair of handcuffs from his pocket and snapped one bracelet

over his own wrist before performing a similar service for Sangster.

The car halted at a checkpoint and its driver, a uniformed member of the People's Armed Police Force, who was also wearing his *koujiao*, wound down the window. At the same time, Proshin and Sangster sat well back in the seat, keeping their faces in shadow. Two guards stepped forward, one on each side of the car. To Sangster, who was listening intently, it seemed plain that the presence of civilians in the police vehicle was causing concern. The driver pushed a sheet of paper through the window and casually lit a cigarette while the guard on his side read it.

The minutes began to pass. Sangster's right leg was trembling slightly. He forced himself to stare down at his lap, as if ashamed of his supposed plight as a prisoner. A movement caught his eye. Proshin's hand, the fettered one, was spasmodically forming a fist and unclenching. With every third clench or so the metal chain linking the bracelets tinkled. Sangster ground his own hand on the upholstery, jerking the Russian into stillness.

The first guard pushed the paper back through the window and began a discussion with the driver. He wasn't accepting the situation.

Sangster felt a bead of sweat burst from under his cap and trickle down his face. He was hot enough to catch fire. His ears contained so much burning blood that they smarted.

The second guard had been slowly walking around the car. Now he bent down to examine the two 'prisoners' in the back seat. Sangster stiffened. Did he have a torch? *Did he?*

The Chinese put his hand on his belt, as if searching for something there. *Was it a torch? Don't let it be a torch, please God, don't . . .*

The attitude of the police driver hardened. He began to swear at the guard interrogating him, although in a genial kind of way – one law-enforcement officer to another. Sangster kept his head down, hoping the man outside would not notice the sweat that now poured down his face into the mask. Suddenly his attention was caught by something on the seat

245

beside him. For a moment he could not believe what he was looking at. He refused to accept that anyone might be that stupid.

Proshin was still wearing his signet ring on the little finger of the hand that had been manacled.

It was no ordinary ring: a great, green pigeon's egg of jade set in white gold that glittered in the light refracted from the overhead floods: enough, more than enough, to attract the greedy attention of the guards. If they saw it.

But they hadn't seen it yet.

Sangster shifted his thigh, ever so slowly, towards the Russian's left hand. Nearly . . . He shifted his thigh again and this time Proshin instinctively moved his own leg away.

The second guard, the one standing outside the rear door, reached out for the handle and tried to open it. Locked.

Sangster jerked his head around to stare at him, simultaneously grabbing Proshin's hand in such a way as to cover the tell-tale ring. At the same moment the driver raised his voice, had the last word, engaged gear and moved off. The second guard jumped back. Sangster heard him shout, but the car did not stop.

The two men tore the masks from their faces with their free hands and gasped for breath. 'Are they following us?' Sangster rapped in Cantonese as he removed the handcuffs.

'No,' the driver replied. 'But I can see' – he frowned at his mirror – 'I can see one of them going into the control-room. He'll call headquarters.'

'What will happen?'

'Nothing, yet. On a normal day, airport security would probably ignore the whole incident. But on a normal day, we would not have been stopped.'

'Is it a problem for you?'

The driver laughed. 'I shall say I was overcome by superior force.' He glanced again in his mirror, only this time he was studying the car's occupants. 'Just don't get caught, eh?'

Up to this point they had been driving along the inside of the perimeter fence, approximately parallel with Baiyun Airport's north-east south-west runway. Ahead of them they could see the low profiles of cargo and maintenance buildings, brightly illuminated by blue, white and orange lights. On top of one such building the letters AMKCF stood out boldly in red fluorescence against the darkness. 'There she is,' the Russian muttered.

Outside the depot a number of planes were parked on the apron. Sangster leaned forward. They were now within three hundred metres of their target. On the left, the line of buildings ranged along the inside of the fence; to the right of that, the road they were following; and to the right of that, between their car and the runway, aircraft. One of them was a Boeing 747-400, parked nose inward.

'Slow,' he breathed. 'Nice and slow.'

Crackling from the radio. The driver snatched the microphone. Reception was poor but Sangster managed to get the gist of it. 'They're coming out?'

'Yes. Twenty containers.' The policeman was no longer in a laughing mood; he faltered over a couple of words, as if his mouth was dry. 'Are you ready?'

'Get rid of that ring,' Sangster hissed to his companion. Proshin hastily pulled it off his finger and stuffed it into a pocket. 'Sorry,' he muttered.

'Caps.'

Both men removed their headgear.

'Masks.' The *koujiao* were replaced.

Fifty metres ahead of the police car, a tractor emerged from the cargo depot and swung across their path, pulling a line of containers. The driver slowed to five miles an hour. Sangster studied the panorama ahead through narrowed eyes, calculating distances. Another five seconds and they would have reached the outer edge of the light cast from the depot . . .

'Window?'

'Down. Yours?'

'Down.'

'Three . . . two . . . one . . . *Go!*'

Both men leapt from the car, unzipped their white overalls and stripped out of them. They bundled them up and ran after the car, throwing their discarded clothing in through the open rear windows. The driver accelerated through the cargo area, then made a sharp right that would take him across the north-east end of the runway and so to the passenger terminal, near where the police had their headquarters.

Sangster and Proshin were now revealed as wearing dark brown AMKCF overalls. The gate-guards would have raised the alarm for two men in white. Not a great device; but when you were buying minutes, seconds, the options were limited.

They tucked themselves behind the row of slow-moving containers and in that way covered the hundred or so metres that separated them from the Boeing.

As Sangster pulled on a pair of thick gauntlets, he began to count, making himself take it nice and slow. One, two, three. A quarter of the way there. On his left, the containers: high, wide, affording total concealment from anyone on the other side. To his right, a huge expanse of apron, several vehicles moving to and fro between rows of green lights embedded in the concrete − a push-back tractor, fork-lift truck, two unmarked cars. No one's looking your way, he told himself, over and over again. Even if they were, they couldn't see one damn thing. But he still wished to God it would rain. The night was fine, the sky clear; the only thing he had to be thankful for was the absence of a moon.

Halfway there now.

Proshin walked a few steps ahead of him and to his right. Nice and casual. *Good.* Colleagues. Friends, maybe. Two guys on shift together, same locker room, same bus to work, same job. Innocent.

The Boeing loomed up to fill his vision. Sangster realized with a start that he had never seen one of these planes from ground level; they were enormous. The cockpit was as high as the attic of a three-storey house. And that's where he and Proshin would have to go. Up.

The tractor driver swung out in a broad arc to come around beside the plane. Two handlers were at work sorting contoured LD3 containers before raising them on the scissor platform to the rear cargo door.

Before leaving, Proshin and Sangster had submitted their

Cantonese to Pete's judgement; he had awarded Proshin the palm. So it was the Russian who led the way over to the handlers and said, 'Give us a lift, will you?'

'Who the hell are you?'

'Flight maintenance. The last crew reported a reversed doppler loop on the Wuzhou/38 NDB but we've checked with Wuzhou and they say no, so it has to be the inflight DC unless of course –'

'Okay, okay. Just hurry up and buzz off out of it.'

'What's a reversed doppler loop, for Christ's sake?' Sangster asked as they rode up on the platform. Proshin shrugged. 'I haven't a clue. But neither have they.'

The two men came out onto the pallet opposite bay 129. The handlers there showed none of the interest displayed by their colleagues on the ground; indeed, one of them pushed Proshin aside in his haste to get at the next container. The upper deck cargo bay was already about one quarter full. Sangster tucked his gauntlets into his belt, then pulled a torch from his pocket and went to the back of the plane, picking his way with care over the metal rails and rollers.

He embarked on a studious examination of the wiring that ran the length of the hull at shoulder-height. 'This plane's hot,' he murmured to Proshin in Cantonese.

'Hot?'

Sangster pulled the torch-switch down a further notch and the Russian heard a low crackle. 'Reading?'

Sangster slid open the end of the torch to reveal a luminous liquid crystal display screen. Proshin gasped in dismay. 'That's a lot of roentgens.'

'Yes.'

Sangster restored the torch to its normal function and briefly consulted his watch. 'We have less than twenty minutes. Move.'

They came back down the starboard side of the plane, ostentatiously examining wires as they went. When they were opposite bay 140 Sangster's flashlight stopped moving. Next second he'd extinguished it.

'What?' Proshin murmured.

Sangster did not answer at once. He was assessing the distance between them and the loaders. A pallet came trundling down and he stepped out of its path. When the pallet came to rest he ducked down behind it, gesturing to Proshin to follow. 'Look up,' he whispered.

He directed a mini-second of light towards the aircraft's ceiling. 'What *is* that?' Proshin breathed.

'Hatch. A round hatch cut in the hull.' Sangster adjusted the torch. Crackling exploded in his hand and he jabbed the switch back so hard that he tore the skin of his thumb. 'Something went wrong here. An accident . . .'

'So you accept the Soviet position?' In his excitement Proshin allowed his voice to rise, and although he was speaking Cantonese, the language of the mission, Sangster angrily signed him to be quiet.

'Let's say my mind isn't as closed as it was. But where in hell's the rest of the equipment? If you're right, they must have taken it out.'

'We're not through yet. Let's move.'

'I need a picture.' Sangster pulled a miniaturized infra-red camera from inside his overalls and quickly snapped the peculiar round hatch. 'Okay.'

The two men rose. As they did so, something scrunched quietly beneath Sangster's feet. He knelt down again and felt gingerly around on the floor.

'What –'

'Mirror. Bits of broken mirror.'

The two men stared at each other. Both knew that one of the major components required for any beam-weapon was an optically perfect mirror. Sangster licked his lips. 'Come on.'

He stood up and risked a peek around the corner of the container that sheltered them. He found himself staring straight into the eyes of one of the two handlers on the upper deck. Sangster stood perfectly still. The light was poor, the distance great . . . the Chinese frowned, then smiled half-heartedly, the kind of Esperanto smile that says 'Okay, mate?' or, 'Howr'ya doin' pal?', meaningless . . .

Sangster nodded and smiled back. Of course the man

couldn't see him smile behind his mask, but perhaps he'd notice how his cheeks moved or his eyes narrowed. Anyway, the Chinese went back to what he'd been doing.

'Forward,' Sangster murmured.

They continued down the hull, ostensibly still looking at wires. Their pace quickened a little as they passed the loading door, but neither of the two handlers bothered to glance in their direction. Ahead of the two westerners stretched the bulk of the aircraft's interior. There was nothing unusual about any of it, as a two minute walk the length of the plane soon revealed.

'What's behind the forward bulkhead?' Sangster muttered. 'Staircase to the cockpit, right?'

'Right.'

'Take a look.'

While Sangster examined a light-fitting, Proshin softly tried the door. It opened to reveal a short narrow passage, bounded to left and right by the forward cargo doors. Immediately ahead of him was a steel ladder clamped to the wall; above was a cavity, evidently the beginning of the flight deck; below . . .

Sangster felt his arm tugged half out of his socket. 'What the –'

'Ssh! This way.'

Sangster scanned the rear of the plane. Activity continued unabated. By now there were so many containers in place that even if anyone had shown curiosity about the two unexpected visitors he would not easily have been able to see them. But no one was curious. The handlers just wanted to finish the job and clock off.

Sangster looked through the door. 'What? I don't see –'

'The ladder leads *down* as well as up. We can get to the lower cargo deck from inside.'

'And they're not loading to the lower deck.'

'Exactly! Why?'

'Could be a million reasons.'

'Or just one. Come!'

They descended the ladder by sliding down its rails, their feet not touching the rungs. The lower deck was in darkness save for small violet emergency lights set into the side of the hull at regular intervals. Sangster flicked on his torch.

'Nothing. Not a darned thing.'

'We'll go aft. Your torch is useless.'

But before they had gone more than halfway down the aircraft's interior they were faced with an obstruction. Sangster directed his torch from floor to ceiling. 'Holy mother of God,' he breathed. 'What is that thing?'

'Serious question?'

'Of course.'

'Then I'd say it bears a marked resemblance to the magneto-hydro-dynamics generator that the Kirtland Weapons Laboratory installed in their converted NKC-135 in 1982 when they wanted to test their airborne laser.'

'Or the one you have in bunker three-slash-A at Semipalatinsk, tied up to the 500 KV switch ring?'

'You're very quick, Mr Sangster, but as we have less than seven minutes left I need an answer. Who shot down the comm sat?'

The American said nothing. Instead he reached for the camera and took a number of shots from various angles, shouldering Proshin out of the way in order to get a clear field.

'No time for gestures.' The Russian's voice was hoarse with urgency. '*Who?*'

'I don't know.'

'*Gene!* What more do you *want?*'

'I don't know. It . . . it's possible.'

Proshin threw up his hands. 'What else do you need to see? What else can I possibly show you in' – he shot out his wrist – 'five minutes?'

'There's no proof,' Sangster said softly. Then he turned to look Proshin squarely in the eye and his gaze suddenly focused. 'Don't you see that? It's incapable of proof. They could have done it; you could have done it.'

'And so could you! So could the French, the Germans, the ancient Greeks.'

'Or the Chinese! That's what I'm *saying*. Why in hell don't

252

you listen?' Sangster fought to master himself. 'They *could* have done it!'

Proshin stared at him with hostility for a few seconds longer. He was about to speak again when suddenly they heard rapid steps overhead and both men looked up.

'Someone coming forward.'

'*Out!*'

Sangster sprang for the ladder, Proshin one rung behind him. As the American emerged from the lower cargo bay he twisted around to find that the first man Proshin had spoken to, the ground-handler, was bending down, hands on knees, towards him.

'You!' the man said in rough Cantonese. 'Who the fuck are you?'

'Maintenance.'

'But these two say they're maintenance!'

Sangster scrambled out and made a great show of dusting down his trousers for long enough to allow Proshin to join him. Furtive glances from under his eyelashes showed him the bad news. All four cargo-handlers were standing in a semi-circle, barring their exit. Behind them were two other men, newcomers, whose overalls matched the ones Sangster and Proshin were wearing.

'What *is* this?' Proshin sounded genuinely angry.

'They say they're maintenance and you're not supposed to be here. They say all that stuff you gave me was shit. Get those masks off. I'm fed up with not being able to see you good and proper.'

Odds of six to two. Six very tough guys, if appearances were anything to go by. So it proved: when neither Proshin nor Sangster moved to obey at once, the surly ground-handler lunged forward in an attempt to snatch the mask from the face nearest him. Proshin jumped back. 'Hands off, shit face! Go fuck your mother.'

The famous Cantonese oath had its usual effect. All six regular AMKCF employees advanced threateningly. One of the genuine maintenance team had been carrying a tool box. Now he dropped it with a clatter and started to roll up his sleeves. At the same time, Sangster and Proshin began to pull on their gauntlets.

Then the 'boss', as Sangster had come to consider the surly man, unexpectedly extended his arm to stop his colleagues. 'No. Hang on.'

He moved forward, piggy eyes creased into the pasty flesh of his face. Something else was clearly troubling him. Sangster had no doubt what it was.

'These two . . .' The man spoke slowly, as if he had trouble crediting the evidence of his own eyes. 'They're not Chinese. They're . . . they're foreign devils! Here you, Ling-chow, you bugger off and get the cops, we'll keep these two busy.'

It was then that the boss made his one mistake.

Ling-chow backed away, keeping his eyes, now wide with astonishment, on the two intruders. The man who had given the orders looked around to see whether he'd been obeyed and must have thought of something else, for he began to speak. Hearing his voice, all the other Chinese momentarily turned their eyes towards him. And away from Proshin.

The Russian dipped his right hand into the thigh pocket of his overalls and pulled out a red tube as a gunslinger might draw: in a smooth, seamless movement. The tube was about the size of a small domestic aerosol, but he acted so fast that none of the Chinese had a chance to see it.

Sangster took a deep breath and pushed the *koujiao* flat against his face, closing his eyes. Proshin held the tube as far in front of him as he could reach, secured his mask with his free hand, closed his eyes and pressed a rubber button set flush with the top of the tube.

A spray of yellow liquid jetted out and instantly vaporized. The six AMKCF men began to cough. Their eyes streamed, they doubled up, already losing the battle to expel mucus from their lungs. As visions blurred and airways constricted, the first intimations of what was happening came home to them and they redoubled their struggles, but only succeeded in exhausting their bodies' resources that much sooner.

The boss was the first to go into convulsions. His eyes rolled upward into his skull, leaving only the whites visible; his tongue came out, he rolled over on the floor kicking and thrashing wildly with his arms. He wanted to scream, but nothing came out of his mouth except strangulated gasps. Suddenly all his limbs simultaneously gave way to a last spasm, he choked out some foul liquid and then he died. One by one his companions followed him, until no one was left alive on the Boeing except Proshin and Sangster. Less than ten seconds had elapsed since the Russian drew out the tube and pointed it at the group of men.

'What was it?' asked Sangster as they sprinted for the door. 'Soman nerve gas?'

'Sort of. But quicker, less dangerous to the user.'

'Jesus!'

'Jesus is right.' Proshin had reached the cargo door a short head in front of Sangster. 'Look!'

As the American came level with him, he saw three police cars racing across the tarmac. The first screeched to a halt at the side of the loading platform. Two men leapt out of the back seat toting Type-64 sub-machineguns. The leader dropped to one knee beside the platform and covered the other while he raced for the control-box.

'So those gate-guards weren't fooled . . . How long do we have to the rendezvous?' Sangster's voice was brisk.

'Three and three quarter minutes.'

'Then I would say we had a problem.'

Simultaneously with the second car careering to a halt beneath the plane, a volley of bullets clipped the metal of the Boeing's hull six inches from Proshin's ear.

TWENTY-FIVE

◇

The man who stepped out into Diana's path after the rape was Chang Ping. He had to slap her before she came to her senses. After that he listened gravely while she gabbled out what had happened. He squatted beside her and gently began to stroke her hair. It was very soothing. Then he knelt down and cradled her in his arms. She made not even token resistance, just keeled over sideways until her head was resting in his lap and her knees could curl up as far as her chest. When at last she opened her eyes it was to find him gazing down on her with the most enticing mixture of tenderness and exhilaration she had ever seen on a man's face.

'You're alive,' she said.

'Of course.'

'No. I didn't mean it literally.'

His face changed, became serious. 'The authorities have lost control now. You can travel without me if you want. But I hope we can stay together. I will take you to Hong Kong, if I can.'

'What are we going to do?'

'Is that a real "we", or a pretend one like last time, before you ran out on me?'

'It's real. I still don't know whether to believe you or not. I don't want to stay with you . . . sorry. But I'm not going to make it by myself.'

His face showed he was pleased by her decision, disappointed at her reasoning. 'Well then . . . we'll wait until nightfall. I want to take a look at that hotel. Maybe we can find some food there. We've still got a long way to go.'

'What kind of "we" was that?'

'A real one. And I don't just mean the journey across China.'

'No.' Diana sighed. 'I know you don't.'

'But now we are going to rest.'

She fell asleep quickly, drugged by her brain's efforts to obliterate all that she had seen. It was dusk when Chang Ping shook her into wakefulness. He gave her some water and waited patiently until she was once more alert.

'Diana, I've been thinking. Controller Sun will be wondering what has happened. He'll send people after us.'

'You make it sound so hopeless.'

'Not hopeless – but we must change the plan. I was supposed to take you to Nanning. Now I think that's not a good idea. The road will be watched.'

'I don't even know where Nanning is.'

'I have a map, remember. Let me show you.' He pulled the tatty bit of paper from his jacket pocket. 'We are here, in Guiyang . . . you can see Nanning almost due south.' He ran his finger in a straight line down the map. 'But the railway out of Guiyang does not go to Nanning, it goes to a place called Liuzhou.' He grimaced. 'Such an unlucky place, Liuzhou.'

'What's unlucky about it?'

'That's where most of China's coffins come from. But the point is that Liuzhou stands on a tributary of the West River, which leads . . .'

Diana followed his slow-moving finger. 'To Hong Kong.'

'Eventually. Once we've managed to bypass Canton.' He refolded the map and looked at his watch. 'We have to cut across country, find the railway where it comes out of Guiyang, and somehow get aboard a train. The railway didn't figure in Sun's original plan. He won't be watching it, I hope.'

'What will Sun do if he catches us?'

He faced her seriously. 'I don't know.'

Chang Ping took charge after that, relieving her of any further responsibility. He foraged in the deserted hotel for food and found a torch; then, with the help of his map, they cautiously began to make their way in the direction of the

257

railway. There was a glow in the night sky: Guiyang ablaze. Diana tried not to look at it.

The next leg of their journey proved easier than they'd anticipated. Chang Ping guided them to a siding that had been made to help trains pass on the single-track railroad; after that, all they had to do was wait. A long goods train hissed its way to a halt not ten feet away from the embankment where they were hiding. He helped her up into an empty truck that stank of pigs, then went to reconnoitre. He was away for a long time; so long that when he finally hauled himself up the stanchions and breathlessly threw himself on the floor the train had already started.

'What kept you?' she cried. 'I was so worried . . .'

'It's a long train.'

Something wasn't right. It showed in his voice. It showed in the way he kept running his hands up and down his folded forearms, as if for reassurance.

'And?'

'And it's okay.'

'No, it's not. I can tell.'

'It's just that . . . there are tanks. On the trucks at the back.'

'You mean . . . army tanks?'

'T-59s. Twenty of them. And . . . troops.'

Diana swallowed hard. 'How many?'

'I managed to count three coaches. Then the train started, I . . .'

He came to sit close by Diana. 'Are you all right?'

'Yes.'

'I want to ask you . . . Why did you run away from me?'

She was silent for a long time. 'Don't know.'

He waited, sensing there was more to come.

'I didn't trust you. You'd told me so many lies. I couldn't work out whether I'd be safer with you or without you.'

'I see.'

'And . . . and I seemed to be such a liability to you, all of a sudden. If you *were* telling the truth at last, I was bound to get you into trouble. I thought, if I ran away, you could say it wasn't your fault. Somehow.'

258

'And now?'

She sighed. 'Now, I don't know. After seeing what happened to that girl, I can't bear the thought of being alone any more. Even though I still don't know what to make of you.'

For a long while after that the only sounds came from the train as it rolled south through the night.

'Strange.'

'Mm?' Diana had been dozing.

'Strange that you thought of me, when you decided to run away. You said you didn't want to get me into trouble . . .'

'Yes.' She understood his meaning. 'I cared about you to that extent.'

'I have to ask . . . do you trust me now?'

'I don't believe it when you say you love me.' She swallowed, knowing she had hurt him. 'Sorry.'

He sighed. 'It would be surprising if you did.'

'And yet . . .' She looked up at where she judged his face to be, but the darkness frustrated her attempt to see his eyes. 'I . . . think something inside you has changed. Your intentions have changed. I don't know why. Maybe it's just because you don't feel safe in China any more.'

'It's simpler than that. You saved my life.' He paused. 'You knew I'd betrayed you. We wcre fighting in the lorry, remember? When we ran into the road block outside Guiyang. Afterwards, you could have driven away. But you shouted to me. Even though you knew I . . . Thank you,' he ended simply.

When she began to cry he kissed her, very gently, on the cheek. Then he slid away to the other side of the truck and lay down, resting his head on his hands so that he could stare at the roof.

Diana leaned back against the wall and aimlessly picked at her denim jacket, snuggling it around her shoulders, 'I love my orphans,' what a joke, what a priceless joke, orphans. No home. No mother.

Like me.

Chang Ping always moved away from her at night. She would have liked him to hold her in his arms, just for comfort, but that would send all the wrong messages. The memory of the rape still simmered in her brain, arming her against any possibility of assault.

I need him. I want him. I'm lonely, afraid . . .

She raised her eyes from the jacket and tried to see him through the darkness.

You want me, I know. And I want you so much. I've wanted you almost from the beginning . . .

It was a trap. It was all part of the same trap, his wanting her . . .

'Chang Ping,' she called.

No response.

Diana got onto her knees. 'Chang Ping?'

His breathing had become steady, a little harsh. He was asleep. Diana slowly leaned back against the side of the truck.

The train rumbled over the points onto the main line, where, to a mounting accompaniment of that gradual assembly of noises and rhythms which marks the start of any rail journey, it settled into the long haul south.

TWENTY-SIX

◇

Proshin flung himself against the side of the hull. Sangster hauled the Russian away and thrust him down to the floor.

'You think bullets can't get through aluminium skin?' he snarled. *'Move!'*

Proshin slithered along the floor towards the flight-deck. Before he had gone a yard, more bullets clanged and pinged against metal; a ragged row of holes appeared above the windows, as if a riveter were doing his work clumsily on the other side. Proshin rolled over twice and struggled on.

Meanwhile Sangster risked a glance at his watch. 'Two minutes twenty seconds to go . . .'

Although the firing had stopped he knew it was only a temporary truce. He had no gun; but somehow he had to divert the attackers, prevent them from surrounding the plane. He monkey-crawled to one side of the door and briefly showed his head, to be met with a long volley. He dived sideways and back, praying they wouldn't read his mind. The next spurt went high, spattering the ceiling opposite and smashing one of the emergency lights.

Then he heard machinery. Of course! They'd backed the scissor-platform away . . . to put their gunners on the platform and raise it level with the loading-bay door . . . *Jesus!*

'Hurry!' he screamed.

'Done!' The Russian was speeding down the row of pallets, weaving between the containers. Suddenly a hailstorm burst under his feet and he jumped high in the air with a squeal; but the bullets must have been deflected by a container, for Proshin emerged without a scratch. Next second Sangster

261

heard high-pitched orders being yelled outside and the firing stopped again. Not hard to guess why: if they shot upward, through the floor, they risked igniting the fuel . . .

Proshin landed next to him with a thud, his eyes squeezed shut in agony. 'Hurt?'

Proshin shook his head. 'Noise . . . terrible.'

'Not for much longer, it isn't. Fuse?'

'Ten seconds.'

Sangster jerked his head towards the starboard cargo door. 'Then *move!*'

Proshin jumped up and ran to the door's lever-handle. As he began to lift it more bullets whined and ricocheted around the hull, only this time they came on a more level trajectory. The platform must be nearly in place.

The door slowly swung open.

'Line!'

Proshin cracked open the lower end of his red tube and produced a hook to latch under the nearest pallet. As he moved away, a wire paid out from inside the tube.

'*Jump!*'

Proshin launched himself into space. The line unreeled, ratcheting him to the ground. Then Sangster slid down the line, using his gauntlets to protect his palms from being shredded. Because the Jumbo's hull bottomed out so close to the apron it was several seconds before the marksmen realized their target had changed. At last one of them, more sharp-eyed than his colleagues, ducked down to see two pairs of legs pumping away from the other side of the plane, and he yelled a warning.

Sangster and Proshin sped faster. Straight ahead of them they could see the main runway. At the north-east end an Airbus was poised for take-off; its engines changed pitch, reached a crescendo; then it was charging between the two strips of light.

Immediately behind it, a Cessna Citation executive jet taxied into position at the start of the runway.

At the same instant the Boeing-747 blew up.

Proshin had planted a small but spectacularly powerful fire bomb just forward of the wings in the centre of the hull, perfectly placed to catch the fuel in the tanks. A wave of heat flung the two men to the ground. They covered their heads, expecting to be deluged with debris, but the fire was still getting under way and not all the fuel had caught yet. They staggered up and ran on. No more shots came: the gunners had been very close to the Boeing when the bomb went off . . .

The Citation's door opened, steps came down. Proshin was first up, with Sangster only half a pace behind him. As they landed on the floor in a heap and the door closed the aircraft was already flashing down the runway, nearing take-off speed.

The two men disentangled themselves but it was some moments before they could speak. 'I don't want ever to do that again,' Proshin managed to get out at last.

'You think I do?'

The plane left the ground. Sangster tried to get up but soon realized that at their present rate of climb it was hopeless, so he merely lay on the floor and grinned at his companion. Proshin began to giggle. 'Where's the stewardess?'

But suddenly a flash of violet and white light irradiated the cabin from one end to the other; they heard a loud clang of metal meeting metal head on; the lights died. Simultaneously the plane tilted to the left and seemed to shudder, as if the effort was proving too much for it.

'What the −'

Sangster grabbed the nearest armrest and somehow managed to pull himself upright. By clinging on to chairbacks he was able to gain the cockpit. 'My God,' he said as he looked inside. 'You . . . !'

'Trotsky' was in the left-hand seat, wrestling with the controls. 'You're late,' he grated.

'What happ −'

'The target went up just as we got off the ground. The initial fire must have reached the main tanks. Something sliced into us. I'm losing −'

'Tower's panicking,' broke in the co-pilot. 'Doesn't know what to do next.'

Trotsky swore. 'Have they scrambled Canton Shadi yet?'

'No military traffic at all.'

The engines changed note; before they had been straining, now they eased off. Trotsky kept pulling back on the stick as if he were trying to wrench it from the floor. 'Got it,' he gasped. 'But we're losing fuel.'

'Do we have enough?' Proshin had joined Sangster in the doorway to the cockpit; it was his anxious voice that posed the question.

'Don't know. I fuelled up with only a small margin.'

'Where are we?'

'Just passed Pingzhou navigational beacon. Zhongshan dead ahead.'

Proshin grabbed the co-pilot's arm. 'What's happening back there?'

'Garbage. Like scalded cats. Everything's grounded, we were the last away. Nothing to come in, everything diverted to Kai Tak International.'

'Damage?'

'Varies. Somebody keeps saying it's a terrorist attack – wait!' He raised a hand to his earphones. 'Yes! They're scrambling Shadi now!'

'Shit, shit, *shit!*' Trotsky slammed his hand against the stick. 'Get up, you bitch, *up!*'

Sangster stared through the windscreen. Suddenly he cried out: something fast and ablaze with light rose from beneath and cut across their course what looked like mere feet away.

'Shadi. F-6bis, by the look of it.'

'Christ, he was close.'

'I think you will find that things get closer than that, Mr Sangster.' Trotsky found time to rub his nose hard. 'And tonight there is no KGB bolt-hole to run inside. So *hold on!*'

As the plane levelled out the co-pilot nudged Proshin. 'Go aft, take a look.'

'What am I looking for?'

'Anything, idiot!'

Proshin re-emerged a moment later with a frown on his face. 'Lights on the ground.'

'Nothing else?'

'Only the rain.'

'It's dry tonight.'

'But the windows are covered in water.'

Trotsky took both hands off the stick and raised them to his temples. 'That's fucking fuel, you *churka*! We're leaking.' He glanced down at his dials. 'Not enough,' Sangster heard him mutter.

'Shadi wants us to land,' the co-pilot announced.

In confirmation of his words another jet-fighter pulled ahead of them from behind, waggling its wings.

'Position?' Sangster asked.

'Roughly . . . Nan-lang. Crossing the coast now.'

'Distance?'

'Forty miles. But we've got another fourteen miles to fly over Chinese territorial water. And we're sinking.' Trotsky tapped one of the glass dials in front of him.

Suddenly the F-6bis flipped over to the left and disappeared. 'Where's that motherfucker gone?' Trotsky asked.

'Behind,' Sangster replied tersely. 'Attack mode.'

But he was wrong. The jet again came out of nowhere, diving down from above just a few short feet in front of the Citation's nose.

'Jesus, that was close!' Sangster leaned against the doorway, loosening his collar.

'If we can fool him next time, we might . . . *might* make Chek Lap Kok beacon.'

'Is that in Hong Kong waters?'

'Yes. If he crosses that it isn't a pursuit any longer, it's war.'

Without ever changing course, Trotsky began to bounce the plane around the sky. He would climb a few hundred feet, then drop like a stone, then climb fifty feet before putting the nose down again.

The same thought was in all their minds. The Citation was leaking fuel like a tank peppered with buckshot. One tracer bullet, maybe even the high-speed passage of a shell passing too close to the outer skin . . .

Sangster held on for dear life. Whenever his eyes came level with the windshield, he could see no signs of the aggressor and nothing to suggest they were being fired on. 'I don't get it,' he cried in Trotsky's ear. 'Why doesn't he shoot?'

The Russian shook his head and flew on without speaking. Suddenly the co-pilot shouted, 'That's why!'

Ahead of them, in the lightening early morning murk, loomed a boiling white wall. 'Low cloud.'

'Height, thirty, sinking fast.'

The radio crackled. The co-pilot began to talk urgently to Kai Tak ATC, explaining their predicament. 'Mayday, mayday . . .'

Then they were into the wall, skimming across the water.

'Not going to make it,' Trotsky laconically announced. 'Time to get your feet wet, Mr Sangster.'

The engines spun to a halt, the nose dipped. Sangster saw a flash-picture of blackness tilting, coming up to meet him, while Trotsky struggled to restore the glide of a moment ago.

'Gene,' he heard Proshin shout close by. '*Gene . . . !*'

TWENTY-SEVEN

◇

When Diana surfaced from the last of many cat-naps the first sight to meet her eyes was Chang Ping sitting beside the door, forearms resting on his knees. The door was open a crack, and a narrow shaft of light shone into the wagon across the top of his head. He did not realize she had woken up, but continued to stare at the point between his feet where sun met wood.

Diana lay still and considered him from under her lashes. Today he looked tranquil, at peace with himself, so unlike most of the men she'd known. But although she didn't understand him yet, she sensed a lot of steel in his make-up. It was a good combination. Maybe she would come to understand him, one day. In Hong Kong . . .

She knew she must guard against these enticing daydreams. They were a rock on which she might founder.

'This truck's filthy,' she said sleepily.

'"Dust will accumulate if a room is not cleaned regularly, our faces will get dirty if they are not washed regularly."'

'Who said that?'

'Mao Zedong.'

'I bet he never travelled swine-class. What were you thinking about then?'

'Mm?'

'When I woke up, you seemed so far away.'

'Oh, that. My father.'

'Tell me,' she murmured.

'The sun,' he said shortly. 'It reminded me of something that happened when I was young. Ten, maybe.'

'Tell me.'

267

The words came hard to him. 'I used to have a magnifying glass. Sometimes I would focus a ray of the sun on an insect.' He glanced at her, divining what her reaction would be. 'One day, my father caught me. He took away my glass.'

'Good.'

'All right, I think so too. But do you know *why* he did that?'

'Because he didn't approve of you being cruel?'

'No. Because he was afraid I'd ruin my eyesight and then I wouldn't be able to study.'

'Oh. Now why on earth were you thinking of that?'

But he just shrugged those classically sculpted, muscular shoulders of his and looked away. Diana wondered what shamed him most – his wanton childhood cruelty, or the coldness of the paternal reaction.

Suddenly the sun went out and the noise inside the wagon bucked several decibels. A tunnel. Now they could not see each other. When the train emerged into daylight a few moments later, however, Diana scrambled across to join him by the door.

Overnight the landscape had changed dramatically. All trace of fertility had disappeared. Diana could see rolling red-brown escarpments coated with crew-cut scrub or patchy grass, and occasionally an isolated tree sticking out as if placed in a crude drawing by some infantile hand. Then her vision was excised by a rough, greyish-white wall of rock as the train rumbled through a gorge, the noise of its passage thrown back at it by boulders that crowded almost to the edge of the rails. Then another tunnel; more rock-wall; a long, long tunnel that seemed to wind on interminably. When at last it did end, miles further down the line, the scenery had been transformed yet again and Diana saw, with a sense of wonder, that they had come to the land of the *karst*.

The train slowed to walking pace in order to cross a fast-flowing river of pale, opaque-green water by means of a wooden-pile bridge. The view that opened up before her eyes could have formed the model for a Chinese scroll painting in all respects save one: the light. Today there was none of the floating, misty remoteness favoured by the ancient artists;

instead, hot, harsh sun burned down on the fantastic scenery, as when a craftily-lit museum tableau is temporarily given over to neon so that the cleaners can do their work.

Yet everything else was there: rippling water, bamboo in thick profusion, cryptomeria, even an occasional pavilion half hidden by a clump of camphor; and far away she could just see a lofty cascade meeting the river in a swirl of spectrum and spray. But above all, the mysterious *karst* . . . those fantastic limestone formations, thin islands of rock jutting into the landscape like engorged stalagmites, each separate from its neighbours while at the same time forming part of a huge, harmonious whole.

Diana unconsciously laid a hand on Chang Ping's shoulder, and he placed a hand over hers, acknowledging the power of an experience shared. Then the river was crossed, the train again gathered speed and another tunnel engulfed them.

After so much light and beauty, the gloom affected Diana's spirits. Things that had not hitherto troubled her now began to assume an all-too-weighty significance. There were tanks attached to the train, and the tanks were guarded by coach-loads of soldiers. The man opposite had admitted himself to be a spy. Her mother was dead. Many miles still separated her from home. China was drifting without leadership . . . so much for the pretty scenery, she thought despondently.

'When will we reach Liuzhou?' she asked.

'Evening.'

'What about the tanks?'

'They may be heading for Liuzhou, or further on, or, I suppose, they are going to some incident between here and Liuzhou. We can only guess.'

'Do we stop between here and Liuzhou?'

'Um . . .I think so, if this train behaves normally. There is a town called Hechi. It's big, the train will stop there, I should think.'

'So knowledgeable.'

Was there a hint of lingering suspicion in that response, she wondered? Chang Ping must have thought so, for he was quick to reply: 'I had to study this area, remember.'

'Of course.' She hadn't.

Around mid-morning the train escaped the last of the lime-stone gorges, crossed a broad river on a double-spanned steel bridge and began to steam across a plain towards a distant horizon of the first industrialization they'd seen since Guiyang. By sitting alongside the door and pressing her head against the side of the truck, Diana could catch glimpses of where they were headed without risking being seen from one of the coaches to the rear. The sight of triple smoke-stacks and a row of electricity pylons fringing a narrow vale drove away consciousness of the pain in her shoulders, the incipient headache, the revolting pig smell, of everything except that here was another peril to be negotiated. Her heart began to beat faster, her throat became prickly dry. She wanted Hechi, by some mysterious sleight-of-hand, not to happen.

First there were isolated settlements, then dusty roads with ox-carts and the occasional lorry; then a row of concrete apartment blocks, each with a large number painted on the side, sprang up into their line of vision.

Chang Ping stood by the door, holding it open an inch so that he could keep watch. 'What do you see?' she cried suddenly, unable to check her anxiety any longer.

'I see the station ahead . . . we're slowing . . . I think we are turning off the main line. Yes!'

Diana rushed to peer out. They were in the heart of the town by now: next to the line was a street bordered by three-storey high blocks of flats, with washing stretched from poles on the upper floors. As she craned her neck the line curved sharply and the wheel-flanges squealed. They were pulling into a siding that ran parallel with the station but was separated from it by two sets of tracks.

She saw something else. The engine had about reached a gap in what looked like a barbed-wire barrier strung on wooden crosses, above which floated the Chinese flag. Soldiers were on guard. One of them raised a baton and waved the driver on. Their train was under military jurisdiction.

She was aware of a burning sensation behind her eyelids.

'What's that smell?' she cried as Chang Ping hauled her away from the gap.

'Tear gas.' The door clicked shut. 'Not close, fortunately, or we'd –

'My God . . . what's happening here?'

He shook his head wearily and sank down on his haunches, brushing the hair from his eyes. 'What are we going to do?' Diana croaked.

'Wait. Be patient.'

'*Wait!* How can you –'

'What do you suggest?'

Diana said nothing, but hugged her rucksack close to her chest, as if it contained a charm against evil.

'This train has two parts,' Chang Ping said. 'There are the soldiers and the tanks. But there are also many other wagons like this one. Whatever the soldiers do, these trucks aren't going to sit in Hechi and rot.'

They were still moving; but now long shadows cast by the barbed-wire barrier infiltrated cracks in the wagon's side. The train shunted itself another two hundred metres or so before it finally clanked to a halt. Diana could hear pressurized steam, complaints from ill-assorted couplings, a far-off rattling noise. Nothing else spoiled the leaden midday silence.

'It's so quiet,' she muttered.

'And we're in the middle of a big town. Yes.'

Voices.

The shouts came from the rear of the long train; evidently orders were being given, for suddenly the wagon gave a big jolt forward, with groans from the bogeys, and as suddenly halted again.

'They're unloading the tanks.'

Diana momentarily brightened up; but then – 'I can hear this funny noise,' she said, without thinking. 'Like an electric hammer, sort of.'

'I wondered if you could hear the shooting. But you didn't say anything, so –'

All the blood in her body seemed to collect in her head, then seep away, leaving her white and shaking. Diana had known that the strange rattling noise was automatic gunfire but hadn't been ready to acknowledge it to herself; now she did and she felt ill.

The train gave another lurch. Silence once more descended, its blanket stifling all but the distant chattering that now had a name.

'I'm going out.'

'You can't! You'll be caught and killed and —'

'We can't stay here and roast. If this train isn't going to move we need to know, so that we can do something about it.'

Before she could think of an answer to that he had gone, slipping through the gap in the door as silently as a cat.

Diana peeked out. Opposite, three sets of tracks separated the train from a grimy brick embankment. To the right, after several other wagons, the engine, but no sign of anyone. To the left . . . far away she could see soldiers milling around on the tracks but Chang Ping had disappeared.

He had been gone about ten minutes when the engine's whistle delivered itself of three long blasts; then the train began to move forward at walking pace. Diana risked another look outside. Only one soldier remained at his post by the barrier through which they'd passed earlier. Then she saw Chang Ping climb from underneath a wagon three down from hers, slithering like a snake between the wheels. He leapt upright as soon as he was clear of the bogeys and began to sprint.

Something, a quick movement in the background, made Diana raise her head. The soldier chose that moment to turn to the left. He caught sight of the running figure and unslung his rifle. 'Hurry,' Diana breathed, but she couldn't warn him, could do nothing except watch impotently while the Fates spun the warp and waft of his destiny.

The train had put on a little speed, but Chang Ping was still gaining ground. The soldier raised his rifle and took aim, only to realize he would have a better shot if he gave himself more of an angle; so he ran back to the embankment wall. The seconds lost were enough to enable Chang Ping to draw level with Diana's wagon.

She leaned out as far as she dared and cried, 'He's got a gun!'

Chang Ping was good, his training held: he did not look around. Instead he lowered his head like a charging bull and accelerated.

The sound of the shot was scarcely audible over the mounting clamour of the train. Diana saw a sliver of wood peel from the box-car by Chang Ping's head. *'Help him!'* she cried; but she could not have said who she was talking to.

He continued to run, his face screwed up in pain. The engine had already reached the points that would reconnect it to the main line, and Diana knew that soon the train would be travelling faster than the greatest athlete could run. The soldier took aim again, realizing this was his last chance.

Chang Ping jumped for the side of the wagon. He got a hold on one of the metal steps. Diana leaned out to grab him. His energy was all spent, he couldn't move to help himself; instead he just hung there, swinging with the motion of the train, and Diana knew that within seconds he must fall. She threw herself flat on the floor and put both hands under his armpits. Chang Ping recovered enough to make one final effort. He kicked with his feet until both were planted squarely on stanchions. Diana heard him gasping as if his heart would explode.

There came the resonant ping of lead on steel, followed by the report of a gunshot. Diana felt something warm flood across her left hand, a splash of crimson lured her eye downward, and 'No!' she screamed. But Chang Ping was half inside and wriggling like a demented seal to drag the rest of himself onto the floor.

A series of shocks ran through Diana's prone body as their wagon traversed the points. She waited for the train to brake, expecting every second to hear the shout of orders outside, a hail of warning shots, but none came. Instead, with a long whistle the engine found its stride and set off down the line to Liuzhou.

She turned her attention to Chang Ping, who still lay on the floor, now breathing more normally. 'Where were you hit?'

But it wasn't his blood that stained Diana's hand, it was her own. The second and final shot had ricocheted, bouncing off the stanchion across her forearm. She stared at it in astonishment. The wound hurt no more than a childhood scratch. It might have been someone else's arm.

'Are you all right?'

'Yes.' He rolled over to lie on his back. 'I'm okay now.'

During the past few chaotic minutes Diana had vaguely been aware of an increase in noise. Now it suddenly thrust itself into the forefront of her consciousness. Shooting. Not like the crack of the soldier's rifle; no, this was automatic fire. And it sounded close.

She raised her head to look through the doorway. She could see a derelict plot of land, littered with piles of bricks and other materials from demolished buildings. Then a line of human figures slid into view. They stood with their backs to the railway, close to a wire fence. All of them had their hands clasped behind them, lending a businesslike atmosphere to the scene. Diana heard the loudest fusillade yet. And one by one, from left to right, the row of people, whose hands, she now saw were bound rather than clasped, tumbled over, like dominoes bringing about each other's downfall at the whim of some child who is tired of his game. They toppled, but no one put them back in the box for another day . . .

Then yet another tawdry, damp-soaked apartment block superseded the killing ground and she saw no more.

'Secretary Zhang, I really cannot see the point of this.'

The white light flooding over the flat, featureless desert made Colonel Lai Jia Yao feel painfully hot. The ambient temperature was well over a hundred degrees Fahrenheit, but that was not the cause of the other burning sensation which had started to flood through his intestines quite soon after he first met Zhang Ming Rong at the airport and learned what he wanted. For it was clear that this young man had brains; what was worse, infinitely so, was that he had all the right bits of properly authenticated official paper – a rare thing, in Lai's experience.

He was also in a tremendous hurry.

'Why do you say that, Colonel?' Ming Rong undid the top two buttons of his shirt and flapped the material gently, letting his chest breathe.

'For one thing, you're only guessing that B-Ten was here.' Lai waved his own hands around, less in an attempt to keep cool than by way of delimiting the desert for the city boy's benefit. 'Those mountains could be ten miles away, or fifteen, or . . .'

'We have high-resolution satellite photographs. And we also have a land navigation system.'

'Surely those things aren't very accurate, though?'

'To within five metres.'

'Five?'

'Five. And for another thing . . . ?'

'What?'

'You said, you cannot see the point of this because "for one thing" I'm guessing the location. What about for another thing?'

Lai stared at the horizon, trying desperately to think of a story that might satisfy this interfering young civilian, armed as he was with the necessary permits. 'For another thing . . . as you can see . . . there's nothing here. The desert has reclaimed its own, hasn't it?'

'Nicely put.'

'And what are you going to do – shovel sand with your bare hands?' Lai forced a laugh, in which Ming Rong joined. 'I mean . . . it's not as if planes could still land here, is it?'

'Ours did.'

'Ah, but we came by helicopter. You can hardly bring in bulldozers – I think you said bulldozers –?'

'Excavators.'

'– with helicopters.'

'On the contrary, here they come now.'

Lai looked to where Ming Rong's finger was pointing. At first he could see nothing, just hear the clatter of rotors rising and falling through the oven-baked air that overlaid Gansu; then dark shapes materialized out of the sun, their loads swinging on cables beneath them, and he swallowed.

Ming Rong surveyed the sweating colonel with interest. What had this man done, he wondered, to merit the Wartime Hero Medal, first grade? And why did he wear the medal itself, rather than the modest breast-ribbon that regulations required? 'You have not seen crane helicopters before?'

Lai shook his head.

'Sikorsky S-64s. Not wonderful by today's standards, but good enough.' Ming Rong glanced over his shoulder to where surveyors had just finished setting up their equipment. 'The excavators will be here soon,' he called to them. 'You can start.' He turned back to Lai. 'That goes for you, too.'

His voice had not changed, but his face had. Lai looked into Ming Rong's eyes and saw neither hope nor any prospect of mistake. 'I . . . ?' he said weakly.

'You can start talking.' Ming Rong raised a hand to shield his eyes from the sun. The helicopters were very close now; he had to shout to make his next words heard above their racket. 'I must impress on you that time is short. We are standing on the brink of war.'

'War!'

'Civil war. The worst kind. I don't exaggerate, Colonel. So it would be better if you told me what you know *before* we dig up the evidence, don't you think?'

TWENTY-EIGHT

◇

The train stopped for a signal by the side of a slow-moving river the colour of water that had been used to wash ashtrays. A single, bare island split the stream in two; beyond that were reeds, an expanse of rice-paddy and, in the middle distance, the beginnings of another *karst* range. With the rain coming down it made a dismal prospect. There was nobody about except for a lone cormorant fisherman poling his bamboo boat across the current.

Diana and Chang Ping jumped onto the track. There were no soldiers or tanks to worry about now, but nevertheless they ran down the embankment on the side furthest from the river, where there was a ditch, and hid until the train had disappeared into the distance.

'Where are we going?'

He pointed to where smoke from their train was still feathering the horizon. Diana saw a few buildings, evidently the start of a town.

'That's Liuzhou.'

'Why couldn't we have stayed on the train?'

'After what happened in Hechi, I don't want to run any risks.'

The wet afternoon wore on badly. They walked for an hour without seeing another soul. After a while Diana plucked up enough courage to ask him the question that had been troubling her since Hechi.

'Why did they shoot all those people?'

'There was a rebellion. When I was under the train I heard the soldiers talking. Twenty-three cadres had their throats cut.

Maybe they deserved it, I don't know – the soldiers seemed to think so.'

'How did you hear?'

'I crawled under the train.'

Had he, she wondered? Had he really? Or was this just another staging post on his mission, the next rendezvous with the Mahjong Brigade?

Chang Ping came to a sudden halt. 'We're nearly there.'

'Oh. What a dump.'

'Yes. But beyond that field, those houses . . . there is the Liu river, and it can take us all the way to Hong Kong. We'll head for that hill: Ma'anshan. You'll be safe there while I ask around for a boat.' He glanced at the sky. 'It's nearly dusk. We'll rest until it gets dark.'

The fields separating them from the outskirts of town were densely planted with corn. They managed to force a way into it and, by trampling hard, make a space. The atmosphere was stuffy with the smell of hot vegetation.

'Strange,' she murmured. 'I've always wanted to see this part of China. Guilin, the *karst*. I never thought it would be like this.'

'Did you know a poet once called the *karst* "blue jade hairpins"?'

'No. That's lovely.' She began to speak but then fell silent.

'Is something the matter?'

'Oh . . . it's just that I can't get it out of my mind that without me you'd have more chance. I hinder you, don't I? I keep thinking of that Chinese birth control slogan – "Two is good, one is better." It's true for us as well.'

'No, it's not. If I was just running away, you'd be right. But as long as I'm in China, I can't be truly safe. Sun Shanwang won't forgive; if he finds me, he'll shoot me as a traitor. So I've got to get out of China.'

He said no more, but Diana filled in the missing link for herself. At the start of their escape she had needed him, but now things were different. She had become Chang Ping's passport to safety and a better life.

'You say Sun wouldn't forgive you, but –'

278

'He wouldn't!'

'You always seem to know so much about him.'

'If you still don't trust me, be open, say so. If you do trust me, act like it.'

She wanted to protest, but his words struck home. In the end she closed her eyes and pretended to be asleep.

At last dusk came. They crept out and skirted the corn field, always keeping the hill before them, until at last they reached the first houses. Many families were gathered outside their homes, playing cards or talking with neighbours beneath paraffin lamps that did nothing to illumine the middle of the concrete road, where the two travellers were hastily making their way towards the park at the foot of Ma'anshan. Diana kept her head well down and walked with a stoop, praying that no curious eyes would pick out her western jeans or long hair.

By the time they reached their destination, darkness had fallen and only a few electric lamps shed light on the dusty, unmade track that zig-zagged up the side of the hill between two low, bamboo-pole fences. Coarse grass alternated with copses of eucalyptus and bamboo on either side. The air was cooler here and it smelled sweetly of camphor.

At last they reached the top. The usual pavilion was there to greet them. Diana unslung her rucksack and looked around. Suddenly she gasped. 'The river!'

It lay before her about half a mile away, encircling the hill like a necklace of light. Whatever happened in Liuzhou evidently centred on the river, for the waterfront was alive with activity. She could hear a band playing and at one place floodlights shone down on an empty quay, as if some great arrival were anticipated. A boat moved slowly downstream, its wash a white froth in the glare of the floods. As she followed its progress, distant fire-crackers sputtered into life.

'What's happening?'

'I don't know. Now, you must wait.'

'*Please* hurry.'

He merely waved and set off, loping down the hill with long, easy strides.

Apart from the raucous hum of cicadas it was quiet in the pavilion. From the steps she had an uninterrupted view of the town and the river that bisected it. Notwithstanding the bright lights and sounds of revelry, she felt horribly lonely in her eyrie. What if he never came back? Suppose he decided she was right, after all, and that he would stand a better chance without her . . . ?

Occasionally a dry twig would break somewhere close by, making her jump. Was someone out there, watching? Could she really hear footfalls in the grass, or was that her overheated imagination? She looked at her watch repeatedly, but the numerals told her nothing she didn't already know: Chang Ping had been gone a long time.

Nearly two hours after he had made off down the hill she heard a commotion coming from the direction of the river. At first she couldn't understand the scene in front of her. A snake of light seemed to be winding its sinuous way through the water towards the town from the south. Suddenly red, green and blue rockets shot into the sky from the centre of Liuzhou, followed almost immediately by a volley of fireworks from the serpent on the river: showers of golden rain, shooting stars, more sky-rockets. At about the same moment the head of the 'snake' hove into view, creeping up to the quay through the huge square of light cast by the floods: a long, fat tugboat, painted white and red, with a train of lighters in tow.

Suddenly another kind of noise snagged Diana's attention and she stiffened. The sound of an engine labouring against the gradient was becoming louder.

She tucked herself into the farthest corner of the pavilion and strained every nerve to listen. The wind blew noises this way and that, but a car, something motorized, was coming up the hill towards her. Then the engine died. She tried to see through the darkness in front of her nose, but there was nothing. No voices, no footsteps. Silence.

'Diana.'

All the muscles in her body joined to produce a spasm that nearly lifted her off the floor, and a dangerously loud gasp forced its way through her lips. 'Who's there?'

'Me. Chang Ping.'

'I can't see you.'

She heard voices muttering; then a torch-beam sprang to life a few metres to her left and she swung around. Chang Ping stood there, holding the torch upright to shine on his face. 'Thank God,' she cried, running to him, 'thank God, thank God . . .'

Then she noticed a second person and stopped short.

The weak torch-beam showed a fat Chinese with a moon face, almost no hair on his head but long, trailing black whiskers on his chin and upper lip. He stank of fish.

'Who's this?'

'His name's Lin. His father runs a line of junks. They're leaving for Canton tonight and he says he can fix up a passage from there to Hong Kong. Diana, we've got a chance.'

Why did she doubt it, she wondered? Lin's stance, his physical appearance, every last thing about him in fact, suggested a feckless approach to life. Lin, she suspected, was a master of turning the fast buck. Without being able to see his hands, she felt sure they would be gnarled and raw, with nails bitten down to the quick; and somewhere he would have an obscene tattoo. The kind of man she used to warn her Korean orphans not to speak to . . .

There wasn't a shred of evidence to support this instant character analysis; but Diana knew she was going to trust her instincts. 'He's a crook,' she said in rapid English. 'Drop him.'

'But –'

'Can't you see he's no good?' She felt her anger rise. He was opposing hunch with reason, but she had to find a way to make him see that this time reason would let him down.

'He's got a pick-up truck,' Chang Ping said quietly. 'He can drive us right to the quay, no one'll see us –'

'But he's *wrong!* Why can't you see that?'

'Because he's all we've got.' Chang Ping's voice was rising now, rough with exasperation at the stupid foreign woman who refused to understand. 'I know he's got to be watched, I *know* that! What else can we do?'

'There's always an alternative.'

'What? Tell me.'

'Anything. Stay here. Wait for another opportunity.'

'There won't be one. Diana, I *know!*'

How did he know? Just exactly who had told him?

They bickered for fifteen minutes, at the end of which time Diana felt certain that if she did not surrender, Chang Ping was going to leave without her.

'Right,' she said, shouldering her pack.

She insisted on travelling in the back of the pick-up. To her relief, Chang Ping at once agreed that it was better for her to keep out of sight, under a tarpaulin, where she would be less prominent than if riding in the cab. As they reached the foot of the hill the driver gunned his engine in an approximation of a racing change and set off hell-for-leather along a road possessed of as many turns as a bent screw. Twenty minutes later they ground to a halt inside a stuffy warehouse on the edge of the river without having even slowed down once.

Diana could hear water lapping against piles and here the stench of fish was paramount. For a moment nothing happened. Then she became aware of voices close by, raised in loud argument.

She shrugged off the tarpaulin and crept down. Her surroundings were lit by a single yellow light bulb, domed by a green metal shade that dangled from the ceiling on a long flex hooked to the wall: tins of paint, a huge rudder, two propellers, ropes of all kinds and thicknesses . . . But these were not the things that held her attention. Ten feet away from her, Chang Ping and the man called Lin were in the midst of a quarrel.

She could see it was about money. Lin kept poking his left palm with his right forefinger, the gesture of a man who counts. Chang Ping was shaking his head and sweeping his arms across his chest: a patent, blatant refusal.

Diana called his name once. No effect. 'Chang Ping,' she screamed.

Both men turned to stare at her.

'How much does he want?'

'Five thousand Yuan.'

'Ridiculous!'

'I've already told him.'

'That's a thousand pounds, give or take. We haven't got it.'

'No.'

'So let's get out of here, ditch the creep.'

'What if he talks?' Chang Ping's air of authority was crumbling. 'Diana, he's not stupid, he knows we're in big trouble. He says if we don't do a deal with him he'll report us to the police.'

'Tell him to go ahead. He will, anyway. And then we can screw him for blackmail. Tell him.'

Chang Ping's face clouded but after a second's hesitation he complied. Lin's expression darkened dramatically and he began to square off for a fight. Chang Ping turned back to Diana. 'It's no good. This guy means it.'

'He does, he does,' said another quiet voice.

Everyone turned to look. Diana found herself mere inches away from a tall Chinese man who was as lean and fit-looking as Lin was fat and pasty. 'You speak English,' she said automatically.

'Little, little.' He was an old man, she realized, and the courtly bow that accompanied his last speech might almost have made him an attractive figure in her eyes at that moment, were it not for the knife he held in his right hand. Now he raised it to eye-level and slowly waved it in front of her face, forcing her to retreat. 'Lin papa,' the old man said. 'Little sister in trouble. Little brother there also in trouble. Yes, I think.'

Diana tried to speak, but he motioned her to be silent. His right eyebrow had been disfigured, no doubt in a fight: the left-to-right downward scar had scrunched up the skin into a wrinkled patch, leaving the white of the eye exposed in a permanent stare. No attempt had been made to recompose his face. It was not one you argued with.

'Have money, take Hong Kong. Have no money, no take. Police, many. Army here, also many. Foreigner come, many police, soldier. You make trouble, you soon find out, no mistake! Come along, little sister.' Now Lin senior was impatient. 'You have much money. All foreigner carry money. I know, I see Hong Kong.'

'I haven't got it. You can search me, if you want.' As she spoke, Diana shuddered; the thought of them pawing her skin clenched all the muscles of her stomach into a knot.

'Yes. I search. If you no have money, have thing. Have thing cost much money.'

It was true: she had her mother's engagement ring.

For a moment the boat shed seemed to spin around her while she fought to keep control of her expression, but the shock of the memory was too great. Old Lin stepped forward excitedly. 'Have! Have! What is?'

It was at this point that Diana's perceptions started to go awry. Suddenly she was wading through treacle. Everything happened twice as slowly as she intended.

She had dropped the rucksack on the floor beside the pick-up. Jinny's ring was buried inside an inner zipped pocket. As she bent down she prayed with all her heart and strength and soul: 'Dear God, dear, dear, God, don't let him snatch it from me. If you never do anything else for me again, *please* do this . . .'

And all the while she was acting in slow motion, every second broken down into milliseconds, each containing its own precise allocation of movement and thought, like a tape designed for specialized editing.

Say two feet directly in front – the old man, knife still raised. Behind her, to the right, Chang Ping and Lin. How far? Approximately four feet. Who was in front? Lin, when last she'd looked. Had they altered position? *Had they?*

Diana picked up the rucksack in her left hand and undid the lace with her right. Then she put her right hand inside, groping for the secret pocket.

She held out the ring to the old man. But when he moved to grab it, greed overriding caution, she flung it behind him as hard as she could.

He spat at Diana, then, thinking she was just a helpless girl, thrust her backwards and turned through a full semi-circle as if to look for the ring. She recovered almost immediately. Her shoe swept up the V between the old man's legs and he cursed her for a she-devil bitch as he dropped the knife and clutched his groin.

Diana flung herself onto the floor, casting about with both hands in search of the knife. She was desperate to know what was happening behind her.

There were sounds of a struggle; clearly Lin and Chang Ping were locked in combat. Diana's fingers found metal and closed around it, but the old mán, reading her mind, wriggled on the floor until he was once more facing her. Diana felt the knife wrenched from her. Then there was a gurgle directly above her, a wet, bubbly sound that she would never forget, and the knife turned bright scarlet in the old man's hand, bathed in a shower of hot blood.

Diana crawled across the floor until at last she reached a wall and could go no further. She dragged herself half upright and turned.

Chang Ping stood by the back of the pick-up. His left arm encircled Lin's pudgy chest. His right was hidden; but Diana knew from the second, crimson mouth suddenly grown by Lin that Chang Ping's invisible hand held his Feng Yuon knife, and that he had used it to cut Lin's throat down as far as the vertebrae.

In the seconds it took Lin's body to slide to the ground they stared at each other, speechlessly. Diana didn't believe Lin had been armed. Chang Ping had killed a defenceless man, them or us, in their situation that didn't matter, *yes it mattered*, she was going to have to think about that, not now, not now . . .

Papa Lin squealed once: rage, fear, hatred, a mixture of all three. Then, holding the knife straight out in front of him he ran forward to lunge at Chang Ping's stomach.

The attack was senseless, utterly unplanned – the gut reaction of a father driven mad. Chang Ping merely did a backward waltz-step, allowing Papa Lin to charge straight up against the side of the truck. That should have been the end of it: Chang Ping still had his own knife, the old man's back presented a broad, temporarily motionless, target. But Chang Ping had discovered a worse adversary: himself. Still shocked by the

285

killing of Lin junior, he could not bring himself to deal with Lin senior.

'Run!' Diana cried. But her warning came too late. The old man bounced back off the truck, sweeping his knife-arm in an arc. Chang Ping jumped aside but the point of the blade caught in his shirt, ripping cloth. Papa Lin raised his weapon above his head and ran forward, as he brought his hand down in a vicious stab. Chang Ping went into a stoop, ducked, and misread the old man's intention, expecting another sideways sweep. Just in time he realized he was underneath rather than to one side of the coming attack and had a pared second in which to correct his stance. He made it, just.

Stand off.

Diana had worked her way around the walls until she reached the double doors to the alley outside.

Chang Ping was moving too slowly, as if he'd suddenly grown tired. As if he'd aged. When Lin came at him again he allowed himself to back against the pick-up: Diana saw the look of mingled surprise and terror on his face as he felt something hard behind him. But he had the sense to turn sideways on, narrowing the target, and lash out with his foot. The old man grunted and tripped. He was on the floor now, helpless. But Chang Ping did not move. Diana saw how his glazed eyes flickered. Then she was running.

She threw herself full-length on top of Lin and got a grip on his scraggy throat. In his panic, he dropped the knife. Diana lifted his head off the ground and smashed it down hard, once, twice. He tried to roll sideways, heaving her off, but Diana somehow transferred her grip to his temples and banged his head down again.

He went limp. She rolled to one side, breathing heavily. When Chang Ping gazed at her as if she were a stranger, she knew that now everything depended on her. She rose to her feet, and snatched the tarpaulin from the back of the pick-up. Without looking down she threw it over the two men on the floor.

Diana clasped Chang Ping's hands between her own. 'Out!' she snapped. 'Now!'

She still had enough presence of mind to collect her ruck-sack; but when, more than halfway down the alley, she re-membered that her mother's engagement ring was lying somewhere back in the filthy old boat shed, she did not even break stride. The ring was the price; and you could not take back the price of anything.

On the one hand, warehouses, tall and forbidding; on the other, grimy shanties redolent of shit and piss, at the far end, light . . . many moving lights. The town square.

There was a crowd. They could lose themselves in a crowd.

As Diana raced into the square, to her left, beside the quay, a tall westerner was stepping forward to greet a group of official-looking Chinese. He stood about fifty metres away from her, his head nodding up and down as if in polite conversation. For a moment Diana merely stood on tip-toe, looking for a way out; then the man turned his head in her direction and with a disabling sense of shock she recognized him.

'Warren!'

Diana thrust herself through the crowd until she was only feet away from Honnyman. She could feel a thousand pairs of eyes picking her to pieces, but her own gaze remained stead-fastly on the American's face. The silence seemed long.

Then he said, in loud and passable Chinese, 'Ah, Diana! I thought we'd lost you back there.' He reached out to pat her arm; and, after so much violence, his friendly touch represented comfort in its purest form. 'Why don't you go bed down those Asiatic pit-vipers, what do you say, mm?'

TWENTY-NINE

◇

When Lo Bing entered Sun Shanwang's sanctum he reckoned it must have contained at least twenty people. Most of them seemed to be having hysterics.

Sun himself was in his usual place at the top of the long table, his back to windows that now were white rectangles of brilliant early-morning sunlight. Both hands rested flat on the wooden surface in front of him and his face had set in an unreadable expression. His eyes were closed. Lo Bing guessed that he was trying to create for himself a place of stillness wherein to renew both stamina and mind.

It was as if Sun sensed a new presence in the room, a fresh disturbance of the already turbulent atmosphere. He slowly turned his head until he was facing in Lo Bing's direction; then he opened his eyes. The General quickly looked away, flushed with that odd guilt that floods through one who watches another wake from sleep.

Sun stood up. The screaming and the table-pounding, the stabbing of files with fingers, died away to silence. He waited ten seconds before speaking; then he issued soft orders and the room rapidly emptied, leaving only the Controller, Lo Bing and Chief of Staff Wang.

Sun sat down again, raising his arms above his head in a long, weary stretch. On this occasion, Lo Bing noticed, unlike the last, there were no histrionics; Wang stood at Sun's shoulder, marking out an unmistakable alliance for their visitor's benefit.

'They're upset,' Sun said wearily, indicating a chair for the General. 'A strange time, isn't it?'

Lo Bing did not take this for a comment on the hour, which was eight in the morning. 'May you live in interesting times.'

'Ah, the old curse . . . appropriate, I think. China hasn't seen many moments like this, not recently.'

'Moments . . . ?'

'Times when power can either change hands, or be diffused through ten thousand different drains into the sewers. They tell me you've had problems of your own, at the campus.'

'Some of the students put up big-character posters.'

'Political?'

'Some directly political; many of them proposing actions of various kinds at the Chairman's funeral next week.'

'Which amounts to the same thing as political. What action did you take?'

'A number of heads got broken.' Lo Bing hesitated. 'They tell me that two of the ringleaders have disappeared.'

Sun looked up at Wang and the two men exchanged smiles. Both appreciated the subtlety of Lo Bing's response: he'd had the trouble-makers executed, making his statement literally true, but no one would ever be able to prove it. 'They tell me . . .' was a particularly clever touch, Sun thought.

'We have a problem,' he said. 'I need someone who's a man of action and at the same time a diplomat.' His pause flavoured the atmosphere with gravity. 'We shall also shortly need a new Chief of Staff. So many needs, so short a time . . .'

Try as he might, Lo Bing could not prevent his gaze from straying to Wang Guoying's face. The present incumbent of the office recently named by Sun stared back at him, lips warped in a slight smile.

'How can I help, Controller?'

'One of my better young prospects has gone astray. He'd been detailed to accompany an Englishwoman down from Sichuan as far as Nanning. The two of them are now missing. The woman was spotted at Liuzhou, a few hours ago. I think she's going to try for Hong Kong, down the West River, quite possibly with my man. And I want them stopped.'

'Stopped . . .'

Lo Bing's monosyllable — judgemental, questioning — hovered in the air for a long time. At last he said: 'I think there are many means available to you for stopping two people who want to get out of China. None of them need involve a brigadier-general.'

'If I thought you intended that as a serious observation I would not have roused you from sleep.'

'Forgive me, but —'

'You're well aware of our present problems. In the midst of all of them, an Englishwoman is making her way south-east through some of the most difficult territory under our command. Perhaps I should say, our *theoretical* command. She went through Hechi.'

'Hechi!' Lo Bing's gaze fell. 'I see.'

'Yes, you see. The question is: How much did *she* see?'

'It would not be convenient to have certain recent events in Hechi broadcast abroad.'

'Convenient! It would be catastrophic! But pursuing those two won't be easy. It could take whoever leads the expedition to the border with Hong Kong. If it does, then, yes, I say to you — I *need* involve a brigadier-general.'

'And a diplomat. Yes. What resources are to be allocated to this expedition?'

'Damn all,' said Wang. 'You know as well as I do, every soldier in Chinese uniform is spoken for at present. Ten men from the Special Operations Group; that's it.'

Lo Bing considered the proposition. 'That's really not enough,' he concluded.

'Against a boy and a foreign woman, both of them unarmed and defenceless?'

Lo Bing said nothing.

'You don't accept?'

'No.' Lo Bing shook his head with a pleasant smile and repeated the word as if he relished it. 'No. You see, Controller, there have been developments since we last spoke together. The few remaining problems over Sledge Hammer have been solved.' He made no effort to keep the triumph from his eyes. 'At the moment, I am afraid I have . . . other commitments.'

Sun stared down at his desk for a long time. Lo Bing, taking it for a gesture of defeat, rose with a satisfied look on his face and made as if to leave. His whole demeanour indicated that he had better, more important things to do than waste time with yesteryear's men.

'Sometimes I don't know what I'd do, without this view. You really must paint it for me one day, General.'

Lo Bing had reached the door. Now he stopped. The tone of Sun Shanwang's voice did not accord with his earlier appearance of submission. There was laughter lurking in there, somewhere.

'View, Controller?'

Now Sun and Wang were both standing with their backs to him, looking out of the windows. 'It's a consolation,' Sun said to the glass. 'When times are bad. When, for example, two foreign spies manage to penetrate Canton Airport and take photographs inside an All Middle Kingdom Cargo Freight Boeing-747 before blowing it up.'

As Sun began to speak, Lo Bing had been in the act of opening the door. Now he closed it again, very softly, apparently afraid of disturbing the sudden, heavy silence that had descended on the room.

'I'm told the photographs are first-class,' Wang said.

'They are, they are.'

Lo Bing cleared his throat. 'These spies you mentioned? They're dead?'

'Alive.'

'Both alive?'

'Yes.'

Lo Bing hesitated a moment longer before moving, crabwise, to a position midway between Sun and Wang. When he looked down at the lakeshore, neither of them overtly studied his face. They did not need to. It was reflected in the glass.

The vista beyond the windows had an eerie familiarity to it: someone sat by the lake, morosely surveying the scenery. But this man wore a colonel's cap, not a marshal's; and although the Wartime Hero Medal, first grade, might have belonged to

291

an officer of any of the three services, his gold-fringed, sky-blue tabs showed he was assigned to the airforce.

Lo Bing was so intent on observing Colonel Lai Jia Yao in the gardens below that at first he did not hear Sun Shanwang sigh and say, 'I miss Secretary Zhang Ming Rong. Such a useful young man. But he is away.'

'Doing what?' Wang Guoying inquired of the windowpane.

'Digging.' Another sigh. 'Always digging, that one.'

There was a long silence, after which Sun said, 'Well, General, I'm sorry to have wasted your time. You must get back to Sledge Hammer.'

Lo Bing was nothing if not deft. 'When you find your general, Controller . . . how would he, in turn, find these people?'

'There's an American-owned barge convoy leaving Liuzhou at first light,' Wang said. 'Our guess is that the fugitives will be on it.'

'Why?'

'First, because the woman's bound to try and make contact with her own kind; secondly, because the barges are going to Hong Kong.'

'It sounds almost like fun. I've not had any fun for a long time; one misses the field, after a while. Might I be allowed to change my mind?'

'You might.' There was neither friendliness nor laughter in Sun's concession. 'Do you or don't you?'

'I'll be pleased to help. Will there be a detailed briefing?'

'In an hour, at general staff HQ,' said Wang. 'We'll have to hurry; it's vital to get you into Canton before nightfall and you've a long journey ahead of you.'

'Then there's no more to be said.' Lo Bing nodded pleasantly, as if they'd all been enjoying a cup of tea and a chat. Wang waited until the door had closed behind him before he spoke.

'I only got Ming Rong's report a few minutes before the meeting. I haven't had a chance to read it properly.'

'But you know what it says?'

'In outline. He found Gansu-B-Ten and started to dig.'

'Fortunately the high-resolution satellite photographs enabled him to do it in more or less the right place.'

'I gather mass graves show up in a special way; something to do with changes in the soil?'

'Something like that. And there they were. Fifty-eight bodies. At that, people started to talk. One in particular.'

'The man out there, Colonel what's-his-name?'

'Lai Jia Yao. He was with *our friend* the day after the "incident", as he so diplomatically calls it. Colonel Lai Jia Yao has decided to remember a great deal more about the whole thing than appeared at the time.'

'So now we've nailed Lo Bing. I still don't understand what he thought he was *doing*.'

'He wanted me, and everyone else, to believe that the Russians had shot down the satellite, so that suspicion would be diverted away from China when he proved his weapon.'

'But surely he'd have wanted everyone to *know* about the beam-weapon. What's the point of keeping a thing like that under wraps?'

'You want people to know when the thing's functional, not at the testing stage. But he didn't only intend to divert suspicion – he had to make sure that Russia and America were at loggerheads while he sorted out China's internal politics after the Chairman's death; with that satellite episode to worry about, they'd hardly be likely to interfere with China.'

'What a risk!'

'Ah, but Sledge Hammer was his one and only bid for power, you see. He didn't have anything else.'

'Why keep it a secret from us, though? Why not come out in the open and threaten us with it, right from the start?'

'Because no one could be allowed to know just how successful his team had been until he was ready to make his move. Not a bad strategy; particularly when you remember that we're still not any closer to knowing how to handle him.'

'What should I tell him to do with the girl?'

'What do you think?'

'I'm for interrogating her. Remember the murder that was

reported from Liuzhou last night? The boatman, what was his name . . . ?'

'Lin.'

'That's something to do with Diana Young, I'm sure of it. That ring they found near the body . . .'

'You may be right.' Sun frowned. 'But we haven't got the girl yet.'

'We will. Lo Bing and ten men, against unarmed civilians . . .'

'Unarmed?' Sun raised an eyebrow.

'Well, obviously I'm assuming –'

'She's travelling on the Statewing convoy. According to dockyard sources, when those lighters left Hong Kong they were ninety percent crewed by ex-United States marines. They're carrying enough weapons to arm a standard infantry platoon. But Guoying' – Sun permitted himself one very tired smile – 'Please don't tell Lo Bing that.'

THIRTY

◇

Leong retracted the portable telephone's aerial and shook his head.

'But he *must* be there!'

'Brigadier-General Lo Bing has gone to Canton and can't be contacted. No one knows what he's up to.'

'No one ever does.' Cumnor wiped his forehead with a silk handkerchief. 'That man's too dangerous to live,' he said viciously.

'What are you going to do?'

Cumnor stared into the middle-distance. 'If he's dropped out of sight, it can only be for one reason: he's ready to make his move. A few hours from now, he'll be in Kowloon, along with half the Chinese army.' He wiped his face again. 'Contact Fomenko, find out what's holding things up at his end.'

'I've already spoken to him. He says there's a problem. They've lost touch with their men inside China.'

Cumnor swore. 'No photographs of the Boeing?'

Leong shook his head.

'All right. All right. We'll play it strictly according to the agreed plan. Lo Bing wants the Club's computer-tape destroyed, sabotaged, anything. I've got to get my hands on it before Young can use it to siphon off the funds.'

'They won't want to give it to you.'

'They will when they've heard me out.' The expression on his face was murderous. 'Let's get this farce over with.'

He emerged from the tunnel and adjusted his jacket-cuffs, entering the underground boardroom in time to hear Simon Young say, '. . . I got the final version of the Scroll of

Benevolence from Ducannon Young Electronics an hour ago. It's ready to run.'

'You've tested it?' asked Tom.

'Yes. It works.'

'So it exists,' Granville Peterson murmured. 'It truly *is*. At last. All that Tom here needs to drain the colony dry. Where is it now?'

'If you don't mind, I'd rather not say until nearer the time.'

Alexander Cumnor fidgeted with annoyance. He checked his Piaget wristwatch, confirmed the reading by the Rolex Oyster worn outside his jacket sleeve and leaned forward. 'It had better work. We go tomorrow.'

The atmosphere in the underground room briefly vibrated with the rustle of men changing position and became quiet. Tom Young cleared his throat. 'Why, when there's still so much to do?'

'Because the market's on its last legs, the Hong Kong dollar has gone through the floor and confidence can't be maintained any longer. All kinds of rumours are flying around – including, I may say, the perfectly true story that some of the colony's richest companies are bailing out.'

'Now just a minute, Alex.'

Tom looked down the table to see who had spoken and with relief identified an ally. Harry Longman was head of one of the largest property groups in Hong Kong. 'Yes, Harry?'

'We all know that things have gone wrong here. When that twopenny-halfpenny bank crashed, there were bound to be ructions. But the Americans and the Soviets seem to be sorting things out.'

Longman, a fat, balding Englishman in his early fifties, looked up and down the table in search of support. He found some, not much. Tom saw how rattled the Club was and clenched his fists beneath the table. Trouble was like strong beer: you could smell it brewing.

Cumnor put forefinger and thumb together and prodded the table. 'I don't understand you, Longman. Did you notice what you had to fight your way through in order to come here this morning? Armed police everywhere, the Corporation cordoned off . . . have you read a paper today? The frontier with the mainland's closed. Reuter's correspondent was expelled from Beijing last night and there are more expulsions on the way.' His voice rose, there was a note of hysteria in it now. 'The Taiwanese press is jumping up and down with glee, they say there's another revolution coming; have you checked the embassy cipher traffic? Do you know what the British ambassador in Beijing is saying to London? And don't pretend you don't know, because everyone around this table has been copied in on it for years . . . they're saying the Thai embassy's been burned to the ground, and that there was a massacre in front of the North Korean legation when some students demonstrated against Chinese imperialism – *Chinese imperialism, my God!*' He flung his arms wide. 'Is anybody listening?'

'We're listening, Alex.' Tom tried to inflect his voice with sarcasm, but the ploy backfired. Someone down at the far end of the table echoed, 'We're listening, all right.'

Cumnor, encouraged, seized the initiative. 'It gets worse. My information is that China was behind the destruction of that telecommunications satellite, not the Soviet Union.'

'*What?*'

But Cumnor raised a hand. 'If that's right, I hardly have to spell out the consequences for Benevolence. The whole project depends on adequate communications with the outside world being maintained during the crucial hours. If China can cut us off –'

'Who the hell told you that?' Tom was openly contemptuous.

'A reliable source.'

'Who?'

'I'm not at liberty to say.'

'Then you can hardly expect us to –'

'Proof is coming. Proof is definitely coming.'

'When? What kind of proof?'

'Tomorrow at the latest. There'll be statements from eye-witnesses, photographs taken inside the plane that launched the attack.' Cumnor looked around the table. No one analysing his haughty demeanour could have guessed the magnitude of his bluff. 'I tell you, I believe this story and I'm going to act on it.'

'Calm down, Alex. We all know that your sources are excellent.'

'Then let's *do* something. Let's get the hell out while there are still some assets to save. Because Red China doesn't only have the means to isolate Hong Kong, she knows about Benevolence as well. Or if she doesn't, she soon will.'

The second of silence that greeted this bombshell was succeeded by chaos. Tom had to stand up and shout before he could restore order. 'All right, Alex,' he said tersely. 'You've had your drama. Now get to the point. What have you heard?'

'Don't ask me.' Cumnor turned until he could stare accusingly at Simon Young. 'Ask your son, over there. Ask him where his daughter is. Ask him what she knows.'

One by one heads turned, until Simon found himself being stared at by every member of the Club. He cleared his throat. 'It's true that Diana's in China,' he began slowly. 'Jinny asked her to take her ashes back to Chaiyang. But she knows nothing, repeat *nothing* about Benevolence.' He paused. 'Unfortunately she . . . she ran into trouble.'

'What kind of trouble?' Longman asked.

'Central Control of Intelligence put a tail on her.' Simon's voice rose and became firmer. 'What matters is that she's nearly home. Warren Honnyman radioed me this morning. Diana got as far as Liuzhou.' He looked at his watch. 'She's coming in on the Statewing convoy, right now.'

'You mean she's still not *out?'*

The room once more erupted. Again, it was Cumnor who found a focus for their collective anger.

'All these years I've known you, Simon, and I never once took you for a fool. Yet now you show yourself up as the biggest goddam fool in Hong Kong. You've been party to a secret that could destroy every man sitting around this table – to say nothing of their families, their employees, their customers and clients. Everyone trusted you; you wouldn't be sitting here otherwise. And now what you're telling us is that you've blown the whole thing to hell.'

No one realized what Mat Young was going to do when he rose from his seat; perhaps they thought he meant to check something on the TV screen. In the event he marched up to Cumnor's chair, hauled him out by the armpits and flung him on the floor.

The fracas lasted no more than a few seconds; many hands disentangled the protagonists, and Mat soon found that he had no stomach for a brawl with an opponent who refused to fight. He was forcibly thrust back into his chair and told to stay there. Cumnor pushed aside would-be helpers with a brusqueness that said far more about his state of mind than his bland expression. One by one the members of the Club returned to the places they'd vacated so precipitously when Mat launched his attack, and turned to the head of the table where their chairman was still standing as if aloof.

He looked at each man in turn. First his eyes ran the length of the right-hand side of the table; then they scanned the left. He was counting.

They had started as a Club of Twenty; now they were nineteen. Warren Honnyman was absent, which left eighteen. Simon and Mat had one vote between them and, in this crisis at least, could be relied on to cast it with Tom. Harry Longman likewise. Three definite votes. Against them, Cumnor – dead against. Which left fourteen uncommitted.

Tom knew each man's business better than the man himself. At this moment, however, it wasn't business that concerned him; instead, his mind homed in on the personal things, the considerations that might make someone want to stay in Hong Kong, or become desperate to leave.

Take Robert Clancy, for instance: chairman of Continental Financial Services, oldest of the participants, a confirmed bachelor without family or ties outside the colony . . . and a beautiful Chinese mistress maintained in a Mid-Levels luxury apartment. Now that the chips were down, how much did he *want* that woman . . . ?

What about Max Weber, vice-president of the largest

German *hong*, former steward of the Royal Hong Kong Jockey Club, with homes in Brisbane and Frankfurt as well as a house in Shek-O?

Or Adrian de Lisle, John Blake, Peter Carrigan and Martin Panmuir-Smith: the four leaders of the next largest English concerns after Ducannon Young itself — men who'd spent their lives chasing crumbs beneath Simon's table and had no reason to love him now. How strong were the ties that held them to Hong Kong?

Tom continued his mental head-count. At the far end of the table, a coterie of money-men: bankers, insurers and investment advisers of one kind or another, who over the years had given the Club sterling advice . . . without ever quite also managing to give the impression that they truly belonged to it. There were only four Chinese members of the Club; all of them with the exception of Cumnor fell into this category. Cautious men; men with strategies that were known to extend far beyond anything the Club might plan or execute. What effect did Cumnor's revelations have on those strategies? Shadowy, unknown quantities at the best of times, what did men like Rameses Wong and Harry Tan *really* intend doing about the mainland?

There were seven in this club-within-a-club. Halfway down the table sat their unacknowledged leader: Granville Peterson, chief executive of the next most powerful bank after the Corporation itself; someone who, in tandem with Tom, exercised autocratic dominion over far more than just the financial affairs of the colony. Tom spent a long time examining Peterson's impassive face. There had been an era when, if you wanted to make serious money in Hong Kong, you ended up talking to Peterson or Young, sometimes both. Each man around this table at least once in his career had been obliged to bow before the colony's banking monarchs. Perhaps they did not feel like bowing now . . .

Tom left the seven financiers and moved on to Roger Sanderson. Head of Splendair, the independent airline that had snatched so much traffic from Cathay Pacific and Dragonair over the past three years: a company said to be heavily indebted to Cumnor, among others. Were the rumours true? What if they were?

Cumnor seemed distressed by his jacket-cuff's untidy habit of riding up: he straightened it a couple of times, peered more closely at the ornamental button and cleared his throat, ready for the kill.

'The situation we find ourselves in,' he began, 'is critical. Thanks to that man, there' – he jabbed a denunciatory finger in Simon's direction – 'we now have to work on the basis that mainland China knows our plans and will do anything it can to frustrate them.'

Mat glanced sideways at his father. Simon sat well back from the table, left arm carelessly flung over the back of his chair, right hand doodling on a scratchpad. The expression on his face indicated polite, if resigned attention to a rather boring monologue.

'But it's worse than that, isn't it?' Cumnor paused, as if expecting a response to his rhetorical question. No one spoke.

'It's worse than that, because Simon Young has put himself in a strange and powerful position. He has contacts with Chinese Central Control of Intelligence, we all know that. Even supposing it's true Diana Young knows nothing about Benevolence, why shouldn't her father go to the Chinese with a deal: free my daughter and I'll tell you about the Club of Twenty? And if that's right, I say he's no longer fit to be trusted with the Scroll of Benevolence. That computer tape's all that stands between us and ruin; I for one am not prepared to see my future left in Simon Young's hands. He's to turn that tape over to the Club. He's to do it now.'

'That's the biggest load of crap I've heard in my fifty years in Hong Kong.'

Granville Peterson. As Tom Young listened to the words, to the tone in which they were spoken, he felt his heartbeat quicken.

'Why?' Cumnor seemed unperturbed; it was as if he had foreseen this interjection and, polished debater that he was, prepared for it. And for the next interruption. And for the one after that.

'First, because Chinese Intelligence haven't yet got hold of Diana, she's with Warren.'

'We only have her father's word for that.'

'Good enough for me.' Peterson's tone did not change. 'I'm not about to start questioning his honour at this time. And I've a second reason for supporting Simon: I know he won't betray us to Chinese Intelligence, even if they do succeed in capturing his daughter.'

'That's your opinion.'

'Yes. I know him better than I know you.'

The studied insult had its effect. It wasn't the kind of thing you said in Hong Kong unless you were prepared to back it all the way and beyond. Cumnor knew he'd just heard himself called. 'Then you'd better be sure you know him pretty damn well,' he murmured politely. 'For my part, I say that at this delicate juncture in our affairs he can't be trusted. Certainly not enough to keep custody of that tape.'

'You're losing your audience.' Max Weber, leaning forward like a conscientious student, anxious to make his contribution to the seminar. 'The situation is serious, we all recognize that; but you're losing your audience.'

Murmurs of assent were audible. Decency and fair play were being questioned by one whose own record in those areas was uncertain. When Simon at last threw down the pencil and pulled his chair closer to the table, the silence deepened.

'I think it's true, what Granville just said: we none of us know you that well, Alex. I rather thought I did, at one time. Jinny's funeral, for example – I liked you then. Things you said made me think of you for the first time as a friend.'

Words that would go home, Mat realized admiringly; words that worked. Cumnor already knew it. His otherwise mask-like face had developed a tic at the corner of the mouth.

'Then again, I've always admired your contribution here, in this room. It's been effective. At times it's been inspirational.'

So simple, so much to the point. Above all, so very, very English: raising your enemy high enough to guarantee that when he fell he didn't just break, he shattered.

'But now we don't need inspiration, we need something

more concrete. I have a plan I think will work. It's a two-part proposal. If someone will second it, there can be a formal vote. I'm in favour of that: it'll clear the air.'

Now Simon folded his hands on the table and paused, as if wanting to ensure the correct formulation of his motion; a motion, everyone realized, that would put him and his reputation – his honour – on the line.

'I propose that my father orders the implementation of first-phase Benevolence here and now, at this meeting. You know the timetable as well as I do: what I'm saying is that we will go, leave Hong Kong, twenty-four hours from Tom giving the nod. I believe my daughter will be back long before then; if she isn't, well . . .' His voice cracked, for an instant he stared at his folded hands, only to recover at once.

'I can't suggest to you that Benevolence ought to be put at risk for the sake of one girl. Even though it's my own daughter we're talking about. Which brings me to the second part of the resolution.'

Simon raised his pencil and pointed it at Cumnor. 'That man says he doesn't trust me. I have to tell you that I don't trust him. Not long after he sweet-talked me at my wife's funeral he tried to suborn Qiu Qianwei, one of my senior employees, although Alex didn't realize I knew that until I just told him. The picture I now have of him is very different from the one I conceived originally.'

Cumnor said nothing in self-defence. His silence weighed against him. Mat looked from face to face. In Simon they were listening to someone who sailed with almost limitless ballast of public confidence. It showed in their eyes.

Simon was speaking again. 'Every man here has traded in the Orient over a long period. There's a certain type of Chinese we've all learned to respect. Because they come clean and they're open in their dealings. They're happy with western commercial ways. We share an international cast of mind, if you like. And then there's another type . . .'

The pause was a long one. When at last he spoke, Simon's voice was tart with rancour. 'The kind who's secretive, and doesn't want to join. The kind that we simply aren't ever allowed to get to know. The sort of man who's as incapable of presenting a straight face to the world as that man *there* – another jab of the pencil at Cumnor – 'is of confessing what really motivates him today.' Simon slowly shook his head. 'I wish I could tell the members of this Club what that was. But I don't know. And yet he's the one who's asking us to take everything he says at face value. He says he can prove that China shot down the satellite. I have to tell you, I don't believe that.' Simon paused. 'I think he is lying.'

There followed three heartbeats of silence. Then Longman guffawed: a searing, offensive series of sounds. 'Lying,' he said. 'I've thought that for years. But now I'll tell you something, Cumnor, and glad of the chance: liar or not, I've never liked *you*.' He nodded forcefully at the Chinese. 'I'll second you, Simon. I can't pretend I'm overjoyed at the timing, and I wish you could have found a way of preventing this – but I'm with you.'

'You haven't heard the second part of my motion yet.'

'I don't think I need to. It involves getting rid of Cumnor, am I right?'

'I want a document out of him. Something committing him to Benevolence that he can't wriggle out of afterwards. Either that, or yes: he's out.'

'Dangerous,' Granville Peterson observed thoughtfully. 'Even if he signs, once he's out of this room he can do a lot of damage.'

'I've thought of that. I'm prepared to have a watchdog by my side over the next twenty-four hours, to monitor every move I make . . . as long as Cumnor's ready to do the same. So what about it, Alex?'

Cumnor raised his right hand and made an elaborate show of consulting one of his wristwatches. 'Time's passing,' he remarked. 'We've got better things to do than discuss this nonsense. Everyone's agreed that Benevolence has to roll *now*. The rest of your proposal . . . well frankly, it's just whistling in the dark to cover up your stupidity. My own suggestion's rather more practical. I want that tape handed over to a committee of the Club, now, at once. I'm prepared to be a member of that committee. So if –'

'Wait a minute. There's a motion on the table.' Peterson's voice was unexpectedly harsh. 'I'm happy to see it taken as a composite resolution, both parts standing or falling together. Mr Chairman?'

'Those in favour of Simon Young's resolution?'

Four hands shot up at once: Peterson's, Weber's, Longman's and one from the coterie of money-men. Simon and Tom were next to vote in favour. Another banker joined them, but with some show of reluctance. Clancy. Eight.

'Against?'

Cumnor, of course. The four leaders of the English *hongs* voted as a block, their faces expressionless. Was it revenge, Mat wondered? Sound commercial judgement? Whatever their motivation, none of them seemed keen to look Simon in the eye.

The rest of the bankers went into a huddle; then two of them raised their hands. Seven against.

'Abstentions?'

Three – including Roger Sanderson, the last man Tom would have relied on.

'The resolution is carried. Simon, if you're agreeable, I'll send one of the Corporation's armoured vans to collect the tape.'

'Fine.'

'Next, arrangements for watchdogs. Someone to keep an eye on you and on Alex as well . . .'

Cumnor stood up and, remembering to button his jacket, walked towards the door. Tom's voice was curt. 'Come back here!'

Simon jumped out of his chair and began to stride around the table. But Cumnor had already reached the door, and when he turned back to face the room he was holding a pistol. 'No,' he said quietly. 'But I'm still a part of Benevolence, gentlemen. You won't be leaving Hong Kong without me.'

Then the door was closing behind him without a sound.

THIRTY-ONE

◇

The noise of the six shots fired within seconds of one another reverberated through the lighter like so many thunderflashes. Statewing's senior convoy-captain lowered the Smith & Wesson and removed a cheroot from his mouth for long enough to say, 'That ought to do it.'

Diana looked. Three holes in the side of one coffin and three in the side of another: each set in near enough a straight line. Impressive. But then she knew that the captain, Lloyd Saunders, had served in the US marines alongside Warren Honnyman. They were going to need those martial skills.

When she asked, 'Do we really have to stay in there?' Warren looked troubled.

'If the Chinese board us, yes! It's your only hiding-place.'

Diana tried to accept his judgement. But breathing below deck in the deep lighter was difficult: the stench of camphor coffins, piled ten high and restrained by rope nets, seemed to saturate the cargo space like concentrated perfume. The thought of climbing into one of them, even though aerated by Saunders' revolver, was too much to bear

She left the two men huddled together, conferring in anxious whispers, and made her way down the nearest aisle, a corridor fabricated by two double-rows of coffins. Chang Ping was sitting by the port side of the hull with his back to the lighter's inner skin, knees up, head cradled on his arms.

Diana flashed her torch at him. Every so often he would mutter something and clench his fists, or restlessly rearrange his arms, before sinking back into lethargy. He had been like that ever since they'd boarded at Liuzhou, the day before.

Since then he'd neither eaten nor slept, although at Diana's insistence he had drunk water. He complained constantly about stiffness of the muscles, particularly around the area of the wound in his leg. She was very worried about him.

Diana sat down. As she stared at the deck she knew without seeing that the convoy was beating its way fast down the West river ran fast and rough, sailing 'by guess and by God', the refuge. Sometimes they traversed broad, flat expanses of quiet water, bounded by the glorious *karst* formations of green-decked rock that made this part of China legendary; and sometimes they plunged through towering gorges where the river ran fast and rough, sailing 'by guess and by God,' the navigator challenging currents that might dash them against the boulders which strewed the banks if he lost concentration for so much as a second. Sometimes, when she looked at Chang Ping, she felt as though the essential Diana Young had chosen a similar journey: one fraught with danger before and behind, below and above and on either side. Enemies everywhere. Danger without end. A voyage into emotional rapids, one without hope.

Somehow she managed to expel these fears from her mind and concentrate on immediate reality — which was bad enough.

Warren had cut short the jollifications at the Liuzhou Hotel by pretending to have mysterious engine trouble, necessitating an immediate return to Hong Kong for repairs. Brushing aside all offers of mechanical aid, he had insisted on supervising the loading of the cargoes personally, thrusting a clipboard into Diana's hands and putting her forward to the curious as his personal clerk. They had finally edged out of the barge-roads just before seven o'clock on a wet-slate morning, keeping their speed down until out of sight of the town and then accelerating to maximum revolutions, a rate of progress they had maintained ever since.

The crew were sinister and silent, but they did something to raise Diana's spirits. All of them had known Warren for years; and the complement of arms they carried seemed astonishing, until Saunders had explained to her, through clouds of thick, throat-tickling smoke, that they had come upriver in the conviction that finding Diana would be one thing, keeping her another.

Around four o'clock the previous afternoon, they'd heard a droning high above them, away to the west.

'Yun-5.' Diana peered up through the hatch-cover from the bottom of the lighter to see Saunders smiling down at them. 'Small bi-plane. Army. Circled twice and went home. We can expect company, Diana. Stay there.'

Now, looking at Chang Ping, she felt sure that when the boarding-party came, she would not force him to take refuge in a coffin. There was a symbolic finality about that which she rejected. Surrender would be more dignified.

Chang Ping raised his head and stared at Diana. The look in his eyes disturbed her. 'What's up?' she asked.

'Nothing. I've been thinking, that's all.' He shivered and looked away.

'Thinking what about?'

'Hong Kong. Are you . . . ?'

'Am I what?'

'Are you really going to help me? Really?' It came out in a rush.

Diana couldn't see his face. 'Chang Ping, what is it, what's the matter?'

'Sometimes I can't believe . . . you, maybe you'll turn me in and then I'll be sent back. Maybe you're pretending.'

His shivers had turned into bouts of shuddering. Diana changed position, working around on her knees until she could look him in the face. She knew she was taking a risk, but – 'Yes,' she said, cupping his cheeks between her hands. 'I'm going to help you.' She pulled him towards her and gently kissed his forehead. 'Really and truly.'

He reached up to hold her wrists and for a moment stared into her eyes as if testing for the truth. Only then did he release her and once more rest his back against the lighter's side.

After a while Diana lay down on the hard steel deck next to him. Her own watch must have broken and Chang Ping's had vanished, but she sensed it was nightfall. The sound of water rushing against the hull brought no sense of peace. This river was an evil stretch of water: it had a voice and seemed determined to speak to her, force her to understand that it was waiting, waiting, could wait forever if need be. The constant 'sssh'-ing sound beside her head was the river's way of lulling her asleep, opening the way for it to strike. She must not sleep. Not sleep . . .

Many feet suddenly pounded along the steel deck-plates, sending metallic echoes ballooning through the hold. Diana was shocked into wakefulness. Chang Ping sat up, convulsed with shivers. His eyes glittered as two white slits in the gloom. 'What was that?' he gasped.

Feet were still racing along the deck, Diana could hear muffled voices coming at her from many directions, as if the crew were deploying along the full stretch of the convoy. Then she heard the first bout of automatic fire. It seemed far away, but next second there came an answering fusillade from the barges and Diana covered her ears.

Only for a moment, however. The thought of facing bullets terrified her, but there was one thing worse: cowering like a rat beside a pile of coffins in what could itself any minute become one huge steel coffin. She made for the ladder beneath the forward hatch, swiftly climbing to the top where she pushed aside a corner of the heavy canvas cover. They were riding in the second lighter from the front. Forward, she could see the tug's navigation lights, and every so often the beam of its spotlight. As her head reached deck-level the light swung around to sweep the left-hand riverbank; and then Diana saw small boats that sat low in the water, about fifty metres away, heading straight for them.

Somewhere deafeningly close came another burst of fire, answered at once from the nearest assault craft. Then she heard more shots, this time from the starboard bow behind her, closely followed by a scream and the clatter of something hard dropped on the deck. They were under attack from both sides.

Once the searchlight beam locked onto the leading craft the firing from the barges, hitherto intermittent, began to come together in a concentrated stream. Diana saw three, maybe four, ghostly silhouettes suddenly go into spasm. One of them stretched upright, as if preparing to dive; the boat wobbled, overturned and swiftly sank.

There were two other assault craft on the port side within Diana's vision. Now one of them peeled off, making for the rear of the convoy, while the other covered it. The spotlight, designed to illuminate a path in front of the tug, could not follow; and seconds later the captain, evidently deciding that the light afforded more of a target than it helped his men direct their fire, extinguished it. Diana, trying to keep her head below the protection of the steel hatch-side and see at the same time, could make out little of what happened next. The volleys coming from the rear of the convoy seemed to diminish, only to re-explode in a continuous roar before dying away altogether. The night was silent.

Diana slid down the ladder and told Chang Ping what she'd seen. He seemed more alert now.

'They must have planned to surprise a lot of unarmed sailors. But this convoy's crewed by an army. So now they're concentrating their efforts on where they think we're weakest: the stern.'

'That's true! I overheard Warren telling Lloyd Saunders to put all his fire-power around this barge, the one we're on. What happens now?'

He shook his head.

Diana did not have long to wait for her answer, however, because within minutes the firing had opened up again. Confused noises could be heard above their heads where the crew fought to defend them. She shuddered as the sound of another cry penetrated the covers; something hit the deck, slithered across it and tumbled into the river.

'They're taking the lighters one by one.' Chang Ping spoke gravely, his eyes fixed on the cover. 'They pick off the defenders on the next barge forward, then use their assault craft to move up.'

'Leapfrogging?'

'In a way. The lighters aren't very close together and we're

310

still moving. That means they can't jump across the gap. But it's bad for Honnyman too – his men can only stand and fight, they can't retreat and consolidate.'

'You make it sound like the attackers are bound to win.'

'The advantage is with them.'

'Chang Ping . . . who *are* these people?'

'They're sent by Sun Shanwang. As to who they are . . .' He shrugged.

Diana stared at him a moment longer. Did he really not know? Or was this just another skein in the web he'd used to entrap her? Then she grabbed the ladder and began to climb again.

Chang Ping caught hold of her leg. 'Come back!'

'I've got to stop it!'

'You can't! No one can stop what's happening outside. Not until somebody wins.'

'I'm going up,' she said rationally. 'My shirt's white. If I raise my hands, I –'

The interior of the barge was suddenly flooded with light. A flare, its brilliance diffused through the green canvas. The next phase of the attack had begun.

This time the racket seemed much closer. There were two sets of feet on the deck now. The defenders were nearest to Diana and Chang Ping; apart from the rattle of their Stens, they made no noise. But the attackers came inexorably forward from the aft swims, their feet pounding, sometimes slithering on the steel plates. Another flare revealed shadows against the canvas, ducking and weaving like dancers in some ghastly ballet.

Suddenly liquid sprayed across the cover, as if someone had flung a pot of paint over it, and a heavy weight fell onto the canvas to form a dark indentation. Diana could not take her eyes off it. She knew the battle was over.

All firing stopped. The silence contrasted so deeply that when Chang Ping swallowed, the sound made Diana jump. Their convoy was perceptibly slowing. A loud voice shouted commands in Chinese. Someone heaved the corpse off the cover and tossed it over the side. Then one corner of the canvas was drawn back and a torchbeam flashed into Diana's eyes.

'Up!'

She obeyed without thinking. Chang Ping followed. On the deck stood half a dozen figures, the torch illuminating their combat fatigues and automatic rifles.

A Chinese who had been standing a little apart from the rest barked a series of instructions. Diana and Chang Ping were bundled into one of the assault craft now moored to the side of the lighter. Moments later, soldiers hustled them aboard the barge next to the tug, where Warren and Lloyd Saunders were standing under guard. Four of the crew sat with their backs to the hatch-surround, hands clasped behind their necks.

The moment Chang Ping reached the deck he fell forward with a groan, fingers scrabbling for a hold. The single trooper following him up aimed a vicious kick at his crotch. As the man's foot swung inward Chang Ping flipped over, at the same time closing his legs in a scissor movement. The soldier gurgled with surprise, teetered, and fell backward into the river. When someone recovered his senses enough to direct a torch to where Chang Ping had lain a moment before, the deck was empty. Only the disturbed corner of the cover showed where he had gone.

Diana stared unbelievingly at the ruffled canvas. Now she remembered what the leading barge carried below. Live snakes in cages. Two thousand of them. All venomous.

The Chinese who appeared to command this attack shouldered his way through his men until he was only inches from Diana. He grabbed her shoulder and began to shake her, squealing and spitting invective. At last, tired of that, he retreated a pace and raised his weapon until it was pointing at Diana's stomach. He shouted a few sentences, then jerked his head at one of the troops. The man spoke hesitant English.

'General Lo Bing has given orders. Your friend is to come up at once. If not, in ten seconds, he will shoot you dead.'

The silence was shattered by the sound of a rifle-bolt being snapped back.

THIRTY-TWO

◇

A few hours before General Lo Bing launched his mission against the Statewing convoy, Qiu Qianwei's mainland contact failed to attend their last appointed rendezvous in Wanchai.

Qiu allowed him the obligatory five minutes' grace, then set off for the Ducannon Young headquarters building. That broken appointment might mean any one of a number of things, all of which Simon Young needed to know about. Qiu's personal interpretation was bleak and admitted of no contradiction: Sledge Hammer was about to come down on Steel Nail.

It was gone two o'clock in the morning, and although the streets of the colony were still crammed with bustlers and hustlers of every description Qiu knew better than to waste time on the front entrance. Fortunately he had a key to the side door next to the Law Courts, the one the directors used because the elevator there went non-stop to the boardroom. He paid off the cab a block short of his destination and walked the rest of the way.

From the first floor upward the Duncannon Young building was illuminated by internal lighting that shone through its green, plate-glass windows to make a giant signal-beacon. Green for Go: a confident, positive message to the other traders of Hong Kong. Qiu had always hated it. The glare reminded him of nothing so much as the sweet, mint-flavoured cordial his son Tingchen used to enjoy. Perhaps still did; Qiu had no means of knowing.

The ground floor was dark. He walked down the lane

in shadow, fishing for the key, and came within fifty feet of the car before registering its presence.

The black Jaguar had parked half on and half off the narrow pavement and its rear door was open. The interior light was either not working or someone had turned it off, but there was just enough glow to activate the red reflector set in the edge of the car's door. Qiu stopped. The street was in complete darkness; what, then, could have made the reflector come alive?

The side entrance to the building must be open.

Qiu had been studying the upper echelons of the DY hierarchy with minute care for many years; he knew that none of the directors drove Jaguars. Instinctively he flattened himself against the wall. His palms were damp.

There was a lightning flurry of activity.

One man ran across the narrow space separating the car from the building and climbed into the back seat. Then came a small group: two men holding a third by the elbows, forcing him into the car. One of the bodyguards, or whatever they were, followed their charge inside and slammed the door. The last man got into the driving seat, the white reversing lights came on and the Jaguar began to move backwards.

Qiu flung himself flat, stretching full-length in the angle between pavement and wall. There was no cover. If the driver turned on his headlights, Qiu would show up in the beam as clearly as if it were noon. *So had he turned on his lights?* No, he wouldn't have, of course he wouldn't, not if he were kidnapping Hong Kong's biggest *tai-pan*.

For Qiu had just had time to recognize the man being rushed into the car. Simon Young. And he was not going willingly.

As predicted, the driver kept his lights off until he'd reversed almost as far as Queensway. Then he did switch them on; but by that time Qiu had gained the safety of the Ducannon Young side entrance, pressed hard into the recess there.

The second the Jaguar completed its turn and began its forward progress into the mainstream of traffic, Qiu was sprinting for the end of the alley. There he had to give way to a security van that was turning off Queensway directly into his

314

path; as it went by he saw the insignia on its side and wondered why the Corporation was calling on Ducannon Young at such an unearthly hour.

He flagged down the first cab he saw, leaned inside the driver's window, said, 'Excuse me' in impeccable Cantonese, and applied expert finger pressure to the man's carotid artery. He shoved the unconscious cabby over onto the front passenger seat before climbing in, thrusting the man's legs off the pedals as he did so.

Qiu's eyes darted this way and that along the flow, but there was no sign of the Jaguar. He pulled up on a red light outside the Star Ferry terminal, avoiding an attempt by a party of drunken Chinese to hail him, then rapidly scanned left, right and centre. Nothing. You could hardly mistake a Jaguar. Qiu swore and wiped a hand across his brow. What to do? Central Police HQ was behind him, better make for that . . .

The lights changed. Qiu looked over his shoulder, preparatory to pulling out into the right-hand lane. And there was the Jaguar, two cars behind him but in the other carriageway, its indicator blinking for the same turn that Qiu had already planned.

· The cab-driver started coming to his senses. Qiu clenched his teeth and swung the wheel hard, cutting across three lanes to the kerb opposite the taxi-rank next to the Star Ferry. He pushed his hapless passenger onto the pavement before accelerating away to the right. Horns tooted angrily, but within seconds he had gained the outer lane and was settling down to tail the Jaguar, now cruising at a steady forty miles an hour along the middle of the highway.

Before long it was clear to Qiu that his quarry intended to cross the harbour by tunnel. He changed lane, seeking to make himself as inconspicuous as possible, and signalled for a turn, appearing to change his mind at the very last minute. Yes! Old tunnel entrance coming up . . .

Once arrived in Tsim Sha Tsui East the Jaguar's driver took the left hand exit. At Nathan Road he turned right and drove as far as Jordan Road, where he made a left.

Qiu's mouth turned dry. They were heading for the sea.

Ferry Street. Almost before he knew it the black car had pulled over to the side of the road at the southernmost tip of Yaumati typhoon shelter and the driver was getting out. Qiu drove straight past without slowing, then turned right into Pak Hoi Street, where he abandoned the cab.

He raced back to Ferry Street in time to see the Jaguar reverse out into the slow lane and drive away in the direction of Mong Kok. Shielded by the shadows of the nearest warehouse wall he could just see a group of men standing with their backs to him, looking out to sea. They were perhaps a hundred metres away, but the street lamps were strong enough to show them bending to pick up what looked like a heavy sack. Then they descended the steps that led down to water level.

Qiu ran across Ferry Street, rested his hands on the railing and looked down. Below him the light was poor, but he could see figures hurrying along one of the walkways giving access to the hundreds of small craft that had sought temporary shelter in the artificial harbour. He raised his eyes and stared out to sea.

Somewhat to his right was Stone Cutter's Island; directly in front, he knew, the main harbour anchorage extended away into the darkness. He could discern many sets of riding lights; here and there some particularly large vessel was lit up from stem to stern, to facilitate the process of taking on cargo. Immediately in front of him, only the occasional weak light glimmered from the few sampans and other boats presently making use of the typhoon shelter. Between the great anchorage and the small, a dark shape hovered on the face of the water, silhouetted against the orange glow generated by a fully-lit tanker.

Qiu took in the high stern, the three pole-masts, the inimitable batten lug-sail, and at last he knew where they were taking Simon Young. He dashed back across Ferry Street, making for a public phone.

'I want to speak to Assistant Commissioner Reade.'

The bleary night-sergeant at the other end of the line

enquired if he knew what time it was before becoming less polite. Qiu cut him short.

'You will get him out of bed and you will tell him, "Wild Goose Pagoda". Understand?'

The night-sergeant did not resume his tirade.

'You will tell him that Simon Young has been taken prisoner by triads who are putting him aboard Alexander Cumnor's junk, off Yaumati. If Reade doesn't act *now*, Young's dead!' Qiu slammed down the phone.

He sped back to the rail overlooking the typhoon shelter. There was no sign of movement.

Qiu might have waited for Reade to show up, briefed him, then gone to bed knowing he'd done all he could for his employer. If it had been anyone but Cumnor, that's what he would have done.

But it was Cumnor's junk riding at anchor out there. And Cumnor somehow had managed to worm his way into the mainland, as far as Qiu Tingchen. Qiu's son. Ever since he had received the two letters from Cumnor's hands, and scrutinized them for long hours every night, and convinced himself that they were not forged, no, by no means . . . ever since then Qiu had been asking himself whether where a letter might go, a small boy might not go also?

Alexander Cumnor represented the only chance Qiu had of seeing his son again. And now he was preparing to up anchor and sail away.

Qiu ran down the steps to hail one of the sampans that were available for hire at any hour of the day or night. A sleepy, gum-chewing girl in her teens asked him where he wanted to go. While Qiu hesitated, a light showed briefly at the junk's prow. Then it began to flash at irregular intervals in a signal of some kind. *Move!*

'Take me out to that freighter, over there . . . the one with the white star on its funnel.'

The girl spat into the oily water which came almost up to the top of the gunwale and nodded. Before long they were gliding silently through the shelter's southern exit.

Qiu asked the price of his passage. They haggled briefly, but silence was worth more to him than money. When he held out the notes she took them without disturbing the even rhythm of her stroke. She showed no surprise at being paid halfway through the journey, or at the subsequent sight of Qiu taking off his jacket and folding it up; life seemed all one to her.

The course he had bought took him within fifty metres of the *Swatow*'s stern. Qiu waited until the last moment before saying to the girl, 'Keep straight on, whatever happens. Go to the freighter, wait five minutes, come back. I'll call for my jacket tomorrow, okay?'

She nodded: when Qiu disappeared over the side she even waved to him, although he did not see that. Perhaps she liked him. Perhaps he imported a degree of excitement into that void between the twin exigencies of childishness and senility.

Qiu battled to keep his head above water. He knew that the harbour was riddled with typhus and every other imaginable kind of bacteriological horror, that the surface of the water consisted of a layer of oil which could kill a man if he swallowed it, or blind him if he let his eyes touch it.

The junk was one of the large, Wusung River craft from the north, and had been stylishly converted to allow for standards of modern comfort. Its stern deck would be where Cumnor had his quarters. Deep picture windows overhung the sea, one at the rear and one on either side, but tonight all of them were shuttered and dark.

No one hailed Qiu. No gunshot-flashes pinpricked the darkness. He got a hold on the huge, hardwood rudder and pulled himself out of the water. As he did so, the deep-throated engines came to life. Just in time . . .

Qiu felt around for a line, a rung, anything he might use to propel himself up. Nothing.

The anchor.

He lowered himself off his perch, careful to enter the sea soundlessly, and swam for the chain. Crawling up, sloth-fashion, was the hardest physical task he'd ever attempted. At last his head bumped against the wooden hull. Qiu uncrossed his ankles, dangling from the anchor-chain. By drawing on

318

his last reserves of stamina he was able to reverse his position, until he was facing the hull-wall. With his right hand, the strongest, he grabbed for the edge of the anchor-port, missed, swung precariously, nearly fell . . . he began to kick, turning his body into a pendulum. One . . . two . . . *three* . . .

On the final count he launched himself forward. His hands grasped the bottom of the port, but there was nothing left in his arms, he was going to fall . . . then his feet landed on one row of the ribbing that ran the length of the ship, and he was safe.

For the moment.

While Qiu was assessing his options he heard voices above and flattened himself further against the planking. Cumnor's smooth, quiet delivery predominated; Qiu could easily follow the *Swatow*'s owner as he moved at the centre of an entourage from the prow to the waist of the ship, where a companionway led down to his suite.

Somewhere on the other side of the hull, not far from Qiu's head, a second engine spluttered into life. Instinct told him, just in time, what its function was: an anchor-winch.

He let go of the port and eased himself sideways. His feet rested on one narrow slat and his hands were gripping another. Because the slats had been preserved in the old-fashioned way with *dammar* oil, they were slippery. *He had to move!*

The anchor was winched in; then the *Swatow* got under way, making due south for the western lanes at the approach to Victoria Harbour. Qiu angled his feet against the side of the hull, like a penguin, and began to climb the makeshift ladder of slats.

The second his eyes came level with the top of the gunwale he ducked down again, out of sight; but one glance had been enough to show him only a skeleton crew at work on the sails. A solitary light glowed forward, in the turret-bridge overlooking the prow.

He waited awhile before risking another look. This time the sails were set, the deck deserted. Qiu scrambled over the side and crouched low in the shadows between the aft deck-house and the gunwale he'd just crossed, using a capstan for additional cover. The *Swatow* veered starboard, setting a course for Kellett Bank. Away from the protection of the main anchorage a light sea was running and she began to pitch a little, all her timbers creaking, as the salt sea-breeze met her head-on.

Apart from red and green running lights, and the solitary glow from the fore-turret, the ship was in darkness. Qiu stumbled along until he was level with the housing over the companionway. Something was stowed on its flat roof. Cautiously he ran his fingers over it. A dinghy, held in place by elasticated ropes.

Keeping his back against the wall he edged around the corner. The deck yawned ahead of him like the stage of a darkened theatre. He crept along the housing until he could go no further without revealing himself at the top of the stairs to anyone who might be keeping watch below. Although he was committed now, there could be no going back, still he dreaded the next move.

He had to look.

Qiu whiplashed his head around the angle of the companionway-door and back again with the speed of a fish, then closed his eyes, allowing the memory of what he'd seen to unfold across his retinas.

A dozen stairs, lit by two pairs of wall-mounted lamps. Carpet. Door at the bottom. Something odd about the door. No human presence.

Qiu opened his eyes. The carpet would deaden the sound of his approach. But he knew his sodden clothes would make more noise than wet skin, so he stripped down to his underpants, rolling up his shirt and singlet inside his trousers before tossing the bundle overboard.

He returned to the companionway, shivering slightly, and reached out to grasp the housing. The *Swatow* dipped into the trough of a wave, sending him reeling across the deck. Qiu cursed his luck and lunged back to grab the capstan.

Seconds later he knew the wave had saved him.

As he prepared to move, he heard voices below and a door slammed. But for those vital few seconds, he would have been going down the stairs in full view of whoever had just opened and closed the door.

Qiu looked for somewhere to hide. But then he heard what sounded like another door being slammed, only the noise was different, muted. A cupboard, perhaps . . .

He eased back to the edge of the housing and risked a glance. Someone stood at the foot of the stairs, sideways on to him, peering at a bunch of keys in his hands. Chinese, wearing a suit. Not Cumnor. Leong.

What had Cumnor's personal assistant been doing with the keys?

Footsteps. Coming up. Coming closer.

Was there anything useful Leong could tell him? Qiu debated the question, Leong's life dangling just as the keys had dangled from his own hands a moment ago.

No.

Leong ascended the stairs and made for the bridge without a backward glance. Qiu came off the wall like a catapulted stone – left hand over the mouth, remembering to pinch the nostrils shut, right hand under the chin, back, back . . . *twist.*

Qiu rolled the corpse to the shadow of the gunwale before setting to work. The keys were in Leong's right-hand trouser pocket. Four of them on a ring. Qiu put them between his teeth and got rid of the body over the side. Only then did he make for the stairs.

He continued to descend until he reached the stern-deck, a carpeted area three feet square marked out by the door, the stairs, and, to either side, wall-mounted cupboards. Qiu tried the handle of one. Locked cupboards.

The lower half of the cabin-door was made of mahogany, the upper panel glazed with bevelled, frosted glass. Its frosting was so thick that not even a shadow-movement betrayed the whereabouts of the cabin's occupants. Qiu could see the space on the other side of the door was lit, but nothing else.

He could not see them. Could they see him?

Qiu dropped to his knees, out of any possible sight-line from within, and placed his ear against the wooden panel. He heard voices rising and falling: two speakers, both men. Cumnor and

Simon. And sometimes a third voice interjected, but Qiu didn't recognize it.

When he stood upright he was sweating. He didn't know where the speakers were, relative to the door, or whether Cumnor had a gun, a panic-button linking him with the bridge, a telephone at his elbow, on the other side of the room, beyond Simon, this side of Simon, close to the third man . . .

Impossible. Suicide.

His gaze lighted on the nearest cupboard. Two feet wide by four feet deep. Again, mahogany, with a surround of gold-leaf embellishment and a highly-polished brass key-plate. The kind of thing in which a mandarin might have kept his jade Mahjong set. Qiu eyed the lock, fingering Leong's keys. The first one he tried fitted. He opened the cupboard slowly, anxious to avoid the squeak of a hinge, but the door swung back in total silence to reveal something that he had not expected.

An armoury.

It wasn't really a cupboard, more of a safe set into but not quite flush with the stairway wall. The ceiling-globe shed only a little light into the recess, but enough to show rifles, eight on either side, and a number of ammunition boxes.

He peered at the nearest rifle-stock. Dragunovs. Of course – the standard terrorist weapon. The rifles were fastened to their racks by steel chains passed through the trigger-guards. He experimented briefly with Leong's keys but knew before he started that it was hopeless: the key required to unlock the guns was minute compared with those on the ring he'd taken from the dead man.

Cumnor was ultra cautious. If anyone had access to the cache, there was potential for mutiny. The other key would be hidden somewhere about Cumnor's body; which meant there was no way of getting at it.

So near, so very near, an arsenal . . . all for nothing.

Qiu closed the door and, very silently, keeping his head well down, moved across to the other cupboard. This one was different. Behind the polished wooden door was a mesh guard, barring further access. The key to this second barrier was also missing from Leong's chain. The dim light disclosed several more cardboard boxes, piled one on top of the other, but no sign of any guns. Qiu was about to close the door again when lettering on the side of one of the boxes caught his eye and he paused.

The nearest box was some three inches inside the mesh, close enough to enable him to read the description of its contents.

He stood up, considering, but this time his attention was directed solely to the mesh-guard lock. It was not as strong as the others. Qiu looked again at the keys. One of them had a flat blade, thin enough to be inserted between the mesh and its flange.

He tried it. The key resisted, then slid into the tight gap. But the mesh rattled dangerously and Qiu shied away, gritting his teeth. He counted up to ten while his heartbeat reduced to normal.

A quarrel was building up in the cabin, however; if the protagonists' voices hadn't been raised, someone might have heard the noise outside. Qiu laid the keys on the carpet and wiped his palms along his thighs. Cumnor wouldn't stay in the cabin all night, he'd come out, or worse – he'd summon Leong. And when Leong didn't come . . .

Ten seconds to break open the mesh gate, three seconds to get inside the nearest box, and then . . .

Suppose the contents of the box didn't correspond with the description? What if it contained oily rags, spanners, eggs . . . ?

From inside the cabin came sounds of suffering – the kind of noise a man makes when he's desperate not to show weakness but pain sends him over the edge.

Qiu wasn't going to get another chance. He thrust the key behind the mesh and levered outward. No effect. Sweat poured down his forehead. Another scream from inside the cabin; this time the victim made no attempt at false bravery, now he was suffering beyond the point where pride mattered. Qiu stood back, raised his right leg and kicked at the mesh. Agony electrified the sole of his foot, but he felt something give. He sucked in a deep breath and tried again.

Inside the cabin, Simon Young was past hearing anything. Cumnor, however, registered. 'What was that?'

The third man, a chunky, track-suited Korean, froze with his fist in the air and looked at Cumnor, who nodded. The Korean wrenched open the door.

'Move,' Qiu said quietly. The Korean, seeing what he held in each hand, obeyed.

Qiu came over the threshold, kicking the door shut behind him. His foot left a smear of dark red on the darker wood.

'Put your hands on top of your head.'

Cumnor and his torturer obeyed, the latter with dogged reluctance. Only when he could see their four hands clearly did Qiu widen his sphere of observation.

The cabin was approximately fifteen feet by twelve, lit with concealed strip lighting and a desk lamp fashioned from a small cannon-barrel. Everything looked plush, down to the velvet drapes and crystal ashtrays. Cumnor's desk was arranged at an angle across one of the corners made by the huge windows; he stood behind it facing the door. In front of the desk was a round table supporting an ornamental compass and sextant. By the other corner of the window embrasure, Qiu could see an illuminated globe mounted in oak casing; immediately in front of that was a deep brown leather arm-chair, edged with brass studs. Simon Young sat there. He was naked to the waist. His chest bore marks of burning. A long cigar still smoked in the ash-tray on the round compass-table; that and the stinging smell were enough to tell Qiu what had caused Simon to scream the way he had.

Qiu slowly bore down on the Korean, who stood six feet away from him, his face expressionless. The man retreated until he reached the window and could go no further.

Simon was conscious. Seeing Qiu, his eyes widened and he tried to sit up. 'Don't move,' Qiu said quietly, before turning his attention to Cumnor. 'I'm surprised,' he went on. 'I've suspected for a long time that you were working for the KGB, but I didn't imagine I would find RKG-3Ms on your ship.'

Qiu raised his voice a fraction. 'I really do wonder what you can want with stick-type anti-tank grenades, one and one quarter pounds of high explosive, impact fuse? Do you find them useful at board meetings?'

Cumnor did not reply. Qiu put a grenade into his left hand, next to its fellow, and inserted his forefinger through the ring at the end of the pin. Cumnor stiffened. The atmosphere inside the cabin became unnaturally still.

'Why?' Qiu nodded at Simon before repeating his question. 'Why?'

'It was . . . it was important not to let him keep control of the Benevolence computer-tape.' Cumnor spoke rapidly as if anxious to please. 'He can't be trusted, you know that, you of all people. He wouldn't tell me where it was, so . . .'

'You decided to torture him.' Qiu saw only part of the truth reflected in Cumnor's face. This man hated Simon Young. It was personal; and Qiu wondered what Simon had done to put that implacable expression into Cumnor's marble-shaped eyes.

'Why did you want the tape?' he asked.

No reply.

'I think I can guess. You were going to destroy it, weren't you? That way, no one else would make it out of Hong Kong.' Qiu grunted, then gave all his attention to the man in the chair. 'Simon,' he said quietly. 'Simon, can you hear me?'

'I hear you.' His voice was weak.

'Go up the stairs. There's a dinghy on top of the deck-house. Go over the side. You will be picked up. Reade's coming.'

Simon eased himself out of the chair and made his way to the door. On the threshold he turned wearily. 'Leong knows where the tape is,' he said. 'No good. Couldn't . . . hold on.'

Not a muscle in Qiu's face twitched. 'Just go,' he said quietly. He waited until Simon had disappeared up the companionway before turning back to Cumnor.

'What do you want?' Cumnor's expression had changed; now it betrayed not animosity, but shrewdness.

'I want my son. That's always been the objective. The only one.'

'Very well.'

'You can help?'

'Of course. There's always a way.'

'You can get him out, perhaps?'

'It should be possible.'

'Or at least arrange for me to see him?'

'I don't see any difficulty about that.'

There was a long pause. Then Qiu laughed.

'You find me amusing?' Something of the hatred had filtered back into Cumnor's eyes.

'I find you . . . contemptible. You would say anything, if you thought it might stop me.' Qiu shook his head. 'I know I'll never see my son again. If you'd been honest . . . if you had tried to be realistic, then perhaps we might have made some agreement. As it is, you played with me. My emotions. My . . . love.'

Again he shook his head and smiled. 'Cumnor,' he said. 'Pick up that cigar.'

When the man made no move to obey Qiu asked him, 'Do you know what will happen if I pull out this pin?'

No response.

'I counted four boxes of these grenades next door. And what looked like mortar bombs. And I don't know what else this junk's carrying, except that it isn't a cargo of dried shrimp.'

Cumnor slowly bent forward to pick up the cigar.

'Smoke it.' Qiu waited. *'Do it!'*

Cumnor put the unlit end in his mouth and took a quick draw. Qiu smiled. 'That's no way to smoke a good Havana. Make it hot.'

The Chinese took three more puffs. Now the end of the cigar was glowing red. The Korean glanced at his master and spoke words Qiu couldn't understand.

'What did he say?'

Cumnor said nothing.

'Tell me!'

'No.'

Qui studied him. 'Let me guess. He said: this man won't pull the pin, because he'll kill himself as well as us.'

Cumnor's face tightened. Qiu laughed; then he tucked one of the grenades under his left arm and gently removed the pin from the shaft of the other, just under the neck. He kept up the pressure, though; as long as his hands maintained their respective positions, the grenades were safe.

Qiu's fishy stare did not waver from Cumnor's face. 'You're wrong,' he said. 'You assume my life is worth living. And you are wrong. Now you take that cigar, and you break off the lighted end, and you eat it.'

Cumnor's eyes swelled. He turned to the Korean in mute appeal, but the man stood with downcast eyes.

'Swallow it,' Qiu said. 'And I will put back the pin . . . see . . . thus.'

Cumnor opened his mouth and raised the cigar. For a moment it looked as if he meant to obey; then he faltered and his hand dropped. But before Qiu could speak, Cumnor had broken the cigar. He dropped the longer, unlit end on the floor. He was staring at the tip in his hand, which still glowed gently beneath a thin outer covering of ash. Then he closed his eyes, his head nodded backward and forward half a dozen times; Qiu fancied he was praying. With a sudden rapid movement Cumnor thrust the remnant of cigar inside his mouth and closed it.

Qiu replaced the pin.

Cumnor had been holding the cigar inside his mouth. Now he spat it out, aiming for Qiu's face. It landed in his right eye. Qiu cried out and dropped the grenades. Cumnor dived to the floor. From behind the cover of his desk he wrenched open one of its drawers. He pulled out a pistol and, still on his knees, levelled it at Qiu. The gun kicked once. Qiu fell without a sound.

'Get Young!' Cumnor dropped the gun and tossed some keys to the Korean, who raced for the cupboards outside. Seconds later he was pounding up the companionway with a Dragunov SVD in his hands.

Cumnor spat, trying to rid his mouth of ash mixed with slivers of charred skin. He reached the door, but then he heard his name called and turned to see Qiu writhing on the carpet. Cumnor's eyes were drawn to an ugly red stain above the liver. Only then did he notice that Qiu was still clutching both grenades to his chest.

'My . . . son. My . . . son.'

Cumnor stared down at him, saw what he was doing, and his scream filled the cabin.

'Cumnor . . .'

He looked around wildly, searching for the gun he'd dropped. In vain. 'Holy Mary,' he had time to whisper. 'Mother of God, pray for us now and in the hour of our death.'

'Cumnor . . .'

Qiu pulled out the pins.

THIRTY-THREE

◇

Diana stared into Lo Bing's face. She knew that this man had his orders. Either he was to kill her, in which case she hoped he'd do it cleanly and now, or he had been instructed to bring her to Beijing. In which case he would not carry out his threat.

The General slowly lowered his rifle. Only then did Diana's knees fail her and she sank to the deck.

She was soon brought to herself by the sound of Lo Bing's harsh voice rattling out orders. The soldier he addressed seemed reluctant; Lo Bing had to cuff him across the face before he abandoned his rifle and slowly made his way to the edge of the hatch. There he pulled back the corner of the cover and felt for the ladder rungs with his feet, while another soldier handed him back his rifle.

Long minutes began to grate through Diana's consciousness. No one spoke. All the torches had been extinguished. Only the sound of water lapping against the lighter broke the deep, dark silence around them.

Lo Bing started to pace up and down the deck, his agitation apparent. Once Diana saw him check his luminous watch; after that he became still more nervous. She looked at Warren, but darkness prevented her from seeing his expression. She wondered if he were thinking what she was thinking: that for unfathomable reasons, time had started to run in their favour.

How far from Canton were they when Lo Bing and his men boarded? How long until dawn brought the river to life, endowing it with curious eyes, potential witnesses . . . if they were within reach of Canton, potential *foreign* witnesses . . .

The scream began at an unnaturally high pitch, as if scalded out of some demon's throat by a hurt beyond imagining. It swiftly degenerated into a series of hiccupping grunts, then ceased. 'Oh no,' Diana heard herself say. 'Oh God, please, no . . .'

A volley of automatic fire ripped its way across the cover, and when Lo Bing directed his torch downward Diana saw more than a dozen holes punctuate the canvas. The General shouted – Diana fancied it was the name of the soldier he'd sent into the hold – but no one answered.

For a moment Lo Bing stood lost in thought. Then he seemed to make up his mind, for he once more approached Diana, beckoning the interpreter.

The soldier listened intently, asked a couple of questions and turned to her. 'The General orders you down. Your friend listen to you. Bring him up. Bring him out.'

She gazed at the man as if still waiting for him to speak. Her brain had so far prevented her from understanding what Lo Bing wanted. Just around the corner of her intelligence there was a message; that much she had grasped. In a minute she would have to decipher it, but not yet . . .

'I can't. Not with the snakes.'

'The General order.'

'Tell him no.'

'He order it. Cannot tell him no.'

Some of Lo Bing's men had been stripping back the canvas cover. Now torches were flashed around in the hold, but they could scarcely dent the darkness below. Here and there a sliver of light would pick out the metal of a cage, or a glinting, serpentine eye reflecting back the beam, but nothing else. Lo Bing seemed upset. Diana sensed he was cursing his motherland, the China that had given the world paper, and gunpowder, but which now could not provide its own army with functional torches.

Time. Everything came back to that. They must find a way of delaying General Lo Bing and his band until dawn. Which was when . . . ? No, never mind, don't think about that, don't

330

think about *anything*, just do as he asks. Manufacture time. Spin it as if you were Rapunzel, with death the price of failure.

Diana took one step forward. Now another . . .

She was on the ladder. Her head came level with the deck. It descended below the deck. What was happening? Presumably her limbs were executing some programme without reference to her brain. Strange. Chang Ping had a word for 'strange'. A Chinese word. *Qi-guai*. It meant strange, in Chinese. *Qi-guai* . . .

The air in the hold was fetid. It felt like a steam bath. Or a laundry. Diana wondered why. Of course: hissing. Like steam, hissing . . .

Her feet touched the floor of the lighter. Sibilance whispered all around her now. She could see nothing, but memory told her what she would see if there was light: metal cages, hundreds of metal mesh cages, three feet long, two feet wide and deep. Each cage contained twenty or thirty poisonous snakes, thrown inside at random. The cages were stacked in twenties, making aisles. Just as the coffins did.

Diana kept her hands on the ladder, staring straight ahead of her. She could not move.

She remembered a tense conversation between Warren Honnyman and Lloyd Saunders, on the quay at Liuzhou. Lloyd was complaining about the state of his live cargo. Some of the cage-fastenings weren't secure. If they hit rough water, a few snakes might break loose. Don't worry about it, Warren had snapped; just don't worry about it . . .

Suddenly Diana jumped back onto the lowest rung and forced her head hard against one of the ladder's uprights. She was crying.

'Chang Ping,' she said to the ladder. 'Chang Ping, it's me, Diana. Can you hear me?'

No answer. Of course – if he replied, the soldiers would be able to locate him by the sound of his voice.

'Chang Ping,' she whimpered. 'Try not to hurt me. I must talk to you.'

Silence.

Diana lowered herself onto the deck once more and removed

her hands from the ladder. For a moment she stood there; then she slowly turned around. Lo Bing directed his torchbeam downward, trying to keep it fixed on a spot in front of her, but so far below decks the light was scarcely more than the hint of a gleam.

She took a step forward. The gleam moved ahead. Another step. Then pandemonium.

There came a quick burst of firing from the hold. Lo Bing's torch dropped with a clang at Diana's feet. More volleys, this time from above . . . but she heard the rattle of cages shaken by someone's rapid passage and knew that Chang Ping was already far away from the place whence he'd fired.

Silence.

A few more shots sprayed down from above, but Lo Bing's shrill voice soon put a stop to that. Diana felt sure he was warning them not to risk harming the girl.

Something slithered across her left foot.

She jerked it back as if she'd inadvertently touched hot coals, knowing in her brain that to move at all was madness, suicide, but she couldn't help herself. Her scream echoed through the steel cavern.

She swung around through what she imagined to be a semicircle and struck out for the ladder. Instead she ran into a pile of the dreaded metal cages: a finger of her left hand actually passed through the mesh, not making contact with anything, thank God . . . She sprang back, only to cannon into another heap of cages. Enraged hissing enveloped her; she felt it had suddenly derived a concrete direction, that it was meant for her and her alone.

Diana held both hands over her eyes and screamed as if she would never be able to stop. Then Chang Ping forced both his palms across her gaping mouth, pinching the nostrils shut with forefinger and thumb.

Diana's feet came off the floor, kicking and floundering, but he merely leaned backward, denying her leverage, until at last temporary unconsciousness supervened and she went limp.

When she came to herself a soft voice was whispering in

her ear. Because she was still half crazy with terror, Chang Ping had to repeat his instructions over and over again.

Diana swayed slightly for a few moments while she summoned up enough reserves to make this, the last journey. A short one.

She advanced slowly, placing each foot exactly in front of the other, until with Chang Ping's fingertip guidance she was once again by the ladder. She reached for the uprights and started to climb.

'General Lo Bing,' she cried, when she was more than halfway. 'We're both coming out now.'

After a pause, the soldier who had translated earlier called down, 'Tell him to throw away the gun.'

Chang Ping hurled his stolen rifle as far as he could. Another long wait; then insipid torchbeams swept the floor of the hold, seeking corroboration that he was no longer armed. Lo Bing must have been satisfied, for at last the interpreter said, 'Come up.'

Diana somehow made her hands and feet obey. Now she could see across the top of the raised hatch-surround. The troops stood well back; no one was taking any chances.

Diana gripped the surround, preparing to lever herself onto the deck. Then she cried out in alarm and slid back until only her head remained above the metal wall.

'Help me,' she squealed. 'He's pulling me down again, I can't – *someone help me!*'

Her voice rose sharply, then degenerated into agonized grunts. By now only one of her hands was still in view. 'Let me . . . *go!*'

Lo Bing advanced a couple of steps. Diana was weakening. He glanced up at the sky, saw grey there and swore. Then he went quickly to the side of the hatch, drawing his revolver; Sun Shanwang would have to be content with only one live prisoner.

Diana was slowly being hauled down the ladder by Chang Ping – that's how it seemed to the General. He knelt by the side of the hatch and aimed his gun vertically. 'Light!' he screeched, and one of his team ran forward holding a torch. Lo Bing leaned over the side of the hatch.

Diana stared up into his malevolent face, saw the gun . . . then something long and curly, a whiplash that hissed and writhed, flew past her head; Lo Bing yelled, a terrible sound comprising hatred, and agony, and terror; the black whip seemed to hang suspended from his cheek, its tail threshing; for one mind-blowing second the snake's body flapped against Diana's hair . . . then Lo Bing and his gun fell together to land on the floor of the hold.

For a split second the troops stood like statues. That tiny flake of time was to cost them their lives.

Saunders knocked the nearest man off balance and snatched his rifle. As the rest of the assault-group came to life, Warren flung himself flat and rolled sideways towards the nearest pair, the full force of his momentum concentrating itself on their calves. One went over the side without a sound; the other tottered, managed to retain his balance . . . but by then Saunders was coolly firing, his aim true. Behind him, the interpreter levelled his gun. Saunders dropped to one knee, allowed himself to fall sideways, then over onto his back, rifle pointing upward. His Chinese adversary had time to loose off only a couple of shots before Saunders' fire criss-crossed his stomach, setting free the intestines in a bloody spew.

Now Warren bounced back upright midway between two troopers: one standing behind the body of the interpreter, the other at the lighter's stern. As both prepared to fire, Saunders cried, 'Hit it!'

Warren went down like a stone. In the same second two volleys shredded the night, neatly cancelling each other out.

One left.

The last attacker raced up the deck, firing wildly from the hip. Saunders was already in position, aiming true. Refusing to be rushed, he took a breath, held it and gently squeezed the trigger.

Nothing happened.

No ammunition.

The Chinese had drawn level with the ladder. Now his teeth set in a snarl, he directed his fire more precisely, the shower of bullets inched up to its target.

Suddenly Diana jumped onto the deck behind the gunman and shoved against him with all her might. Thrown off balance, he panicked, flailing around in search of a target. But before he could work out where this dervish had come from, Warren leapt forward to snap his neck.

Diana fell down and lay on her back, staring at the heavens. The pink heavens: dawn had crept up on them without her noticing. Then she turned her head and caught sight of something else. A power station, belching smoke, seen across a wide expanse of silt-ridden, coffee-coloured water; beyond that, some forlorn-looking paddies. She sat up. Lorries on a highway. Houses, rickety wooden jetties sticking out into the current, oil-drum rafts, smoke rising from early morning stoves, factories, tenements.

Chang Ping wearily climbed out of the hold. As he came to sit beside her, Diana nodded her head towards the starboard side and said, 'Canton.'

THIRTY-FOUR

◇

Gene Sangster couldn't master his breathing, it was the one thing that gave him away and he found it irksome, because he wanted to die courageously.

This was a strange way to go to execution: jogging through the misty dawn in the western hills beyond Beijing, with a Russian agent and twelve Chinese soldiers for company. They maintained a regular stride through the damp grass, making for the razor-edged crimson disc that had just begun to slot its way into the far horizon. The air was cool and freshly sweet in his nostrils, the pace easy: only the dryness that extended all the way down the back of his throat, that and the problem he had filling his lungs, spoiled what might have been decent early morning exercise.

When the officer stuck out an arm his contingent wheeled left, heading for a copse of birch trees on a rise to one side of the track. Sangster glanced at Proshin. The Russian's face gave nothing away. He looked worn, but neither of them had shaved in a while. Was he, too, remembering other dawns at boot camp, weekend fun runs through the pine forests outside Moscow . . . ?

The officer lifted his chin and shouted, the words falling on the air in time with the pace. The soldiers to Sangster's left answered him, clapping the stocks of their rifles; then the refrain was taken up by the file on the right. Sangster couldn't make out the words.

'Rah . . . rah . . . rah-rah-*rah!*'

Sangster, startled, managed another glance at Proshin. The Russian was grinning. Seeing Sangster look at him he made a

336

fist and nodded his head in time with the jog. 'Rah . . . rah
. . . *rah-rah-rah!*' they chorused.

The officer turned his head in surprise and grinned at them.
Then he lifted his thumb. Sangster thought that, given the
choice, he'd rather be shot by the Chinese than anyone else.

'Here we are,' Proshin muttered. Sangster looked. On the
other side of the birch copse the ground fell away to a lake,
its surface a flat sheet of tarnished tin in the pallor of early
dawn; by the side of it stood parked an army lorry. For the
bodies. Dead people couldn't jog . . .

'How've you been doing, buddy?'

'Fine.' Proshin's mouth twisted in a rueful smile. 'They
didn't even torture me. Unless you count not letting me smoke
my pipe. You?'

'No. Not one question.'

'No opportunity for a hero's resistance.'

'No far, far better thing . . .'

Then Sangster saw something else; and it didn't marry up
with expectations.

Beyond the lorry, until now concealed by it, was an old-
fashioned tea-pavilion, complete with a jetty that stuck out
into the lake. Its three pairs of doors were closed, but the broad
terrace contained several low, square tables on which pots and
cups were set out, as if many guests were expected. In front
of the tea-house two elderly Chinese gentlemen faced each
other, doing their early-morning exercises.

The officer called a halt and while his soldiers rested on their
rifles the prisoners sank down, gasping for breath. Both the
Chinese gentlemen simultaneously finished their routine. One
of them climbed the steps to the tea-house terrace and the
other walked towards the newcomers with what might have
passed for a smile of welcome.

'Mr Proshin. Mr Sangster. Excuse me. I don't speak Russian
at all. My English is so-so, as you can hear. I believe you both
speak Chinese. Can we use *putonghua*, please?'

They stared at him. For a moment neither man could understand the message. Then Sangster awkwardly stood up, followed a second later by Proshin. 'Yes. *Shi de.*'

'Come along inside.'

The old man led the way up the steps to the centre doors and pushed them open. As Sangster set foot on the threshold his eyes widened. A moment ago he had been feeling sick to his stomach; now he was winded.

The second Chinese gentleman stood with his back to the trio who had just entered, surveying a montage of photographs. Each print had been enlarged many times, but nothing in the way of resolution had been lost.

It was like being back in the Boeing-747 again.

'We had your films developed. I hope you don't mind. They're good, aren't they? Given the circumstances in which they were taken, I really must congratulate you both. Fine work!'

Sangster revolved until he could see the speaker's face. There was no trace of sarcasm in his expression.

'I'm sorry you both have to leave us now. I would have liked to talk longer with you.'

Hearing that, Sangster began to whistle. It had to happen soon. *Why in hell didn't they do it?* He knew. He knew. It was because they thought if they put the end off for long enough he'd lose control, cry, make a fool of himself. Well, he wouldn't. *But why the hell didn't they just do it?*

'Come and have some tea.'

The Chinese who had been studying the photographs heard the invitation and turned away rubbing his hands. He passed the prisoners with a pleasant smile and a nod of appreciation. Sangster looked at Proshin. After a long pause, both men walked outside. The officer in command of their escort handed around steaming cups. Sangster took one, but the china was too hot, his hand shook, he couldn't hold it properly. He damned himself to hell, wondering if Proshin had noticed.

'Would you like to take the prints with you, or just the negatives?'

Sangster subjected their host to a hard stare. The speaker wore glasses and seemed a year or two older than his companion, who had not yet spoken. The host was studying his guests with a quizzical smile, as if he seriously expected an answer to his question.

'I'm sorry to rush you, but we really are very busy today. Forgive me, I forgot the introductions. This is Marshal Wang Guoying, chief of staff of the People's Liberation Army. I'm Sun Shanwang. I head up the Central Control of Intelligence, also known to you, I believe, as the Mahjong Brigade?'

The implied request for confirmation was ignored by both men, who were staring as if they fancied themselves to be in the presence of a lunatic but weren't quite sure.

'I've had it written down for you,' Sun Shanwang said. He leaned forward and Sangster saw two rectangles of white card lying in the centre of the tea-table. Sun picked them up and handed them to his 'guests'.

'My business card, in a way. I'm thinking of having a few hundred run off. What do you think?'

Sangster stared between the old man and the card in his hand, struggling vainly to understand.

'I hope it's clear enough . . . I had it done in Chinese and also in *pinyin* . . . there's the telephone number, telex . . . Fax. In the past, it was difficult to do business with your organizations. That was partly our fault: we worked too hard to make ourselves inaccessible. But now there's a lot of business to be done . . .' The old man tailed off, sensing that he'd lost his audience. 'Something wrong?' he enquired.

At last Sangster found his voice. 'What kind of joke is this?' he rasped.

'Joke?'

'We're spies. We blew up one of your planes. You bring us out here, you're going to shoot us, right? And you —'

'*Shoot* you!' The two Chinese exchanged looks of amazement, then broke into roars of delighted laughter. 'What good would that do?' Sun said, wiping tears from his eyes. 'You can forget about the plane: if you hadn't destroyed it, we'd certainly have had to do it ourselves. And — "Dead men tell no tales", isn't that what you say in the west?'

Now Wang spoke for the first time. 'And we want you to

tell tales,' he said encouragingly. 'You're no use to us dead. So drink your tea before it gets cold, and listen . . .'

Warren lowered his binoculars with a toss of the head. 'I'd give one helluva lot to be on her right this minute,' he growled; and Saunders nodded.

The two men stood on the bridge of the tug, surveying a mist-shrouded stretch of the Pearl River estuary. Visibility was poor. The object of their immediate attention was the Statewing hydrofoil, cruising slowly from right to left across their field of vision, near the end of her run between Kowloon and the port of Canton. She was travelling slowly, her bow scarcely frothing the flat, red-silted river. Within minutes she'd breast the last of the major islands and exit Lingding Yang; then her captain would start negotiating a passage through the crowded northern approaches to Zhoutouju Pier. Long before that, however, she was lost from sight in the soft white pride-of-the-morning fog that floated above the sea like a cotton wool quilt.

'I just hope this is a good idea,' Saunders muttered. His face was worried; rightly so, Warren concluded. For they were moored opposite Songgang, in the mouth of one of the myriad outlets where the West River debouched into the estuary proper, still separated from the safety of Hong Kong's territorial waters by too many miles.

They were waiting for a replacement tug. When it arrived, they would hand over the convoy to the new captain and continue to Hong Kong on their original tug, leaving the new crew to backtrack as far as Canton and offload the cargo as if nothing untoward had happened. Warren looked at his watch. Ten o'clock. Benevolence would start to roll in less than half an hour; he wanted to be away.

'Where *is* he?'

Before Lloyd could answer, however, the helmsman called, 'Cutter approaching. Customs flag. Hell, more than one – those look like fast-attack craft.'

Warren snatched up the glasses again. 'Shit! Headed right this way . . .'

340

'Jesus Christ.' The two men stared at each other. 'What are we going to do?'

Warren bit his lip. 'Maybe they're not interested in us.'

But they were.

Tom Young set up the conference telephone call at ten-fifteen precisely. He waited until all the remaining members of the Club had logged on, then cleared his throat. 'I think the first thing we have to do, gentlemen, is synchronize watches.' He looked at the grandfather clock by the door. 'On the word "mark", ten-seventeen exactly. Three, two, one . . . mark. At ten-thirty I shall bring Benevolence on line. After that, the programme takes over. Ensure that your computers are ready for it, please. Questions?'

There were none.

'Very well.' Tom paused. He wanted to say something suitable to the occasion, but time was ticking by and they were committed now. 'Good luck, then,' he grated.

At ten twenty-three, he unlocked his personal safe to remove the computer tape which had been programmed by Ducannon Young Electronics and delivered by his son earlier that morning. He put this into a briefcase, then took the lift down five floors to where his Director of Information Technology was awaiting him. Together they entered the main computer-room and approached the Cray mainframe. Without a word, Tom handed the tape to the director, who read its label with a smile.

'So this is the famous "Scroll of Benevolence" at last, is it? We're used to rather more prosaic descriptions here.'

Tom eyed the wall clock. Ten twenty-eight.

The next two minutes seemed very long to him. He stared out of the window, trying to visualize the whirlwinds that were descending on eighteen major offices throughout the colony. It should have been nineteen, but with Cumnor dead . . . he frowned. What had caused the junk to blow up like that?

He glanced again at the clock. For nineteen of Hong Kong's biggest traders, time had finally run out.

'Run it.'

The Cray took nine seconds to sort out the various commands. The first thing it did after that was round up the computers belonging to the members of the Club and connect them to Hong Kong's domestic equivalent of CHAPS. Then it linked both of them to SWIFT. The Central Clearing Houses Automated Payments System (CHAPS) was the mechanism whereby clearing banks shuffled billions of pounds each day between themselves. SWIFT, the world-wide financial message switching service, could extend that operation to anywhere on the face of the globe. As long ago as 1987 it had been calculated that the two systems, operating in tandem, could drain Britain of sterling in a quarter of an hour. They took much less time than that to empty all the money out of eighteen Hong Kong companies and divert it to safer homes.

The three banks that were part of Benevolence fell into a separate category. Sufficient funds were left to allow them to honour their immediate commitments while at the same time guaranteeing reserves large enough to satisfy the stringent official requirements as to deposits; without that safeguard, none of them could have continued to operate. Once those provisions had been met, however, the picture changed; from that moment on, the banks became branch offices with control resting elsewhere.

After a while, Tom grew tired of watching the spools spin and whir. He had a board meeting at eleven-fifteen.

First, however, he wanted to make sure the gold got off all right.

He took the lift to the ground floor and approached one of the side exits, where an armoured pantechnicon was already backing down the ramp to the underground vaults. Tom stood between the armed guards to watch the loading begin. It surprised him to see how little metal there actually was; but then if all the gold ore ever mined were brought together in one place it would not fill St Paul's Cathedral. The foreign currency reserves took longer. Even so, the process was nearly complete by the time he went back upstairs to the boardroom to find his son waiting.

'Your life is never dull, is it?'

Simon shook his head with a smile. He expected that to be the end of the topic, so it surprised him when his father approached and put both hands on his shoulders.

'You're looking well for a man who was tortured.'

'Peter Reade came on the scene very quickly. Thanks to Qiu.'

'Ah, yes. A remarkable character.'

'He saved my life. And the tape – Cumnor sent Leong to fetch it, but he must have gone up with the junk, I assume. Coming to terms with Qiu's death won't be easy for me. So many deaths . . .'

'Don't brood, it's a waste of time.' Tom dropped his hands, his manner changed. 'Any news of Diana?'

'Nothing.'

'What do you want to do?'

'Go on, of course.'

Tom looked at his son and was met with an implacable stare. 'Very well. Let's have the others in. Ah, gentlemen . . .'

Three directors were waiting in an anteroom, along with various lawyers and a Hong Kong magistrate. The latter's presence was required by the Corporation's articles of association, which laid down that no Founders Shares in the bank might lawfully be transferred unless the document was witnessed by a judge. Simon and Tom quickly executed transfers of their holdings into the names of Singaporean nominee companies before Tom and his fellow directors conveyed the entire undertaking of the bank, lock stock and barrel, to an entity called The Pacific & Cantonese Banking Corporation (Singapore) Limited. Tom signed board minutes authorizing the conveyance. It was as simple as that.

'Welcome to Singapore, gentlemen. Alan, would you kindly have all these faxed to the branches?'

Alan Sanditon acted as Simon's personal lawyer; in this matter he was also retained by the Corporation. As he went out, one of the 'boys' was waiting in the corridor. 'The package from Bradbury Wilkinson is here,' he said.

'Bring it in.'

Tom waited until the door had closed behind the boy before ripping open the parcel's wax seals. 'Ah yes . . . first page proofs . . .'

Simon looked over his father's shoulder and whistled. 'Quick.'

'Not bad. Letters to staff, letters to customers . . . creditors . . . notice of closure for the Gazette . . . yes, it's all here. When you consider that this was still in code until the Benevolence tape came online at ten-thirty it does become somewhat remarkable, I agree. But that's the security printing industry for you. I assume that –'

He was interrupted by the sound of an aircraft flying low overhead. All the men in the room instinctively ducked, then turned to the window. An enormous plane was drifting over the rooftops to land at Kai Tak, its blue and yellow Statewing tail livery mirroring sunlight into their eyes.

'So that's the biggest cargo-jet ever built . . . well, we can't accuse Warren of underestimating demand. What do they call that thing – anyone know?'

It was Simon who answered. 'That's a Super Guppy.'

Tom snorted, then looked at his watch. 'When are you breaking it to staff?'

'We did our senior management over breakfast. The rest get notice after lunch.'

'Same here. Everyone feels better after lunch and there's fewer excuses for slipping out to make private phone calls then.' Tom grunted. 'Cynical but sound. Key personnel?'

'Out this morning. I've reserved a few places on Warren's flying circus, just in case.'

'Which is about due.' Tom looked at his watch again. 'Kai Tak's closing to commercial traffic in fourteen minutes.'

'What excuse are they giving?'

'Air traffic control computer malfunction. Which in a sense is true: Benevolence is about to introduce itself to Hong Kong ATC and cause more than a malfunction. Look, if you'll excuse me . . .'

'Yes. We've all got a hell of a lot to do between now and three-twenty.'

'Some of it pleasant, some of it less so.' Tom paused. 'I'm seeing all the "boys" now.'

Simon stopped, his hand on the door-handle, and stared at his father. 'Why?'

When Tom made no reply, Simon came a couple of steps back into the room. 'In the name of God, why? All these years you've despised the Chinese, made fun of them, treated them like dirt –'

'I know.'

'So why?'

Tom stared coldly at his son. 'Because I have to,' he said at last. 'Good morning, Simon.'

As Simon made for the lift he met Alan Sanditon coming back along the corridor with a look of anxiety on his face.

'Your father's outer office is already fending off the press. Someone spotted the gold being loaded at Kwai Chung container terminal.'

'I'm surprised it took them so long.' Simon's voice was calm. 'There were bound to be leaks, especially after last night.' He looked at his watch. 'Warren's planes will be stacking over Chek Lap Kok. Better get down to it, I suppose.'

'Diana?'

'Nothing.'

'What are you going to do?'

'I'm going to do the only thing I can do, in the circumstances,' Simon said as he pressed the 'down' button. 'I'm going to wait.'

In Beijing the day had grown hot. By noon Sun Shanwang was feeling exhausted. But he did not care; for at last there was an end in sight.

'So the capitalists are finally going,' he said slowly.

'Yes.' Wang Guoying's voice sounded distant at the other end of the line, as if he were holding the phone some way from his mouth. 'Do you want me to do anything?'

'There's nothing you can do. It's just as we feared. They'll have bled Hong Kong white by dinner time.'

'What's the news your end?'

'All well. I have contact.'

'What, already? From Moscow –'

'And Washington, yes.'

'*And?*'

'And . . . they're angry, as we expected. Both Sangster and Proshin have made preliminary reports by telephone. There was a lot of grumpy talk about verification, but it's clear that America and the Soviet Union accept we have beam-weapon technology to equal their own. I explained to them about our maverick friend and I apologized.'

'Did they believe what you were saying?'

'The Russians are used to wayward generals, and in any case it wasn't their satellite that got shot down; no problem there. In the Pentagon they take a different view of these things, but they'll come around.' He chuckled. 'They really have no choice!'

Sun savoured Wang's hiss at the other end of the line. That was, for the moment, the only recognition he could enjoy. It more than sufficed.

'Then the way's clear?' Wang asked at last.

'If the Army is loyal –'

'It is, it is!'

'Then the way's clear. Guoying, there is one loose end and it's troubling me a lot. Can you spare anyone at present?'

'For what?'

Sun picked up the report that lay at the very top of the pile on his desk. 'The girl did pass through Hechi, we've had confirmation. Bearing in mind all that happened there, we can't afford to let her go now. Not while I'm trying hard to sell us to the rest of the world as a civilized nation. Then Lin, the man who was attacked, whose son was murdered, remember . . . ?'

'I remember.'

'. . . He's given the police a description that fits Diana Young. What's more, she and her friends appear to have succeeded in liquidating our "dream culture" colleague, you know who I'm talking about?'

346

'Yes. But how —'

'A good question. Certain factions won't be pleased to hear about the bodies left floating in the river for all to see. I'm going to need a scapegoat. A foreign murderess would do nicely.'

'What about the Americans on the barge convoy?'

'Leave them out of it. I'm busy making friends with America.'

'So my orders are what?'

'Capture my man, Chang Ping; and Diana Young as well. Use whatever means you have to, short of starting a war. Dispose of them.'

THIRTY-FIVE

◇

The wait in Canton would have been nerve-racking enough under ordinary circumstances. With Chang Ping now very ill and Chinese immigration officials standing not two feet away from them, Diana knew real terror.

In the cool of dawn it had seemed such a wonderful idea. Warren spotted the Canton-bound Statewing hydrofoil on the tug's radar and flagged down the captain. Bob Kerrick was a friend, as well as an employee; he had readily undertaken to secrete Diana and Chang Ping aboard his craft, thus getting them off the lighter-convoy, which by now must be red-hot. The changeover took mere minutes and then the hydrofoil was away, creaming into Canton behind schedule but not late enough to arouse suspicion. Diana knew they were taking a risk, but she felt safe. The Chinese might search the barges, but they would never suspect that the two fugitives had back-tracked into an enemy city.

She had not faced up to the reality of the two hour wait at Zhoutouju pier.

Kerrick's tiny dayroom was behind the bridge; it contained a fold-down table, recessed bunk and precious little else. He locked his unofficial passengers in there, warning them to stay quiet and keep out of sight. The second part came easy; it was the first that troubled Diana.

Chang Ping had a fever; more of an ague than an ordinary temperature. His whole body would quake with shivers for minutes at a time; then he would come to the boil, with sweat pouring down his face, and incoherently talk to her, to himself, to the devils who haunted him. Once or twice now he had suffered convulsions. On each occasion his lips drew right back to reveal his teeth. His jaw and neck were very stiff.

She made him lie down in the bunk and tried to keep him dry with Kerrick's towel, but in less than half an hour it was soaked. The room had no window and, despite the air-conditioning, the interior felt like a Turkish bath.

Diana couldn't understand what was wrong with Chang Ping. He'd been sick since the death of Lin, back in Liuzhou, but this was illness of a different order. He drifted in and out of consciousness; his waking dreams were terrible. Once she had to sit on his legs and use the weight of her body to prevent him from rolling onto the floor.

She kept remembering their conversation about tetanus. 'Have you had tetanus jabs?' she'd asked him; and he had replied: 'I'm not sure. Maybe as a child . . .'

What were the symptoms of tetanus? How long did they take to show themselves? Could it be snake-bite?

He urgently needed hospitalization. Diana knocked on the door, meaning to ask Kerrick how much longer they'd have to stay in Canton, but got no response. Chang Ping was temporarily quiet. He seemed to have sunk into a doze; his eyes were shut and, although his breathing was laboured, at least it sounded regular.

Then she heard Chinese voices outside.

Diana killed the light and jammed her ear against the door. Men tramped along the deck, now they came over the raised threshold onto the bridge. They were in the middle of an argument.

There seemed to be three speakers: Kerrick and two others. Kerrick's Cantonese was fluent but Diana sensed he was making no headway. The discussion became more heated.

After a minute or so, they reached an impasse. Diana heard footsteps approach the door. Kerrick was muttering to himself. 'Passport, passport, fucking passport . . . if you've seen my passport once you've seen it a hundred times, I'm telling you.' He shouted the next few words, and Diana realized with a stab of alarm that he meant them as a warning to her. 'All right, all right, I'll *get* it!'

He pushed open the dayroom door.

Diana slid back against the wall, making herself as thin as possible, but it was a tight squeeze. She breathed in deeply, trying to ignore the pain where the door jammed against her arms, and prayed.

Only a narrow shaft of daylight intruded into the darkness of the cabin: certainly not enough to illuminate the bunk, which was to one side, its end touching Diana's calf. Kerrick did not switch on the electric light. He made for his coat, hanging from a hook behind the door, and collected his passport.

He had rehung the jacket and was about to exit when Diana saw something block out the light that filtered through the wire-thin space between the hinge side of the door and its frame. Someone was looking into the room.

She did not dare breathe. If Kerrick opened the door an inch wider, the wedge of light would expand to take in the bunk.

Then he was out, pulling the door to behind him. But he did not close it completely. Diana stared at the strip of light on the floor, now narrower but still palpably there. *Idiot!* Chang Ping was sensitive to the least sound, he might wake up any minute, or suppose the officials on the bridge took that open door as an invitation to explore the inner room . . . ?

Suddenly she understood why he'd left the door open. It was to lull suspicion: his way of saying, 'Look, I have nothing to hide.'

At that moment, Chang Ping woke up.

Diana heard his feet move underneath the thin cotton sheet. When he clicked his teeth and swallowed, she knew that the next thing he would do was groan. She fell onto the bunk and placed both hands over his mouth. 'Chang Ping,' she hissed into his right ear. *'Don't move. Hush.'*

For a moment he lay quiet. Then he began to struggle.

Diana could still hear voices outside. They sounded calmer now, as if some difficult passage had successfully been navigated.

She knew she had to do anything, *anything*, to stop Chang Ping making even the slightest sound. She stayed on top of him, hoping his weight would be enough to keep him motion-less. But he didn't realize who she was. He had woken in a dark, stuffy room; he was frightened. It was like trying to quieten a very young child.

She pinched his nostrils shut and rammed her right forearm down on his mouth, almost weeping in frustration because he was about to give them away. She'd come almost to the gates of Hong Kong and surely she hadn't got this far, this close to safety, only to be thwarted now . . .

'*Ho-leh, ho-leh*,' she heard someone on the bridge say; and she dredged up enough of her childhood kitchen-Cantonese to recognize this as a sign of approval. The officials were going away. Footsteps. Fading voices, chatting amicably now. Silence.

Diana rolled off the bunk and covered her eyes.

'Why?' His voice sounded weak.

'I had to,' she replied dully. 'There were people outside. Police, I think.'

Before he could respond, the engines fired. Diana slowly forced herself upright and went to peer through the crack in the door. Kerrick turned away from the chart spread out in front of him for long enough to shoot her a tense smile. 'Was he having a heart attack, or something?'

'You heard?'

'Damn right I did! I'll never know how Immigration missed it.'

He turned to his first mate and nodded. The Chinese leaned out of the port and gave orders to cast off. Then they were moving.

'The radio's been busy.' Kerrick addressed the glass but Diana knew his words were meant for her. 'I used code, don't worry. There's a reception committee lining up on the border between Chinese territorial waters and the Hong Kong Sea Defence Area, just in case. Two police launches, and the Royal Navy's sending a "Peacock" class patrol boat, HMS *Swallow*. She's equipped with Seariders.'

'With what?'

'Avon Seariders. Inflatable rubber dinghies.'

'What good will they do, if there's trouble?'

His shoulders twitched in a shrug. 'They carry Sterling sub-machineguns and gas grenades as standard armament. You never know.' He spoke to the helmsman – 'Keep a weather-eye lifting and steer small' – then turned to face Diana. 'It gets rough, so hold on. I want you in the cabin with the door shut; I also want you ready to move at a second's notice. Understand?'

The hydrofoil slowly navigated away from the quay and forged a path through the approaches, littered with freighters and junks, with sampans and launches, with great boats and small. At last the shorelines on either side began to open out, exposing a clear passage through the Pearl estuary. Only an occasional buoy or fishing boat enlivened the dull stretch of water ahead. The morning mist had disappeared; a yellow sun crisped the landscape, making the rice-paddies glitter bright mint green.

The mate's hand dropped to the twin throttles; he eyed Kerrick expectantly. 'Cleared for foiling?'

Kerrick picked up his binoculars from the shelf and swept the landscape. Suddenly he saw something in the distance, far away where the headland began its curve around to Huang-ko, and he froze in mid-sweep.

'Jesus *Christ! Go!*'

'What the hell are you doing here?'

Reade had to shout to make himself heard above the scream of helicopter rotors. Simon Young grabbed the Assistant Commissioner by his lapels and hauled him close. 'I might ask you the same question,' he cried. 'What's happening?'

'The navy's on standby, we've an alert. A border incident.'

The nearest helicopter took off in a maelstrom of dust, hovered, then rapidly made its way north-west, towards China. Reade shook himself free of Simon's grasp and with an impatient gesture signed to the hangar at one side of the main terminal building, where the Royal Hong Kong Police airborne watch was stationed. Normally the helicopter crews spent their time quartering Deep Bay in search of illegal immigrants. Today they were being despatched on a more difficult enterprise.

'It's Diana, isn't it?' Simon said as they gained the relative peace of the hangar. 'Honnyman's office alerted me.'

'We think so. Simon, I'm already late for Captain-in-Charge Hong Kong and I want you out of here.'

'Let me go in the chopper.'

Reade looked at his face, saw how desperate he was and made a discreet sign behind his back. Two policemen approached at a leisurely pace.

'You're not a father, Peter.'

'No. Simon, I —'

'First Jinny, then Diana. I'm appealing to you, I *beg* you . . . let me go with them.'

'They'll be observing, that's all. Your presence couldn't alter anything.'

'You don't send out the Fifth Cavalry just to observe.'

Reade turned on his heel. Simon tried to grab him, but the two officers at his elbows restrained him before he could bring his arm up level. Reade heard the scuffle and glanced back. 'I'm sorry,' he said shortly. 'I'm not in the mood to do you favours.' He tossed his head towards Kai Tak's runway, where a Boeing-757 in Statewing livery was turning at the harbour end, ready for an inland take-off. 'It's a brilliant operation. The secrecy, the organization, they're incredible. I'd like to discuss it with you one day, find out how you did it. Somehow I don't think we'll have an opportunity, do you?'

'You could make one. You could hang me on the end of a rope, like you did poor Qiu Qianwei. Why don't you do that?'

'Yes, that would justify everything, wouldn't it? You could tell the world: see what shits the Royal Hong Kong Police really are! Torture, oppression.' Reade's voice had become bitter. 'Just how do you think we've kept it going for you over the years? With *habeas corpus* and the rule against self-incrimination? Eh? You've lived here on the edge of a volcano, while I and men like me struggled to keep you from throwing the world into chaos, doing the job as best we could no matter how hard you tried to thwart us . . . you've made a fortune out of it. And now, at the end, no thanks for me? Not a single word of gratitude, before we part?'

He laughed and stalked off. Then a thought seemed to strike him, for he came back until he was only inches from where Simon still stood pinioned.

'Goodbye,' said the Assistant Commissioner, holding out his hand.

The officers dropped their guard and retreated. Simon gazed into Peter Reade's face for a long time before wheeling around and walking swiftly to where his car awaited him on the other side of the security fence.

The unit commander was young, very stiff, very straight. Unusually for a People's Liberation Army cadre, he sported a moustache and this worried Lloyd Saunders more than anything, because it suggested quite outstanding individuality.

The commander listened to his senior NCO's report. Then he slowly walked to the tug's stern and looked over the flat hinterland of the estuary.

Saunders lit a fresh cheroot and nodded to where the replacement tug from Hong Kong rode at anchor some fifty metres off the starboard bow. 'Waste of time, bringing her up.'

'Yeah.' Warren Honnyman yawned and stretched, then did a couple of knee-bends, much to the delight of the Chinese soldiers lined up on the deck. Warren lazily smiled back before sauntering over to the rail to join Saunders.

Two Huchuan fast-attack craft kept the convoy within easy range of their guns. They had come out of nowhere to flank the Canton customs cutter, which now stood moored to the tug's side; within minutes of arrival their crews were swarming down the line of lighters on rubber rafts. Then the search had begun.

They were thorough. Nothing was left uncovered. They even wore thick rubber gloves, useful for handling cages of live snakes, and Warren knew they must have been thoroughly briefed. But they'd found nothing suspicious; he and Saunders had made doubly sure the lighters were clean long before they entered the network of waterways that bypassed Canton on the way to the South China Sea. The guns had been dumped. So had the passengers – and Warren guessed it was the passengers who mattered. But it remained in the realm of guesswork, because the unit commander wasn't talking.

Now the officer came back down the deck. He looked smart in his well-pressed white uniform and peaked hat, held in place by a tight chin strap. What did the single gold star mean, Warren wondered?

'Mr Honnyman, I will ask you some questions.'

His English was slow; obviously it came hard to him. But Warren had no excuse to misunderstand.

'Shoot.'

'When you left Liuzhou?'

'Seven o'clock in the morning. Couple of days ago.'

'How many men crew?'

'Oooh . . . say a dozen?'

'Now have one-two-three-*four*.'

'Four, yup.'

'Where go?'

'Where . . . the others, you mean? We put them on a Statewing freighter passing by.'

'Why?'

'Engine trouble's been holding us up. Those men have other assignments, I wanted to be sure they'd get back to Hong Kong on time.'

This proved too complicated for the officer; he and Warren had to break it down into bite-sized chunks before he understood.

'You with a woman left Liuzhou.'

'Yes, we did.'

'Called what name?'

'Diana Young.'

'She is where?'

'On the freighter I just told you about.'

'I do not think so,' the officer replied quietly.

Warren shrugged. Diana was not aboard the lighter-convoy,

355

that much was certain. For the rest, the officer could believe him or not, as he chose.

The Chinese ran a hand through his hair and thoughtfully replaced his cap. He showed no sign of preparing to leave. Instead he began to pace out a rectangle on the deck, six feet by four. Along-down-along-up ... the frown on his face deepened with each circuit.

Suddenly Warren felt Lloyd stiffen beside him. He counted to five before turning slightly to see what had attracted his captain's attention.

Far away in the distance, the dark but unmistakable shape of the Statewing hydrofoil rode silently across his vision, its high bow-wave folding and enfolding the placid waters of the estuary like a ploughshare. As Warren raised his head, the hydrofoil's stern sank and she accelerated away. Then she was planing.

The Chinese naval officer wondered what was causing the American to smile in that strange manner. He followed his gaze and caught sight of the hydrofoil water-jetting towards Hong Kong. Warren turned back to face him and his smile became lopsided, just for a second; but in that second the officer saw the corner of his mouth twitch.

He shouted orders. In less than three-quarters of a minute the first Huchuan was racing after the hydrofoil with its sister ship hard astern, leaving Warren and Saunders to survey a deck that had emptied itself of men with speed bordering on the miraculous.

There was little to choose between hunters and quarry: they were all hydrofoils. Approximately fourteen nautical miles away from the Statewing vessel's present position, Hong Kong's territorial waters and Sea Defence Area began. Kerrick knew from his radio that the Royal Navy would be waiting for him at a point four miles north-west of Lan Kok Tsui, 'Black Point', not far off the Bao-An peninsula, which was mainland territory.

He also knew about something called 'Hot Pursuit'. The Chinese might try to cross into British waters, arguing that it was necessary in order to arrest wanted criminals. Or they might not even trouble to invent an excuse. All these things were going through his mind when he gave the order for maximum revolutions. And so the flight began.

Three miles separated the Huchuan fast attack craft from the Statewing hydrofoil. The two pursuers spread out, each seeking to come up alongside their prey from a different direction, but the manoeuvre proved too dangerous. It brought the port Huchuan too close inshore. This estuary was thick with silt at the best of times and even for shallow-draft vessels the shoals were hazardous. When the captain of the second Huchuan realized this he was forced to drop back and fall in line, astern of the lead pursuer.

Kerrick quickly assessed the situation building behind him and banged on the dayroom door. 'Out, quick!'

Diana stumbled onto the bridge. The noise was excruciating. Ahead of her she could see nothing but a sweep of yellow water stretching as far as the horizon under a sickly blue-white sky. The hydrofoil was bouncing up and down, trying to cope with the strain of an operational speed for which it had not been designed.

'Where's the boy?'

'He –' The hydrofoil pitched to port, diesels screaming, and Diana fell awkwardly, banging her head. She was only dimly aware of Kerrick helping her up. 'He's ill, he can't stand . . .'

'Well drag him, then! The Navy's waiting around that headland, there, to the left. If it gets too hairy I may have to ditch you.'

'You mean . . . in the *sea?*'

'That's what ditching usually means. Now get ready!'

'But he'll dro –'

They both heard it at the same instant; their eyes assumed the same faraway look of disbelief, then they were on the floor with Kerrick's arm around Diana's shoulders.

The shell slotted neatly into the sea some seventy metres off the port side, a little ahead of them. The Chinese mate wrested the wheel to starboard and in the instant before he could make a correction the hydrofoil seemed to slide through the sea

357

on her starboard hull. Then, miraculously, she was running straight again.

Kerrick staggered up. 'Firing on an unarmed civilian ship, my God!'

Diana hauled herself upright by clinging to his legs and managed a swift glance out of the windscreen. Bao-An headland was looming now; beyond it and to the right she could see a large ship, surrounded by lesser craft and hovering helicopters: a king attended by courtiers. As she looked, one of the helicopters began to move away from the flotilla, heading towards her.

The second shell landed much closer, dispelling any hope that these were warning shots. The hydrofoil rocked on her beams, all but turned turtle. Kerrick flung open the nearest port and leaned out, training his glasses on the pursuers. 'They're closing,' he snapped to the mate. 'Give her all you've got.'

'No more, Captain.'

They were almost there. Diana could see the markings on the Royal Navy ship now, could even see the Union Jack at her stern; it was less than a mile away, with a hovercraft too, and seven or eight black inflatables bobbing about in the water. The helicopter was overhead, the beat of its rotors adding to the noise inside her brain.

'Why don't they come?' she breathed. *'Why don't they come?'*

'Because they don't want to start a bloody war! Christ, look out!'

The leading Huchuan had drawn almost level. As Diana turned to look through the starboard port she saw men on a wing of the bridge doing something to a machinegun. Then the twin 25 mm. midship guns slowly swivelled until their barrels were pointing directly at the Statewing hydrofoil.

Kerrick nodded wearily at the mate, who understood and cut the power. The vessel took much less time to stop than Diana had imagined would be the case.

'Sorry,' Kerrick said abruptly. 'I can't let a boatload of passengers be shot from under me.' He glanced at the mate.

'Hoist a blue shirt, will you? May as well tell the world we need assistance.'

While the crewman rummaged in the flag-locker for the international distress signal, Diana pleaded with Kerrick, knowing it was hopeless. He was right. But it hurt to see that beautiful British ship, proud and impotent at the same time, now riding less than half a mile away.

The leading Huchuan pulled around forward of the State-wing hydrofoil, barring her course. The second patrol boat came alongside until only a few feet of frothy water separated the two craft. Diana was close enough to see the officer on the bridge raise a bullhorn to his mouth. 'We are putting a line over you,' he shouted. 'Do not resist.'

'Diana!'

She turned, alerted by the urgency of Kerrick's tone, and saw he was pointing forrard. She gasped; for one of the inflatable Avon Seariders was creaming over the water towards them.

'The idiots! . . . What in *hell* do they think . . . get the boy.'

'But —'

'Don't argue. Just *get the boy!*'

The helicopter pilot circled while his observer mapped the seascape for posterity. The UN would require a report; contemporaneous accounts were best. His words, spoken into a hand-held microphone soundproofed against outside interference, were taped back at HMS *Tamar* and also on the Sea King's inflight recorder.

'Statewing seven-zero-eight is stationary. Estimate decimal seven five of one mile from British territorial water. Two Huchuans in position, one fore of Statewing 708, one mooring to starboard side. Second Huchuan is sending a dinghy across. One of our Seariders approaching the first Huchuan, keeping a wide berth. Now being challenged . . . first Huchuan opening fire on our Searider . . .'

The Sea King SH-3D hovered lower, its rotors whipping fine spray off the surface of a sea made choppy by its approach.

'I see activity on the bridge of Statewing 708 . . . someone has entered the water . . . the Searider is attempting a rescue . . .'

The observer put his hand over the microphone and yelled to the pilot, 'Christ! Who gave the green light on *that*?' Then he took his hand away and looked down. 'Got him! The Searider has picked up, I say again, the Searider has picked up man overboard. Leading Huchuan is coming around now, to cut off the Searider . . . I see men on her deck . . . the Searider is away . . . *Grenade attack on the Searider!* . . . the Huchuan is homing now . . . direct hit . . . and we are coming under fire from enemy craft . . .'

As the first volley whistled past the port side of his cockpit the pilot climbed steeply away, banking out to sea. For several minutes contact was broken while they fought to recover position. At last the Sea King was coming in again on a straight approach, but higher this time, and to one side of the international incident now entering its final phase below.

To the observer they looked like toy boats in a bath tub. Through his binoculars he could just make out the black remains of the Searider, blown to pieces by a direct hit from a grenade; then he homed in on a figure floating like a broken rag doll, a body that rippled, offering no resistance to the waves.

'I see one, I say again one, body floating face down. HMS *Swallow* is approaching at full speed. *Swallow* has fired on the leading Huchuan. Enemy forces in retreat now. Both Huchuans have declined combat and are withdrawing.'

The pilot began a slow circle of the Statewing hydrofoil. Suddenly there was a swirl of white water at her stern as the vessel got under way, making course towards the fast-approaching HMS *Swallow*. The observer waited until he was sure, then said: 'Statewing seven-zero-eight entering Hong Kong Sea Defence Area now.'

The radio came to life. 'Spectator One, this is *Tamar*, do you read me, over?'

'I read you, *Tamar*, over.'

'What about the body in the water, over?'

The observer peered down. 'The body . . . Long, dark hair, denim jacket, bullet wound in the back . . . no, that is wrong . . .' He adjusted the focus. 'It is a heart, a red heart, there is lettering around it . . . no survivors visible, I say again, no survivors . . .'

THIRTY-SIX

◇

'It says here, some guy name of Sun Shanwang is going to be next chairman of China's Communist Party Central Committee.' Gene Sangster lowered his copy of *Ta Kong Pao*, the pro-mainland Hong Kong newspaper, and beckoned a waiter.

'You don't say. Thank you.'

Proshin's last two words were addressed not to Sangster but to the waiter, who had brought more hot water. Now the Russian lit his meerschaum, stretched out his legs and folded his hands behind his head the better to savour both pipe and surroundings.

They were sitting in the lobby of the Peninsula Hotel, daintily taking afternoon tea. This was a long-standing ambition of Proshin's and Sangster had been glad to indulge him. The circumstances were very pleasant. High, square pillars supported an ornately corniced ceiling which had not changed since Victorian times, those legendary days when a boy would carry your bags the few yards from the hotel's front entrance to the railway station, where you could embark for Calais. The carpet was deep rich maroon; the mirror opposite their table brilliantly reflected golden light filtering down from strips concealed behind the architraves. Proshin picked up a teaspoon, fingering the engraved hotel logo, and was tempted to pocket it. Then he saw Sangster watching him and shrugged with a slight smile, knowing he'd been caught out. He was going to miss this man.

'Yes,' Sangster went on. 'Sun Shanwang, someone – it says here – who does not appear to have held high office before. A

362

dark horse.' He folded up the paper without further comment. Proshin laughed.

'This is nice,' he said, looking around. His expression was hungry, but Sangster, who had watched him put away one of the Peninsula's assault-course teas, knew that the craving on Proshin's face had nothing to do with food.

'It'll go on a while longer, I guess.'

'Is that a reference to the success of our project?'

'Uh-huh.'

'I wasn't sure they'd find our portfolio of photographs convincing.'

'In our world, what evidence is ever wholly convincing?'

'What is truth . . . ?'

'Said Pilate. Jesting.'

'Mm. Your people and mine can go back to sleep. Until next time. But what about China?' Proshin waved airily, wreathing smoke around his head. 'Will China be content to leave all this in place?'

'Sure, why not? She's going to be a prosperous country herself soon. It isn't so hard to figure out what happened. The big boys took a look at the photos and realized China's one of them now. They've got to come to terms with it. So they'll put together an aid package, make China an offer she can't refuse, solve her food problems. Sun Shanwang stitched it all together, I shouldn't wonder.'

'And got the number one job as a reward?'

'It's possible. He'll be remembered as the guy who brought China into the big players' league.'

'I would like another chocolate eclair. And a tea cake. With apricot jam this time, I think.'

But before Proshin could attract the waiter's attention the orderly progress of tea at 'The Pen' was interrupted.

The intrusion began as a wave that started by the main doors and billowed inward until every niche and crevice of the lobby was filled with humanity. Flashbulbs spattered, microphones were held aloft, three or four video-cameramen in the van of the flood walked backward, relying on colleagues to clear them a path.

'Oh, my!' said Proshin as he jumped onto his chair. 'Elizabeth Taylor. I must look!'

'That's not Elizabeth Taylor, that's . . . that's Thomas Young, the old man. And his son.'

'Who?'

Sangster had to shout the next words; the level of noise in the lobby had become intolerable. 'Tom Young's chairman of the biggest bank around these parts. His son, Simon's, one of the old-style *tai-pans*. And there's *his* son, too. Hong Kong's royal family . . . Take your hat off.'

'But I'm not wearing a hat . . .'

They heard a commotion by the stairs, where Mat was vigorously forcing a passage for Simon and Tom into the hotel's main conference suite. Hotel staff, worried by the bleak looks on the faces of regular guests, were trying to instil order, but the task was hopeless.

Tom managed to climb a few stairs. He raised his hands for silence. The decibel level dropped, but only a fraction.

'Press conference . . . be told in the proper way . . . prepared statement . . .'

Then came one of those statistically impossible moments when everyone in the crowd paused for breath at the same time. A reporter used the opportunity to shout his question; Sangster caught the fag end of it.

'. . . that about twenty of the largest *hongs* have quit Hong Kong today?'

'Yes. Quit isn't the word I'd use, but . . .'

Tom's confirmation locked the silence. Now no one spoke. The same questioner pursued his theme.

'Is it right that you've dismissed most of your staff? Is it true that Statewing commandeered the airport this afternoon to airlift men and material out? Can you confirm that the Taiwanese airforce has been covering your retreat. Is it –'

'Is there a connection between the incident earlier today between the English and Chinese Navies?' A woman's voice, strident and strong. 'Simon Young, is it right that your daughter is missing?'

Now Sangster, too, was standing on his chair. He saw a

man younger than Tom emerge from the sea of heads as he climbed the stairs. He looked tired, unhappy, unwell.

'She's missing.'

'Was she aboard the Statewing hydrofoil that was machine-gunned this morning?'

'I'm not aware of any machine-gunning.' Simon's face was the colour of lambswool.

'Do you know where she is?'

'She is —'

He fell silent. Everyone fell silent.

Simon Young's eyes had become fixed on the main lobby doors. One head turned to look, then another, then several, then everybody was staring at the doors. At first what attracted attention was the clean starkness of the British naval officer's whites and his ratings' tropical Number Sevens; then a murmur began, low at first, background noise; but soon it swelled into a chorus of operatic proportions.

For a woman had entered the lobby. She did not fall into the category of typical Peninsula guest. The denizens of this crowded, famous hotel usually wore fine clothes; she did not. Her shirt was soiled with blotches and sweat-stained; her jeans were holed in places; her canvas rucksack would not stand comparison with the piles of Luis Vuitton and Gucci luggage stacked by the concierge's desk.

She strode down the lobby, and people gave way. They parted respectfully, for despite her shabby apparel she walked with head erect and shoulders back, like a soldier.

Like a queen.

She reached the lower step. The three men were staring down at her in disbelief. Simon's lips moved soundlessly. Diana Young unshouldered her rucksack and held it by the straps in front of her, while she looked at them. Then she spoke.

'I couldn't jump, I was too afraid.' Her voice sounded husky and low, but she spoke like an Englishwoman and every word went into the waiting microphones clear and distinct. 'He wasn't afraid. But he was cold. He was so cold. I gave him my jacket, because he was cold, and I had to help him.'

Diana dropped the rucksack and allowed herself to fall forward into her father's arms. 'He loved me, you see.'

Only then did she begin to cry.

*With this cold night-rain hiding the river, you have come
   into Wu.*
*In the level dawn, all alone, you will be starting for the
   mountains of Ch'u.*
Answer, if they ask of me at Lo-yang:
'One-hearted as ice in a crystal vase.'

Wang Ch'ang-ling
'At Hibiscus Inn; parting with Hsin Chien.'

Fontana Paperbacks: Fiction

Fontana is a leading paperback publisher of fiction.
Below are some recent titles.

- ☐ JUSTICE Ian St James £4.50
- ☐ FIRST STRIKE Douglas Terman £3.99
- ☐ NOW AND THEN, AMEN Jon Cleary £3.50
- ☐ THE SHEIKH AND THE DUSTBIN
  George MacDonald Fraser £2.95
- ☐ FLASHMAN AT THE CHARGE
  George MacDonald Fraser £3.50
- ☐ BLACK WIDOW Bart Davis £3.50
- ☐ PAPER DOLL Jim Shephard £2.95
- ☐ TRAPP AND WORLD WAR III Brian Callison £2.95
- ☐ THE LAZARUS FILE Stuart Prebble £2.95

You can buy Fontana paperbacks at your local bookshop or
newsagent. Or you can order them from Fontana Paperbacks,
Cash Sales Department, Box 29, Douglas, Isle of Man. Please
send a cheque, postal or money order (not currency) worth the
purchase price plus 22p per book for postage (maximum postage
required is £3.00 for orders within the UK).

NAME (Block letters)_____

ADDRESS_____

_____